Don't Stand So Close To Me

by

A. C. Bentley

Grosvenor House
Publishing Limited

This book is published by
Grosvenor House Publishing Ltd
Link House
140 The Broadway, Tolworth, Surrey, KT6 7HT.
www.grosvenorhousepublishing.co.uk

A CIP record for this book
is available from the British Library

ISBN 978-1-78623-836-8

Author information

Born in Aldershot in Hampshire, A. C. Bentley taught Modern Languages in numerous schools and colleges in the South of England over a period of 20 years. **Don't Stand So Close To Me** is his first book.

Acknowledgements

I'd like to thank the following friends, most of whom trawled without protest through my entire 173 000 word manuscript and offered invaluable feedback:

Simon Brooks
Lucy Cole
Neil Harding
Kat Lailey
Zoë Lynch
Andrew Neill
Remo Ranken
Victoria Sindall
Lucy Walpole
James and Deborah Whelan.

I'm also grateful to *Silvia Peduto* for the cover designs (*silvia.sperdi@gmail.com*).

My final thanks go to my family, whose love and support has never wavered – a rare constant in the crazy roller-coaster ride of life.

All chapter titles and song excerpts were taken from compositions by *Lennon/McCartney*, apart from **All Things Must Pass**, which was written by *George Harrison*.

With a few notable exceptions, all the names used in the book are fictitious.

Life is what happens to you
While you're busy making other plans.

From *Beautiful Boy* by John Lennon

Norwegian Wood

(Year 1)

I once had a girl,
Or should I say,
She once had me?

AUTUMN TERM

It's fast approaching 7.45 on a balmy, sun-blessed early September morning in 1992 and I – Alan Bentley – can barely contain my excitement as I sprint down the dual carriageway in my cherished Italian classic, an Alfa Romeo Alfa Sud. Red, of course. Having survived three demanding yet at the same time rewarding years serving my apprenticeship in two secondary schools, I'm about to embark on a whole new chapter in my teaching career.

Thanks to selling myself successfully at a competitive interview back in April, I've landed my dream job of French and German teacher at *Mardall's*, one of the county's leading Sixth Form Colleges. In a sixteen-plus environment, with a predominantly A level focus, I'll now have a perfect opportunity to fully exploit my language skills and, perhaps, even play a small part in helping to reverse the British reputation abroad for linguistic incompetence.

Following the post-interview celebrations, there were still three months of my old contract to honour – time enough to bid a gradual farewell to the many delights of the secondary sector. Even now, it's hard to believe that assemblies, cover lessons, detentions, disruptive pupils, school uniform and, of course, the illicit fag behind the bike shed will soon be little more than 'fond' memories.

As I swap lanes to ease past a slow procession of rush hour traffic, I remember, no doubt with a hint of sentimentality, a brief conversation I had during my probationary year with thirteen-year-old Ricky Norton.

"What's 'e poin', sir," he asked suddenly, interrupting my explanation of the perfect tense, "o' me learnin' French if I'm gonna be a brickie?"

Searching frantically for an appropriate riposte, I found myself umming and erring before suggesting rather tentatively that he may one day secure a lucrative building contract in France and need to communicate with the customer.

"Yeah, but they all talk English out there, sir," Ricky said wearily. "Me 'n' m' dad've been to Frogland loads o' times 'n' we never 'at to speak no French."

Unable to find an answer to this smart but not entirely inaccurate retort, I returned defeated to the next irregular verb on my list.

"At least I won't have to justify my existence in a Sixth Form College," I say to my passenger, with an air of unbridled optimism. "Yes, I'm certain this'll prove to be a wise career move."

Okay, I'll come clean – there's no passenger. I just have a habit of talking to myself.

Whilst few could dispute that my professional life is currently on the up, the same can hardly be said of my love life. A handful of fleeting relationships between eighteen and twenty-four, then girlfriendless for two years. Not exactly much to write home about. Hell-bent on drawing a line under this gold-medal-winning performance at celibacy, I jetted off to Corfu in July with my best friend, Scotsman Mario Campbell. Since we met working as language assistants in Austria back in '86, this was the first time Mario had been properly single. Convinced that 'sharking' in tandem with such an experienced lady-killer would help me take the island by storm, I'd gone away with my tail wagging. But then I've always been one of life's eternal optimists.

Within twenty-four hours of setting foot in Durrell's childhood paradise, Mario was clocked by Liza, an Anglo-Italian who'd escaped from England alone for a fortnight to nurse a broken heart. Before bracing herself for an approach, she'd assumed from appearances that I was German and Mario my Turkish *Gastarbeiter* (immigrant worker) companion. Realising at once that she didn't have a friend in tow, Mario nobly rejected his latest admirer's amorous advances out of loyalty to his old mate. Liza, however, obviously undeterred by 'Romeo's' polite rebuff, latched on to us for the remainder of the holiday – a move which, I'm sure, cramped our style and put paid to my hopes of that long-awaited kiss. Or maybe more …

Partly through years of dedication to my studies and competitive gymnastics, but also as a result of inheriting the moral values of my parents' and grandparents' generations, I have – shock, horror – never had sex. I've often wondered how many other young adults have been through the whole modern university experience without ever 'doing it'. With the onset of my new job and the imminence of another birthday, it's suddenly become a major issue. How can I contemplate facing classes of acne-ridden sixteen- to eighteen-year-olds on a daily basis, aware that the majority will almost certainly be more sexually experienced than I am? Besides, what if I don't meet my soul mate until I'm fifty? I can't possibly hold out that long ...

"It's no good," I tell the dashboard in front of me as I turn into the College drive. "I'll have to pull my finger out and try a bit harder from now on."

I find a parking space in front of the building's imposing red-brick façade and reverse into it.

With a large Slazenger bag in my right hand and a buzz of anticipation in my step, I cut through the main ex-grammar school building out to the covered way at the rear, which provides dry access all year round not only to my destination, the *Grosvenor Building*, but also to the split staff/student canteen opposite and the Design Technology workshops further down. If I remember rightly from my last visit, the *Grosvenor*, a two-storey block of modern design, accommodates the English and History Departments as well as Modern Languages.

At the top of the *Grosvenor* stairs, I run into two important characters from the day of my interview – Desmond Willis, a German specialist and the overall Head of Languages, and Marilyn Butcher, the Head of French. Desmond's short, raven-black hair and matching pirate beard belie the fact that he's a shy, softly spoken man at heart. Blackbeard's younger brother, perhaps. Marilyn, on the other hand, with her brusque, somewhat sarcastic manner, could hardly be described in such moderate terms, her prominent cheekbones and mop of closely cropped silver hair only serving to reinforce her authoritative, if not intimidating, presence. "Not one to be crossed lightly," I remember noting back in April.

After a warm welcome, Desmond escorts me directly to my permanent teaching base, a narrow, rectangular classroom occupying a corner position on the top floor, overlooking the rear of the main building.

"Cramped but cosy," I mutter under my breath.

Peering out of one of the windows, I notice that it's just possible to see the periphery of the grassed quad that lies at the heart of the campus to the right and the edge of the staff canteen to the left. In the distance beyond the canteen, I spot a rather lonely-looking pavilion at the far side of a vast field, offering the prospect of staff cricket in the summer term.

My two new bosses then introduce me to the rest of the language team – two other full-timers and five part-timers. I shake hands with each in turn, but fail to register all their names first time round. They seem a friendly enough bunch, though.

With initial introductions out of the way, we all head off together to a staff meeting in the Main Hall.

"Should be an ideal venue," I observe as we take a seat, "for the extra-curricular gym and trampolining clubs I promised to run at interview."

As the towering, six-foot figure of the Principal, Avril Cunningham, launches into her 'welcome back' and 'welcome to new colleagues' speech, I can't help noticing as I glance around that the other departments mirror my own in that they aren't exactly overrun by eligible young ladies under the age of thirty. Mind you, I suppose finding someone to … well, you know, 'sow wild oats with' could hardly feature prominently on my staff development request form.

Anyway, there's hope on the romantic horizon in the shape of the new language assistant, Claudia Schmidt, who's due to arrive from former East Germany in October. With a twinkle in his eye, Desmond grants me a sneak preview of Claudia's photo once we've returned to the department to prepare for the year ahead.

"Mm … yes, very attractive young lady!" he says with a nod of approval, almost as if seeing it for the first time.

As a happily married man, he's obviously taking his role of mentor very seriously, with his junior colleague's best interests firmly at heart.

At midday, Desmond invites the whole language team to join him for lunch at the local pub. As the new boy and 'baby' of the department, I receive the full red carpet treatment.

"Oh yes," I tell myself. "I'm definitely going to fit in here."

Our after-lunch administrative activities are interrupted by the unexpected visit of a slip of a girl with a real baby. There are "oohs" and "ahs" all round, and my lady colleagues take it in turns to hold the cute little fellow.

"She was one of our French students last year," Desmond explains once the visitors have left. "The Chairman of Governors' daughter, in fact."

"The poor young lady had no idea she was pregnant until she went into labour," Marilyn says. "With her small frame, nobody noticed her bump. And she did a sponsored parachute jump at five months."

I'm tempted to enquire about the identity of the baby's father, but I decide against it. Suffice to say, the infant displayed no detectable signs of pirate-like stubble.

In contrast to my previous jobs, where teaching kicked off from day one, a further three whole days are taken up with the enrolment and induction of new students, all armed with their GCSE result slips. The majority have achieved their predicted grades and are signed up without difficulty. There are, however, some borderline cases that have to be referred to Desmond or Marilyn. It soon becomes clear that a high proportion of those enlisting for A level language courses are female. I'm also amazed at how much older everyone looks without the restrictions of uniform and with the disguise of make-up.

"So, Al, is there anything else you need to know before all hell breaks loose on Monday?" Desmond asks mellifluously once the enrolment process is complete.

I reflect long and hard.

"Steady on, old lad!" he says. "You don't want to overtax the little grey cells just yet. There's a gruelling term ahead."

Whilst my new boss may well be a relatively shy man, he certainly doesn't lack a sense of humour. I smile and say: "Erm … as it happens, I do have one question."

"Fire away. I'm all ears."

"Er, it may seem a strange thing to ask, but how are the students expected to address us? I mean, I'm obviously used to surname terms from the secondary sector, but my cousin's just joined the Sixth Form College I attended myself what … eight years ago and, apparently, all of the staff are now insisting on the use of their first names. Hm, would've been frowned upon when I was there."

"Ah, you'll notice a change of attitude in the modern Sixth Form College sector. Gone are the draconian days of the authoritarian teacher and the subservient student."

"Thank goodness!"

"Oh yes, we've had to move with the times. The push for social equality is rearing its ugly head in Further Education, all right. Interaction with students must now be conducted on the grounds of mutual respect and understanding."

"Surely that's not altogether a bad thing."

"Yes and no. Anyway, to answer your question, Avril is happy to leave the term of address to the discretion of individual teachers. We are old fogies here in the Language Department and have tended to stick with surnames."

With this final piece of information under my belt, I'm now ready to start teaching on Monday.

The first few weeks at the College run remarkably smoothly and convince me beyond any shadow of doubt that I'm going to be happy in my new job. The students, apparently appreciating my exuberant style of teaching, are enthusiastic and well motivated, and my new colleagues friendly and supportive. What's more, I feel very much at home in a more informal, 'adult' environment. However, as I discovered in my other posts, there's never any question in this profession of being broken in gently as a new member of staff. One of the four Lower Sixth French groups that I'm sharing with part-timer Nancy Harris – all French groups here are split between two members of staff – contains the daughters of the Vice-Principal and Head of Careers.

"Hm, let's just hope I won't be making an appointment with the latter next summer to discuss alternative employment," I mutter, not entirely in jest.

Claudia Schmidt's arrival at the beginning of October to take extra conversation classes serves as further confirmation that I've made a sound move. I immediately volunteer to take her under my wing, on the grounds that the management will surely be impressed by my willingness to assume extra departmental responsibilities. I soon discover that Claudia is not only as petite and beautifully Aryan as her photo suggested but also a lovely young woman with an endearing personality. We strike up a friendship at once and seem to have a lot in common. Well, that's until she touches on the subject of relationships, of course. Although on her application form under *marital status* it reads *single*, this is misleading. In reality, she's got a long-term boyfriend back home and – I can hardly bear to hear it – a daughter.

"But ... but you look far too young to have kids," I tell her.

It wasn't intended to be a compliment, but she takes it as one. Not for the first time, my hopes are well and truly dashed. After all, my upbringing has led me to believe that women in steady relationships never look at other men, especially when they've got children. I console myself with the thought that the gorgeous Claudia probably doesn't fancy me, anyway.

As is often the case in life, good fortune arrives when I least expect it. Shortly after the letdown with Claudia, I'm presented with a perfect opportunity outside College to fulfil my mission and gain some much sought-after sexual experience.

It's a Saturday night like any other. After a few drinks at a couple of my locals, I drift towards *Clifford's*, the small but popular wine bar just up the road from my flat, which has recently been granted an extension until 1.00 am. In tow is Simon Lennon, the tall, wiry, enigmatic Lancastrian art teacher from my previous job. He's a couple of years older than I am and a real 'man of the world'. The place is as crowded and smoky as ever.

Just before midnight, I get chatting to an *au pair* from France called Juliette who I've conversed with in French on several occasions over the past year. Unbeknown to me, she completed her stay in England several months ago and is, therefore, just over for the weekend visiting friends. As we're jabbering away, I'm totally oblivious of her body language until Simon, far more experienced in affairs of the heart, has a quiet word in my ear.

"Get in there, lad!" he says. "She fancies the pants off you."

My reply is almost instinctively dismissive: "Yeah, right – good one!"

But on this occasion, Simon's observation proves to be spot on. Nevertheless, without further encouragement from my mentor and six pints of Strongbow, I would no doubt have successfully bottled it and wouldn't find myself an hour later collapsed in a drunken heap on my sofa with the blonde, pallid, sylphlike figure of Juliette perched over me.

"We make love now?" she says brazenly, clasping my limp right arm in both hands and tugging it in the direction of the bedroom door.

"What, you mean … you want to … to actually … *do* it with me?" I ask with incredulity. After all, I'm not the type of bloke who's used to such benevolence from women.

"Comment?"

Damn! In my disbelief, I'm gabbling my words. Or is it the alcohol? I try a different approach: "Euh … tu … euh, tu veux *coucher* avec moi?"

"Mais oui, bien sûr!" Juliette says before adding somewhat impatiently: "Bon, on y va."

Miraculously, the onset of a premature hangover is immediately thwarted as I lead her expectantly, although also a tad apprehensively, through to my bedroom. Whilst she's busy undressing, I clench my fist in anticipation of an historic moment, uttering a virtually inaudible "Yes!" in the process. With a name like Juliette, surely this must bode well for the future.

However, what I'd hoped for years would be one of the most treasured experiences of my life turns out to be one of my most disastrous and humiliating. I am, of course, a total washout, yet it has little to do with the quantity of alcohol in my blood or inexperience. In my exuberance, my understretched foreskin retracts so far that it becomes well and truly jammed behind the head, exposing the hugely sensitive area underneath for the first time. And boy, is it sore! I try desperately to relay my predicament to Juliette, but somehow degree level French just hasn't equipped me with the necessary vocabulary to cope with such an emergency. And they told me Southampton was one of the trendier universities. I'm suffering, but she just won't stop the relentless upward movement of her hips, apparently mistaking my cries of discomfort for unparalleled pleasure. Weary and extremely sore from her indiscriminate thrusting, I finally decide to 'fake it'. Further relief eventually arrives in the form of sleep.

I surface some five hours later with that unpleasant dryness on my tongue that often accompanies a night on the tiles, especially when there's cider involved. It isn't long before I'm reminded of that all too familiar burning sensation down below. Involuntarily, I gently cradle the afflicted area with my right hand. Unfortunately, my oblivious tormentor of earlier is also awake and interprets this as a clear indication that I'm eager for further action.

"We make love again?" she says in her de Caunien English.

To my dismay, I have to endure the whole excruciating experience once more, determined as I am not to appear disinterested and disappoint her. But as before, the suffocating effect of my foreskin ensures that I'm deprived of ultimate gratification – if you catch my drift.

As if my situation can't get any worse, I finally withdraw to discover to my horror that the blessed condom has magically vanished. It's wedged inside her. In my despair, I curse my luck for ending up with a French girl. Surely English women don't have such a veracious sexual appetite. I mean, twice in one night – incroyable!

Except it's not unbelievable at all, it's very much reality. And, although I'm not usually averse to a spot of slapstick humour, I just can't bring myself to see the funny side.

Still ailing down below and distraught at the thought that I might've leaked enough to make her pregnant, I drive a bewildered Juliette back to the pub where she's staying. It's still dawn. We avoid eye contact and barely exchange a word. Having thanked Juliette – I'm not sure what for, exactly – and bid her "au revoir", I return to my flat to contemplate my fate.

"Thank God she's off back to France tomorrow!" I sigh, confident that this will leave her too little opportunity to spread word of my sexual inadequacy. My hometown is too small and my self-esteem too fragile to risk that on top of everything else.

It's at this point that I suddenly remember Juliette's revelation in the early hours that she'd slept with Glen Moore, the local stud and prominent member of the 'hundred plus' club. I'm starting to panic.

"Oh no!" I mutter under my breath. "I can't see him giving a monkey's about a condom."

My attention is now diverted from the threat of unwanted pregnancy to the fear of AIDS. I'm in a real state. It just doesn't seem fair that I should have to endure this nightmare when I've resisted temptation before for so many years waiting in vain for the right girl to come along. My protests are loud and clear, but fall on deaf ears.

It's mid afternoon and I can't help noticing that my foreskin hasn't budged an inch. The sensitivity of the exposed area is so acute that any form of underwear proves extremely uncomfortable. After much deliberation, I decide to swallow my pride and ring Mario. After all, what's your best mate for if you can't call him for advice when your foreskin gets trapped trying to lose your virginity? I prepare myself for laughter, but not the full ten minutes it takes to convince Mario that it's not a wind up.

"Well, you could try smothering it with soap and massage it back into place," he says.

"You're still taking the mickey," I reply, unconvinced that the hilarity has finally ceased.

But it has. So it's off to the bathroom to follow his instructions. Lather, lather and more lather. It's no good. No matter how hard I rub, no amount of Imperial Leather is going to dislodge this stubborn bugger.

An hour or so later, I make up my mind to phone Simon who, I figure, will be eagerly awaiting some form of feedback by now, anyway. I think he must sense the exasperation in my voice since he manages to withhold anything more than a snigger and feigns genuine concern.

"Ya best bet is to run cold bath and sit in it," he says.

So it's off back to the bathroom for contingency plan number two. I can't believe it. Most young men spend hours contemplating the size of their 'thing'. In fact, I read recently that extensions will one day be available on the NHS and here I am, at the beginning of winter, freezing my butt off in six inches of ice-cold water, trying to shrink the sodding thing.

"Any more of this and I'll need a sodding shrink!" I curse aloud.

Just to make matters worse, I'm also starting to feel guilty about my rather immoral conduct last night. Call me old-fashioned if you like, but I know my doting grandmother, who died about this time last year, would've been disappointed by my actions. And I so hated letting her down. There's no way her strict Christian moral code would've condoned sex outside marriage, let alone outside a loving relationship. Not that I think for one moment that my current misfortunes are a result of her wrath from somewhere up above. She was far too kind and loving to ever consider inflicting punishment on anyone, but it appears that she still has a hold on my conscience. Her younger sister, Auntie Flo, lives in the flat above mine and often cooks for me.

In spite of all my efforts, by the time I head for bed on this unforgettable Sunday night, it still hasn't shifted. There's no denying it, something isn't quite right. I'm going to have to seek medical advice. Only, how will I explain to a GP who's known me since I was in nappies that my foreskin got stuck attempting to have sex for the first time at the age of almost twenty-seven? Sometimes, when the whole world is against you, there's nothing more you can do but turn in and pray that the morning will bring better fortune.

It's Monday morning and it's breaktime. On my way to the Staff Room in the main building, I stop off at the Gents for a pee. My sense of relief reverberates throughout the whole building. It's gone back and normal service has been restored. Gott sei Dank!

My relief is short-lived. I suddenly realise that I still won't be able to risk 'doing it' again, so later in the week I pluck up the courage to consult the family doctor. Having rehearsed my story carefully beforehand, I survive the encounter. But then Dr Frost has always been the very best that the NHS can buy. He refers me to a specialist, but he can't see me until after the German work experience trip to Hamburg in November.

This is particularly unfortunate since I run into Glen Moore later in the week. I tap him confidently on the shoulder and announce: "You and I've got something in common."

"Oh yeah?" he says. "So what's that, then?"

"The name Juliette ring any bells?"

"Huh! Not you as well?"

I hold my head aloft, proud that this stud doesn't have a monopoly of all the desirable 'local' women. "Yes, a few days ago."

Glen throws back his head and emits a hearty roar, his mouth as round as a crater. "You 'n' me 'n' the rest of town!"

With the wind taken firmly out of my sails and definitely not amused, I slip away, more panic-stricken than ever. Surely I must be in one of the high-risk groups now.

On the ferry to Hamburg, Rebecca Carter, the shyest member of the small Exchange party, suddenly goes AWOL. The rest of us carry out an extensive search of the ship, but there's still no sign. However, just as rumours start to spread amongst her fellow students that she's fallen overboard, she miraculously reappears, noticeably the worse for wear.

"I've been batting with the charman," she says, slumping into the chair beside me.

My more experienced colleague, Thelma Parker, and I are anxious to establish that she's okay. She passes our examination with flying colours by insisting on divulging the most intimate details of her mother's sex life. I listen in carefully but discreetly in the hope that I may pick up some practical tips. Thelma, however, an unassuming mother of two in her mid-forties, tries unsuccessfully to change the subject, no doubt envisaging her embarrassment at the next Parents' Evening.

On our arrival at the German school, the students are each allocated an Exchange partner to live with and informed of a work experience placement for ten days in one of the local firms. I get to stay with a female German teacher, her greying English hippie husband and their eight-year-old daughter, Veronika. As usual, I try to capitalise on the opportunity to practise my German. Unfortunately, one evening at dinner, Mr Hippie overindulges on Liebfraumilch and attacks me verbally for monopolising the conversation – much to his wife's horror. Okay, I confess, I can be a bit of a chatterbox at times.

A couple of evenings later, Lisa Thomas, one of the students who's in my form for registration back at College, rings to invite me to join her and the others at the cinema. Seeing as his other half isn't home and I have to leave almost at once to catch the bus, my host kindly offers to shove a frozen ready meal in the microwave for me. I accept, but then feel uncharacteristically subdued all evening.

During the night, I'm violently sick. I remain under the weather for two or three days. Considering that I only drank one bottle of beer after the film, the students must think that I'm the biggest lightweight in history.

Although this is the first time I've suffered from food poisoning in my life, it is, rather embarrassingly, the second time that I've thrown up in somebody else's house. The first was at my friend's seventeenth birthday party when a brass table lamp mysteriously fell on my head and upset my stomach. His mother just happened to have been my O level German teacher. The poor woman then found herself washing my corduroys in the middle of the night. To this day, I remain indebted to Mrs Davies not only for her laundry skills but also for inspiring me to learn such a great language. It simply didn't do justice to her teaching skills that all three of her offspring failed to gain a qualification in the language.

Anyway, it isn't so much my stomach that detracts from my enjoyment of the trip, but a constant preoccupation with the thought that I might be HIV positive.

Back in England, they announce on the news that AIDS will one day be the largest epidemic in the western world. I really don't need to hear this right now. Maybe the specialist can reassure me. I'm seeing him in the morning.

I've just seen the willy doctor and it's official – my foreskin is unnaturally tight, so he's booked me in to be circumcised in January. Sounds excruciating! The good news is that he reckons my chances of being HIV positive are minuscule. No one hundred per cent guarantee, but enough to put my mind at rest. Thank God! I can now contemplate a future.

I'm still slightly puzzled about Juliette, though. She was so eager I got the impression that she really liked me. Didn't seem like the promiscuous type at all. But then what do I know about women?

After the drama of that bizarre Saturday night before the Exchange, a certain degree of normality has returned on the romantic front. In other words, I've reassumed my former role of Mr Invisible.

It's Friday night in late November and I'm alone propping up the bar at the scene of my recent triumph, trying to appear cool and confident. Since it now looks like I may well live beyond the age of thirty-five and haven't heard from Juliette to say she's pregnant, my state of panic has largely subsided. After all, it was a turning point. Not quite as I'd envisaged, perhaps, but a turning point, nevertheless. The only thing is, I'm not exactly sure if ... well, you know, if it really *counts* seeing as I didn't ... Oh well, too embarrassing to ask anyone, I guess. Although my 'thing' will effectively be out of action until after the op, there's nothing to stop me practising my pulling technique. As they say, "practice makes perfect".

It's an unusual evening. Having lived in the town from the age of two and a half, I can generally guarantee bumping into at least one person I know. But not tonight, apparently. Never mind, it's Karaoke and that's normally fairly entertaining. With no-one to chat to and considering that not a single girl has bothered to grant me a second look, I start to reflect. What was it that made me stand out on that 'Juliette' evening? Did I look trendier – I was wearing my new safari shirt? Or was it my hair – it was a tad longer then? Or was my demeanour more upbeat, my smile more radiant? Mm ... maybe I just drank in greater volume. Or was it Simon's influence? Come to think of it, I wasn't even aware that Juliette fancied me until he pointed it out, so perhaps I have been noticed in the last few weeks, but just haven't noticed myself. Oh bugger! I'm doing it again – analysing everything too much. How many times has Jayne, my sister, reproached me for this?

"C'mon, Al. Just chill out, man, and have a laugh," I mutter in an effort to chivvy myself along.

After a while, Karaoke begins to lose its appeal and I become restless. Since there's still nobody I know in the club and I'm in high spirits, I persuade myself to 'have a laugh' by putting my amateur dramatic skills to the test. At this point, I see a girl nearby who I find attractive. After several faltering attempts to approach her, I take a large swig of beer and a few deep breaths.

"Come on, Al," I say to myself. "If you can take an assembly in front of several hundred school kids, you can do this."

I move towards her diffidently.

"Having a good time?" I ask in a fake, 'chilled out' sort of way.

"Yup," she replies without catching my eye.

"Not singing, then?"

"Nope."

There's an awkward silence.

"Um ... nice talking to you, but...," she says, then turns and scampers off.

What does she mean "nice talking to you"? But for once, I'm not offended.

After downing another pint, I'm itching to resume my little game. Looking round, however, I can't see anyone else I like who's not with a bloke. As I extend my search, I notice that my 'friend' from earlier is heading back towards my end of the bar, looking 'fitter' than ever. What if she was playing hard to get and I just didn't spot it? After all, I've always been pretty hopeless at that sort of thing.

Before I get chance to think before I speak, I speak before I think: "Can I get you something?"

"No … thanks," she says tersely. "My mate's just got the drinks in. Look … um … I'll see ya round, yeah?"

Before she has chance to scarper, I follow her in an attempt to prolong our chat. I grab her arm gently and say: "Okay, if you won't talk to me and you won't let me buy you a drink, maybe you'll let me take you out to dinner tomorrow?" My manner is unmistakably bold, but I'm just acting out a part, of course. Hope she hasn't noticed.

The girl swivels rapidly and looks at me for the first time with a 'this guy's either foreign or incredibly slow on the uptake' type of expression. Then comes her response: "No … no way! I … I don't fancy you, okay? You're just not my type."

"Oh, aren't I? Er, look, thanks for being honest," I say politely, still persevering with my 'chilled out' game. "I appreciate that."

She appears perplexed and I wonder whether she was expecting fireworks. I turn to go, but she stalls me. For the first time, I detect a relaxing of her stance.

"So it's all right if I talk to you again?" she says. "I mean, you're not pissed off or anything?"

"No, not at all."

We exchange names briefly, then my new acquaintance nods, smiles and returns to her friends.

Back home, I decide that just because a girl doesn't fancy me it doesn't mean that she's not a nice person. I feel proud that, for a self-conscious bloke who never usually has the courage to approach women he doesn't know, I've been quite daring tonight, even if it wasn't the real me. I contemplate myself for a few seconds in the bathroom mirror, the extremities of my mouth smothered with toothpaste froth.

"Huh! Wasn't exactly a big deal," I tell myself.

I go to bed alone, but vaguely contented. I wonder what it was, though, that Juliette saw in me that she didn't.

As is common practice in most educational establishments, all full-time members of staff at *Mardall's* are expected to take charge of a form for registration in addition to teaching their own subject. It's known as a 'Set' here and consists of a mixture of Lower and Upper Sixth students – first and second years – of varying abilities. There's a range of other duties that befall a Set Tutor, such as passing on messages, chasing up invalid absences, dealing with course-related queries and compiling university references. The latter is a major undertaking and, as a newcomer, Desmond has been showing me the ropes.

Although time-consuming, I actually find my role as Set Tutor an interesting extra dimension to the job, particularly when it comes to dealing with any problems or concerns any of my tutees may face. Consequently, I don't think twice about keeping my period one German class waiting outside the classroom one Tuesday morning at the end of November when Helen Ferguson, a shy redhead with crimson cheeks, requests a confidential chat immediately after registration.

"So are you worried about one of your subjects?" I ask, interpreting the anxious expression on her face.

"No," Helen says nervously. "It's nothing like that. It's just … I think you …"

She pauses, her head dipping as if to suggest there's something far more serious to report, something she may well be ashamed of.

I reassure her gently: "It's okay, Helen. Take your time."

There's a further pause before she raises her head slowly, bites her bottom lip, and then says somewhat hesitantly: "I think you … you ought to know that I … I'm pregnant."

I'm completely taken aback.

"Pregnant? Oh, right … er … are you absolutely sure?" I ask, for want of something better to say. After all, this wasn't one of the role-play scenarios I was required to act out during my teacher-training course.

"Yeah, positive. I did a test at home. And I've had it confirmed by my doctor."

"Okay. Sounds pretty definite, then."

"Yup."

"Does … does anybody else know?"

"I've told my mum."

"Well done! That was very brave." I'm still bluffing my way along. "How did she react?"

"She … she's been really understanding, but … but she doesn't know if she can afford an abortion."

"An abortion? Is that what *you* want?"

"Yeah. It happened at a party. I had quite a lot to drink and this bloke he …"

She breaks off mid-sentence.

"Did … did he force himself on you?" I probe cautiously, focussing my eyes on hers. She glances away. "Helen, I don't wish to pry, but if …"

"I don't wanna take it any further," she says finally, flashing an assertive glance back at me.

"Are you sure cos ...?"

Again, I can't quite get my sentence out before she cuts me off, this time even more assertively than before: "Yes, totally!"

"Okay, then. Look, what I'll do is make some enquiries about abortion, then give your mum a ring. If that's all right with you."

"Thanks," she says with a puff of relief.

At breaktime after period two, I inform Clive Morgan, one of the four Senior Tutors responsible for the smooth running of the pastoral side of the College, about Helen's misfortune. Clive is a lovely, compassionate man who possesses the unique quality of being able to time a meeting down to the very last second. Sadly, he's inflicted with a rapidly deteriorating case of tunnel vision, which may well compel him to take early retirement in the not too distant future.

"Oh dear, poor Helen!" he says with genuine concern. "Yes, I think you should make a few calls first about her options – I'll give you some numbers – then get on to her mother straight away."

I follow Clive's instructions. Helen's mum is most grateful, but explains that her daughter would prefer to leave the College and start somewhere else next year. It occurs to me that the bloke responsible for Helen's condition could well be one of her fellow students, maybe even someone in the Set. Still, without her consent, there's very little I can do.

For the rest of the week, Helen's unfortunate situation leaves me feeling rather shell-shocked. I can't help thinking that, had luck not been on my side, I may well have found myself having a similar conversation about unwanted pregnancy with Juliette just a few weeks back. It seems that my private and professional lives are not as far detached as I previously thought.

It's Monday again and I'm feeling guilty. Two weeks till we break up for Christmas and I still haven't fulfilled my promise to take Claudia, the German assistant, out for a drink. And she's returning to Germany soon for the festive season. After all, it's not her fault that the Berlin Wall prevented her from coming to England before she met her boyfriend. Besides, she's a guest and it's the right thing to do.

I tentatively suggest Friday. Claudia looks pleased and accepts. I tap anxiously on my bottom lip with the finger tips of my right hand as if attempting to play a keyboard.

"Great. The thing is ... er ... I've only got a ... a one-bedroom flat," I add, "so I'll have to take you home afterwards. Or ... er ... I could borrow ..."

"Al, it's fine," she says placidly, her hand on my shoulder. "I'm very happy to sleep by you."

I'm suddenly stirred by the image of a scantily clad Claudia sleeping 'by me', but it's not long before my excitement is tempered by the realisation that she's translated literally from the German *bei dir* meaning *at your place*. Shame.

When Friday evening finally comes round, Claudia and I go for a drink at one of my locals, *The Combine Harvester*. Whilst there, we bump into a small contingent of my French students from College. They're initially shocked to see a teacher engaging in a pastime generally associated with normal human beings, but they soon come to terms with it. Any potential awkwardness is avoided through Claudia's presence and I begin to enjoy the opportunity to chat with them in a more relaxed, uninhibited fashion. Claudia provides us all with a fascinating insight into life under a Socialist regime. Not quite part of the students' usual Friday night billing, I'm sure.

I know that the holier than holy mob probably wouldn't approve of a teacher condoning under-age drinking. However, I made a decision in my first job that, seeing as I'm not a policeman, it's not my place to interfere with something that's happening in virtually every pub throughout the country at least every Friday and Saturday night. I'd only make myself unpopular and achieve nothing in the process. What's more, I'd rather witness students trying to be grown up in a controlled public environment than hear horror stories of excessive boozing and drug taking in private. Rightly or wrongly, that's my stance.

After an hour or so, Claudia and I move on to *Clifford's*. We're fairly early and manage to get a seat. Having knocked back a few drinks and had a fun time with the students, we're both in dazzling form, exchanging anecdotes in both languages. Claudia compliments my spoken German, which further bolsters my mounting confidence.

The next hour is hazy, but involves further drinking and laughter. There's no time to analyse the situation and, before I know it, I find myself kissing Claudia passionately and she's reciprocating.

"This can't be real," I tell myself as I stare into the mirror in the cramped, dwarf-sized toilet just inside the main entrance. I half expect to see that I've been transformed into a tall, dark film star, yet the incredulous figure looking back at me is short and blonde and definitely not a celebrity.

I relieve myself quickly and hurry back to Claudia to check that I haven't been hallucinating. To my relief, she's waiting for me and hasn't sobered up or had second thoughts during my brief absence. We start kissing again.

A short while later, I resurface for air. There's a girl at the table opposite, staring at me. It's my 'friend' from last week. I can't help beaming at her smugly, but she just glares at me with an expression of total disbelief written all over her face. I know I'm a sad case, but anyone who's been ignored or rejected as frequently as I have over the last two years will understand what a sweet moment this is.

Back at my flat, I offer Claudia the z-bed that I've borrowed from mum and dad. She declines it and, to my unexpected delight, I get to sleep 'by' her after all. Part of me senses that she's feeling a bit guilty. Anyway, I'm not exactly in a position to take things further, so we just restrict ourselves to kissing. What an exquisite body she's got, though. You'd never believe she'd given birth.

When daylight reappears, there's no apparent awkwardness between me and Claudia. What a contrast to a few weeks back with Juliette. I drive my guest home.

Back in my flat, I am for once brimming with romantic confidence. I look in the mirror and wonder why I've always had such low self-esteem when it comes to my attractiveness to women. After all, I really don't look that bad this morning and I'm pretty confident in most other areas of my life. Odd one that.

As the day wears on, I can't get Claudia out of my head. I decide that there are five possible scenarios as far as she's concerned.

1) She was missing her boyfriend and I was just a substitute.
2) She loves her boyfriend, but fancies me.
3) She likes me more than her boyfriend.
4) She's away from home and just wants to exploit her freedom.
5) She was very drunk and didn't know what she was doing.

I finally arrive at the conclusion that, however frustrating it may seem, it's unlikely that I'll be able to establish which of these is true until the start of the spring term. I've no choice but to put the sumptuous Claudia out of my head until then.

Crashed out on the settee after we've broken up for Christmas, I find myself mulling over the events of this last term. Apart from the fact that I'm unbelievably happy in my job – and I think everyone likes me – I've had more excitement romantically over the last three months than in the last three years. For some bizarre reason, moving to a Sixth Form College seems to have changed my fortune. Roll on '93!

SPRING TERM

It's happened at long last – I've had the dreaded chop. I was in and out earlier today and, despite repeated jibes from friends that I'd be walking like a cowboy for weeks, my walking is just fine, thanks very much. And to my profound relief, it's not unbearably sore either – just a tad uncomfortable when I go to the loo. I am, however, a bit apprehensive about the night ahead.

It's now 2.00 in the morning and, as I feared earlier, I'm struggling to fall asleep. In an attempt to avoid unnecessary pressure on the afflicted area, I'm having to lie on my back with my legs apart, thinking of England. And I've never had much joy before sleeping in this position. I'm trying desperately to divert my attention from any thoughts of Claudia, Kylie Minogue or Brooke Shields. After all, if the stitches were to burst …

As the hours tick by, I can't help going over stuff. You know, as you do when sleep proves elusive. Inevitably, my train of thought takes me back to May '91. As a generally sound sleeper, this is the last time I remember suffering from insomnia. I'd been gym training in preparation for the British Past Masters Championships, then rushed over to a pub near the school to join a couple of colleagues who were both celebrating their birthday. I quickly downed a pint and a half of lager, and was contemplating accepting an offer of another swift half, when I suddenly remembered I still had a final batch of practice French essays to mark for the Upper Sixth. Considering they were due to go on exam leave the next day, it couldn't really wait.

As a conscientious 'rookie' teacher, I made my excuses. I then hurried back along the familiar but damp country lane, only to skid out of control at the wheel of my mid-engined Fiat roadster whilst exiting a sharp left-hander. The car then clipped a tree and flipped onto its roof. Wobbling like a jelly, I managed to crawl out on my stomach unscathed through the shattered off-side window. I then found myself inadvertently wrapping my arms around the middle-aged man in the car behind who'd stopped to alert the police. This is, I promise, the one and only time in my adult life that I've been intimate with someone of the same gender. Maybe that explained his hasty exit from the accident scene. I think I was just seeking confirmation that I was still in the land of the living.

Standing alone in the obscurity, watching passing cars swerve to miss my mangled wreck of a two-seater stranded in the middle of the road, sent a cold shiver hurtling down my spine. What if one of them had been heading towards me as I spun out of control? At this point, a police panda car arrived in a blaze of flashing blue lights.

As the passenger door swung open, a strangely familiar voice called out to me: "Hey, I know you, don't I?"

It was Mr Ledbeater, my Science teacher from secondary school who'd abandoned us for the Force.

"You're lucky," he said, glancing down at me from his tall, lanky frame, his blonde 'perm' every bit as curly as I remembered from my school days. "The last poor bastard we pulled out of here was decapitated."

But then he always did have a way with words – when he could be bothered to teach us, that is. Even at the tender age of fifteen, I knew that if I did go through with my plans to become a teacher I'd actually attempt to stand up and teach my classes, not settle for setting copious amounts of note-taking from textbooks as Ledbeater was prone to do. He was, however, brave enough to bring his guitar along to the Easter Concert and sing *Leaving on a Jet Plane* with a 5th Year girl in front of the whole school. In a strange sort of way, the best and worst of Ledbeater helped me determine what kind of teacher I'd endeavour to be.

After an agonising wait, my breath test proved negative. Ledbeater and his colleague agreed to drop me back to the flat, leaving Kevin Baker from the school year above to load my three-thousand-pound heap of scrap metal onto his breakdown truck. Not exactly the cheapest and most memorable of school reunions.

As I lay awake in bed afterwards, it really hit home how fragile our lives can be. Had my careless misjudgement been combined with bad timing, then twenty-five-years' worth of life would've been blown away in seconds. And for some less fortunate souls, it is. What a chilling thought! Needless to say, I got up early the following morning to finish marking those essays, despite a sleepless night and my zombie-like state. After all, a teacher has to get his priorities right.

In the days that followed, I began to appreciate my life more than ever before – my family, my friends and all the great things around me. And to think I could've died a virgin. I promised myself that I'd never again be guilty of taking things for granted, that every day from then on would be lived to the full. *Carpe diem* would be my new motto. I'd even get my act together and find a girlfriend. But then how often are our good intentions swallowed up amidst the high-pressured frenzy of modern-day life? Twenty months on, I'm usually so wrapped up in my day-to-day routine that the many miracles around me pass by unnoticed. What's more, I still haven't got a girlfriend, although you have to give credit where it's due – at least I did have a fair stab at trying to rectify the virgin issue. The only lasting impact of my near-death experience is that I now always remember to take out an *uninsured loss* option with my car insurance policy. Funny how material things often have the last word.

Incidentally, good old Simon Lennon later confessed to leaving the pub soon after I had and driving past the scene of my accident. Concerned that he may've had one too many, he'd ducked his head and continued on his way.

"I saw someone talking to copper," he said in his soft Lancastrian tones, "so I assumed it were you and you weren't injured."

Thanks, mate!

It's morning again and my hours of reflection are over. It doesn't feel like it, but I suppose I must've slept a wink or two. As I throw back the duvet, I'm slightly alarmed to discover that a fair amount of blood has soaked through the dressing. Just to be on the safe side, I peel back the bandage and take a quick look. Ugh! It's very raw and very exposed. But the stitches haven't ruptured, so I cover it up again rapidly and prepare myself for work. There's no way such a minor operation is going to keep me away from my beloved students.

Claudia returned from Germany a few days ago, but I've been too preoccupied with other 'private parts' of my life to have that serious chat with her. Actually, that's a fib. I'm just a big coward living in fear of the truth.

By the end of the week, the truth is out. No heart to heart or tête-à-tête, just a couple of passing comments that spare my blushes and tell me all I need to know. Back in Germany during the Christmas holidays, Claudia was tormented by pangs of guilt, so decided to spill the beans by confessing all to her boyfriend, only to discover that he'd been up to the same tricks with other women. Moreover, according to the French assistant, Isobelle Dupont, I wasn't Claudia's only bit on the side either. Before Christmas, she'd pulled another Englishman. Looks like my theory number four was closest to the truth. I wish I could've been her only secret lover, though. I'd have felt far more special that way. Inevitably, I suppose, I had to be brought back down to earth at some point. I'm disappointed, although not entirely surprised. Maybe one day I'll meet someone who doesn't feel the need to share me with her boyfriend or half the local community.

Good news. Two of Claudia's female friends are coming to visit next week and, apparently, one of them is single and looking forward to meeting me. Every black cloud …

Claudia's friends turn out to be sisters. Their visit is short, but very sweet. It's true that the softly spoken younger one, Katja, is single and we seem to hit it off almost immediately. Unfortunately, there's little opportunity to spend any time alone together, so we exchange numbers and promise to stay in touch. Katja is keen to organise an extended stay in England sometime in the not too distant future, so I tell her I know a man locally who'd be more than willing to put her up. She approves, so … watch this space.

With the departure of Claudia's two friends, February soon arrives and my life becomes more hectic than ever before. In addition to my full timetable of French and German teaching, I'm now voluntarily running a trampolining club during two lunch hours and an after-College gymnastic club. Then there's my private, recreational gym club that I've been in charge of for almost four years. It's held in my old secondary school hall and involves three hours' coaching on a Friday night and a further three the following morning if the Saturday coach cries off sick – not exactly an infrequent occurrence. Add to this a good hour for setting up and dismantling the equipment. Since I began my own gym career there back in 1973 and received fantastic support from a number of dedicated parents – above all, my own – I don't begrudge the time. But it can be knackering after a heavy week at work. I've also had my arm twisted about offering private language tuition to some friends' children. At the moment, this amounts to two hours on Saturday and two on Sunday. I do get paid for my efforts, though.

The other week, I attended auditions for a bit part in the local amateur dramatic society's Easter production of *The Secret Diary of Adrian Mole*. By pure coincidence, Guy Harper, one of my French students, landed the part of Barry Kent, the infamous bully. I hope he doesn't get any big ideas about rehearsing his moves on me in class. Just to prove what a complete nutter I am, I found myself agreeing to take on a fairly major role. How I'm going to find time to plan all my lessons and keep my marking up-to-date once rehearsals get underway, I haven't a clue.

There is, however, one positive aspect to being so busy – there's scarcely a moment to brood over my non-existent love life. In fact, I haven't had a second to think about the opposite sex for days – apart from when I'm in bed, of course.

Towards the end of February, nineteen-year-old Howard Parish, one of my coaching assistants at my private gym club, brings his band to College on a Tuesday lunchtime. It's a beautiful day and, in my capacity as Functions Organiser for the Student Activities Team – another sideline I forgot to mention – I manage to persuade the Vice-Principal to authorise an open-air concert in the quad.

The group gives a remarkably polished performance for such a junior outfit, but then at the end, Howard embarrasses me by insisting over the mic that I provide the vocals for a version of *Wild Thing*. Surrounded by expectant students, I have little hope of escape. Since singing comes as naturally to me as sprinting does to a snail, they get to witness a self-conscious side to their teacher that would never rear its ugly head in the classroom.

A few days later, I discover that my character in *Adrian Mole* is expected to perform a solo. If it weren't for his superior height, I could ask

Howard to deputise during this scene. Maybe he'll give me some singing lessons instead.

On the following Friday, Louise Wilson, one of my star gymnasts and trampolinists from College, fulfils her promise to make an appearance at my evening gym club for extra training. She gets on really well with Howard and by the next gym session, they're an item. What it is to be a pop star. Now, I wonder when I could squeeze in those singing lessons ...

In March, Marilyn invites me to join her, Isobelle Dupont and one of the part-timers, Diana Lewellyn, on the French Exchange. Marilyn, Diana and the students – among them some of *The Harvester* crowd – head off by coach to Poitiers, with Isobelle and me in hot pursuit in her ageing Renault 5. Her parents live fairly close to our destination, so she's wisely decided to kill two birds with one stone by paying them a visit.

None of us gets much sleep in the lounge during the overnight crossing – all the cabins were booked up. Consequently, I find myself nodding off in the passenger seat of Isobelle's car on the other side of the Channel. Suddenly, I'm awoken by the deafening squeal of brakes and the jolt of her Renault 5 swerving into the lay-by before coming to an abrupt halt.

"What the hell's going on?" I ask, turning to face my visibly shaken chauffeur.

"I am so sorry," she says, gasping for breath. "I fell asleep at zhe wheel. When I woke, I saw we were about to 'it zhe lorry in front, so I braked. It is a miracle zhat I wake zhen."

Having survived my second near-death experience in two years, I make light of it and encourage Isobelle to press on. Needless to say, I keep my eyes firmly open for the remainder of the journey.

On the first morning in Poitiers, as we're assembling in front of the lycée, three or four of the *Harvester* girls rush over and greet me with cries of "Bonjour, Al. Ça va?" Then, in full view of my two lady colleagues, each one in turn kisses me audaciously on both cheeks.

"I see my young man has found himself some admirers," Marilyn says good-humouredly.

Over the last year, I've come to realise that her brusque, somewhat intimidating manner is very much a front. Below the surface, she's a warm-hearted woman of sharp wit. I wonder if the girls were deliberately trying to embarrass me. If so, they certainly succeeded. Of course, I just pretended to take it in my stride.

The trip is a success. We all return to England to see out the last few weeks of term in buoyant mood. For my part, I'm just relieved to make it back in one piece.

With my currently manic lifestyle, April arrives before I know it. The BBC broadcasts highlights of the World Gymnastic Championships and I get to see Neil Thomas, my old adversary, win a silver medal for his floor routine – an outstanding achievement. My claim to fame from now on will be that I once outscored a world class gymnast in the compulsory section of the British Youth Championships. Of course, I'll fail to mention that Neil was fractionally younger at the time. Anyway, it should sound a bit more impressive than my previous boast – that a former British Women's Champion once sat on my lap at a disco several years before her triumph. We were both on a training course at Crystal Palace at the time.

Adrian Mole is a hit at the box office. Eager to experience another hilarious attempt at singing by their teacher, a whole crowd of College students turns up to watch me on Friday night. Marilyn Butcher, the Head of French, is also in the audience along with Patricia Bates, one of the receptionists.

On the Saturday, good old Mario travels all the way from Manchester to support me, unaware that the play won't be the only spectacle he'll be witnessing. Given that he played such an invaluable role in reassuring me after my 'accident' with Juliette before Christmas, I decide that it's only fair he should be the first to gain a sneak preview of my healing war wound. Whether this has anything to do with his uncustomary lack of appetite at dinner is hard to say. I hope he's not going down with something. We've got a full weekend of boozing ahead of us.

Having won the competition for selling the most tickets, Cliff Rose, the producer, presents me with a large bottle of champagne at the cast party. Oh yes, students do occasionally have their uses. I think I'll be needing this to lubricate my ailing vocal cords. Or maybe I'll hold it back for my next proper romantic encounter. On current form, it should be a real vintage by then.

After the excitement of the three performances, the blues start to set in on Sunday morning. This prompts Mario and me to have one of our familiar discussions on the meaning of life and our plans for the future. Almost predictably, we touch on the subject of our year in Austria and how we threw away so many romantic opportunities. I like it when Mario is around. He's on the same wavelength, reminding me that I'm not the only nostalgic lonely heart in this crazy world.

SUMMER TERM

Free from play rehearsals and, therefore, with more time midweek to complete lesson preparation and marking, my weekend social life starts to pick up again after Easter. On a visit to *The Combine Harvester*, I bump into Isobelle Dupont, the French assistant, quite legitimately drinking with a large crowd of College students.

"I now 'ave … euh … some good friends among zhe students," she tells me. "I meet zhem 'ere offen."

I'm pleased for her, given that life in a foreign country can be rather lonely at times. On top of Howard's continued romance with Louise, this means potentially that I could find myself mixing with various members of my language classes and extra-curricular groups on a regular basis on a Saturday night. I'm not aware of any College rule against this, so I think I'll tread carefully and see how it pans out before deciding to abandon my favourite drinking hole.

Despite my initial fears that my charges may start to show less respect for the student-teacher relationship, the opposite proves to be the case with most of them actually working harder in class. Who said that familiarity breeds contempt? After a while, they begin to accept that, because of my position and their age, there's one condition to our out-of-office encounters – I won't be buying them any drinks.

June is a sad month. James Hunt, one of motor racing's great characters, dies prematurely at forty-five and Edith Matthews, a former employee of mum and dad's, and an important part of my childhood, passes away at almost twice this age.

At Mrs Matthews' funeral in early July, I recall sentimentally what my much-missed late grandmother once said to her when she was ill: "If you die before me Edith, I'll kill you."

Mrs Matthews obviously took this threat seriously, delaying her passing for as long as possible. Only eleven of us are there to pay our last respects, but this has nothing to do with Mrs M's lack of popularity, just the fact that she outlived most of her contemporaries. I'm not sure I'd fancy this. It seems such a high price to pay for a long life. Maybe a short life like Hunt's, crowned with fame, fortune and glory, and spared the injustices of old age, does have some plus points, after all.

In similar fashion to the aftermath of my terrifying car crash, the spate of deaths prompts me to analyse my own existence and wonder whether I really am making the most of it. During my period of reflection,

I remember that I still haven't fulfilled my long-standing promise to visit Petra, my Norwegian friend from four years back.

Petra and I met in the summer before I started teaching whilst I was temping for a company that organised summer schools for foreign students. Petra was only fifteen at the time. The mornings were spent teaching English. Then, after lunch, I was required to accompany the students on a wide range of excursions. Once a week, a full-day trip was arranged. One of these to Brighton coincided with a visit to England by my fourteen-year-old Norwegian second cousin, Ingrid. There was space on the coach, so she came along for the ride.

Petra and Ingrid got on famously and, feeling responsible for the latter, I spent most of the free time in the afternoon with the two girls. Petra's maturity impressed me and, given her almost perfect figure, bright blue eyes and long, blonde hair, I couldn't help wishing she were five years older. But she wasn't, so I kept my thoughts to myself. However, on her last night before returning to Norway, Petra suddenly and totally unexpectedly burst into tears, flung her arms around me and declared that the thought of leaving me was breaking her heart. I tried to console her by suggesting we could correspond on a regular basis and maybe see each other again sometime in the future. It was a very touching moment.

Although we've exchanged letters several times a year ever since and often talked about meeting up, we haven't managed to get our act together yet. Now Petra is nineteen. Admittedly, that's only a fraction older than the Upper Sixth, but she's mature and there is an eight-year age gap between mum and dad.

I pick up the phone spontaneously and dial Norway, Ingrid's parents first, then Petra. The conversation with the latter is initially a little strained, probably due to the fact that she's just completed a year in Brazil as an *au pair*, speaking almost exclusively Portuguese. However, her impressively fluent English soon returns.

"Petra, Ingrid and her family are keen for me to come to Norway this summer," I tell her slightly tentatively. "And … er … I just wondered whether I could combine it with visiting you."

"Al, it would be wonderful to see you again," she says. There's a definite note of excitement in her voice. "When will you come?"

I throw some dates at her that I know suit my relatives. To my relief, there's a week at the beginning of August that's convenient for both of us.

"This will, however, be the time that I move from home into a university hostel," she says. "And so we'll have to share a room, if that's okay with you."

This is a tricky one. On reflection, I decide that if push came to shove I could probably just about tolerate such an intimate arrangement. I hang up, proud of my spontaneity.

During the middle of July, my first year at *Mardall's Sixth Form College* draws to a close with a staff-student cricket match. I can't deny that I'm looking forward to catching my breath and recharging the batteries during the six-week holiday, but I feel sure that come September I'll be raring to go again. With hindsight, the small amount of A level teaching I did in the two secondary schools, with tiny groups and covering only a fraction of the syllabus, didn't really prepare me as well as I'd hoped for managing classes of twelve to fifteen students and teaching all aspects of the course. However, I think I've been largely successful at learning 'on the job'. There's certainly been no talk of replacing me, anyway. I really am very lucky as I can't imagine a more rewarding way of earning a living. The more informal approach of the modern Sixth Form College sector suits me down to the ground. I never was much good at telling kids off on a day-to-day basis.

But this is not quite my last teaching role of the year. Immediately after breaking up, I appear as a teacher in three outdoor performances of *Our Day Out* by Willie Russell. Rain threatens to spoil the party on each night, but we survive, as does my attempt at a Liverpudlian accent – thanks to good old *Brookie*.

On the following Wednesday, a complimentary review of the play appears in the local paper, along with a photo of me in the company of two adoring young ladies. Just like real life, then. Hm.

A day or two later, mum jets off to China with dad, concerned that should they not return Jayne and I will a) not be able to find the key to the metal box containing their will or b) fight over the will's contents.

The following morning, my radio alarm wakes me with news of a plane crash over China. In a panic, I sit bolt upright in bed and turn up the volume. It transpires from the report that all the passengers were killed, including *one* Briton. Although an obvious tragedy, my sense of relief is immeasurable.

About ten days before setting off for Norway, I drive to a nearby town to collect some medals for the impending annual gym club championships. As I'm searching for a place to park, I notice an old man with a stooped back walking up the road with two sticks at about three inches at a time. The lady in the trophy shop tells me he makes the same journey at the same snail's pace to and from the local pub twice a day. Good lad! I'm really touched by such dogged determination in the face of adversity, a real Absurd Man in Camusian terms. As it happens, I've been studying a novel by Albert Camus with one of my Lower Sixth French groups. Rather bizarrely, the man's plight reminds me of my as yet fruitless quest for true love.

Finally, the day of my long-awaited trip to Norway arrives. I head for Harwich in my first ever Japanese car, a Honda CRX. The overnight crossing to Gothenburg in Sweden threatens to be a fairly lonely affair since there don't appear to be that many other passengers on board, certainly not younger ones who are prepared to brave the bar and disco.

In the bar after dinner, however, I catch sight of a small, attractive young lady of Scandinavian appearance who seems to be on her own. Like me, she looks as though she's at a loose end. In typical Al fashion, by the time I've plucked up the courage to move across to talk to her, four Geordie lads have beaten me to it and invited her to join them at their table. I castigate myself for being so hesitant.

But all is not lost. Shortly afterwards, the girl nips off to the loo, so I craftily jump at the opportunity to ask the lads if they happen to be from Newcastle. They are and allow me to sit with them. I'm glad I didn't opt for Sunderland as the thought of front crawling it to Sweden doesn't really appeal.

The girl returns and, within ten minutes, has lost interest in chatting to the Geordies. She turns to me.

"Hi, I'm Erika," she says confidently, offering her right hand.

"Oh, hi," I reply. "I'm Alan … Al."

"Pleased to meet you, Al."

"You too. So … er … are you travelling alone?"

"No, I'm returning home to Sweden with my mum, stepdad and half brother. How about you?"

"I'm on my way to Norway to visit a friend. On my own."

After a while, the two of us go for a stroll outside in the moonlight and listen to the waves crashing up against the side of the ship. It's a beautifully romantic setting, but, close up, I can see that Erika is about the same age as my Lower Sixth students, so I decide to repress any thoughts of an emotive kiss beneath the stars. Anyway, I'm on my way to visit Petra.

"How come your English is so good?" I ask. "You don't seem to have an accent at all."

"That's because I'm half-English," she says proudly. "My real dad comes from England."

"So did you get chance to visit him whilst you were there?"

"I'm afraid not. He walked out on us years ago and hasn't been in contact since. I haven't got an address or anything, although he was last heard of in the county of Somerset."

"Oh, I'm sorry …"

"That's okay. I would like to try and find him one day, though."

We continue talking for another ten minutes or so, then decide it's time to turn in.

"Will I see you tomorrow?" Erika asks as we're on the verge of parting. "I'm sure we'll be on the main deck sunbathing."

"Okay, I'll come and find you."

I head for my cabin, wondering why it is Scandinavian girls seem to be so grown-up for their age.

The weather is excellent the following morning. After introducing me to her parents, Erika asks if I'll join her at the on-board pool to watch over her little brother whilst he paddles. Over the next hour or so, I get a taste of what it'd be like to be a parent and it's a hugely positive experience. Erika and I talk a lot more and by the time we've reached our destination, I'm genuinely disappointed to have to wave goodbye to my new-found friend. We do, however, exchange addresses. She slips the scrap of paper containing mine inside the English book she's been reading.

I return to the car deck, buoyed up by recent events.

"I've got a good feeling about this holiday," I tell myself. "Norway, here I come!"

The first week with my relatives is just perfect – amusing conversation, delicious home cooking and a fair amount of sun. I'm sorry to leave them so soon, but excited at the prospect of my stay with Petra.

I drive directly to Petra's parents' house and we have an emotional reunion. At first glance, I'm disappointed that she's cut her beautiful long, blonde hair – I don't say so, of course – although it hasn't detracted in the slightest from her stunning looks.

"If it's okay with you, Al," she says, "I thought we could stay here tonight, and then move my belongings to the university hostel in the morning."

"Sounds good to me," I reply, trying to appear cool about the prospect of sharing a room with this nineteen-year-old Norwegian beauty queen. Things are really looking up.

Before turning in, we reminisce for hours whilst listening to the tape of ballads I sent her a while back. Just like four years ago, Petra seems more serious than most English girls I know and remarkably caring and passionate about life. What's more, I think she's definitely still interested in me.

However, just as I'm starting to believe that a holiday romance could well be on the cards, Petra makes an unwelcome announcement: "Al, I just want you to know now that I think it's best if we're only friends whilst you're here."

"O…kay," I nod slowly, failing to conceal my disappointment.

She places her hand on my knee affectionately. "I hurt so bad when I left you last time. I can't allow for that to happen again. And you are only here for one week."

And so, out of respect for Petra's wishes, I refrain from getting too close. Once we've transferred to her new accommodation, I make up a bed on the floor.

After a couple of days of sightseeing in and around Oslo, Petra decides to introduce me to her older sister, Solveig, who's attending the same university. We go for a pizza.

After knocking back several bottles of wine between us, Solveig, a darker, slightly bigger built version of Petra, throws an unexpected question at me: "So how come you are not married, Al?"

"You're not the first person to ask. Er, I don't know really. I wasn't that bothered about girls when I was younger as I spent all my time training for gymnastic competitions."

"Oh, right."

"Mind you, I was really smitten with my first girlfriend, but she broke up with me soon after I went to university. Took me a long time to get over her."

"And you didn't meet any other nice girls at university?"

"I had lots of friends who were girls, but I never got the impression any of them really fancied me."

"Really? But you are not that bad looking and you have a good body."

"Oh, thanks. That comes from all the gym training."

"And now? You don't know any nice women of your own age?"

"Most of the women of my own age that I meet are either married or have a serious boyfriend. Having said that, when I was twenty-four, I did go out with a thirty-year-old. She was separated with two children."

"Well, what happened to her?"

Is this twenty questions or what? "She couldn't have any more kids."

"And so?"

"So there was never any future, as far as I was concerned. Anyway, if possible, I'd like to meet someone who hasn't been married before and doesn't already have children."

"Maybe you are too fussy."

"Mm, perhaps. Thing is, if you're going to commit yourself to one person for life, surely you can afford to be choosy, can't you? That's what I reckon, anyway."

Throughout my hard-luck story, Petra remains a passive observer, her grey cells working overtime.

Once we've said goodbye to Solveig and returned to her room, Petra steps forward suddenly and throws her arms around me.

"Please forget what I said the other day," she says. "I've decided that I want to make the most of the few days we will have together, after all."

I can scarcely believe my change in fortune. As soon as Petra heads off along the corridor to the communal bathroom, I rummage frantically through my suitcase for that carefully concealed pack of …

"Oh, bugger! I don't believe this," I curse. "Where the hell is it?"

I search further and further, tossing my clothes out onto Petra's bed like a man possessed. But to no avail. There's no hiding it, I've done the unthinkable and forgotten to pack the most important item of all after my passport, tickets and money. How could I have been so stupid?

"Why the bloody hell didn't I make a list like mum always does?" I cry out in my frustration.

"What's up?" Petra asks on her return to the room.

"Oh, nothing," I reply and pretend that I'm searching for a T-shirt and shorts to sleep in. After all, I don't want her thinking that I'm taking things for granted.

And so it happens. I get to share a bed with the gorgeous Petra. We kiss intimately and there's a bit of fumbling in the dark. I desperately want to make love to her and I'm so tempted to risk it, yet despite what the doctor said I can't be completely sure that I'm infection-free.

"You can't do this to her, it just wouldn't be fair," my head tells my highly eager and now presumably fully functional tool. "C'mon. Calm down, boy!"

Eventually, we fall asleep and I'm relieved of my misery. But then I wake again in the middle of the night and agonise over my unbelievable absent-mindedness. Feeling Petra's warm, sexy body pressed up firmly against mine and hearing the gentle sound of her breathing is sheer torture. Then I have a positive thought: "I'm here for another four days, so I'll find a vending machine in the morning. All is not lost."

The following evening, Petra takes me to an all-night party at a large log cabin in a stunning location by the sea. She tells me it belongs to a friend's parents. This time, I'm well prepared and looking forward to a night of unbridled passion.

"My boyfriend of two years that I told you about in my letters will be here later with his new girlfriend," Petra informs me over our first bottle of beer.

I pause mid-swig.

"It's fine. I'm over him now."

Reassured, I follow her over to the buffet table on the veranda. When it comes to entertaining, Norwegians, just like the Germans, never do things by halves.

As the evening progresses, I have a great time chatting to Petra and her friends under the star-lit sky whilst knocking back plenty of beer for Dutch courage. Everything seems to be running perfectly until, that is, the ex suddenly makes an appearance with his new woman. Before the bat of an eyelid, Petra dives for the toilet.

When she fails to return, I go off in search of her and discover that she's locked herself in. I knock several times before speaking: "Petra, it's Al. What's up? Are you feeling sick?" Has she really had that much to drink?

"Go away, Al!" she says from behind the barricaded door. "I don't want to speak with you." This is followed by a succession of audible, almost exaggerated, sobs.

"What's the matter? What've I done wrong?"

"Nothing. It's not your fault. I'm still in love with him and I don't want to talk to anyone."

"*Him?*"

"My ex-boyfriend, of course. Who else? Just go away and leave me alone."

Naturally, I'm upset. Glancing round, I can't fail to notice that virtually all the other guests have paired off. Feeling mercilessly rejected, I sit alone over another beer, gazing desolately out to sea, hoping that Petra will come to her senses and re-emerge. But my wait is in vain.

Eventually, I renounce all hope and head for bed, more abandoned than ever before and fed up that once again another bloke has come between me and potential romance.

"Why does it always happen to me?" I ask myself. "And surely it can't be normal for a nineteen-year-old to change her mind so frequently during the course of four days."

In the morning, Petra adopts an unusually cold manner towards me, making no attempt whatsoever to apologise for her behaviour of the previous evening. On account of her reluctance to talk openly and share her feelings – which is so out of character – I begin to feel increasingly isolated and uncomfortable.

For the remainder of my holiday, I make a severe error of judgement. Instead of abandoning ship and returning to the warm, hospitable environment of my relatives' house, I decide to stick it out with Petra in her box-like room. And it's a disaster. Tantrum after tantrum, initiated by the smallest things – like the fact that she's a fork short in her cutlery set, for example.

"You have no idea how traumatic it is for me coming to university!" she shrieks when I tell her she should be able to manage with five forks for the next week or so until her parents visit.

It's no good, whatever I say is wrong. All attempts to conduct a reasonable, adult conversation like we had so many times before in England fail miserably. And, needless to say, there's no sex – not even a kiss on the cheek. It appears that I had my one and only chance and blew it. What's more, I'll just have to wait that little bit longer now to establish if the op really has been a success. It certainly hasn't dampened my appetite, that's for sure.

My journey back to Gothenburg, complete with an unopened two-pack, is a sad, dispirited one. After all, Petra and I always seemed like soul mates. I felt so positive about the whole trip, even though I always knew I'd have to return to England without her.

"Unlucky at cards, lucky in love!" mum used to reassure me after I'd just lost all my pocket money at the family Christmastime game of Knockout Whist. Looks like I'm destined to be unlucky at both.

On the ferry home, I remember Erika and feel pleased that I found time to send her a postcard from Norway. She seemed such a lovely, genuine girl. A pity she wasn't a bit older, though. Then again, she'd almost certainly have had a boyfriend in tow. As the ship approaches Harwich, I find myself wondering if our paths will ever cross again.

Do You Want to Know a Secret?

(Year 2)

Listen, do you want to know a secret,
Do you promise not to tell?

AUTUMN TERM

Believe it or not, with the new academic year at *Mardall's Sixth Form College* barely a week old, here I am back in the confessional for the second autumn in succession. Only, on this occasion, I'm pretty confident I won't end up on a slab with my manhood at the mercy of a surgeon's knife. Whilst undoubtedly less nauseating, this year's 'secret' is, nevertheless, no less embarrassing. You see, I've met this ravishing young lady by the name of Maria who, for some inexplicable reason, turns my head like never before. Excellent news on the surface, perhaps, but there's a wee snag – she just happens to be one of the new students at College.

This is typical of me – doing everything back to front. After all, isn't it the female students who are supposed to have a crush on the young, 'unobtainable' male professional? In my world, however, as I've discovered many times before, nothing ever goes quite according to plan as far as women are concerned. And there I was just a few weeks ago after my disheartening trip to Norway vowing to give them up as a bad job. Mind you, I suppose the consequences of heartache are very much like the aftermath of a heavy drinking session: you swear publicly that you'll never go there again, fully aware that it's only a matter of time before you re-indulge.

It all started a couple of days ago during the annual enrolment process. I was 'on duty' with a couple of colleagues in the language area when a polite, well spoken, South American-looking girl with a smile to die for came in to sign up for A level Spanish. Spotting from her GCSE result slip that she also had an A* for French, I tried to persuade her to opt

33

for two languages in view of Britain's ever-increasing role in the EU. My efforts were in vain, but as I was making my case I couldn't help becoming aware of a shortness of breath, a rush of blood to my head and a sharp tingling sensation in every sinew.

This is so unlike me. Whilst I may well be a bundle of nerves in the company of desirable women I meet in the outside world, I'm normally completely in charge of my emotions in a work situation. Maria is, admittedly, very attractive, but then she's hardly the first female student with this quality I've encountered in my four-year teaching career to date and none of them has had the same unsettling effect on me. This is most peculiar. I must be going down with something.

By the end of week two, the new timetable is up and running and I meet the second of my two new Lower Sixth French groups for the first time during the last lesson of the morning. It contains not only the daughter of one of the Senior Tutors but also a French native speaker called Delphine Leblanc whose cousin, Natalie, is the star of one of my second-year classes. On top of this, there's a familiar face from the past, beaming away in the back row. It belongs to Jonathon Freeman-Hardy, a bright, conscientious pupil from my probationary year. He was only twelve at the time and in a dream group I introduced to German and also took for French. I was so proud of their progress, I had to think long and hard before abandoning them at the end of the year for a more lucrative position at another secondary school closer to home. Looks like I'll now have an opportunity to finish what I started. Well, with Jonathon, at least.

With the period over and the last student out of the door, I set about wiping the board and filing away the resources. There's a smile on my lips as I reflect on a highly promising introductory lesson. The students were, almost without exception, able, enthusiastic and eager to contribute – a teacher's dream, in fact. My train of thought is interrupted by the arrival of three girls in the doorway.

"Is it still okay to sign up for the trampolining club?" one of them asks.

The voice seems familiar. As they approach, I notice a beaming brunette leading the way. It's Maria. As if by magic, I sense the sudden appearance of goose bumps all over. Anxious that I might be blushing, I turn away.

"Mm, don't know about that," I tease in a further attempt to deflect my embarrassment. "I'll have to check the numbers first on my list."

I rummage nervously through a pile of random papers on my desk. As I glance back, I detect a sign of disappointment all round, so I smile and tell the girls they're more than welcome to come along.

"Do we have to wear leotards?" Maria asks, looking directly into my eyes.

"No, 'course not," I reply with a reassuring smile, trying desperately not to imagine her in one. It's just that if I were to break out in a hot sweat in front of them, well, then I'd definitely give the game away.

I grab my list and start to write down their names.

"You're Maria, aren't you?" I ask after taking the details of her two friends

She screws up her forehead. "How d'you know that?"

What, she doesn't remember me? "Well, I signed you up for Spanish the other day, didn't I?"

"Yes, you did, but you must've spoken to loads of other girls."

"True," I reply with several short, sharp nods, finally regaining my composure, "but it's part of my job to remember names."

As the girls leave the room, I can't help wondering whether Maria has picked up on something already. After all, women are so much more perceptive than men when it comes to realising someone likes them. It's almost as if they've got a sixth sense.

"What I'd give for this quality at the moment," I mutter to myself as I sprint down the stairs, through the covered way and into the canteen for lunch.

All afternoon, I can't stop trying to figure out why it is this Maria throws me off-balance so easily. What is it exactly in the human brain that enables us to decide who we do and don't find attractive within fractions of a second of meeting someone, even if it is an inappropriate person? How I'd love to know the scientific explanation for this. Maybe one of my colleagues in the Chemistry Department can enlighten me.

The first lunchtime trampolining session of the term gets underway on the Wednesday of the third week. Maria shows as promised with her two friends – minus leotard – and signals her arrival with a stunning smile that all but melts me on the spot. As for the flirtatious flick of her exquisite ebony locks that follows – well, nothing short of breathtaking.

It's a good turn-out and I soon notice two girls from the Jonathon Freeman-Hardy French group lining the edge of the bed – Rachel Hill and Amanda Redpath. Rachel, a slender, tanned girl with a pretty, angelic face and silky, waist-length chestnut hair, has already stood out as the shyest member of the French class. I'm surprised by this as, in my experience, the more attractive students tend to be amongst the more confident, outgoing ones. Apparently not in Rachel's case.

When her turn arrives, she clambers hesitantly onto the bed, her whole body quivering with nervous anticipation.

"First time?" I ask.

She nods timidly.

I explain briefly how to get going. As she depresses the springs to initiate her first tentative bounces, I find myself looking on like an overwrought parent, almost expecting her matchstick legs to buckle and then snap under the modest weight of her rake-like frame. Gradually, though, her confidence mounts as does the height of her bounces. Judging from the intense concentration betrayed by the lines on her forehead, I'd guess that she's a real trier. I wonder if she'll demonstrate such dogged determination when doing French.

Maria takes over from Rachel and leaves little doubt that she's an accomplished, if slightly ragged, performer. As a firm believer in steady progressions, I have to curb her enthusiasm slightly. She listens carefully to my advice, her radiant smile never far away.

Before we know it, the lunch hour is over. With no time to change out of my trackie bottoms and sweatshirt, I return hurriedly to my classroom for afternoon registration. Matt George, one of the friendliest lads in the Set and a regular at *The Combine Harvester*, is already there, eager to bring me up-to-date on his love life.

"Al, you know that girl in my English class that I've been after for a while?" he says somewhat dejectedly as I sink breathlessly into the chair behind my desk. He's one of an increasing group of students who've elected to use my first name.

I raise my head and say: "Oh yes."

"Well, I've made a complete tit of myself in front of her."

"You, Mr Smoothie, make a fool of yourself? I don't believe a word of it."

"Just get this, then. I was chatting her up this morning at break when she suddenly asked me what I had next. Seemed a harmless enough question, so I told her I had Geography with that miserable old bastard Hurst."

"And?" I ask, guessing what's coming next, but not wanting to spoil his story.

There's no missing the note of exasperation in his reply: "Well, he only happens to be her old man, doesn't he?" With these words, Matt slumps down onto the corner of the desk nearest to mine, his broad, rugger-player frame curled up in disappointment.

"Mm, looks like you're definitely in there, Matt. Just don't forget to include me in your wedding celebrations, okay?"

He flashes me a look of mock disapproval. We then chuckle away together until the remainder of the Set start to file in and take their seats.

Later in the week, as I'm making my way across the car park at the end of the day, I spot a female student climbing into the passenger seat of an old Vauxhall Cavalier. As it speeds off, I notice that the driver is Rob Hurst, the rather fearsome Head of Geography. I wonder if Matt George is also unlucky at cards.

One breaktime shortly afterwards, I tell Nic Reynolds, the staff cricket captain and Business Studies teacher – in priority order, of course – about Matt's misfortune. He then goes on to relate a similarly amusing story involving my language teaching colleague, Phil Harris – who's married to Nancy – and a teacher from New Zealand called Des Wright. Like his wife, Phil teaches French and Spanish, but during the course of his twenty-five-years' service at the College has acquired additional roles of responsibility. Not only is he the Chief Admissions Officer, but he also oversees the running of exam invigilation. These extra duties have earned him his own private office next to Finance at the front of the main building.

"Well, apparently Des went up to Phil one day last year," Nic begins, using his index finger to slide his black-rimmed glasses further up his nose towards his curly blonde fringe, "nudged him with his elbow and said: 'Come on, you jammy old sod. Who's that hot bit of stuff I've seen waiting to cavort with you in your office after hours? Go on, spill the beans. Have you given her one yet?' Anyway, from what I was told, Phil blew his top completely and sent Des packing in no uncertain terms. 'That's my daughter, you stupid Kiwi prat,' he bellowed at him."

"No wonder Des scarpered after a year," I say, wondering if Phil would really have used such language.

Phil and Nancy are devout Christians, so Des could hardly have chosen a more inappropriate person with whom to share his humour. At this point, there's a buzz of activity in the Staff Room, signalling the start of period three, and our conversation ends.

By the fourth week, the events of the summer holiday are all but forgotten and my desire to have a 'proper', legitimate girlfriend – and maybe if I'm lucky, put my new 'tackle' to the test – is as strong as it was before. But as is always the case, the harder I try to chat up girls who catch my eye down the pub or at *Clifford's*, the more I get the cold shoulder. The likes of Juliette have, apparently, gone into extinction.

When Saturday evening comes round, I stroll down to *The Combine Harvester* with Howard who's enjoying his last few weeks of idle abandon before embarking on a university Law course next month. I know I'll miss his assistance at the gym club as well as our amusing chats afterwards over a pint. It seems like a lifetime ago when his parents first moved to the area and he joined the gym as a precocious nine-year-old, boasting that he would regularly change gear in his dad's BM from the passenger seat whilst scanning the pages of *The Telegraph*. It appears that some people are just born to be self-confident and Howard, aided by his pop star good looks, hasn't had the slightest difficulty attracting the ladies since splitting up with Louise over the summer.

With its heavily knotted oak beams and perilous low ceilings, *The Harvester* recaptures perfectly the character and charm of a bygone era. The one-time watering hole of the pipe-smoking gentry, no doubt. It scarcely seems possible that in late 1993 it's become the number one meeting place of the fashionable under twenty-ones, not to mention a twenty-seven-year-old teacher. And yet every Friday and Saturday night, what seems like the entire community of local young people descends on it religiously, adorning the tiny car park with BMWs and Golf GTis, borrowed from mummy or daddy if not personally owned. Surely no other south-eastern suburb could lay claim to a superior legacy of Thatcherism.

Tonight, the interior of the pub is more crowded than ever. After a twenty-minute wait to be served, Howard and I escape to the smoke-free haven outside, overlooking the car park. Suddenly, there's a deafening screech of brakes combined with an earthquake-like rumble from a top of the range stereo as an Escort Convertible dives into the car park in search of a prominent parking space in front of the main entrance. Judging from the youthful appearance of the driver and the car's other occupants, this could easily be a Sixth Form College outing. With a wry smile, my attention reverts back to Howard.

"So where d'you reckon I'm going wrong, then?" I ask, forgetting as I always do that he's not much older than the Upper Sixth. "You know, with the ladies?"

He raises his lips from his beer and says: "You really want me to tell you?"

"Course. Why else would I ask?"

Howard places his pint glass carefully on the edge of the nearest picnic bench, then gives me the once-over. "All right, then. Well, you could do something about your appearance, for starters."

"Oh, thanks a bunch, mate, but somehow I don't think a teacher's salary would stretch to plastic surgery."

"I don't mean that," he says with a half-grin. "Okay, I do think it's a definite handicap being short, but I'm talking about your dress sense."

"Dress sense? How d'you mean?"

"Er ... well, take your jeans, for example. How much d'you pay for them?"

"Not sure, really. About a tenner in the sale, I think."

"There you go!"

"I don't follow."

"Well, they're basically too long for you and the cut's crap, to put it bluntly."

"Oh, cheers for the compliment! So … what you saying?"

"Come up to town with me next Saturday and I'll sort you out with a decent pair of *Levi's*. If you want to impress the ladies, you've got to show you take your appearance seriously. It's all about image."

"But they'll cost a fortune, won't they?"

"Probably set you back about thirty to thirty-five quid. But hey, man, who said women come cheap?"

As Howard passes both hands through his slightly unkempt mop of wavy brown hair, I detect a twinkle in his large, hazel eyes. I pause to consider my itinerary for the following weekend.

"Okay," I say with a business-like nod. "You're on."

Later that evening, as I'm heading home over the river bridge, I start to question what Howard meant about my height being a disadvantage. I'm taller than Dustin Hoffman, Tom Cruz and Michael J Fox, and it doesn't seem to be a problem for them. Maybe I should knock the jeans idea on the head and invest the money in extra drama lessons instead. Come to think of it, even Howard has appeared on TV, licking his lips in a lasagne advert.

By the following weekend, Al is a transformed man. Complete with an expensive pair of properly fitting *Levi's*, I'm ready to break hearts amongst the local female population. I must admit, though, it was a bit embarrassing hitting the clothes shops with Howard. Every time I tried on a new pair of jeans, I had to come out of the fitting room and parade in front of him. I'm sure the bloke serving us thought we were … well, you know, more than just good friends.

October is here again and brings with it two new language assistants, both very pleasant if not quite from the Claudia mould. Anne-Sophie, the French one, originates from an isolated farm in Provence and immediately presents the language department with an unusual dilemma – she has a severe personal hygiene problem. The whiff that she leaves behind in the small conversation room defies belief. Marilyn is fully aware of the situation, but eager to pass the buck.

"You're much closer to her age, young man," she tells me at the end of one of our lunchtime departmental meetings. "She'll take it far better from you."

"Yes, but I'm sure it mentions in the small print of your HoD's job description," I jest, "that combating unpleasant odours is in fact your responsibility."

Needless to say, neither of us is prepared to back down and take on board this unsavoury task, so the poor students will have to face the prospect of a further seven months of delightful aroma during their weekly conversation class. You never know, it might even assist with those elusive nasal sounds.

Although I would never claim to be an expert Sixth Form College teacher, the hands-on experience I've gained over the past year has ensured that I can now approach each working day with confidence rather than trepidation. However, it's Monday morning of the last week of this half term and I have to admit to feeling uncharacteristically nervous. This is down to the fact that it's the first day of our charity fund-raising Rag Week and, as Functions Organiser for the Student Activities team, I'm struggling badly to flog tickets for this evening's Rag Ball. The College Reps and I have had posters up for weeks, sent messages in all the registers, and plugged the event at break and lunchtimes in the canteen. Yet in spite of our efforts, we've only sold a handful of tickets – nowhere near enough to cover even the deposit I've had to pay *Razzmatazz* nightclub in the nearby City for hosting the event.

"Don't worry, most of them will buy their tickets on the door," Hannah Murray, the Head of the SA team, reassures me in her broad Glaswegian accent.

I wish I could share her confidence. According to the Reps, those members of the Upper Sixth who are already eighteen are reluctant to fork out for a party that'll only offer a juice bar.

"Can't the club rope off an area for the over eighteens and check passports?" one of them asks perfectly reasonably.

"I'll have to check with Mr Malcolmson," I reply, well aware that he's unlikely to play ball, even though he's a prominent member of the staff cricket team.

The club actually suggested this when we first booked, but as the senior member of staff with the final say Peter Malcolmson wasn't keen. I broach the subject once again, on the grounds that ticket sales would receive a timely boost. But I'm wasting my breath.

"There's no way," he tells me in an exaggeratedly authoritative tone, "that I'm prepared to sanction that. End of story."

Although over fifty and one of the 'twenty-five years at the College' brigade, Peter still considers himself a bit of a hit with the female students. There have been rumours of indiscretions in his younger days, but as a married man with his wife now working on the same site he'd be extremely foolhardy to risk anything untoward. There was a similar husband-wife pairing in my previous job. He had such a bad reputation for eyeing up the Sixth Form girls that the Head would only authorise his involvement in the summer Out of Bounds trip on the condition that his wife tagged along too. I never did find out whether she was aware of the reason behind her requested presence. I really hope I don't end up like that.

I relay the bad news to the Reps and accept that I'll just have to take the flack if the over eighteens decide to boycott the event.

"So how's it going, then?" asks an expectant female Scottish voice, interrupting my counting.

I look up from my position at Reception just inside *Razzmatazz* nightclub and see the prematurely white-haired figure of Hannah Murray heading towards me. It's now 9.00 pm and I've been frantically selling tickets for the Ball for the last two hours.

"Unbelievably well," I reply, beaming triumphantly. "In fact, I reckon there're now almost five hundred of them inside getting paralytic on coke and lemonade."

"Well done! That's fantastic!"

"You were right about last-minute ticket sales. I was panicking unnecessarily."

"Well, when you've been doing this job as long as I have … Any problems?"

"Oh, just a few tipsy lads trying to sneak a *Tesco* bag of beers past the bouncers."

"That's okay, then. Right, why don't you go inside and enjoy yourself. I can take over now."

"All right. Er, if you're sure."

Following an enthusiastic nod from Hannah, I head off into the club and make for the nearest bar, relieved that my first major function has been a real money-spinner, after all. When I arrive, I'm immediately accosted by Maria and her two friends, Natasha and Louise.

"Are you going to buy your lovely, adorable trampolining girls a drink?" Louise asks boldly.

"Oh, scrounging off a poor teacher now are we?" I reply, feigning a tut of disapproval.

Then Maria chips in: "You can't be that poor, you've got two cars."

"How on earth d'you know that?"

"You mentioned it at trampolining when we were talking about hobbies."

"So I did. Oh well, I spose I could just about afford to splash out on a coke or two without having to call in the receiver."

Once I've got the drinks in, I'm surprised by the girls' continued presence. Surely they don't want to waste their time chatting to an old fogy like me with so many fit young lads in the club.

"So have you got a girlfriend, then?" Maria asks, giving me that now familiar flirtatious smile.

"No, I'm afraid I'm just a sad, lonely old bachelor," I reply, seeking mock sympathy with a dip of my head and an exaggerated protrusion of my bottom lip.

"You're not that old," Louise says kindly. "What type of women d'you go for, then?"

"Oh, I'm not that fussy really – just beautiful, intelligent ones."

"Blondes or brunettes?"

"No preference."

"Tall or small?"

"Well, I'm not exactly a six-foot giant, so probably small, I guess."

I wonder where all this is leading. But I'm not left in suspense for long as Maria opens her mouth suddenly and says with complete nonchalance: "I normally go for short men."

I try desperately not to look at her in case I give something away, but was that a mischievous grin I perceived out of the corner of my eye?

"Is she just having a laugh winding up the gullible teacher," I contemplate, as the conversation ends and the girls disappear onto the crowded dance floor, "or have my new *Levi's* transformed me into a sex God overnight?"

Throughout the remainder of the evening, I'm inundated with students coming across for a chat. I can't help noticing that most of them are female.

"Must be because languages, gymnastics and trampolining attract more girls than boys," I decide. "If only I could be this popular with the opposite sex in the 'real' world, though."

Towards the end of the evening, Cara Mitchell and Mandy 'Mandarin' Bailey, two high-flying linguists from one of my Upper Sixth French groups and regulars at *The Harvester*, achieve the impossible by coaxing me onto the dance floor in a sober state. And for once, I actually manage to relax and not feel too self-conscious. Howard, you're a guru!

By the time I've got home, I'm high as a kite and I can't help reflecting once again how fortunate I am to have such a varied and rewarding job. What's more, Hannah will almost certainly be putting in a good word for me with the Principal.

Still buzzing, I fail to drop off straight away once I've hit the sack and find myself reliving the evening's events, including, of course, my interesting encounter with the lovely Maria. There really is something about this student that I find unbelievably appealing, and yet I still can't quite put my finger on it. Okay, I take my job too seriously to ever consider doing anything about it. That just wouldn't be right. Besides, she's too young. But … but she just captivates me like no other girl I've ever met.

"Has my late-starter status confused my emotions?" I ask myself. "Or am I just a bit of a freak?"

Whatever the answer, one thing is certain – life with Maria in the world is so much more exciting than it was without her. And anyway, if I can't make a move on her, then my hopes can't be crushed, can they? It could be my longest romance yet.

On Tuesday morning, Hannah stops me in the corridor on my way over to the *Grosvenor* for registration.

"I forgot to ask last night whether you'd be prepared to take part in the rest of the week's lunchtime fund-raising activities," she says, her face lit up with enthusiasm.

"Er, you mean Blind Date?" I reply.

"Aye, Blind Date this lunchtime, Mr and Miss Sixth Form tomorrow. Oh, and the Slave Auction on Thursday."

"What, all of them?"

"Why not? It'd be a laugh. I think the students would appreciate it."

"Well, okay, then. Provided I can find a partner for tomorrow."

By lunchtime, I find myself sitting at one end of the stage next to two strapping seventeen-year-old lads sporting back-to-front baseball caps. There's a large partition to our right, concealing a desirable female chooser that we haven't seen. The host is, as planned, none other than Peter Malcolmson, clad in his very best Cilla outfit. In reality, however, he looks nothing like the famous host having refused to don a wig to cover his thinning mop of greying blonde hair. In fact, he looks much more like ... well, Peter Malcolmson in drag, I guess. I'm also slightly disappointed to discover, as he introduces us to the large audience, that he's sticking to his own voice. Consequently, I make a last-minute decision to revive my Scouser accent from the *Our Day Out* production back in the summer.

After the familiar three questions to each contestant, the member of staff behind the screen, whose voice I recognised at once as belonging to my colleague, Rebecca Piper – a loveable punk from the Media Studies Department – chooses ... not one of the macho young studs, but me. She appears genuinely taken-aback by her choice. Hopefully, surprised rather than disappointed.

Our date consists of a trip out to the quad, with some of the College Reps serving us cake and a drink. Not quite an exotic island, but enjoyable enough. Needless to say, Rebecca is firmly attached – to a biker.

On Wednesday lunchtime, it's the turn of Mr and Miss Sixth Form. I parade up and down a catwalk-like platform extending out from the stage with a heavily breasted Matt George on my arm. We receive a loud cheer from the packed crowd, but fail to impress the judges. This is, I'm sure, entirely Matt's fault – absolutely nothing to do with me flaunting a pair of trendy Christmas shorts. Howard would not have been impressed.

On Thursday, it's the Slave Auction. Carly Walsh, a melodramatic but loveable half-American girl from my Set, offers to pay fifty pence for a feel of my biceps. Things then start to hot up as Maria's friend Louise promises to donate a pound if I drop the loud beach shorts I'm wearing. I glance across at Hannah for support, but she just shrugs helplessly, her palms turned to the ceiling. Someone in the audience then yells "Get 'em off!" This is followed by a series of deafening wolf whistles.

Whilst I'm trying frantically to recall exactly what colour briefs I put on before leaving the house this morning, I suddenly remember that my top half is covered by an extra large T-shirt that would almost certainly prevent me from revealing too much of my upper thighs, amongst other things. With an elaborate twist of my hips, I slowly discard my shorts and Louise's pound coin disappears into the bucket to a deafening cheer. To my profound relief, there are no further bids, so I make a hasty exit.

Later on, the entire rugby team turns out in force. Needless to say, the size of the donations more than quadruples. By the end of the lunch hour, the bucket is impressively full, signalling the conclusion to a hugely successful Rag Week. I wonder if Maria was with Louise when she made her bid. With everyone jumping up and down, it was impossible to tell.

During a visit to *The Harvester* over half term, I get into conversation with a girl who seems to know some of the *Mardall's* crowd. It doesn't take long for her to establish that I'm their French teacher.

"I don't spose you'd happen to know someone called Maria Grey?" she asks.

"Why's that?" I reply.

"Oh, it's just that we used to go to the same school. In fact, we were good friends."

At first, I smell a rat, but the girl seems so genuine that I can only assume her enquiry is nothing more than a bizarre coincidence. Incredible that, of the six hundred plus female students enrolled at the College, the one name she just happens to mention is Maria's. I flash a quick look around the pub to make doubly sure Louise or Natasha haven't put her up to this, but I've never seen them here before and there's no sign tonight either.

"Well, I don't teach her, but she does come to my lunchtime trampolining club," I say finally.

"Oh, okay. Well, she's a really nice person."

Before the girl has chance to elaborate, someone calls her away. This rather strange encounter leaves me wondering whether Maria has been discussing me with her friends behind my back.

Immediately after half term, Cara and Mandy 'Mandarin' stay behind after one of their lessons, and present me with a joint birthday card. I wonder if they call her 'Mandarin' because she's small and sweet. Cara, on the other hand, is a giant of a girl. I haven't exactly broadcast the fact that I'm only two years away from the dreaded three zero, but they must have remembered from the first lesson last year when I introduced myself in French and the group had to make notes – a gentle introduction after the three-month lay-off post GCSE.

Since the beginning of this term, they've both been particularly friendly. In fact, after a visit to *The Harvester* one Saturday night, they offered me a lift home with one of their male friends, Marcus, who also attends the College. They persuaded me to invite them into my flat for a non-alcoholic drink and stayed chatting for about half an hour. I'm sure there are some long-serving colleagues who wouldn't approve of this, but both girls are very mature, hard-working grade A students. What's more, it's become clear over the past year that a Sixth Form College is a far less stringent environment than a secondary school with a sixth form. If it were Maria that I was inviting back on her own, well, that would obviously be another matter altogether, however attractive the idea may seem.

Despite the age gap, I can quite easily imagine forming a long-term friendship with Cara and Mandy once they've left College. Cara, no doubt aided by her height, is a useful club tennis player and has challenged me to a match in the spring. I'm very much a part-time, self-taught player, so I could be up against it.

At the start of the lunchtime trampolining session on the Friday following my birthday, something slightly bizarre happens. Karina Prince, a tall, blonde French student from last year, who surprised me with an enormous bear hug on Leavers' Day, comes bounding through the hall door as if there's something she just can't wait to get off her chest. I'm not wrong.

"Hi there, Al. How you doing?" she says, as chirpy as ever. "I heard this rumour you were engaged and I just had to find out for myself if it was true."

For once, I'm lost for words as I finish unfolding the trampoline and kick the leg braces into place. Then I turn to face her, finally finding a reply: "You are kidding, aren't you?"

"No, I'm deadly serious. Heard it down the pub."

"Who on earth from?"

"Oh, some girl in the Upper Sixth. Can't remember her name. So isn't it true, then?"

"Er, I don't think so, somehow," I titter, revealing a ringless left hand.

"Oh well, never mind. It's good to see you, anyway."

"You too. So what've you been up to?"

Karina brings me up-to-date on her university course. Then, realising that the tramp group is waiting eagerly to start bouncing, she announces that she's got other members of staff to see and disappears.

"Me engaged?" I chuckle under my breath. "At the current rate, the Pope's more likely to marry Madonna in a registry office – no offence to either."

You know how they say things often happen when you least expect them? Well, shortly after my quip about Madonna and the Pope, and just as I'm contemplating asking for my money back on my expensive, 'pulling' *Levi's*, a person of the opposite gender actually agrees to go on a date with me. Well, sort of. Caroline Field was a pupil in my first job who, with her friend Jenny, has written to me on and off since I left the school over four years ago. By chance, Caroline has become an avid fan of the non-league football team that plays at the ground next to the gym club where I train for my Past Masters competitions.

Earlier in the week, as I was walking towards my car after another gruelling training session, I bumped into Caroline. She was uncharacteristically down in the dumps having recently been given the elbow by her long-term boyfriend. To cut a long story short, I was in a bit of a hurry and suggested we met up sometime for a drink. She looked as if she could do with cheering up. She reacted positively and, in the end, we decided to go to the cinema together at the weekend.

On my way to pick up Caroline on this third Saturday in November, I can't help acknowledging how easy it is to ask someone out when a) they know and respect you and b) you haven't actually got designs on them. Not that my 'date' isn't attractive.

Caroline and I get on well from the outset and after the film, sit in my car for a good twenty minutes, discussing her ex. I feel fairly relaxed in her company and have no hesitation in asking her back to my place for a drink. She's happy to accept.

When we arrive, however, I find that the only alcohol I've got in the flat is that bottle of champagne I won for selling all those tickets for *Adrian Mole* last Easter. To my relief, Caroline is not averse to the odd glass of bubbly. It's not long before her face brightens.

"Let's not talk about my boyfriend any more," she says. "Tell me what's going on in your life."

So I proceed to inform her about work, gym and amateur dramatics, carefully avoiding any mention of my many failed romantic exploits. It's not that I mind referring to them generally, but she was my pupil and I can't help feeling a little uneasy about disclosing more intimate details of my life. Just like with *The Harvester* crowd, I suppose. I sense, however, that Caroline is more comfortable than I am with the change in role and is anxious for me to open up.

"You not drinking any more?" she asks when I refrain from refilling my glass.

I shake my head. "I'd better not. I've got to drive you home, remember?"

"That's a pity."

Caroline looks disappointed and, if I'm being honest, so am I. Another glass might well help to loosen my tongue. What's more, it'll take me a good hour to drop her home.

"Unless, that is, you don't have to be back tonight," I say suddenly, not wanting to be a party-pooper. "I've got a z-bed or you could have my bed and ..."

"Okay. That'd be nice."

I'm as surprised by her decisive response as I am by the boldness of my question. Surely she doesn't fancy me. I mean, I'm just a friend and a sounding board, aren't I?

As I empty my third glass of champagne, I start to chill out. With it, I notice a mounting attraction to the young woman next to me on the sofa. Incredibly, over a year has passed since I sat here with Juliette. I smile at the recollection of what followed. At the same time, however, I'm anxious that my ever-increasing light-headedness will lead me to do something that will cause embarrassment, possibly even offence. And it would be a shame to ruin what has been a lovely evening. Did I imagine it or have I got the shakes?

As if sensing my unease, my more confident drinking partner edges towards me along the settee. Our thighs touch. She then turns her head towards mine and gazes longingly into my eyes. It's at this point that I realise beyond any shadow of doubt that there's no way my actions, however extreme, are going to offend this young lady tonight. I lean towards her assertively. As our lips come together for the first time, it feels as if a lifetime's worth of self-doubt and frustration have been lifted from my shoulders. Okay, she was my pupil. She's only nineteen. She's just split up with her boyfriend and almost certainly on the rebound. She's away at uni most of the time. All valid reasons for not allowing anything further to develop. But then she's a consenting adult and ... and I'm too high and too far gone to halt the inevitable trek through to my bedroom and history repeating itself. Well, not entirely, please!

It's now Sunday afternoon and I have to pinch myself repeatedly to believe the events of last night. Never in my wildest dreams had I imagined that my innocent trip to the cinema with Caroline Field would result in a night of passion. And one free of technical hitches, to go with it. I can now declare officially that I'm the very proud owner of perfectly functioning sexual apparatus and definitely no longer a virgin. Even the condom stayed on. Of course, my conscience is still there, trying desperately to spoil my moment of glory, but I think this is something I'm just going to have to learn to live with. All afternoon, I've had this incredible feeling of light-headedness and well-being. However immoral casual sex might be in the eyes of some, it certainly seems to be good for the soul.

It was all very amicable between Caroline and me this morning. She's off back to university later today and we both promised to stay in touch. A pity I'm not as bowled over by her as I am by Maria. Still, I'm sure the timing wouldn't suit her, anyway.

It's now the end of November. As I make my way to the car park at the end of another long but entertaining day's teaching, I see something that I've been dreading for quite a while now, although in my capacity as a teacher I have no right whatsoever to feel this way. Striding down the main drive in front of me is Maria, arm in arm with a bloke. In fact, it's not just any old bloke. It's one that happens to be over six-foot tall.

As I drive past the cavorting couple on my way out, I recognise her new man in the rear-view mirror. He's part of an A level PE group that I've been coaching for gym an hour a week since half term and hasn't exactly made a favourable impression. Gymnastics, it seems, is just not cool enough for his taste and every week so far, he's feigned an injury in order to skip the session. To make matters worse, he's on the arrogant side too and really fancies himself. Dave Salkeld, the Head of PE, is not happy with his attitude and has already threatened to throw him off the course unless he can provide a doctor's certificate confirming his injury.

What is it that attracts pretty, intelligent women to the pompous, macho types when there are plenty of modest, down-to-earth blokes out there? If I could have a pound for every woman I've met who claims to be attracted to 'jack the lad', I'd ... well, you know, I'd have them flocking after me for my money.

I try to convince myself on the way home that I'd be much happier if Maria were going out with one of the friendlier, more humble male students like Matt George or a salt of the earth character like Ian Thompson from one of my Upper Sixth French groups. But I think I'm probably kidding myself. When you're bowled over by someone as much as I am by Maria, I guess it's always going to hurt seeing them with someone else, even if you're hardly in a position to do anything about it. I wish I could be confident that it was only younger women that go after the brash, laddish types – many of whom seem to treat women badly – that it was a phase they eventually grew out of. However, you only have to look at the world of showbiz to see that this is often not the case.

"It's the challenge of trying to tame them," a seasoned 'bastard hunter' once informed me.

Okay, I'm overreacting, lashing out for the fact that I'm a twenty-eight-year-old teacher who a) can't find love in the 'real' world – just a one-night stand with an ex-pupil on the rebound – and b) is besotted with a current student who's just revealed a bad taste in men.

"Al, you have seriously got to pull yourself together," I tell myself firmly.

After a gym training session later in the week, I go for a swift pint with one of my Past Masters team members, forty-four-year-old father of three, Jim Headley. We're joined by the club Chairman, Cyril Granger, also a dad. In response to Jim's enquiry about Al and girlfriends, I find myself relating not my encounter with Caroline but my crush on Maria. The two men listen attentively.

"In a strange sort of way," Cyril says, once I've paused for breath, "I think her new bloke's probably saved your bacon."

Ah, the voice of experience. He's right, of course. I just wish my heart could see it that way.

Later, as I'm about to jump into the car, Jim places a reassuring hand on my shoulder.

"I do understand," he says. "It's not easy loving someone from a distance."

I'm taken aback.

"But it can't possibly be love, can it?" I ask. "I mean, surely it's not possible to love someone that you hardly know."

Jim smiles omnisciently and says: "Oh yes, I'm sure that it's perfectly possible."

"Right. One, two, three and I'll take you," I instruct in early December from my supporting position at the side of the bed, a female student's hand clasped firmly in mine.

There's an eruption all round the trampoline.

"Have I missed something?" I ask, a picture of innocence.

One of the group repeats my words with a subtle thrust of her hips. It's at this point that I get it. I raise my head to the high hall ceiling in search of divine intervention. It's at times like this that I'm relieved to be a teacher of French and German and not English. There are simply too many sexual double-entendres in the English language. I focus again on the student and, on the count of three, take her over for her maiden front somersault. There's loud applause.

"Just as well it wasn't Maria I was supporting," I reflect afterwards with relief. "Would've been even more embarrassing."

Finally, this highly eventful term comes to an end with the staff pantomime. I'm almost relieved to have the opportunity to escape temporarily from the daily sight of Maria with her new boyfriend, not to mention the skipped heartbeats that accompany her gorgeous smile.

Having never been a particularly organised person and certainly not one to have all his Christmas presents wrapped up by September, I head for the nearby City on 22nd December to start my shopping in earnest.

Once I've parked the car, I make for the High Street. As I'm walking down it, I immediately come across a hugely familiar face that at first I'm convinced is a mirage … only, the smile is too real for it to be that. I smile back instinctively and, without the exchange of a single word, Maria vanishes amongst the busy crowd of last-minute shoppers. Considering that she lives near the College – a good five miles from here – it's another strange coincidence. It reminds me of when you buy a new car. All of a sudden, you start spotting ones of the same colour, make and model wherever you look. Not that there's more than one Maria, of course.

Throughout the remainder of my two-hour shopping spree, I bump into two of my cousins, Susannah and Toby, but not a single other student from College. My heart tries to tell my head that this latest encounter with Maria is more than just a coincidence, but my head is sticking to the new, level-headed approach and dismisses the suggestion at once.

On New Year's Eve, I return to the scene of my shopping expedition after Simon Lennon has invited me to kip over in his newly acquired flat, located within walking distance of the town centre. He tells me that there's a buzzing nightlife, but that we may not be able to get into all the pubs because of a 'ticket only' policy.

He's right on both accounts. However, we still manage to find a busy, central drinking hole that's selling tickets on the door for two pounds. Simon introduces me to spirits for the first time and we have a fun three hours or so reflecting on the joys of teaching and putting the world to rights.

At five to midnight, we down our drinks and hurry through the back streets towards the cobbled pedestrian precinct where, according to Simon, there's a traditional annual gathering of about two thousand people under the large clock. He's not wrong.

After the final chime, there are handshakes, hugs and kisses all round, as if all the world's woes have been sidelined for one tiny moment in time and peace on earth reigns supreme. As we fight our way through the animated throng, even Simon and I are kissed warmly on the cheek by several passing strangers. And then it happens. Out of the corner of my eye, I suddenly spot Maria and Louise, standing just a few feet away. For a split second, they freeze at the sight of me, but then Louise takes an assertive step forward and wraps her arms around me in a warm New Year embrace. Maria follows suit and, with the woman of my dreams unexpectedly in my arms, my vodka-distorted brain can't help entertaining an array of seriously illegal thoughts.

"I can't snog you, can I, cos you're a teacher?" Maria says, completely out of the blue.

I'm stunned by the audacity of her comment, yet every nerve in my body urges me for once in my life to be bad and escort her away for an illicit kiss in one of the side alleys.

"Would it really matter in the history of the universe?" I ask myself. "After all, it's New Year's Eve and all around me there are people behaving out of character."

I gaze wistfully into her gorgeous dark eyes, realising more than ever how stunningly beautiful she is. And that smile – I can't imagine ever being able to forget it. I want to kiss her so badly and judging from her comment – and this is what makes it even harder – she'd be up for it too. Or is she just bluffing? But I'm a teacher bound by professional responsibilities and in spite of my inebriated state – it was good stuff that vodka – kissing students is nowhere to be found in my job description. I brace myself.

"Er … yes, that's right. You can't," I say finally. "So where's your boyfriend tonight, then?"

"Oh, he's out with his mates. He wants to shag me, you know. What d'you reckon, Mr Bentley? D'you think I should let him?"

Before I have chance to answer this impossible question, I'm rescued by French student Ian Thompson who waddles over towards me with a shout of "Al". Ian suffers from spina bifida, with one of his feet angled outwards, hence his highly characteristic gait.

"Happy New Year!" he says, full of festive cheer. "Cara, Mandy 'Mandarin' and the others are over there. They'd love to see you."

With an apologetic shrug, I reluctantly leave Maria's clutches and follow Ian over to the rest of *The Harvester* gang, with Simon still in tow. There are further seasonal hugs with some of the girls repeating the kiss-on-both-cheeks routine they started on the French Exchange back in the spring. However, unlike last spring, there's no embarrassment this time. My thoughts are too far away for that, wondering whether I'll ever be granted another opportunity to kiss the girl of my dreams. Or have I missed my one and only chance like I did when it came to sleeping with Petra on that fateful night back in Norway? My only consolation is the fact that I can return to work in a few days with a completely clear conscience and with my job still intact. But will this reassure me when I'm on my death bed, looking back on my loveless twenties?

At this point, I bump into about half a dozen of Jonathon Freeman-Hardy's contemporaries from my first teaching job. It's great to see them again almost five years down the line. They just about have time to fill me in on what they've been up to before Simon gives me the nod that he's ready to turn in. What an evening! I've got a feeling that '94 might be a very special year.

SPRING TERM

The onset of a new year has prompted me to seriously consider some wholesale changes to my current lifestyle. Since I've definitely found the job of my dreams at *Mardall's*, priority number one is to give up my rented accommodation in mum and dad's back yard, and get on the property ladder. There's no way a teacher's salary will stretch far enough for me to buy locally, so, reluctantly, I've started looking further afield. In fact, there's a smallish market town about twenty-five miles further south – but still only about twelve from the College – which has ex-council houses that fall into my price bracket. And I've already seen a three-bed, end-of-terrace one that I like. With a double length garage and off-road parking for at least another three vehicles, it's tailor-made for a car enthusiast like me. At fifty-seven grand, I reckon it's a bargain.

It's the prospect of becoming a homeowner at long last that's occupying my thoughts on the last Saturday of January. It's 10.00 in the evening and I'm surrounded by about twenty seventeen- and eighteen-year-olds in varying states of inebriation. Only, on this occasion, it's not the College or *The Harvester* that's providing the setting, but my Uncle Thomas' house. It's his daughter Susannah's eighteenth birthday party. I'm already feeling a bit out of place in my role as cousin rather than teacher, but I've been promised the settee for the night, so I think I'll just down a few more cans and continue planning my future in the privacy of the dining room. It was sweet of Susannah to invite me, though.

A little later on, after I've finished helping myself to another plate of food from the buffet table, a skinny, giant of a girl with longish blonde hair approaches me suddenly.

"So you must be Susi's older cousin, then," she says, looking down at me – literally, not metaphorically.

"Oh, er … yes. That's right," I reply, hurriedly swallowing the remainder of a sausage roll. "Hi, I'm Al."

"Yeah, Susi told me. I'm Hayley, by the way."

At this stage, I'm convinced Susannah has sent her friend over purely on a mission to keep me company. Another thoughtful gesture.

For the next few minutes, we go through the usual pleasantries. Then, rather unexpectedly, Hayley removes the paper plate from my left hand and signals in the direction of the lounge with a gentle toss of her head. This has the effect of covering her face with errant strands of streaked blonde hair. All rather alluring.

"Come 'n' have a dance," she says.

I hold up both hands. "Oh, I … I don't know … I … I'm not …"

Before I have chance to complete my mumbled excuse, Hayley grabs my hand and leads me through onto the makeshift dance floor. I feel self-conscious at first, but then remember the Rag Ball and how I managed to overcome my inhibitions about dancing. What's more, I've got my demon *Levi's* on this time too.

As if by magic, the DJ – Susannah's younger sister, Rosie – puts something considerably slower on and Hayley leans on me as if to suggest the effects of the booze have finally got the better of her. By the middle of the track, her arms are wrapped firmly around my neck and mine around her waist, bringing my forehead and her chin within close proximity of each other. A second smooching song follows the first and before I have chance to plot my escape, Hayley has kicked off her heels to come down to my level and planted her lips firmly onto mine. Slightly taken aback, I decide to oblige. After all, it'd be extremely impolite to back off after she's made all the running. Besides, I can feel something stirring down below.

Our lips part with the last beat of the song and, with excitement getting the better of me – or was it that last can of Heineken? – I nip off to the loo. Just like a couple of months back with Caroline Field, I have to pinch myself to believe my dramatic change in fortune. All of a sudden, I'm brimming with confidence again.

When I return to the dance floor, I notice at once that Hayley is missing. I glance around the room and spot her sitting on one of the two large settees, being chatted up by Susannah and Rosie's tall fifteen-year-old brother, Toby.

"Cheeky little sod!" I mutter under my breath.

I pop off to the kitchen to grab another can from the fridge. I return to the shocking sight of Toby in the middle of a passionate kiss with Hayley ... my Hayley. Considering it only seems like yesterday that I was pushing him in his pram on a typical family walk, I'm not overly impressed. My self-confidence plummets instantaneously.

Once she's aware of my return, Hayley abandons Toby's side and ambles across to me, her tail between her legs.

"Whoops!" she says with a shrug of guilt. "Sorry!"

For the remainder of the evening, Toby pursues Hayley relentlessly each time I've turned my back. To my relief, however, she manages to resist his repeated advances – at least when I'm within view. I may well be ten years older than her, but losing out to my little cousin really would be the last straw. It's amazing how a bit of competition can heighten one's interest.

Before I know it, all the guests have made tracks and I find myself crashed out on the sofa nearest the door with a half-naked Hayley lying beside me.

"Aren't you sposed to be sleeping in Susi's room?" I ask, wondering what my auntie and uncle are making of all this in the bedroom above.

It's not that I'm desperate to get rid of her, of course, but she is only eighteen and ... I'm a teacher. Not *her* teacher, admittedly, but a teacher, nevertheless. Would I be feeling so uneasy if I were a brickie?

Hayley shrugs. The problem is, I'm drunk and, with her sexy body pressed up against mine, my conscience has a real battle on its hands.

"I'm too far away from work for it to leak out," I then reason, duly easing Hayley's head closer to mine for another kiss. And in addition to the pure physical pleasure of intimacy, I'm starting to feel so much more comfortable with an inflated ego.

For the next couple of hours, the kissing continues, accompanied by a small amount of foreplay. But despite my reasoning, I just can't bring myself to go any further. In my mind's eye, I can see my grandmother sitting in the chair opposite at Christmastime and ... she always loved Christmas so much. Anyway, as much as I've got a taste for this whole sex business, I've no intention of becoming a male tart, especially when every member of my family would get to hear about it.

Hayley eventually slips away to join Susannah upstairs and, in spite of the intense physical frustration, I'm relieved I managed to hold back. Now that I've already got one proper sexual experience under my belt and proved beyond doubt that my tackle is in normal working order, I think I'd rather revert to my original plan of saving myself for a Maria equivalent who I'm actually going out with. One thing has become clear, though. It's a hell of a lot harder controlling my animal instincts now that I'm no longer a virgin. I guess what you don't know, you don't miss.

On my way home the following morning, I can't help wondering why it is eighteen- and nineteen-year-old girls seem to fancy me now when they wouldn't even spare me a second look when I was that age myself. It's not as if I'm a suave, smooth-talking older man with loads of experience and a fat wallet. This whole female sexual attraction thing, it really is beyond me.

Although a conversation with Susannah during the week after the party betrays the fact that Hayley has no interest in seeing me again, I suppose I can derive some solace from the fact that she must've found me vaguely attractive in the first place. Anyway, my thoughts are elsewhere at the moment. I've taken the plunge and committed myself to buying that ex-council house with the large garage. My initial offer was rejected, so fifty-seven grand it is, then.

For Valentine's Day, the College Reps organise an internal postal service. When two of them appear at my classroom door at the start of the lunch hour, I assume it's to report on the extent of its popularity. But I'm mistaken.

"Looks like you've got a couple of admirers, Mr Bentley," one of them says, handing me two white envelopes.

"Mm, that's funny," I reply. "I don't remember informing my mum and sister about your service."

"You must be more popular than you think," his female accomplice says kindly with a smile.

Once they're out of sight, I open the two cards with intrigue. The first is simply signed *From the three of us*. Since most of the female students I'm associated with hang out in pairs, my immediate suspicions fall on Natasha, Louise and Maria. Nice gesture! The second card has an interesting pattern of lipstick prints all over the envelope and contains a mysterious rhyme followed by a large question mark.

> *When I'm sad and weary*
> *When all hope has gone*
> *When I walk down the corridor*
> *I think of you with nothing on!*

(I fell in love with your bum, but the rest of you isn't bad either!)

Gazing out of the window with this bizarre yet hugely flattering message still in my right hand, I find myself hoping that it's from … well, you know who. Not so that I can lower my standards and attempt to initiate an illicit romance, but so I can still live with the flicker of hope that something might materialise between us once she's left College and everything is above board. Once again, I know I shouldn't be thinking along these lines, but … but I just can't seem to control my emotions at the moment. Maybe Jim Headley was right, after all. Perhaps I am actually in love with Maria. I wonder if I'd be any good at laying bricks.

Two days later, my relatively new friend, Martin Studd, who was outstanding as the lead in *Adrian Mole*, accompanies me to work to view some History lessons. He's in the middle of a teacher-training course and wisely considering the possibility of working in the Sixth Form sector once qualified. I leave him in the capable hands of my 'neighbour', Michael 'Bomber' Lancaster, whose short temper and booming voice have occasionally interrupted my language lessons, thanks to the paper-thin nature of the adjoining wall. Does he raise his voice to help combat his stammer?

At lunchtime, Martin joins me for trampolining. I confessed to him about my 'thing' for Maria over a beer last night and he can't wait to give her the once-over. When the lady in question appears, however, sniggers break out all around the bed. On one side of her neck is just about the largest love bite I've ever seen. Not that I've seen that many, of course.

"Been carrying out secret rendezvous with vampires again?" I ask with a grin.

Maria feigns embarrassment, but I sense that, deep down, she's actually quite proud of her new identity mark. I can't help wondering whether it's a clear indication that she's finally allowed her boyfriend to have his wicked way with her. It's none of my business, I know, so why does the thought of it hurt so much?

Martin really enjoys the day's experience, although he admits to being at a loss as to why I'm so besotted by Maria. I guess there's no accounting for taste.

I'm not exactly sure why, but the rest of February has left me feeling rather uninspired and down in the dumps. Maybe I'm lovesick or maybe I'm just a touch sad at the prospect of leaving a town that's been my home for more than twenty-five years. Whilst I accept that the time has come to move on, the fact remains that I've been incredibly happy here. My childhood was particularly magical. I reckon I must've been one of the few students at Southampton University who couldn't wait to leave the campus and head home at the end of each term. Not that life at uni was that bad. Home life was simply superior.

March begins badly with both my cars being off the road at the same time. I manage, however, to arrange a lift in to College with Victoria Brook, one of my Upper Sixth French students who lives just round the corner. She owns a smart Vauxhall Astra.

At the end of the day, one of her classmates, Pete Sargent, drops me back in a Peugeot 205. I can't help noticing that both cars are considerably newer than any of the ten I've owned. Hm, maybe I should consider giving up teaching and returning as a full-time student. Still, at least I'll have my own pad before long.

Just before this year's Exchange trip to France, Maria accidentally whacks my knee whilst I'm supporting her for a backward somersault on the trampoline.

"Oh, I'm terribly sorry," she says, showing what appears to be genuine concern. "Are you okay?"

"Yes, I'll be fine," I reply. "I'm a pretty tough lad."

"Really? Well, in that case, maybe I should give you an arm wrestle."

And sure enough, before the tramp is folded away at the end of the session, I take on Maria in a battle of brute force. The strength of her resistance impresses me.

"I'll beat you one day," she says, gracious in defeat and I can't help wishing that one day there'll be wrestling of a slightly more intimate nature between us. "Oh, and have a good time in France! You can keep an eye on Natasha for me."

It's strange, but for the first time since I clapped eyes on Maria back in September, I sense real affection in her voice. I appreciate it, of course, but it doesn't half add to that feeling of hopeless longing. If only I could establish whether she had anything to do with that Valentine's card. Unfortunately, there's absolutely no way I can put her on the spot. The problem is – and I've encountered this before – when you really, really want something badly, it's so easy to misinterpret signals and rearrange the world to conform to your own blind desires.

I'm back from the Exchange in one piece. Although it was great to temporarily escape the pressures of lesson preparation and marking, nothing particularly exciting happened, apart from a reunion with my old English teacher and Head of Year, James Wattingham. Whilst at secondary school, I was one of a small group of lads invited on a Norfolk Broads trip with James and the school's Deputy Head, Clifford Potterton. James, a confirmed bachelor in his thirties at the time, continued to include me and several others in his holiday plans after we'd left the school and, on more than one occasion, we tackled the south-eastern waterways in a long boat. One evening over a beer, James disclosed to his former charges that he thought he'd 'missed the boat' as far as women and marriage were concerned. Shortly afterwards, he was reunited with a former teaching colleague and the pair went on to tie the knot. I was delighted to be invited to the wedding celebrations. Weary of teaching, the couple emigrated to France after starting a family, where they took on a small campsite and adjoining restaurant.

Given that the new home was only a short train journey from Poitiers, I managed to slip away from the Exchange party and catch up with James, Mary and their two young daughters. They appeared to be thriving in their new life and I left on an overwhelmingly positive note. Whenever I lose heart after another failed romantic exploit, I always think of James and it helps me find a second wind.

In Poitiers, I stayed with a forty plus Economics teacher called François, his diminutive wife, Claudette, and spoilt eight-year-old son, Laurent. The food was sublime and my hosts really went out of their way to entertain me at the weekends. However, François is unbelievably serious and it was impossible to get him to lighten or open up for even a nanosecond. I tried my utmost on numerous occasions to persuade him to join me for a drink in the evening, but he always declined as if it were completely against his religion.

Considering that I'll have the space to accommodate guests by the time the French party visits England in May, I'll be obliged to put up François for the duration of their stay. That's only fair, of course, but it could be the longest, most uneventful ten days of my life.

Rachel Hill – or 'Damon' as I frequently refer to her – and Amanda Redpath were a delight to be with on the trip. They remind me so much of Cara and Mandy from the Upper Sixth. Since both now do gym with me as well as trampolining and French, it looks like we'll be seeing a lot of each other in the months ahead. Rachel really is a stunner.

The last day of March is designated for In-Service Training (INSET). I manage to slip away at lunchtime to collect the keys to my new property. Although I won't actually be moving all my belongings until tomorrow – April fool that I am – standing in the empty building fills me with a wave of excitement, an expectation of something new and very special just round the corner. Staring out of the vast upstairs bedroom window, with its rusting metal frame and secondary double-glazing, I can see a towering block of flats directly opposite and houses all around that betray their continued council ownership through identical replacement PVC windows and tile cladding far more modern than my rather drab asbestos version.

"Not quite the estate of my dreams," I tell myself, "but at least it's a start."

I just hope Guy Harper – alias Barry Kent from *Adrian Mole* – was pulling my leg about the number of criminals that share my postcode.

Whilst my mood at the moment is one of returning optimism, a staff meeting shortly after our INSET day provides possible cause for concern. According to Avril Cunningham, our revered Principal, the Government will shortly be introducing an alternative funding formula for Sixth Form Colleges. It's to be based on units of study rather than the number of students on roll. Apparently, this is a major cost-saving exercise in disguise that will not only dramatically reduce the amount each department is entitled to spend on resources but also have far-reaching implications for staffing.

"Regrettably, this will result in larger class sizes than we are enjoying at present," Avril announces rather sombrely, "could make some minority subjects such as Latin no longer financially viable, and ..." She then pauses for a sip of water before placing her head on one shoulder and continuing in an Oscar-winning display of compassion: "And, more seriously, we may well at some stage in the future have no alternative but to entertain the possibility of redundancies in certain curriculum areas."

The length and breadth of the Staff Room, the atmosphere can be cut with a knife as a gathering of some eighty professionals grapple to come to terms with something that, until this moment, has always seemed inconceivable – redundancies in education. A heated discussion ensues, with particularly poignant comments from Julian Horvath, the Classics teacher. In the run-up to the next election, the Tory Government will no doubt attempt to hoodwink the electorate by producing statistics to confirm that funding in education has risen substantially during its term in office. The reality, it seems, is quite different. Anyway, sixth forms in secondary schools have always been better funded than Sixth Form Colleges.

As I leave the building, as shell-shocked as everyone else, I convince myself that as a junior member of staff with the flexibility to teach both French and German to A level – not to mention my extra-curricular contributions – my position should be secure.

My first few nights out in my new town prove to be relatively unspectacular, although it hasn't escaped my attention that there are plenty of attractive women here of all ages. I must admit that I've felt a bit isolated without friends or family nearby, but enough of them are threatening to visit soon, so I'm sure I'll survive. Anyhow, one of the objectives of moving was to make some new friends.

It's on one of my evening visits to the town centre over the Easter holidays – about ten minutes' walk away – that I catch sight of a pretty, bubbly brunette who appears to be part of a wide circle of friends in their early twenties. I can't help overhearing their conversation and it doesn't take long to establish that they're a friendly, seemingly approachable crowd.

Just as I've sunk a third pint of lager and plucked up the courage to introduce myself, the more outspoken of identical ginger twins suggests perfectly audibly that they move on to *Alfredo's*. Since this was mentioned to me before as a 'cool' place to hang out and I've no idea where to find it, I decide to follow the group inconspicuously.

Alfredo's turns out to be a small, modern, rather chic wine bar on two levels, connected by a spiral, wrought iron staircase. More importantly, it's bursting at the seams. Access to the bar is hampered not only by an almost impenetrable wall of high-spirited bodies but also by a thick cloud of cigarette smoke that's impaired visibility considerably. After several deep inhalations of breath – for oxygen as well as Dutch courage – I manage, however, to squeeze my way through the crowd to take up a position at the bar right alongside the attractive brunette.

I tap her gently on the shoulder and say rather awkwardly: "Hi there, I'm new to the town and … er … well, to be honest, I've just followed you and your friends from the pub. Thought you'd know the best places to ... er ... to go. Hope you don't mind."

The girl places her mouth barely inches from my left ear to make herself heard above the surrounding din.

"No, not at all," she says. She then proceeds to wriggle her shapely physique as if to deliberately draw attention to it. "So what's your name, then?"

"Oh, yes – sorry. I'm Al. Al Bentley."

"Hi, Al. I'm Emily. I'll just get myself a drink, then I'll introduce you to the others."

With handshakes all round and repeated coverage of the usual formalities – you know, who I am, where I come from, what I do for a living and why on earth I'd want to live in a dump like this – I soon realise that my initial assessment of the group was spot on: they are indeed a particularly friendly bunch. We spend the rest of the evening together.

At chucking out time, we stand in a huddle outside the kebab shop, contemplating our next move.

"So then, Al, have you got your own place?" one of the twins asks, breaking the temporary silence.

"Yes, I've got a house on the Dandelion estate," I reply.

"A council house?" one of the other lads enquires, his broad, bouncer-like frame perched on the back of a tall, rather shy girl who I assume is his other half.

"Well, an ex-one, yes."

Then Emily's best friend, Delilah, a rather loud, heavily built girl, pipes up: "So it's back to your place for a party, then?"

"Er ... I ... I'm not sure. It's just that I haven't really got to know the neighbours yet and ..."

"Don't worry about that." There follows a drunken, dismissive wave of her hand. "We won't make a lot of noise."

In reality, I'm pleased with my evening's work and hardly ready to hit the sack, so it doesn't take much further persuasion to win me over.

Within half an hour, ten of my new-found friends have descended on my pad and transformed it into the scene of a totally unexpected house-warming party. Delilah raids my record and considerably smaller CD collection, and then automatically assumes the role of DJ, selecting what she deems the most appropriate sounds for the occasion. Her appreciably older brother, Daniel, who's already greying at the temples, lights up a rather smelly cigarette, which prompts several others to follow suit. The few cans of lager I had stored in the fridge and two unopened bottles of wine are rapidly consumed.

"You haven't got anything to eat, have you?" Emily asks suddenly, running her hand gently down my backside. "I'm starving."

At this point, I remember the rhyme in my Valentine's card and feel encouraged that she too seems to have noticed my newly discovered asset. In my mildly intoxicated state, I'm eager to please the sexy Emily who appears to be giving off the sort of vibes I could scarcely have dreamt of when I first spotted her just a few hours ago. Looks like a change of surroundings has changed my fortune. Problem is, I can't see her doing anything with her friends around. I'll have to try and get her on her own.

"How about some oven chips?" I say, guiding her into the kitchen away from the others.

"Listen up, everyone. Al's doing oven chips," Emily then announces with a flourish over her left shoulder. Oh, bugger!

Needless to say, Emily isn't the only famished soul at the party and, within seconds, there's a mad rush towards the kitchen door. An entire kilo bag of frozen oven chips is devoured, of which the host and principle chef receives about four.

Even with her stomach full, Emily seems to have ants in her pants – she's a dance teacher, by the way – and foils my numerous attempts to talk to her alone. Maybe she likes to take things slowly. After all, she has only just met me. I think I'd be wise to back off for tonight. Wouldn't want to scare her away.

The events of this Saturday night are repeated the following weekend almost down to the tiniest detail, including Emily's spontaneous transition from flirt to flight.

It's not until surfacing on the Sunday morning, when I'm confronted once again by a sitting room that reeks of stale cigarette smoke and looks like a bomb has hit it, that I begin to question the wisdom of my hospitality.

"It wouldn't be so bad if they'd offered to supply some booze," I mutter irritably as I pick up a wine glass full of fag ash and transfer the contents to an empty beer can.

My thoughts are then interrupted by the shrill sound of the doorbell. I open up to find Delilah's brother, Daniel, a plumber by trade, standing in the doorway looking completely done in.

"Sorry to disturb you, old son," he says. "I just wondered whether you'd come across a large lump of gear." He makes the shape of a golf ball with his thumb and middle finger. "I think I must've mislaid it here last night."

"Er, pass. I haven't got round to clearing up yet," I reply, realising all of a sudden why his fags appeared to have such a characteristic twang. "You'd better come in and take a look for yourself."

"Good man. There was about ten quid's worth there."

Daniel searches thoroughly, but in vain. He leaves shortly afterwards with a resigned shrug of his shoulders.

"By the way, if you ever need any plumbing or your heating serviced, Dan's your man," he says kindly before turning and disappearing down the hill.

Judging by the sight of him this morning, I can't help feeling that he'd be well-advised to give his own body a thorough service before tackling any ailing heating systems. Now, now! It's just that I've always had an aversion to illegal substances. I'm not sure whether it's due to my upbringing or the fact that doping in sport always seemed to me to be the most unforgivable form of cheating. Mind you, I have to confess that I did once have a brief puff outside *The Harvester* – just to be able to say I'd tried it.

That 'Dan the man' thought he could smoke pot or whatever it was in my house without asking permission only adds to my frustration on this Sunday morning. There's no escaping the truth. In my eagerness to make new friends and find a girlfriend to help deflect thoughts of Maria, I've allowed myself to be taken advantage of. They're a nice enough crowd, but why is it when you give some people an inch, they take a mile?

The remainder of the Easter holiday is taken up with the marking of French coursework – thirty-six essays of a thousand words, in fact. I would've started on them weeks ago had it not been for my move and all the administrative palaver that accompanied it. With the submission date for moderation fast approaching, I can't delay any further. Given that there are three separate marks out of ten for content and three for language, it's taking me much longer than anticipated – almost an hour to complete each piece.

It wouldn't be so bad if the temperatures outside hadn't decided to dip to almost sub-zero figures. Now I know why mum and dad expressed reservations about the lack of central heating in the house. There are these strange heaters with bricks inside in some of the rooms, but when I switch the button to *on*, nothing seems to happen for hours. Next year, I'll start marking my coursework well in advance, probably in the warmth of the College without the need for gloves and a woolly hat.

SUMMER TERM

On the morning of the first day back, Marilyn scowls at me when I confess she'll have to wait until the end of the day for a full list of coursework marks. Despite my efforts in the arctic conditions of my study – the box room at the front – there are still two essays left to correct.

I do, however, manage to finish them off later in the day during a free period and successfully appease my leader.

"Thank you very much, young man," she says in a typically brusque manner. Her face then softens as she adds with a half-smile: "I do find it difficult to be cross with you for long."

With the weight of those wretched coursework essays off my mind, I'm in particularly good spirits the following weekend for the maiden visit of my former colleague, Simon Lennon. After a curry at the Indian on the way into town, we do a circuit of my locals. It isn't long before we bump into the gang. I introduce Simon.

At closing time, my new friends hurry off to Delilah's house for a party, with no sign of inviting the two of us. Slightly offended after my hospitality of recent weeks, I persuade Simon we should gatecrash.

As we're heading back home from Delilah's in silence some two hours later, Simon opens his mouth to speak.

"Didn't like that Emily at all," he says with an air of authority. "And she's got a big arse for a dance teacher."

I flash him a look of surprise.

"You reckon?" I say. "I must admit, I can't quite make her out. One minute she's flirting with me like crazy, the next she can't wait to run away. Maybe she's scared of …"

"She's just not interested, mate."

He adjusts his glasses and passes a long, skinny hand through his grey-streaked raven black hair.

"What, did … did she say something tonight, then?"

"Didn't need to. It's blatantly obvious she doesn't fancy you. But yeah, as it goes, Delilah did mention that your advances have been the subject of amusement amongst the group."

I'm hacked off, of course, but also mystified as to why Simon seems to be able to read the signs so clearly when I'm always left completely confused by them.

"She's just a tease, mate," he adds as we turn into my road. "Forget about her."

On account of the fact that I seem to have made a bit of a fool of myself in front of the gang, I view the arrival of the French Exchange party at the end of April, complete with the dour, uninspiring François, as a welcome distraction. He may well have as much in common with me as I have with sign reading, but at least I'll have an excuse to distance myself from the group's clandestine mockery over the next ten days or so.

"Tu as envie de m'accompagner au pub ce soir?" I ask once he's unpacked his bags and we've had a bite to eat.

"Non, non, non!" he replies emphatically, placing both hands together to form a steeple, then resting one side of his head on it with a mock yawn. "I am ... a bit ... euh ... comment dire 'crevé'?"

"Knackered."

"Ah yes, sank you. I ... euh ... rest 'ere and sleep. But ... euh ... but you go."

After protesting in vain about leaving him alone on his first night in England, I head into town, realising more than ever what a bundle of laughs François' stay promises to be.

The following day is a Saturday. In the evening, I propose to François that we pop into town for a meal. After careful consideration, he agrees – on the condition that we go somewhere that's not too rowdy.

I take him to *Ten Tenths* wine bar and bistro, which serves particularly good traditional English food. The bar can get busy after 9.00, but that's a couple of hours away, so there shouldn't be anything to upset my little olive-skinned guest. To my relief, there are only about ten people sitting inside the Harvesteresque building drinking unobtrusively.

"Would you like to sit downstairs in the bar or upstairs in the restaurant?" the polite young waitress asks.

I'm about to translate, but François' comprehension of the English language proves far superior to his ability to speak it.

"I sink we go ... euh ... up zhe stairs," he says. "Zhere is ... euh ... much ... euh ... noise 'ere."

So, reluctantly, I follow the young girl and François up the steep, narrow staircase, away from the imaginary din. My guest selects a table by the window, overlooking the High Street.

"Has this man got no sense of adventure whatsoever?" I mutter under my breath. "You'd never believe he's barely into his forties."

Although in a way I envy his cosy family life, if this is what marriage does to a person's spirit, then maybe my single status isn't so unattractive, after all.

During the course of the meal, we manage to keep the conversation ticking over – mainly in French – covering such exhilarating topics as the English weather, food and architecture. My attempts to switch it to a more personal level fail miserably.

Once we've finished the dessert, François rises from his seat.

"Où sont les toilettes?" he asks, mopping his lower lip and chin meticulously with one of the cotton serviettes.

"En bas," I reply, pointing towards the stairs.

Judging by his agitated state on return from the Gents two minutes later, I half expect a protracted criticism of the hum from the floor below and a request to procure cotton wool before our next evening excursion. But I'm forgetting that life can often prove extremely unpredictable and that A. C. Bentley is not exactly the world's finest judge of character.

"Allez, allez!" François cries, gesturing frantically in the direction of the floor below. "You must come quickly. Zhere are girls, many, many beautiful girls. Allez!"

Once I've explained to the waitress that we're transferring downstairs for further drinks and not doing a runner, I follow François in pursuit of his 'remarkable' discovery. Not once during my ten-day stay with him and his family in France did I detect a sign that the screwed up forehead and intense frown would ever leave this dreary, unexcitable Frenchman. And yet all of a sudden, here he is now in a distinctly noisy and smoky wine bar in England on a Saturday night with his eyes popping out of their sockets and a grin normally associated with the proverbial Cheshire cat.

And from this point on, there's no stopping him as we do a circuit of the local bars, one pretty girl after another finding herself on the receiving end of the charms of my metamorphosed guest. My initial assumption that they'd run a mile, given his age and broken English, proves to be way off the mark as they listen with a degree of captivation and interest that only my students seem to grant me.

"How the hell does he do it?" I ask myself with a mixture of intrigue and good humour. "Maybe it's easier when you know there's someone else to go back to. Nothing to lose."

Before we know it, last orders are called and I have to drag a reluctant François away from his most recent victim.

"I see you again ... euh ... very, very soon," he says before kissing her on both cheeks.

As we're negotiating the ten-minute walk home, both slightly the worse for wear, François suddenly stops in his tracks.

"How far you say it is to zhe next disco?" he asks, his English more fluent than before.

"Oh, about eight miles," I reply. "Thirteen kilometres."

"And you are certain you cannot drive zhere?"

"I don't think so somehow. Not after six pints of lager."

We continue for another hundred yards or so before he stops again and grabs my arm. "Maybe I could drive your car?"

"François, you've had as much to drink as I have. The police in this country are very strict about drink-driving."

"C'est dommage, ça!"

"Yes, it's a shame all right." I pause to reflect. "I tell you what. I'll drive you to a nightclub next Saturday, if you like."

He nods slowly, a sombre, intense expression returning to his Mediterranean-featured face.

A hundred yards further on, François pipes up once more: "Tell me, Al. Zhe girls 'ere in England. Do zhey carry ... euh ... les ... euh ... *préservatifs?*"

Needless to say, my guest is a new man following his exploits on that first Saturday night. On several occasions during the following week on return from the various planned excursions with his students, I'm required to provide confirmation that our trip to a nightclub is still on. However, in the company of his female colleague and on the phone to his wife, I overhear François referring to his first weekend in England as "a couple of quiet drinks with Al and an early night".

One morning in the car on the way to College, I put on the soundtrack to the film *Philadelphia*. As soon as the opening bars of the song *Streets of Philadelphia* kick in, François comes to life.

"I love zhis song," he says. "You could maybe write me ... euh ... *les paroles?*"

Later in the day, during a free period, I fulfil François' request by jotting down the words on a small piece of paper, which he duly slips into the inside pocket of his blazer.

On Saturday, I keep to my promise and drive an excitable François to *Razzmatazz* nightclub where the Rag Ball was held. It's a busy night full of many attractive women dressed to the nines. But in contrast to the similarly alcohol-free night of the Ball, I'm unable to rediscover the same degree of aplomb. As much as I hate to admit it, the whole business with Emily has dented my self-confidence. Not that it's ever been that high when chasing women, anyway. In the end, I resign myself to watching the incorrigible old master at work. Once again, he waves aside his age, marital status and limited communication skills, and moves in on the opposite sex as if it were as easy as boiling an egg. To my amusement, he's sent packing at the first few attempts, but perseveres doggedly throughout the whole evening.

Shortly after 1.00, I spot François from a distance, deep in conversation with a girl some twenty years his junior. Only, unlike the others before her, she seems to be hanging on to his every word. All of a sudden, he reaches into his blazer pocket and pulls out a scruffy piece of paper. At this point, I lose sight of the pair as an extremely merry crowd cuts off my line of vision.

Some ten minutes later, however, François reappears in a state little short of ecstasy.

"I do not believe it," he squeals, waving the familiar piece of paper under my nose and jumping up and down on the spot like a Jack-in-the-box. "She sink I write it for 'er, she sink I write for 'er!"

He then proceeds to read what's before him with the force and passion of a Shakespearean actor, be it one with a strong French accent.

I was bruised and battered
Could not 'elp what I felt
I was unrecognizable to myself
Saw my reflection in a window
Did not know my own face etc, etc

When he reaches the end, I'm initially lost for words, unable to comprehend how a married man some fifteen years my senior could be so easily taken in.

"Oh, François, there's no way she wouldn't know the song," I say finally, shaking my head. "It was in the chart for weeks and the film ..."

"Non, non, non!" he says impatiently, persevering with his Zebidee impersonation. "She believe I write it, I promise you."

Realising that it'd not only be futile but perhaps unkind to continue to spoil his moment of glory, I settle for a nod of agreement. The bard returns to his young admirer, but as on previous occasions doesn't get to discover whether English women do in fact carry condoms about their person. In a way, I'm relieved – partly for his devoted partner back in France, but also for my flagging ego.

A fortnight ago I'd never have believed that I'd be saying this, but with François' departure, my life seems incredibly ordinary all of a sudden. Nevertheless, I've resisted any temptation to socialize with my new group of friends outside pub opening hours, and so avoided a repeat of my farcical pursuit of Emily. The thought of the others having a laugh at my expense only makes my blood boil. Surely I can expect better than this.

Just to remind me exactly how much of a late-starter I am, I attend an early summer wedding at the beginning of May at no place other than *The Dorchester*. The lucky man is Owen, an old school friend, who has overcome modest A level results to achieve great heights as a businessman in London. On the way there, I accidentally leave the present on a bus, which sends the driver into a wild frenzy. Concerned that it may be a terrorist bomb, he abandons his vehicle and chases after me, sweat pouring off his brow. I reassure him that it's just a table lamp and we return to his bus to collect the mislaid item. Silly me.

At the reception, I get into conversation with a pretty half Welsh, half Oriental girl of twenty-three called Denise Luck. Full of gratuitous champagne and convinced that her surname must be a good omen, I try to turn on the charm. At the same time, I mimic Simon Lennon by looking out carefully for possible signals – you know, facial expressions, body language and all that. And I have to say, the signs are really good.

Having chatted through most of the sit-down meal and enjoyed a couple of fast, jazzy dances together, I chance my arm at the end of the evening by asking for Denise's number.

"I don't know it," she replies dispassionately as if it were a perfectly normal response.

I throw her an incredulous look and ask: "How come?"

"Well, I've just moved into this new place." She looks in the opposite direction and plays uncomfortably with a beautifully embroidered serviette from the table. "And I don't know it yet."

Determined not to win a prize for naivety, I acknowledge that I've been fobbed off and abandon my mission. I try my best to put a brave face on my disappointment. After all, it's Owen and his wife Julie's special day, not mine. But once the initial effects of the alcohol have worn off, I'm fighting a losing battle.

On the bus back, I start to wonder what it is exactly that enables me to attract initial interest from so many women, only to be spurned so easily. After all, I have a bath or shower once, sometimes twice a day, use deodorant regularly and never ever forget to brush my teeth. Maybe in my efforts to prove that there's nothing fundamentally wrong with me, I'm just trying too hard. Thing is, when I don't try, I don't even get a start.

Back at College the following week, I head over to the Drama Studio one lunchtime to check it out for size. With A level exams threatening and the prospect of the Main Hall being unavailable until the end of June, I need an alternative venue for my gym and trampolining clubs. By pure coincidence, Maria and Natasha are there, rehearsing a sketch from an Ibsen play for their Theatre Studies practical.

"Have you got time to watch us do a quick run through?" Maria asks, as polite as ever.

"For you, I have all the time in the world," I think, but refrain from voicing.

Instead, I pull up the nearest blue plastic chair and, placing it carefully in front of the two performers, form a solitary mock audience. The sketch is relatively short, but both girls act it out with such skill that their amateur dramatic abilities can be left in little doubt. Maria plays the part of a woman in love, and does so with a degree of emotion and sincerity that leads me to wonder whether her off-stage romance with her boyfriend has really taken off.

"Excellent!" I say, clapping my hands furiously. "Very well done."

"You really think so?" Maria asks excitedly.

With a nod of confirmation, I rise to my feet and make for the door.

"Keep up the good work. Oh, by the way. The ceiling's high enough, so we'll definitely be doing trampolining over here during the exams."

Later in the afternoon, I pass Maria in the corridor between lessons. She treats me to a smile that surpasses any of her many previous efforts. What a cruel world it is!

In early June, one of my tutees, Clive Jacobs, invites me to his eighteenth birthday party at *Opportunity Knox*, one of the nightclubs just round the corner from *Razzmattaz*. It's midweek and the club is virtually empty apart from Clive's crowd, but we have a good time, nevertheless. With marking to do back home, I stick to two pints of shandy and only stay for a couple of hours. The birthday boy seems happy enough, though.

On my way out, I have a brief word with the General Manager, a Mr Steve Whately, about possibly using the club for future College functions as an alternative to *Razz*. He warms to the idea immediately and has no hesitation in offering the facility free of charge. I'll have to mention this to Hannah Murray in the morning. I'm sure she'll be delighted at the prospect of saving four hundred quid. It'd mean more money for charity and the Student Activity funds.

In view of the threat from local drug dealers who, apparently, have been coming onto site and targeting our students, Avril announces the employment of a full-time security guard called Trevor Phillips. He's a tall, solidly built individual in his early forties with a large, bushy moustache.

Trevor and I get chatting later in the week in the covered way and I soon discover that he's a likeable character with a keen interest in sport. I tell him about the imminent staff cricket matches and his eyes light up.

"It's years since I've played," he says, "but maybe you could bowl a few balls at me sometime over there in the nets."

He points towards the far side of the field.

"Sounds good to me," I reply. "The second-year A level students start their exam leave after half term and the first years are also off for a week then during their internal exams, so we should be able to squeeze in a net or two."

In the last few weeks, I've also become friendly with another member of the non-teaching staff, Charles Spackman. He's one of an increasing number of IT technicians employed by the College. His rather rugged, Viking appearance – shoulder length brown hair and a beard – masks a warm, gentle character underneath. He is also a good sport and has made it along to some of the recent trampolining sessions. I'm sure he'd hate me for saying this, but my star bouncers, Rachel 'Damon' Hill and Amanda Redpath, pointed out the other day that, with both feet turned slightly outwards, he walks rather like a duck. From their vantage point on the wall outside the staff canteen, which they've made their own since the start of the summer term, they don't miss a trick.

I have to say that Rachel has gained appreciably in confidence since Christmas. Whether this has anything to do with her recently discovered bouncing abilities, I don't know. It's amazing, though, how many parents at my out-of-College gym club have mentioned over the years that their shy offspring only began to come out of their shell after starting gym. It's an observation that always puts a smile on my face.

Half term brings with it exam leave for the Upper Sixth. This means effectively that the four A level French groups that started at the same time as I did have reached the end of their course. Although I'll see them all again during the exam period, I can't help feeling a bit sad. I guess it's just part of a teacher's lot. You meet up with large groups of young people day in, day out, form close working relationships with them, and then, all of a sudden, they've gone – off to brave university and the world of work. The one consolation for me, however, is that it's not always a permanent separation, given that I still bump into some ex-pupils and students from my two previous jobs.

With the Lower Sixth also on leave for their end-of-year internal exams, the campus feels like a ghost town during the first week back. It does, however, enable Trevor, Charles and me to get in some much-needed batting practice. I soon discover that Trevor has a teenage daughter from his first marriage and this goes a long way to explain his obvious ability to click with the students. They've responded well to his presence and been spotted enjoying a fag with him at breaktimes in the smoking area – ones containing tobacco, of course.

It's on the Friday of this uncharacteristically uneventful week that I pass Maria sitting by herself at one of the picnic benches near the quad.

"What're you doing looking all lost and alone?" I ask unceremoniously.

She looks up at me and delivers that magical smile once again.

"I've got my Spanish oral later on," she says.

"Oh, right. I'd better not disturb you, then." I turn to go.

"It's okay. It's not for a couple of hours and I'm well prepared."

Considering that this is the first opportunity I've ever had to talk to Maria on a one-to-one basis and, therefore, get to know her a bit better, I'm relieved by the reply. I straddle the wooden seat opposite her. Scarcely have I done so, however, when Trevor comes whistling past on one of his rounds. At first, I'm confident that he'll be busy and soon on his way, but

I'm wrong – he has all the time in the world. Over the next twenty minutes or so, the conversation is directed principally by Trevor who proves that, sober, he can even outdo a drunken Al in the verbose stakes. We touch on a series of random topics, but it's not until Trevor questions Maria about her future plans that my ears really prick up.

"So you planning to get married and have kids, then?" he asks.

"No way! I never want to marry," she says emphatically, shaking her head vigorously in the process. "I just get bored of men too quickly."

Even though I know she's only seventeen and probably repeating the words of many now happily married women at her age, I sense a sharp stabbing pain in the centre of my chest.

"Then again, at least she can't be that serious about her current boyfriend," I reason, in an attempt to soften the blow, which I hope I've managed to conceal from the other two.

After what seems like an eternity, Trevor finally hauls his bulky frame off the wooden seat and mutters something about having work to do. At last, I'm alone with Maria.

"What about you, then?" she says. "D'you think you'll ever get married?"

"Well, I'd like to eventually, but obviously only if I live long enough to find the right person," I half-jest.

She contemplates me intently for a few moments before adding rather strangely: "I think you'll have a very long life."

I smile with a nod of acknowledgement, yet in reality I've no idea what she's implying. "Thanks. I hope you're right." In my head, I hear an additional, unspoken line: "But just not long enough to win my affections."

I decide to change the subject. "You really should come along to the gym club sometime. I can tell from your trampolining that you'd be excellent."

Whilst I'd love to see more of Maria, of course, I'm actually telling the truth.

"I've always wanted to be able to do a back flip. Would you be able to teach me?"

"Yup, no problem."

"But isn't the gym club after College on a Monday?"

"That's right, it is."

"Mm. I finish at lunchtime on Mondays and normally go straight home."

"You could always come to the club where I do my training. They have a class for adult beginners and intermediates on Thursday evenings."

Maria appears genuinely interested and requests further details.

"I'll have a think about it and let you know before next Thursday," she says finally.

I sense that this is probably a good point to leave and get on with some internal exam marking.

"I hope your oral goes well," I say in parting.

She gives me a half-smile. "Thank you."

As I head back to the *Grosvenor*, I can't help feeling rather deflated. If Maria is attracted to me, then she's doing a very good job at disguising it as something purely superficial. What's more, if she's confident none of the six hundred-odd strapping lads here at College would be able to command her interest for that long, what hope does a failed romantic like me have once she's left? I'm just living in cloud-cuckoo-land.

The following week at one of the trampolining sessions, 'Damon' Hill overrotates slightly doing a front somersault and almost lands on top of Charles who's spotting at the front end of the trampoline. There's good-natured laughter from all sides. Charles turns a deep shade of crimson.

It's not until Charles comes over to my place at the weekend for a pub crawl that I'm made aware of the significance of his sudden change in complexion – he's got a mad crush on Rachel. In return for his confidence, I decide to come clean about my feelings for Maria. What a sad pair we are! Somehow, though, it's a real comfort to know that someone else understands what I'm going through. Whether as a member of the non-teaching staff it'd be acceptable for Charles to date a student, I'm not exactly sure.

A couple of days before the A level French reading exam, there's high drama. Desmond informs me that Delphine Leblanc, the native French speaker from one of my Lower Sixth classes, and her cousin, Natalie Lafayette, from the Upper Sixth – both grade A French students – narrowly escaped death when Natalie's parents' house burnt almost to the ground during the night. Apparently, the boiler in Delphine's room was faulty and caught fire. Had she not suffered from excessive perspiration and been unable to sleep, none of the occupants would've got out alive. The insurance company has arranged to put up the family in a local hotel.

I'm on the list of invigilators for the French reading exam in the Main Hall. Once the students have been told to start, I take a glance at the paper. Almost unbelievably, the first article is about a fire in a small bar and how the lady owner only just managed to escape from her upstairs flat. I look across at Natalie and am reassured by a calm, if incredulous, smile on her lips.

During the following week, I pass Maria on numerous occasions around the campus and see her for our usual weekly trampolining session, now in the Drama Studio as planned. She's as friendly as ever, but there's no mention whatsoever of Thursday night gym. Reasoning that it'd probably give the wrong impression – or do I mean the 'right' one? – to pursue the issue, I decide not to raise it again. With hindsight, she'd probably end up falling for one of my taller, darker, more confident – and, of course, more eligible – team-mates, and that really would be the last straw.

When Thursday evening comes round, something slightly bizarre happens – not during the gym session itself, but afterwards at the pub where we have a customary pint before hitting the road. For some reason, the men's Past Masters team is joined by nineteen-year-old Leanne Bishop, the daughter of one of the girls' coaches. She sits next to me and explains in no uncertain terms that she's separated from her long-term boyfriend.

I offer some words of consolation: "Oh, Leanne, I'm sorry to hear that. You must be really upset."

"I am a bit," she replies in her broad north London accent. "But 'ey, shit 'appens." She edges a notch closer to me on the seat before adding confidently: "What I need now is someone to cheer me up."

I observe her closely. "If I didn't know you better, Leanne Bishop, I'd think you were coming on to me." My lack of embarrassment surprises me, but then I did train well tonight and that always serves as a fillip.

"Maybe I am."

"Well … er … maybe you'd like to come out with me sometime, then?"

Wow, was that really Al Bentley talking?

'Sometime' turns out to be Saturday two days later. Although I harbour some reservations about our compatibility and feel concerned that Leanne's mum may not approve, I'm not exactly in a position at the moment to turn down a 'date-on-a-plate'. When I spot her from the lounge window stepping out of her white Metro, dressed glamorously in a low-cut top, mini-skirt and high heels, any lingering doubts are immediately dispelled.

We walk into town for a meal chez *Ten Tenths* – the source of Francois' aphrodisiac a few weeks back – then pay *Alfredo's* wine bar a visit. My ego hopes that the gang – especially Emily – will be there to witness my exotic date. Alas, it's left disappointed.

Standing at the bar, Leanne glances down at me from her towering height. Why did she have to wear heels?

"I've always liked ya, ya know," she says suddenly.

"How d'you mean *always*?" I ask. "You were only about twelve when your mum first started coaching at the club."

"I was thirteen, actually. But I fancied ya even then."

Although it was common knowledge Leanne was way ahead of her years, I'm rather taken aback by her revelation.

"So what d'you like about me now?" I ask, fishing for much-needed compliments.

"Well, I fink you're really friendly. You've got a nice muscular body, which I like. And you're good-lookin' too."

I kiss her instinctively on the cheek. Never before in almost twenty-nine years of existence have I been described as "good-looking". Well, not to my face, at least. I always thought I scored nought out of three in the tall, dark and handsome stakes.

As if by magic, the self-doubt and inhibitions that have played havoc with my love life in the past evaporate and I begin to feel more enamoured of the young woman beside me than I believed possible before her visit. Before closing time, there's a fair amount of proper kissing.

When we get back to the house, I'm aware of the biting influence of the booze and the strong physical urge for intimacy, yet my conscience is never far away.

"I don't want to lead you on," I whisper as we climb into bed and Leanne removes her skirt and skimpy top.

Straddled across me with her bulbous breasts spilling out of the outer extremities of her bra, she leans forward, covering my lips with her index and middle finger. She then replaces them with her mouth and kisses me with a degree of passion that leaves little doubt of her intent. I'm turned on now, really turned on. I cradle her in my arms, searching clumsily for the clip on her bra strap. Sensing my eagerness to view her assets at close quarters, Leanne rolls over slightly to assist me in my mission. As her bra finally flops onto my chest, I'm overwhelmed by the size of her boobs. Never before have I seen such a prominent pair in the flesh. Like a small child with a new toy, I find myself fondling them excitedly before rolling her over onto her back. I remember in passing my good intentions of resisting casual sex, but the desire to feel wanted is irresistibly strong on this Saturday evening in June.

Now stripped of our remaining clothes and with me on top, I finally give way to my animal instincts. As I thrust away frenetically, I become aware of a dramatic increase in the volume of Leanne's breathing.

"I don't believe it. Looks like she's about to have an orgasm," I think, proud of my skilful approach. "And I've only watched *The Joys of Sex* video twice. I must be a natural."

If ever I needed a morale booster, Leanne Bishop is providing it in abundance tonight. Or so it appears.

Over the next five minutes or so, Leanne's breathing takes on a progressive harshness that I eventually come to recognize only too well from my childhood. I pause to check that she's okay, levering my body away from hers.

"Al, it's … no … good," Leanne wheezes. "I'll … I'll 'af to … go down … to the car … 'n' fetch … me in'aler."

She climbs into her skirt, throws on her top and makes cautiously for the stairs. I follow her, anxious that she might lose her footing.

I switch on the landing light and ask: "Is there anything I can do?"

"No, fanks. I'll … be fine … wive me in'aler."

Leanne returns from her car almost immediately, shaking her head slowly: "I 'aven't … got it wive me. I'm … gonna 'ave to go back. I'm … really sorry, Al."

And so it happens. My evening of unbridled passion is brought to a premature conclusion by a severe attack of asthma. Having established that she's okay to drive and doesn't need a taxi, I wave goodbye to the unfortunate Leanne.

I ring the following day to check that Leanne is all right. To my relief, she's made a full recovery. The conversation is more than amicable, but there's no suggestion on either side that we should try again.

Once the exams are over and the Upper Sixth have kept up with tradition by decorating the campus with flour and eggs before departing for good, the remaining few weeks of term are spent with the returning Lower Sixth.

One day after College, towards the end of June, Charles and I are joined in the cricket nets by 'Damon' Hill and one of her other friends. They're determined to have a go, impressing with their underarm bowling. Afterwards, I can't help reflecting on whether 'Damon' has picked up on Charles' interest and is keen to get to know him better.

Having decided to move to Germany with his German wife and two young children, Desmond Willis, the Head of Languages, suggests a picnic on the nearby river for his send-off. Marilyn books three four-man rowing boats and the entire department heads off downstream early one evening in July to explore the local navigation. It's a peaceful, relaxing event – a perfect way to bid farewell to our shy, unpretentious yet highly effective leader.

By pure chance, we come across Rachel and Amanda, strolling down the bank just as our expedition has ended and we're in the process of disembarking. They stop briefly for a chat with Marilyn and me, their two French teachers.

"What a coincidence we should bump into those two," I say to Marilyn once they've disappeared cheerfully back down the towpath.

"Yes, indeed," she says in a blatantly sarcastic tone. "I can't imagine for one moment why they would want to bump into us."

It's only later that I recall telling the girls at gym that I'd have to shorten the session because of a staff leaving party on the river. Maybe Rachel had assumed Charles would be there.

For financial reasons, there are, apparently, no plans to replace Desmond in the short-term. Starting in September, and for the foreseeable future, Marilyn will assume the responsibilities of Head of Languages and Thelma Parker will be acting Head of German with the able assistance of Alan Bentley. Although I'm genuinely sorry to see Desmond go, his departure will result in an increase in my quota of A level German teaching, which until now has played second fiddle to French. Since the third year of my degree was spent predominantly in Austria, this is a situation I'm more than happy about. With the prospect of a more even balance of the two subjects, I'm looking forward to September already.

In the staff-student cricket match during the last week of term, my hopes of a visit to the wicket and some extended batting practice are foiled by an innings of outstanding courage and longevity by Marilyn. With virtually no backlift, she manages to block or fend off everything the exuberant Sixth Form lads can 'throw' at her. Her efforts are only marred by the unfortunate run-out of one of her batting partners, Michael 'Bomber' Lancaster, my short-tempered History and Politics neighbour. He retires to the pavilion to wash his mouth out with soap and water.

A succession of towering straight sixes and bludgeoning fours from Dave Salkeld, the Head of PE, plus useful contributions from Trevor Phillips on his debut and Peter Malcolmson ensure an impressive staff total for the students to chase.

Despite a series of dropped catches in the deep off my gentle off-spin bowling – 'Bomber' being one of the culprits (more soap and water) – I still manage to finish with a three-wicket hall. One of my victims has had trials with the County, but I won't mention how many runs I conceded in the process of dismissing him. The remaining wickets are shared amongst three or four of my colleagues and the students are sent packing well short of their target.

All in all, a perfect end to a year that's been as enjoyable as it's been eventful. How can I complain about my social life and lack of proper romance when I'm blessed with such a fantastic working environment? There's just no pleasing some people.

Every Little Thing

(Year 3)

When I'm walking beside her,
People tell me I'm lucky.
Yes, I know I'm a lucky guy,
I remember the first time.
I was lonely without her,
Can't stop thinking about her now

AUTUMN TERM

Right, let's get one thing straight. With a new academic year already underway, I have no intention whatsoever of continuing to bore everyone to tears with further declarations of my love – or whatever it is – for student Maria. I do think it's worth mentioning, however, that our paths crossed briefly during the summer at the *Opportunity Knox* nightclub. My dream girl stopped for a friendly chat, but was soon lured away by the persistent attentions of a tall, dark-haired lad who I didn't recognise. When the smooching songs came on at the end of the evening, Simon Lennon and I found ourselves hovering on the periphery of the dance floor, hoping to spot a female lonely heart equivalent. It was at this point that I caught a glimpse of Maria, lost in a passionate embrace with her new hunk. I tried to feel sorry for him, reasoning that if her words from last June rang true he'd soon be on the scrap heap. But funnily enough, this was a sentiment that in the circumstances proved elusive.

On reflection, this latest encounter with my all-time number one heartthrob has forced me to be practical and think ahead. Even if Maria did by some miracle happen to really like me – and I mean 'miracle' – what future could we possibly have? A summer together after she'd left College, perhaps. And that's assuming that I managed to maintain her interest for that long. Then she'd be off to university and, faced with constant attention from other tall, swarthy hunks, I'd soon be history, wouldn't I? Although she's occupied my thoughts majorly for a year now, I reckon it's high time the fantasy stops before I end up in a padded cell. Whilst I accept that this is almost certainly an unavoidable final destination, it'd be nice to be able to put it on hold for at least a couple more years.

"It's no good, sonny Jim," I tell myself firmly. "You're going to have to pull yourself together and start living in the real world."

Whilst contemplating future love with a current A level student may not be the most recommended pastime of a single teacher, remaining good friends with a few students once they've left College can be rewarding as I discovered at the end of August. Following their thoroughly deserved grade As for French, Cara and Mandy 'Mandarin' accepted my invitation to dinner at *Ten Tenths*. Where else? Charles Spackman joined us and we had a richly entertaining evening – far less nerve-racking than if Maria and Rachel Hill had been our guests, I'm sure. C and M really are two of the friendliest girls I've ever met, and I'd like to think we won't lose touch once they've left home for university.

During the customary enrolment and induction period at the beginning of the first week back, two familiar faces provide a welcome break from the constant influx of new young blood. It's the dynamic duo Cara and Mandy once again.

"Hi ya, Al," they chant in chorus. "We've come in for our breakdowns."

They are, of course, not referring to a serious mental condition, but the marks for the four individual components of their A level French exam: reading, writing, speaking and listening.

"Hi there, you two," I reply, dipping into my bag for the list of marks.

"Thanks again for the other night," Mandy says whilst I'm still searching.

Then Cara adds kindly: "We had a really great time."

There's no doubt that I'll miss them both this year, not only for their friendship but also for the outstanding levels of commitment and enthusiasm they displayed in French lessons. It really is true, familiarity doesn't always breed contempt.

Whilst perhaps not quite in the same league linguistically, Rachel Hill and Amanda Redpath have, nevertheless, become two carbon copy replacements. Both girls turn up as promised for the gym display scheduled for the lunchtime of Induction Day. Unfortunately, Rachel develops a severe nose bleed just before the start and has to watch from the sidelines with a screwed up tissue pressed against her nostrils. That leaves just three students and the coach with the task of impressing any prospective members to the club. The dozen or so spectators are appreciative of our efforts and a few add their names to my list.

Incidentally, Rachel and Amanda have become so enthusiastic about trampolining that they've joined a club at the Sports Centre in the City. According to the latter, Rachel immediately caught the eye of the young lads in the group. Given her stunning looks and sweet, gentle personality, this doesn't surprise me. What does surprise me, however, is that none of the lads here at College seems to have noticed her many qualities. With all the basking in the sun by the busy covered way she and Amanda indulged in last term, how could she have possibly escaped attention? Maybe the male students are just too much in awe of her beauty.

My regular Thursday night gym training session brings with it some surprising news – Leanne Bishop and her boyfriend have resolved their differences and announced their engagement. Maybe heavy breathing in his company signals something other than the onset of an asthma attack. Leanne appears over the moon and is just as friendly towards me as before, so no harm done, I guess.

On my return from work at the end of the second week, Alicia Burns, one of Cara and Mandy's old classmates, calls round to the house to size it up for cleaning. When I ran into her over the summer, she was whinging about financial hardship, so I offered her the opportunity of ridding my pad of the mounting dust and grime. After a brief inspection of all the rooms, she agrees to take on this unenviable task during the three weeks leading up to the start of her university course. This is very lazy of me, I know, but I'm extremely allergic to dust and … well, I'll be doing Alicia a favour.

Alicia is another friendly, gregarious student and I'm of a cheerful disposition when I head into town after her visit. In a moment's weakness later in the evening, I allow the gang to descend on my home once again. Any hopes that they may have had chance during their lengthy absence to resolve to show a little more respect and even consider volunteering some booze go up in a familiar cloud of smoke – some of it illegal, no doubt.

To my frustration – and irritation – Emily resumes her harsh teasing game from where she left off before the holidays. As ever, this only fuels her appetite and Al finds himself dipping into the freezer once again, this time for pitta bread. I resurface and hurl a rock-solid piece in Frisbee fashion towards Emily who's positioned by the toaster. Unfortunately, she's not paying attention and it inadvertently strikes her on the right temple. Had she witnessed my throwing in last summer's staff-student cricket match, all thoughts of me taking careful aim would be dispelled at once. I'm not a vindictive soul, me.

On Saturday, I drive a recovered Emily, clad in a short skirt and knee-length boots, Delilah and the ginger twins to *Opportunity Knox*. The generous Door Manager, Mr Steve Whately, who's obviously pleased that the College has accepted his offer of the facility for the Rag Ball later this term, grants me a queue jump and free entry.

In many ways, the evening resembles a past Rag Ball with Cara, Mandy, Alicia, Maria and Ian Thompson amongst the large contingent of College-related partygoers. I have a long discussion with C and M – but not Maria – as this will almost certainly be our last meeting before their departure. It's hard to believe that almost two years have passed since Claudia and I first spotted students at *The Harvester*, and I felt hesitant about socialising with them. It's such a common occurrence now that I don't even spare it a second thought.

At long last, the property development company that's constructing part-ownership houses on the piece of wasteland next to my pad erects a brand new wooden fence to replace my towering ten-foot hedge that it erroneously cut down back in the summer whilst I was on holiday in Devon. It doesn't look anywhere near as impressive, but I guess for a non-gardener like myself, it should prove low maintenance. The houses themselves are springing up really quickly, so it shouldn't be long now before I have new neighbours. Single women in their early to mid-twenties would be just what the doctor ordered.

One morning at the start of break, I bump into a familiar face amongst the group of new students streaming out of Michael 'Bomber' Lancaster's History lesson. It belongs to Elisabeth Pascal, the much younger sister of an old school friend, Lee. She recognises me at once and, although quite shy, brings me up-to-date on her brother's married life in Canada, including the birth of his first child last December. Apparently, Lee is planning to come to England with the family for a few weeks sometime next year. Elisabeth promises to keep me informed.

In our Sixth Form College days, Lee and I used to go running on a regular basis, sometimes at 6.30 in the morning. To help relieve the tedium, we'd make up stories involving our other friends and attempt to predict our own futures. I wonder if his life has panned out as we imagined it might. It'll certainly be good to see him again.

My encounter with Elisabeth provides me with a perfect opportunity to wind up 'Bomber'. A few days later, I catch him at the end of the day staring out of his classroom window.

"Hey, Michael," I call out. "D'you fancy some hot gossip?"

"Lll…looks like I'm going to ggg…get it, anyway," he says, turning towards me with a wry smile.

He's a moderately overweight individual with unkempt greying hair and a prominent burn-like birthmark on one side of his neck and lower jaw. A real character, though, and someone whose company I enjoy.

"Get this," I begin with mock excitement. "One of the girls in your Lower Sixth History group asked me if I'd go to bed with her."

"Wh…wh…wh…which one?" he asks, his facial expression betraying a cocktail of horror and intrigue.

"Elisabeth Pascal. Virtually pleaded with me she did."

"I ddd…don't bbb…believe it. You hhh…have to be ppp…pulling my leg."

"No, I'm deadly serious. She also requested that I read her a bedtime story."

Sensing that my face is about to crack, I look away. But it's no good – I just can't keep it up. I turn back towards 'Bomber' and say: "Mind you, she was only three at the time and I was her babysitter. Played me up something rotten she did. Wouldn't stop crying until I agreed to climb into her bed like her brother did and read one of her favourite fairy tales."

I go on to explain how I know her family and the excitement of potential scandal evaporates from my colleague's bemused face.

"You sss…sod!" he says, shaking his head in recognition that he's been 'had'.

On the penultimate Friday in September, Charles Spackman and I go for a drink at the cider house close to the College and who should we bump into but Rachel Hill, sitting outside with a couple of friends. She immediately invites us to join her table, causing Charles' eyes to light up.

The conversation is relaxed and good-humoured, yet I'm beginning to wonder if I was wrong about Rachel reciprocating Charles' romantic interest. She's certainly not giving anything away. Then again, with my track record, I wouldn't recommend placing any bets with her namesake.

Charles is rather subdued on the way home. You don't have to be brain of Britain to sense that he too has picked up on Rachel's vibes and is suffering from the pain of unrequited love. He has my unreserved sympathy.

Back at work on Tuesday, my as yet unblemished record as Functions Organiser for the SA team takes a bit of a bruising. At my invitation, a couple of male singers, who perform cover versions of popular tracks and are a major hit at *Alfredo's* wine bar, make an appearance at lunchtime in the Main Hall for a reasonable hundred quid. Typically, it's a sunny day and not one student is prepared to cough up the modest fifty pence entrance fee.

Rather than allow the two entertainers the humiliation of playing to an empty house, I make an executive decision and let the students in for nothing. In the end, we manage to assemble a rather paltry audience of about seventy-five.

"Don't forget that we'll be saving four hundred pounds by not having to pay a hire charge for this year's Rag Ball," I say to Hannah Murray, with egg all over my face.

At *The Barley Mow* the following Saturday, I meet a couple of *au pairs* from Holland called Betty and Eva who are employed by the same Dutch family. I spend most of the evening chatting to them much to Emily's disapproval. She responds by flirting with me in the most overt fashion imaginable, which leads me to question Simon's rather pessimistic assessment of our situation. Surely she wouldn't have reacted so jealously if she didn't fancy me at all. Women, eh!

At the end of September staff meeting, Avril depresses us once again with a further reference to teacher redundancies long-term. Apparently, our contingency budget should ensure that we'll be okay for the remainder of the current academic year and some, if not all, of the following one. Beyond that, however, the situation looks considerably less auspicious.

To counter the gloom and doom, Avril concludes the meeting by reading aloud a letter of complaint received from a local resident whose property backs onto the rear extremity of the field, directly behind the cricket nets. It seems that her peaceful August afternoons were regularly interrupted by the sound of willow on leather. Further investigation revealed an elderly gentleman bowling quickly at a young boy – presumably his grandson – who barely rose above the height of the stumps. When questioned about the legitimacy of their presence, the old codger had responded with language that wasn't fit for public consumption. It's not until she reaches the end of the epic account that Avril discloses the identity of the two harmony breakers – Peter 'ladies' man' Malcolmson and his ten-year-old son. Despite the humiliating insult to his age and virility, Peter joins in with the general hysteria that fills the Staff Room. Education really does mirror life itself – tears and laughter all rolled into one.

It's now 6.30 on the first Monday in October and I'm about to return to the College for my maiden session as a French Evening Class tutor. Given their family commitments, none of my colleagues was keen to volunteer his/her services beyond normal working hours. I could hardly offer this as an excuse. Anyway, the pay isn't bad and it'll keep me out of the pub on a Monday night.

Just as I'm on my way out of the door, the phone rings. It's Cara Mitchell.

"Hi, Al," she says, as high-spirited as ever. "I'm off to Bristol in the morning, so I thought I'd just ring to say goodbye."

"Oh, hi there, Cara," I reply. "Good to hear from you. So … er … you finished packing yet?"

"Yes, I have, thanks. Well, more or less."

"Excited?"

"Mm, sort of. A bit scared too, though."

"Oh, that's quite normal. But listen, you've got nothing to worry about. You'll make loads of new friends."

"It's the course I'm more worried about, Al. What if all the others are better than me?"

"Cara, you're one of the most able students I've ever taught, so there's no way that's going to be the case."

"D'you really mean that?"

"Absolutely!"

Conscious of the time, I have to cut Cara short. I wish her good luck.

The adult group is composed of eight people all eager to revive their schooldays' French. They're a friendly, easy-going bunch and the two hours pass quickly. Not a bad way of earning thirty-seven quid. It'll also make a useful addition to my CV.

The following weekend proves to be one of the most memorable of my life as I win my third National Past Masters Gymnastic Competition. Unlike with the previous two victories, I have to share the title this time round. However, this is hardly an issue as it's with an ex-British international who was number two in the country for several years. To crown a perfect moment, my old friend Neil Thomas, two times World Championship silver medallist on the floor and arguably the most talented British gymnast ever, is there to present the medals to the sound of Tina Turner singing *Simply the Best*.

I'd be lying if I said I didn't envy Neil's outstanding achievements, but I've come to realise that in a truly amateur sport considerable sacrifice has to be made in the pursuit of excellence. If I'd followed Neil's path, it's unlikely that at the age of twenty-nine I'd have a degree in modern languages, my own house, an album full of photos of sporty Italian cars that I've owned and, perhaps most importantly of all, a job in education to die for. On reflection, my childhood ambitions of being a world champion gymnast and racing driver as well as a top dairy farmer were maybe slightly unrealistic. The great thing about my current lifestyle is that I get to experience a little of all the things I enjoy most, even if my racing is limited to the confines of the public road and my livestock farming to a pair of guinea pigs.

Back at work on Monday, I'm buzzing like never before. There really is nothing quite like sporting success for lifting the spirits onto a new plane.

For me, it's like a drug – one that retains its effect throughout the rest of the month.

At the end of October, I receive a mysterious, forwarded letter with a Swedish postmark. On the back of the envelope is the name and address of the sender – Erika Peterson. It doesn't take long to register that this was the girl I met on my way to Norway fourteen months ago. I'm puzzled since I sent her a postcard before leaving the country and a Christmas card from England, but never heard a word. Seems odd she should want to make contact after such a long silence. I peel open the envelope and pull out the contents with intrigue.

> *Dear Al,*
> *I hope you remember me. We met on a ferry to*
> *Gothenburg the summer before last. Unfortunately,*
> *I lost your address. It was only when I started*
> *re-reading the English book I had with me at the*
> *time that the piece of paper with your address fell out!*
> *I'm so sorry!*

Trust me for failing to include my contact details on the back of the Christmas card envelope. I read on.

> *This is most unfortunate because I was in England*
> *for a few weeks last summer. I really wanted to meet*
> *you again but I couldn't remember exactly where you*
> *lived. I looked in some telephone books but there were*
> *so many Bentleys.*

Once more, I seem to be jinxed. However, as I read further, it becomes clear that all is not lost.

> *Anyway, I'm hoping to get a job as an au pair in England*
> *next summer, so maybe we can meet then. I'd like*
> *this very much! I should hear in the next month or two*
> *if I have a place. I'll write you as soon as I know.*
> *It would be good to receive your news so if you do*
> *remember me and have time to write …*
>
> *From Erika*
>
> *P.S I'm sending a recent photo of me and my friend.*
> *I'm the one on the left!*

I take a close look at the black and white photo she's sent and, although she definitely looks older, there's no mistaking the rather cute, happy-looking face I remembered from my trip. I love it when something totally unexpected like this happens. It reminds me of the most exciting thing about life – the unpredictable. Of course, bad things can happen unpredictably too, but this is something I try not to dwell on.

A couple of days later, my new Dutch friends, Betty and Eva, come back to the house after an evening together at the pub. With her olive skin and gorgeous dark features, Eva cuts an attractive figure, although she's noticeably shyer than her blonde, buxom friend. Both girls are so friendly and easy to talk to that it doesn't take long for me to forget my rather unpleasant previous encounter with a girl from the Low Country.

Marieke was also an *au pair* and I used to chat to her frequently at *Clifford's* a year or so before starting at *Mardall's*. We were getting on really well, so one day after a few drinks, I managed to pluck up the courage to ask her out for dinner. She accepted without hesitation. I was looking forward to the evening, but found Marieke in an uncharacteristically sombre mood. However hard I tried, I could barely induce more than a "yes" or a "no" out of her throughout the duration of the meal. Acknowledging that she probably regretted her decision to come out with me, I paid up and offered to drive her straight home.

"Oh, I was hoping we could go to a pub for some drinks," she then announced in her first full sentence of the evening.

I obliged. When we got to *The Harvester*, I found myself providing my date with a continuous supply of spirits. I was disappointed at first that she didn't at least offer to get one round in, but judging from the positive change in her demeanour reasoned that it was a small price to pay for an end to the embarrassing silences of earlier. The upswing in Marieke's mood was enough to convince me that she was probably just nervous at dinner, so on dropping her home I dared to ask if she'd like to go out again sometime.

"No way!" she barked, shutting the passenger door with a thud and storming up the drive without the hint of a wave goodbye, let alone a word of thanks.

With an empty wallet, I limped back to the flat to lick my wounds. I hate experiences like that – ones where you never really know where you went wrong. Not only do they hurt your pride but they leave little scope for improvement. But Betty and Eva are different kettles of fish, of that I'm almost certain.

"Eva and I would like to invite you over to our home," Betty says cordially as they're on their way out. "But first, we have to ask the lady of the house."

Before I know it, it's November again and my twenty-ninth birthday. Given that I'll be busy with my Evening Class tonight, I had a mini-celebration with the family yesterday. Betty and Eva are, however, keen to meet up later.

I'm not back home until gone 10.00, so I drop the car off quickly and hurry into town. They're waiting for me at *Alfredo's*.

"We've got a present and card for you," Eva says, "but maybe you should open them later."

After a couple of drinks, Betty drives us back to my place and I get to open the unusually shaped parcel. Inside, I find an assortment of Dutch beers – Grolsch, Oranjeboom etc.

"Ah, you're real stars, you two!" I say with genuine delight. "Thanks a lot."

"That's okay," Betty says. "Thanks for being a good friend. We were beginning to think that English people didn't like us very much."

Considering that I haven't known the girls for long, I'm touched by their generosity. We stay up chatting and drinking until 1.00. I've got work tomorrow, of course, but this time next year, I'll be over the hill and probably turning in at 10.00 on a regular basis, so I might as well make the most of my fading youth.

One of Delilah's friends, John, shares his birthday with me. On Tuesday evening, about eight of the gang plus Charles and I go out for a joint celebratory meal. The restaurant is located on the main cross-country road to work. I hitch a lift there with Gary, the bouncer look-alike, and his fiancée, Kathy. As soon as we're seated, a familiar face appears at the large table to take our drink orders – Katherine Savage, one of the more reserved girls in my Set. Escaping work is never as easy as it may seem.

The food meets with my approval, although one or two of the others are not so impressed. After some six months of friendship, Emily astounds us all by offering to buy me a drink. What is the world coming to? Once we've settled up, we head back to *The Barley Mow* for last orders.

My busy week's social life continues on Thursday with a trip to Betty and Eva's residence/workplace to meet the overly formal 'lady of the house'. I'm on my best behaviour and survive her rigorous questioning.

Afterwards, I drive the two girls to the Sports Centre in the City where Rachel Hill and Amanda Redpath partake in their out-of-College bouncing. Betty has a water polo match, which means I'll be alone with Eva in the viewing gallery for over an hour. Perfick!

All buoyed-up, ready to charm the lovely Eva, I find her in an uncharacteristically reticent mood, resulting in an unusually strained encounter. Memories of my meal out with her fellow countrywoman come flooding back, and I start to feel all nervous and uncomfortable again.

"I'm really, really tired," she says on at least three occasions.

I suppose this should put my mind at rest, but I can't help feeling that even after a week of sleepless nights, I'd still manage to summon up at least a hint of enthusiasm when talking to a girl like Eva. As much as I hate to admit it, I reckon this is just her way of 'blowing me out' gently. For the umpteenth time in my life, it's as if the pure act of revealing interest in the opposite sex triggers off a non-reciprocation button. I really don't know why I bother.

With her match over, Betty catches up with the two of us in the canteen. Eva's normal, cheerful demeanour returns miraculously. This only serves to confirm my depressing theory that she just wants to be friends.

The following day, I make the customary journey from work over to the gym club to set up the equipment for the present coach and his team.

After dinner with mum and dad, I then head back home to change before meeting up with Emily, Delilah and the ginger twins in *The Barley Mow*. For the second time in a week, Emily excels herself by offering to drive us all back to the pub where we had the birthday meal on Tuesday. Keen for a change of scenery on a Friday night, we pile into her Fiat Uno before she has a second to reconsider her generous offer.

The atmosphere inside the pub is excellent. Shortly after our arrival, I spot Gavin McDonald, a sensible, mature lad who was in my Set last year. We spend a good ten minutes catching up before it suddenly occurs to me that his stepdad, a games master at the illustrious private school round the corner from *Mardall's*, may be a useful contact if I decide to follow up an idea I've had recently.

"Gavin, I've been thinking about expanding my gym coaching outside College," I say, "and I was wondering if your old man's school would be interested in paying someone to run a club one or two evenings a week."

"Don't see why not," he says with the trace of a public schoolboy accent. "I can ask my stepfather for you and give you a call, if you like."

"Thanks, I'd appreciate that."

"I'll just grab a pen and piece of paper from the bar."

Gavin stops to exchange a brief word with a girl whose face is obscured, then returns and jots down my phone number.

As is always the case when you're having a good time, the evening is over before we know it. On my way out, a girl I don't recognise stops me in the doorway.

"I hear you're a gymnast," she says with a hint of admiration.

"That's right," I say proudly. "How d'you know that?"

"Ah, that'd be telling. I like gymnasts, though. They've got really fit bodies."

I introduce myself properly to the girl whose name is Lauren. Just as I'm beginning to realise how incredibly sexy my mystery woman is, Emily shouts from her car to hurry me along.

"Sorry, that's my lift home. Nice meeting you, though."

"Yeah, you too. I work at the pub up the road on a Saturday night. You know, the one that does Thai food. Come in and see me sometime."

"Yes, okay – I will."

As I turn to go, I can't fail to notice a hugely seductive smile light up a face hidden only partially by strands of wavy blonde hair. Did I imagine it or did she run her bright blue eyes up and down my body as if trying to undress it?

"No, I must've had one too many," I tell myself as I climb into the back of Emily's Uno.

Mum and dad pay a visit on Sunday. As ever, it's great to see them, although on this occasion I have to endure a seemingly endless barrage of complaints about the state of the house – you know, unwashed dishes, dust on the furniture, unmowed lawn, that sort of thing. How I miss Alicia, my domestic help, now that she's at university. Their gripes are perfectly justified, of course, but with my busy lifestyle I just can't seem to find the time or summon up the motivation to do anything about it. I'm sure living on my own doesn't help either. Maybe I should consider taking in a lodger. It'd also provide a timely boost to my finances.

In *The Barley Mow* the following week, a tall, skinny bloke resembling a cross between Rodney Trotter and Hugh Grant suddenly descends on the table I'm sharing with the Dutch girls and addresses both of them.

"Hello there, ladies," he says confidently. "You're far too lovely to be from England. Don't tell me, you must be Belgian or Dutch. Mm, probably the latter."

"How did you know that?" Eva asks with raised brows.

His reply is uttered in a near perfect London accent, be it more Del Boy than Rodney: "Intuition, darlin', intuition." He then draws on a cigarette before releasing the unwanted smoke in the direction of yours truly with a goldfish-like yawn. This is followed by a smug cackle.

"No, seriously, I worked in Amsterdam for a couple of years," he explains in what I assume is his own voice, still Del Boy but with the benefit of elocution lessons. "Dutch girls are much friendlier than English ones. Sexier and more beautiful too."

He leans forward and places his right arm around Eva.

"So what you doin' later, darlin'?" he asks with a further cackle, this time revealing a set of large, partially nicotine-stained teeth. "I'm Rupert Stanley, by the way."

Eva flicks her fringe out of her face with a nervous giggle. From my position of innocent bystander, it appears that in a mere thirty seconds Rupert Stanley has made more of an impression on the lovely Eva than I've managed in weeks of friendship. If only I could be so smooth and self-assured.

Later in the evening, Rupert strikes up a conversation with me.

"Sorry about earlier," he says, "but it was pretty clear you weren't involved with either of the girls."

"That's okay," I say half-truthfully. "They're just friends."

He nudges me and emits the now familiar cackle. "But you'd like more with the brunette, eh?"

"Is it that obvious?"

"Blatantly, Mr Bond, blatantly! I can read you like a book."

Although I find myself envious of his charm and intuition, the more I talk to Rupert, the more I have to acknowledge that I quite like him. Beyond the supremely confident, smooth-talking exterior lies an apparently honest, genuine man. On top of this, he's only a year older than I am, studied at university and has a German mum, so we've got plenty in common.

"Not got a girlfriend, then?" I ask.

"I have," he replies, "but she's back home in Austria at the moment."

"Known her long?"

"About two years. She was an *au pair* over here."

I probe further, wondering if Rupert poses a serious threat to my pursuit of Eva: "Must be hard with the distance."

"I must admit, I have cheated on her a few times. I'm not proud of it, but I did confess afterwards."

"And she let you off the hook?"

"Yeah. Cried for a day on each occasion, then forgave me. Guess that's love for you. Look, you probably think I'm a real bastard, but I've been treated badly by girls in the past and, well, I always look after Astrid properly when she's over here." He lowers his head as if tormented by the recollection of his acts of infidelity.

He's right. I do disapprove of his behaviour, yet I leave the pub at the end of the evening uncertain whether it's more through envy than for moral reasons. Rupert Stanley, it seems, has the ability not only to attract women at will but also to hang on to them – qualities that have eluded me all of my adult life.

Back at work the following Friday, my spirits are lifted by a series of rewarding lessons and the charming company of Rachel, Amanda and co at the after-College gym club. More than ever before, this draws my attention to the enormous contrast that exists between the high confidence

I feel with students around me at work, and the despondency and insecurity that have come to dominate large chunks of my social life. It's almost as if I'm living in parallel universes.

It's already dark by the end of the gym session, so I offer Rachel and Amanda a lift home en route to my private gym club. They accept without hesitation.

On the first Friday in December, Rachel and Amanda make use of my taxi service once again. In the car, Amanda betrays the fact that Rachel is now going out with one of her admirers from the Sports Centre trampolining club.

"Stone the crows! My little Damon's got a man. I don't believe it," I say facetiously. "I hope you're taking things slowly. I mean, I don't want to hear that you've been holding hands for at least a month." In the rear-view mirror, I can see Rachel blushing. Her head dips. "Don't tell me you've had hand contact already? I don't know, the girls today – no morals."

Rachel lives slightly further from the College than Amanda. As she climbs out of the car, she thanks me politely with a warm yet slightly embarrassed smile.

On the way over to the other gym, it occurs to me that it'll do Rachel's confidence no harm whatsoever to have a boyfriend. I'm pleased for her, of course, but I've become so fond of the two girls that I can't help feeling a little protective towards them. Just hope her new man treats her well.

"Poor old Charles – he'll be devastated," I remember later as I'm wheeling the trolley of mats out of the gym club garage and into the Main Hall.

My thoughts are interrupted by the arrival of fourteen-year-old Kayleigh Yearwood, one of the coaching assistants, who I've known since she was six. She brings news of the sudden death from a brain tumour of a former club member. He was only fifteen. Although not a natural gymnast, he was a super lad from a superbly supportive family and always gave one hundred percent.

This heartrending discovery prompts me to recall another gym-club-related loss from the distant past. When I was still a teenager, there was a lovely American couple who used to bring two of their four children along for training. Appreciating my struggle to make a name for myself nationally as a performer from a small club, the father, a larger than life figure working for a major oil company, offered some kind words of encouragement on our last meeting before his transfer to Scotland.

"Hang on in there, Al!" he said, shaking my hand with a vice-like grip. "The folks who make it in this life are the ones who never quit trying."

Not long afterwards, he was dead – killed outright when the car he was travelling in collided with a lorry. His words, however, have never left me.

Sometimes, there really is no justice in this world. And there's me thinking I'm hard done-by because I can't find a girlfriend. Get a grip, Al!

Friday night's sad news puts a different perspective on my meeting with Betty and Eva at the weekend – there's no way I'm going to end up feeling sorry for myself. The lady of the house and her husband own a small flat in London and have allowed the two girls access to it for a couple of days. Having passed her ladyship's rigorous examination, I was granted permission to join them. I catch the train up on Saturday afternoon.

In the evening, we go for a meal, then have a few drinks in a nearby pub. Reminded of the importance of living for the moment, I brave a question to Eva when Betty is in the loo.

"How about you and I going out alone sometime?" I ask, placing my hand confidently on her knee and looking her right in the eye in typical Rupert Stanley fashion. "You know, without Betty."

"Yes, okay," she replies dispassionately.

"What, you don't mind?"

"No. Why should I?"

Rupert, you're a star!

Back in the flat, the two girls set up a couple of airbeds on the lounge floor. Betty then throws me the bolsters from the settee.

"Here, you can arrange these at the bottom of our beds," she says. "If you want a proper pillow, you can fetch one from our employers' bedroom."

I head off to the master bedroom and discover a large piece of rope residing on the bedside table. I grab it, along with a pillow, and return to the lounge.

"D'you think we'll be needing this?" I ask with mock sincerity, dangling my find in front of the girls' noses.

Every bit as aware as I am of the exaggeratedly formal, somewhat prudish manner of the lady of the house and her husband, they're shocked by my discovery. The mental image of the pair indulging in bondage ensures that all three of us hit the sack in high spirits. What's that saying about never judging a book by its cover?

Eva looks decidedly sexy in her T-shirt and skimpy shorts. What's more, the thought of her lying just a few feet away is almost more than my sexually starved body can bear. Why can't I get that piece of rope out of my head?

Back home the following day, Gavin McDonald rings to inform me that his stepdad likes the sound of my gym-coaching plans.

"The school is in the process of building a new sports hall for its own and public use," he says. "My stepfather's confident they'll be needing extra sports coaches."

"Thanks, Gavin," I say. "That's exactly what I was hoping to hear."

"Oh, by the way, Lauren Stewart – you know, the blonde you met on the night I saw you – thinks you're really fit. You're well in there, mate."

"Ah, so it was you who told her I was a gymnast."

"That's right, she's a friend. She works at the Thai restaurant up the road."

"Mm, so I gather."

"Then I'd get along there next Saturday, if I were you. She's a seriously tasty woman."

"Yes, I think I might just do that," I say coolly. "Look, thanks for speaking to your stepfather and for the ... er ... tip-off."

"No problem. Any time. Good luck, mate!"

I hang up, intrigued. I had intended to call in on Lauren, but my confidence has been so shaky recently that I haven't quite managed to steel myself for a visit. However, Gavin's words of encouragement have given me genuine hope and, anyway, I'm still supposed to be in *carpe diem* mode.

On the following Saturday evening at 10.00, I drive over to the Thai pub/restaurant. Sure enough, Lauren is manning the bar and recognises me instantly.

"So you made it eventually, then," she says good-humouredly.

"Yes, I'm here at last," I nod, trying to conceal my unnaturally fast heartbeat. "Sorry it's taken me so long."

"Hm, I'll let you off. So what can I get you?"

"Well, I'm driving, so I'd better just have a ... er ... pint of lager shandy, please."

Lauren serves me my drink with a friendly smile. Then, after a brief chat about nothing in particular, she leaves me on a barstool.

During the course of the next forty-five minutes, Lauren ignores me almost completely whilst dividing her time between serving the handful of other customers and collecting glasses. Then, perhaps detecting my restlessness, she approaches me again.

"I'll be at the *Watermill Inn* later after I've finished here," she says.

"Oh, right," I reply. "Er ... I'll probably see you ... er ... there, then."

I finish my drink leisurely before strolling up the road to the *Watermill*, also a pub-come-restaurant. As I enter, I remember having checked it out on one previous occasion. For some reason, it manages to stay open until 1.00 at weekends – illegally, I'm sure – and is, therefore, a popular venue in an area bereft of nightclubs.

For once, there are no familiar faces to help pass the time, so I stand alone daydreaming until Lauren appears just on midnight. She sees me at once and comes across to say hello, placing her hand affectionately on my shoulder in the process.

"I need to say 'hi' to a couple of mates," she says before I have chance to offer to buy her a drink. "Back in a sec."

A moment or two later, I catch sight of Lauren flirting with a series of tall, good-looking men in their earlier twenties. I contemplate going across to join her, but, fearing the competition, hold my ground.

After a while, I become irritable once more. Tired of waiting around, I move out into the lobby as a precursor to making tracks. I stare through the vast glass cabinet housing the giant waterwheel and watch it rotate slowly and reliably.

"If only my love life could run so smoothly," I reflect.

After several minutes, I make up my mind to return to the main bar, only to witness more of Lauren's excessive flirting with her so-called friends. My confidence sinks.

By 12.30, I'm convinced that Gavin has got his wires crossed, so I decide to call it a night. I head for the door. As if by magic, however, Lauren spots my planned escape and comes after me.

"Where you off to?" she asks.

"I ... I thought I might make a move," I reply, signalling the exit with my thumb.

Lauren then runs her hand down my left arm before clutching on to my index and middle fingers. "You can't yet, you're taking me home. Just give me a minute to say goodbye to my friends. Wait there, yeah?"

She bustles off to hug and kiss each member of her large group of predominantly male friends. My mood switches instantaneously from one of resignation to one of nervous anticipation.

"Maybe she was just playing hard to get," I tell myself. "Trust me to be so negative."

Five minutes later, we arrive outside Lauren's house and sit for a split second in silence, save for the loud thud of my heart. Lauren then rummages through her bag before turning out the contents of her jacket.

"What's up?" I ask.

"It's my keys," she says impatiently. "I don't seem to have them on me. Shit, they must've fallen out of my bag."

"D'you want to go back?"

"No, it's okay. We'll never find them in the dark."

"Is there no-one else in?"

"Just my sister, but she'll be pissed off if I get her up at 1.00 in the morning."

It's at this point that Mr 'You-couldn't-be-more-slow-on-the-uptake-if-you-tried' Bentley finally gets the message – she wants to come back with me. Yes, a lucky break at long last!

Anxious not to miss out on such an opening, I turn to her and mumble awkwardly: "Well, you … you're more than welcome to stay at … er … my place."

"Mm, I'm not sure."

Ah, I know this game – she doesn't want to appear too easy. "I mean, I've got a spare bedroom. Two, in fact."

That's better – a much more confident delivery.

There's a moment's silence whilst Lauren contemplates my suggestion. "No, I'd better not. I've got work in the morning."

Talk about playing hard to get. "What time?"

"My shift at the pub starts at 12.00."

"That's no problem. I can drive you back well before then."

She stops to reflect once again. "Mm, I really don't wanna wake my sister up. But then … um … no, it's okay, thanks. I think I'll ring my friend. I'm sure she'll let me stay."

"Are you sure cos … ?"

"Yeah, I'm sure."

There's a protracted pause as I try to come to terms with the fact that, in spite of all the apparently blatant hints, Lauren is genuinely not even prepared to stay in my spare room.

"D'you want me to drive you there?" I ask eventually in defeat.

"It's okay," she says. "She's just round the corner."

With a rapid peck on the cheek and an equally rapid "Thanks, I'll see ya around", Lauren climbs out of the car and vanishes down a side road. I sit motionless for a few moments, trying to fathom what the hell was going on in her head. Had she really lost her keys? Did she fancy me or didn't she? What exactly had she said to Gavin? He's not the sort to play practical jokes.

On the way home, I find myself reliving the events of the evening with an overwhelming feeling that somehow I must've done something wrong. How could I have blown such a great opportunity?

"Maybe I wasn't persuasive enough?" I tell myself. "Then again, in the short time I've known Lauren Stewart, she's hardly appeared reserved or indecisive."

As I climb wearily into bed, I decide that it's now official – I really don't understand women at all. How other men manage to suss their cryptic minds, I'll never know.

It's now 30th December and I'm back home after spending an unusual festive period in Wales with mum, dad and my brother-in-law, Joe, waiting for my sister, Jayne, to give birth. Considering that the baby was due on about the 20th, we were all pretty confident we'd be spending Christmas Day in the company of the new addition to the family. Baby Chloë, however, had other ideas and refused to leave the womb until prised out by Caesarean section early in the morning of the 27th. She's a gorgeous little thing with the cutest yawn I've ever seen. It didn't take long for us to forgive her for the fact that we had to wait until the 28th for the taste of turkey. I'm now a very proud uncle.

As is usual towards the end of a school holiday, my attention is drawn towards piles of marking in my school bag that has to be tackled before we go back on 3rd January. Part of me feels that I should retire to my office – the box room at the front – and make an early start. But there's another part that fancies a swift pint. I head upstairs and empty the contents of my bag out onto the large teak desk. The sheer enormity of the task ahead hits me right between the eyes.

"Oh, sod it! I've still got a couple of days to get through this," I tell myself. "Might as well make the most of the time off whilst I can."

I grab my wallet and ageing leather jacket and head off to *The Barley Mow*.

I return soon after 11.00 to find the top of my road buzzing with activity and a large area incorporating my property sealed off by the police.

"What's going on?" I ask one of my neighbours who I find assembled with a small crowd of onlookers.

"Geezer in the flats opposite's bin done ova," he replies dramatically.

"Who by?"

"Oh, by some lads from the estat', apparently. Pissed up they were. Kicked 'is 'ead in good 'n' proper."

"Is he … er … really badly hurt?"

"Yeah, mate. One of 'is eyeballs was right back in its socke'. In a coma, poor bastard. P'lice don't reck'n 'e's gonna make it. Got a couple o' kids too."

With the permission of one of the numerous police officers, I step over the tape and retreat to the sanctuary of my house. Once safely tucked up in bed, my mind is working overtime.

"Flipping heck!" I mutter to myself. "If I'd stayed in and got started on that marking, I would've witnessed everything. Maybe I'd have been able to do something."

I spend another sleepless hour or so wondering exactly what sort of estate I've moved onto. Looks like Guy Harper – Barry Kent in *Adrian Mole* – wasn't pulling my leg, after all, when he warned about the plethora of criminals in my road.

When I head for the bathroom at 7.00 to relieve myself, I notice that the police and forensic are only just preparing to leave.

After breakfast, a couple of junior officers drop in for a statement. They ask if there's anyone who could confirm my whereabouts last night. Fortunately, I'm able to pass on the name of one of the bar staff at *The Barley Mow* who served me.

New Year's Eve proves to be almost a carbon copy of last year in terms of location and company. Even Maria repeats her sudden appearing act as Simon and I arrive at the cobbled High Street just before the stroke of 12.00. But there's a notable difference this time. At the mere sight of us, she turns and disappears, sparing me the agony of another moral dilemma under the influence.

Shortly afterwards, Simon and I lose each other in the jubilant crowd and I'm approached by Laura Palmer, a girl who came to me for private German tuition about four years ago. She's matured into a stunning blonde and I'm really taken aback when she flings her arms around me, pressing her lips up against the edge of my mouth.

"Hi ya, Al," she says confidently – she was rather shy four years ago. "It's really good to see you again."

"You too," I reply, aware that a mere four hours ago before we hit the pub, I was also appreciably shyer. "You look great."

Laura moves towards me again. Before I know it, we're both lost in an exceptionally passionate kiss. She's very good at it and I can feel my heart pounding furiously against her breasts. Within seconds, I'm transformed into the million-dollar man. But then I become aware of the taunting of her friends in the background and it isn't long before Laura withdraws, presumably out of embarrassment. I try to take hold of her again, desperate to continue where we left off, yet her friends are now in full swing.

"Teacher, teacher, teacher!" they chant.

Back down to earth, Laura rediscovers her shy demeanour of former times.

"I'm sorry, I can't," she says awkwardly before releasing herself from my clutches and returning to her friends. "Bye."

The girls then turn and vanish amongst the crowd.

Dizzy from my brief but highly emotive encounter, I set off in search of Simon. I soon stumble across him in the company of a small group of youngish women who I don't recognise. At the sight of me, he rapidly makes his excuses and leaves them.

"C'mon, lad," he says decisively. "Time to turn in."

Back at his flat, Simon extracts some oven chips from the fridge-freezer and places them under the grill. I nip off to the loo. On my return to the kitchen, I spot my toothbrush sizzling away nicely alongside the chips. I toss back my head in laughter.

"Oh, Mr Lennon," I say, "you're such a comedian!"

With our stomachs full and my teeth brushed with a peculiar, shrivelled v-shaped gadget, it's time for bed. I stretch out on the camp bed in the centre of Simon's curtainless, furnitureless lounge, my head full of Laura Palmer and our magic moment beneath the New Year moon. Well, my magic moment, at least.

"Definitely the prettiest girl I've ever kissed," I say under my breath, my confidence the recipient of a timely boost.

I stare through the large window in front of me at the clear, star-studded January sky. 1994 really has been an action-packed, if frustrating, year. I wonder what delights '95 has in store.

SPRING TERM

The first day back at College brings with it a surprising revelation. According to two of my confident, outgoing Lower Sixth French students, Mr Serene himself, Simon Lennon, pulled one of their friends on New Year's Eve. I'm sceptical at first, on the grounds that he's always insisted seventeen- and eighteen-year-old girls are far too young and immature to deserve even the remotest sniff of attention. But then I remember his mysterious disappearing act and the fact that I caught him amongst a group of young ladies. Hm, he's a dark horse, that one. Just wait till I next see him.

With the Upper Sixth mock exams underway, I'll only be required to teach the Lower Sixth over the next fortnight. This doesn't mean, however, that I'll have loads of free periods as there's exam supervision or 'invigilation' to be done. In fact, I've been clobbered for two periods later on today. Unlike a number of my colleagues past and present, I don't object to invigilation. It provides a perfect opportunity to chill out and do some serious thinking. In addition, there are fun games to be played with the other invigilators, such as trying to be the first to reach a student requesting more paper. I also enjoy working out what percentage of the students present is left-handed and whether the figure is higher for boys than it is for girls. It's just about the only chance I get now to apply some of my mathematical skills. Okay, I'm a sad case, I know.

In between teaching and invigilating, I arrange to see Avril, the Principal, to discuss my plans for the future. As much as I love my job here at *Mardall's*, I've come to realise over the last few months that I'm struggling to improve as a teacher because of the extent of my commitments. By teaching French and German to A level standard full-time, with all the preparation and marking that it involves, and coaching gym and trampolining for nothing, I feel I'm spreading myself too thinly.

This is very much a personal opinion and certainly hasn't been pointed out by anyone else. It probably stems from years of competing at such a perfectionist sport as gymnastics.

"So I wondered whether it would be possible to switch to part-time here next September to enable me to pursue my gym and trampolining coaching on a professional basis," I say to Avril after filling her in on the background to my decision.

"I can't foresee any reasons why this shouldn't be feasible," she says avidly. "Have you had any ideas about where you might do your gymnastic coaching?"

"Well, I'm exploring the possibility of taking over my old out-of-College gym club as a small business concern. And I'm also considering offering a coaching service to local schools."

"That's a splendid idea. Of course, we may well be able to offer you some paid coaching here in the not too distant future if our plans for the new Sports Centre materialise."

"Really? That'd be ideal."

"Okay, Al. Well, thanks for sharing your ideas with me. I'll run them past Clive [the Vice-Principal] and see what we can come up with."

As I close the door to Avril's office, it occurs to me that she was far more enthusiastic about my proposals than I'd expected. Maybe she sees a reduction in my teaching hours as a means of easing the looming financial crisis, a move that could help to avoid redundancies in my department.

I'm in a mischievous mood on returning to the house. Once inside the door, I give Simon Lennon a call. As soon as he picks up, I launch into a protracted mock criticism of his conduct on New Year's Eve, pulling his leg in every direction possible. To my disappointment, however, he denies any recollection of the incident with the seventeen-year-old girl. However, did I detect an uncomfortable tone in his voice?

My good humour is severely dampened later in the evening when the young bloke who works part-time at the local shop informs me that the hospital have had to switch off the life-support machine connected to my neighbour who was attacked on 30th December. Apparently, two lads from my estate have been arrested and charged with ... MURDER. How fragile our existence can be.

On the Friday of the first week back, I'm tied up all day with the conduct of German mock orals. All but one of the candidates is from Thelma or Marilyn's group, which enables me to compare the standard with my own class. I've often thought that I'd relish being an oral examiner for one of the Boards, but it's only for a limited period in the year and not that brilliantly paid. Consequently, I'd have to squeeze it in on top of everything else.

At the end of the day, I have to disappoint Rachel, Amanda and co by cancelling the trampolining session – for the simple reason that I need time to pop home and change into my suit for this evening's Prize Giving/Speech Night. For my normal, everyday teaching, I generally make do with a pair of black trousers and a smart shirt with or without a tie. Some of my colleagues in other departments wear jeans. Our dress code is very different from the one existing in most secondary schools and below, and is indicative of the more informal approach adopted in a modern-day Sixth Form College. It is, after all, supposed to be a stepping stone to university.

The evening proves to be a fairly mundane affair, with only a handful of language students amongst those filling the pews in the local cathedral. Fortunately, Cara and Mandy 'Mandarin' are present, and I manage to have a few words with them at the reception that follows. Both have settled in really well at uni and made loads of new friends. It's great to see them again, although I sense that moving away has put a strain on their previously close friendship. Something has definitely changed between them, which is a shame. I'm also disappointed to discover that I failed in my bid to win the staff sweepstake on the length of the MP guest speaker's address.

As a College Rep, Maria's friend Louise is on duty all evening and asks at the end if I'd be able to give her a lift home. I oblige and find her in a really chatty mood.

"It's a pity that you and Maria have stopped coming along to trampolining," I tell her when she pauses for breath.

"I know, it was a laugh," she says. "It's just that there're so many other distractions at lunchtime."

"What, like little boys, you mean?"

"Actually, I was referring to my College Rep duties."

I refrain from mentioning it, but it hasn't escaped my attention that Maria now seems to spend a lot of her free time in the designated smoking room. Doesn't look like I'll be seeing the two girls again on the trampoline.

On Saturday, I attend Howard Parish's twenty-first birthday party, held at his mum's house. Among the thirty or so guests is Annette Enquist, a lively, attractive Swedish girl who used to train and help coach at my out-of-College gym club. There was a period a few years back when she used to flirt with me ostentatiously at *The Combine Harvester*, insisting on sitting on my lap and bear-hugging me at every opportunity. However, when I went to kiss her, she ran a mile. Surprise, surprise! She tells me she's hoping to be a physiotherapist. If I continue to compete at gym well into my thirties, I may well have to call on her services at some point in the future. You know, to treat those ailing muscles. It's an enjoyable evening and I appreciate the chance to catch up with Howard as well as Annette.

The following weekend, I head off to Southampton, the scene of my degree and teacher-training course. On the Saturday night, I visit Lisa Thomas, one of my former tutees who took part in the German Exchange trip to Hamburg in November 1992. Her dad also used to manage *Razzmattaz* nightclub. She writes to me every now and again and, in her most recent letter, insisted I pay her a visit.

I turn back the clock by joining Lisa and her uni friends in the Union Bar. Although I've always been aware that Lisa has a soft spot for me, I'm surprised by the extent of the flirting that ensues, given that she's supposed to have a boyfriend. As the booze starts to bite, we're drawn closer together.

Back at her student house, we start kissing in earnest and the evening ends with both of us lying sardine-like in her single bed. Fortunately, Lisa imposes limits on the degree of her infidelity and I'm spared a situation where my desire to feel wanted overtakes my determination to avoid casual sex – if you know what I mean. Tired of my tossing and turning, Lisa kicks me out of bed during the night. With nowhere else to go, I curl up on the floor until morning.

Lisa and I part amicably at lunchtime on Sunday. Before returning home, I call in on one of my former university chums and his Australian wife. They're off to live in Oz in three weeks, so I'm grateful for the opportunity to catch up on their news, view the wedding photos and reminisce.

Back at College on the Monday after my interesting weekend in Southampton, Rachel twists her ankle badly during the lunchtime trampolining session. It starts to swell alarmingly and she's in considerable pain, so I decide she ought to get it checked out at Casualty. I'm fully prepared to drop her there myself until one of the ladies in the Main Office informs me that teachers are not supposed to drive injured students to hospital. Another of the latest government-inspired Health and Safety initiatives, no doubt. I find one of Rachel's mobile friends and arrange for him to take her instead.

In the evening, I give Rachel a quick buzz at home. She seems really pleased to hear from me and relays some good news – no broken bones, just torn ligaments.

"They've even given me crutches," she says finally with an involuntary laugh.

It's now the first Monday in February and a couple of weeks have elapsed since Rachel's mishap on the trampoline. As is often the case when you take the mickey out of someone, something else happens soon afterwards, which leaves *you* at the centre of ridicule. At the end of afternoon registration, Ruth Sutton, one of the louder, more outspoken girls in my

Set, informs me with delight that she knows Laura Palmer and has had the low-down on my antics on New Year's Eve. Is nothing ever sacred? Sorry, Simon – all is forgiven!

The following day at registration, Ruth asks if I can lend her fifteen pounds for a driving lesson.

"The instructor's meeting me from College and I forgot to ask my mum for the money," she says. "Don't worry, I'll pay you back tomorrow."

I scratch my head uncomfortably, sensing a potential case of blackmail on the horizon. Then again, I am entitled to my private life and how could I have known that Laura had contacts at *Mardall's*? After all, she does live about twenty miles away.

Ruth hands over a rather trendy black leather jacket. "Look, you can take this as security, if you like."

After a close inspection of the jacket, I decide to accept her offer. Once she's out of the room, I try it on for size. It fits perfectly.

"With any luck, she'll forget the money for a few days and I'll get to wear this at the weekend," I chuckle to myself. "Combined with my *Levi's*, how can the ladies resist me now? It's all about image, old son."

At the weekend, I return to the scene of my birthday meal, complete with *Levi's* and trendy leather jacket. No sooner am I through the door than I clap eyes on Lauren Stewart. She freezes at the sight of me, then legs it to the far side of the pub. Maybe she's an animal rights supporter.

Not wishing to experience any further humiliation, I make a hasty exit, then head directly back to town and the more familiar surroundings of *The Barley Mow*. The Dutch girls, who've been far too busy since New Year to meet up, are there sharing a joke with Rupert Stanley. I join them for a drink.

At a convenient moment, I subtly remind Eva that we still haven't arranged our date.

"Oh, I was going to ring you," she says, "to say that I saw my ex-boyfriend in Holland over Christmas and that we are sort of back together now."

Just to rub salt into the wounds, Emily targets me again with her excessive flirting. I'm on a downer after the events of earlier and I find myself responding, only to be rejected in familiar fashion once she tires of her little game. Feeling rock bottom, I grab her arm and pull her towards me.

"Why d'you keep doing this to me?" I rage. "You tease me until I'm really turned on, and then you … you throw me away like … like I'm a piece of … a piece of shit."

Suddenly taken aback by the extent of my outburst, I release her arm. All round, there are confounded expressions on the faces of the other members of the gang and, in our corner of the pub, silence reigns supreme. No-one, it seems, has ever witnessed Alan Bentley lose his temper.

"Go on, then, be honest. What's wrong with me?" I ask, desperately trying to regain control. "Tell it to my face. Tell me why you won't let things go any further. C'mon, I want to hear it. Am I just not tall or good-looking enough for you, or what?"

Emily turns away awkwardly. I place my hand on her left shoulder and attempt to spin her round. There's no way she's ducking out of this one. She resists. I try again. This time she yields and swivels on the spot to confront me.

Then she says firmly: "All right. If you want to know, then I'll tell you. No, it's got nothing to do with the way you look. And I think you're a nice bloke and all that. But ..."

"But *what?*"

"It's just that there's ... there's something missing, that's all."

"What *something?*"

"Dunno. I can't put my finger on it. But whatever it is, you haven't got it. Sorry, mate!"

During the following week, I have three consecutive dreams featuring Maria Grey. All above board, of course. Since she continues to prefer the smoking room at lunchtime on a Monday to the Hall for trampolining, I haven't seen a great deal of her lately, so I'm surprised that she's managed to penetrate my subconscious. Why is it that dreaming about someone you really like often has the effect of reinforcing the infatuation? All of a sudden, I can't get the wretched girl out of my head again. Somehow, my thoughts always seem to return to her when I've got the blues. Maybe it's easier being 'in love' with someone you can't have. After all, fantasies are generally blessed with happy endings, aren't they?

By Saturday 11th February, it's official. If I weighed thirty-five stone, were as bald as a coot, had a severe acne problem, warts all over my face, jug ears, a hooter for a nose and an IQ of under fifty, I couldn't possibly feel more unattractive to the opposite sex than I do right now. Any attempts to feel positive about my popularity on New Year's Eve and in Southampton simply aren't working. Let's face it, both girls were drunk and probably just wanted to pull an older man as an ego boost.

In the evening, I attend the party that Lee Pascal's parents have organised to celebrate their son's two-week visit to England with Canadian wife and fifteen-month-old baby daughter. By pure coincidence, the house is just a few doors along from where Marilyn Butcher lives and she's there with her husband, a university lecturer.

It's great to see my old school friend again after so many years, and to finally meet his attractive wife and gorgeous little girl. I'm rather shocked, though, to see that the wiry frame that served him so well during our morning jogs a few years ago – not to mention the Paris and London marathons – has given way to a physique resembling a medium-sized beer barrel. I'm sure this wasn't one of our many predictions for the future. The important thing, however, is that his wife obviously loves him and that he's found real happiness. Having had a rocky period in his late teens, when he ran away from home and later deserted the French army, this is particularly good to see. Inevitably, Lee's parents question me about my lack of wife or girlfriend, which I struggle to explain convincingly. Somehow, "I just haven't met the right person yet" sounds so feeble for someone approaching thirty.

My mood of self-pity continues when I wake on Sunday morning. I spend a large part of the day moping around the house with the longest face I can muster. I really don't know why, but other people seem to find it so much easier to meet their soul mate than I do and I'm starting to develop a major inferiority complex. If only I knew what makes me such an unattractive proposition to so many of the girls I like, I could do something about it. Emily's recent comment has left me in despair because it was so intangible. If I were overweight or suffered from BO or bad breath, I could take combative steps. But how do you go about trying to rectify a problem as abstract as my one?

It's only after a few glasses of wine in the evening that my usual spirit makes a welcome return – only, this time with a vengeance. For some bizarre reason, I find myself with an overwhelming desire to do something out of character, to break free from the shackles of decency and respectability, let alone predictability.

"I'm just too inhibited, too constrained by social conventions," I tell myself.

Maybe if I weren't so obsessed with toeing the line all the time, I'd be more appealing to the opposite sex. After all, the guy that Emily has got her eye on at the moment is a real Jack the Lad.

Still high from the cheap plonk, I unwrap a blank tape and make a recording of the Simon and Garfunkel ballad, *Kathy's Song*. I place the finished product in a padded envelope that I find lying around and copy the address of the parcel's destination from the phone directory. Uncertain of the weight, I stick on two first-class stamps for good measure. Before I have chance to sober up and back out cowardly, I stumble along to the nearest post box to deliver my potential minefield.

"This year's Valentine's Day will signal the start of the new adventurous Al," I announce with a sense of victory.

On my way to work on the morning of Valentine's Day, I'm 'shitting bricks' as they say. Without the prop of alcohol, my bold, daring act of Sunday night suddenly seems unnecessarily suicidal.

At breaktime, College Rep Louise tracks me down in the main corridor, ostensibly to collect more tickets for the Valentine's Ball later in the week.

"Did you send any Valentine's cards, Al?" she asks as I hand over a further batch.

"Valentine's *cards*? No, not this year, Louise," I reply with perfect honesty.

She gives me a broad, knowing smile, then heads off to the canteen to flog the tickets. A little later on, Natasha asks me the same question.

"How the hell did they suss it so quickly?" I ponder, scratching my head.

I should be quaking in my boots, I know, but somehow the early morning jitters have given way to a profound sense of calm and release. Probably for the first time in my adult life, I've wilfully done the wrong thing – although I could probably plead diminished responsibility – and yet I'm not wracked by guilt. In fact, I feel incredibly pleased with myself. Maybe that padded cell is beckoning, after all.

I return home later with the hope that there'll have been a second post, delivering a pile of Valentine's cards from mystery admirers. Yeah, right. Dream on, Al!

The following morning, Louise corners me in the entrance hall by Reception.

"I was pleased to see that you sent Maria a song," she says without batting an eyelid.

I spin round to scan the area, anxious that someone may have overheard her. But she's chosen her moment very carefully. The teacher in my head advises playing the innocent, but Louise is a smart girl and, anyway, nobody really wants a Valentine's message to remain totally anonymous, do they? Otherwise, what's the point? But then, on the other hand, this is no ordinary amorous scenario. I'm torn, really torn between the old and the 'new' me, my head and heart fighting a ferocious battle. In the end, I settle for a sheepish smile, not wanting to confess verbally and potentially incriminate myself any further.

"We guessed it was from you because it was an older song," Louise explains.

I smile sheepishly for the second time and utter a feeble: "Oh, I see."

Suddenly, a crowd of students barges through the swinging doors and we're no longer alone. I glance at my watch impatiently, then mumble an excuse about needing to press on. Louise smiles understandingly and we part.

"Why did she say she was pleased about what I'd done?" I ask myself as I jog across to the *Grosvenor*. Then I have an anxious thought: "I hope they don't assume I want something to happen before Maria's finished her A levels."

It's Parents' Evening after College. By chance, I'm given a table in the staff canteen next to my Spanish-teaching colleague, Gillian Jones, who I notice has *Mr and Mrs Grey* written half way down her list. At *Mardall's*, the students are encouraged to attend with their parents and, sure enough, Maria appears midway through the evening with her South American mum and English dad. I'm keen to eavesdrop on the conversation. Unfortunately, the early arrival of my next appointment renders this impossible. However, out of the corner of my eye, I can't fail to catch a glimpse of Maria's pretty, olive-skinned face adorned by a ravishing smile. The news is obviously good. Once more, my heart melts and I have to call on all my experience of amateur dramatics, as well as teaching, to disguise it from the couple sitting attentively in front of me. Oh bugger! I really have got it bad again. How inconvenient!

"Just hope her parents haven't been granted a hearing of *Maria's Song*," I worry suddenly as they shake hands with Gillian and leave the room.

As the evening progresses, I'm reminded repeatedly of the respect that the majority of local parents have for teachers here and my conscience receives a severe blow. I return to the car soon after 9.00, with my new daring approach falling apart at the seams.

"What on earth possessed me to send that tape?" I castigate myself as I leave the College grounds. "It was so unprofessional. Let's hope Avril doesn't keep fingerprint detection equipment in one of the drawers of her desk."

At the students' request, the Valentine's Ball is back at *Razzmattaz*. As now seems customary, a large number of tickets are sold on the door. There's no sign of Maria, but Rachel and Amanda are there in force.

Later in the evening, I join them for a dance. The staff represen-tation is significantly better than usual with Peter Malcolmson, Nic Reynolds, the cricket captain, and Rebecca Piper, my blind date from last year, amongst those present. Even Avril makes a brief appearance towards the end and grants me a nod of approval after scanning the crowded dance floor.

With another successful student bash under my belt, I find one of Cara and Mandy's old friends, Merv Fitzgerald, stranded on the pavement outside the club with no lift home. Although it'll involve a major detour, I see it as my duty to drop him back. On the way, he reveals an interest in my rally-derived Lancia Delta HF 4x4 and an interesting discussion ensues about cars. Merv, it transpires, is keen to become a racing driver. Good lad!

Back home, it occurs to me how much I missed Maria tonight. However, there's no doubt that her absence helped to ease my mounting conscience. I really am an emotional wreck at the moment, switching involuntarily between my recently discovered liberalism and the conservatism of old. Unable to sleep, I start to count the takings from tonight's Ball. It's 2.00 am by the time I turn out the light.

I'm really washed out in the morning, but spurred on by the thought that this is the last day before the half term holiday. How I need a break to sort my head out and re-establish a grip on my life.

Rachel, Amanda and a handful of others are there as usual for gym at 3.30. Rachel's torn ligaments have now healed completely. In the middle of the warm up, Natasha comes into the Hall to collect some sheets that I've photocopied to assist her with her French coursework. As I'm handing them over, I spot Maria standing by the door, waiting for her friend. Natasha heads off with the photocopies followed by Maria.

About half an hour later, however, the two girls return and spectate from the doorway for a few minutes. I'm in the middle of coaching at this stage, so I just send a smile and wave of acknowledgement in their direction.

At the end of the session, Rachel and Amanda accept the now customary lift home, along with Rebecca Piper whose Jeep is temporarily off the road. In between Amanda and Rachel's house, Rebecca remarks that she can't see what's so special about the Lancia and I end up approaching the next corner, a sharp left-hander, far too rapidly. My passengers are sent into hysteria, although the car copes admirably. It wasn't a rally champion for nothing. Needless to say, Rebecca revises her view on the virtues of the Lancia Delta HF 4x4.

When Rachel steps out of the car by the alley way that cuts through to her road, I apologise for my boy-racer impersonation. She smiles warmly.

"Thanks for the lift," she says. "Oh, and have a nice half term!"

With everything that's been happening lately, I forgot to mention that Katja Müller, Claudia Schmidt's German friend who came to visit England two years ago, will be staying with me during half term. She's keen to find a job in London as a social worker and wants to call in on a few offices to assess the prospects. I promised to lend a hand.

After a rapid house-tidying operation first thing on Saturday morning, I shoot off to Heathrow to fetch Katja. On the way there, I remember our previous meeting and how I'd been convinced that something would've happened romantically had her stay been longer. Mind you, two years is a long time and a lot can change. Anyway, it'll be good to have some female company to distract me from recent goings-on at work, even if it proves to be purely platonic.

Right from the outset, however, Katja adopts an encouragingly tactile manner towards me and I begin to wonder whether this may, after all, turn out to be the romantic opportunity I've been searching for. With her smart, short brown hair, petite figure and warm, gentle personality, Katja certainly is my type of woman. Not that I have a problem with larger women or long hair, of course.

Throughout the remainder of the morning, Katja continues to flirt with me. After lunch, we fall asleep together on the settee against each other.

On awakening, there's more flirting and, feeling mildly aroused, I lean across to kiss her. She doesn't turn away, but balks at anything venturing beyond a simple peck on the lips. After a while, I decide that I'm probably coming on too strongly, too soon and back off.

"Come on, Al," I tell myself firmly. "She's here until Thursday and you don't want to rush things."

In the evening, I take Katja out for dinner at *Ten Tenths*. We communicate mainly in German and continue to get on famously.

Later, we catch up with the gang at *The Barley Mow*. I'm slightly concerned to discover that Rupert Stanley is there licking his lips ominously, but I decide it's only polite to introduce my guest to him as well as to the others. What I'd hoped would be a confidence-boosting night out in the company of an intelligent, attractive woman transpires to be a highly jittery one as Rupert turns on the charm big time in an attempt to woo Katja. Every trip to the toilet is accompanied by the inherent fear that I'll return a few minutes later to the devastating sight of Rupert with his tongue down her throat. After all, he's not the sort of bloke to settle for a meagre peck, I'm sure.

To my profound relief, closing time arrives without the realisation of my worst nightmare. I walk home with Katja, trying to recall if I was anything like this paranoid two years ago. Somehow, it seems that I've taken several steps backwards in this area. I feel a sudden rush of guilt for doubting Rupert and Katja's integrity. My train of thought is interrupted by the sound of Katja's tiny voice.

"Your friend want me to go back to his house," she says.

"What?!" I exclaim, suddenly overcome by a suffocating feeling of panic.

"Your friend, Rupert. He want me to leave with him. I think he quite like me."

I take a deep breath, aware that my initial reaction probably exposed my vulnerability. I then say more calmly: "I'm sorry, he's like that with a lot of women that he meets."

"That's okay. I think he is nice."

Seeking reassurance in the light of Rupert's now genuine threat to my potential week of romance, I make a subtle move on Katja again back at the house. But her response is the same as it was earlier in the day – an abundance of hugs and 'innocent' kisses, but no more. Just after midnight, she declares that she's ready for bed and retires to the spare room.

On Monday, I accompany Katja up to London by train in the hope of finding her a job. I'm not overly optimistic about her chances, but she does have a long list of social service offices to visit and appears confident herself.

We spend the day moving from one office to another. Unfortunately, none of them is in a position to offer anything concrete. We do, however, manage to compile a list of further contacts.

"Maybe it is possible to just telephone with these other offices tomorrow," Katja says wearily at the end of the afternoon.

I tell her it's a good idea and we set off home. After another full day of Emily-like teasing, I'm frustrated. I decide to confront my guest once we've returned to the station car park.

"Why do you flirt with me all the time," I ask, "but not allow me to kiss you properly?"

Katja glances out of the window as if searching for the most tactful response. After a few seconds, she looks back at me and asks: "Can I say it in German? It's not so easy in English."

I nod and she launches at once into a highly complex explanation of what appears to be a very straightforward stumbling block – she's got a boyfriend in Germany who she met just a few weeks ago. At first, I'm consoled by the realisation that the problem doesn't stem from any lack of a vital ingredient on my part. But then later, over dinner with mum and dad, I can't help acknowledging privately how unlucky I always seem to be with timing.

Having said goodbye to my parents, I take Katja to the *Opportunity Knox* nightclub. Almost from the moment we've arrived at the top of the stairs, I'm accosted by a whole array of *Mardall's* students, predominantly girls, wanting to know who my lady friend is. I'm slightly taken aback by the extent of their interest, but then again, this is the first time any of them have seen me in the company of a woman.

After a while, Katja seems genuinely put out that my focus is no longer on her. Surely she can't be jealous of a group of college students. In the circumstances, I reason that it won't do any harm to lap up the attention from around. And I'm not wrong. Before long, Katja takes me to one side, eases my head towards hers and kisses me passionately – tongues and all – for a good five minutes. I look up to find the posse of girls witnessing my big moment. My initial embarrassment soon gives way to the recognition that their presence has done me a huge favour. Thanks, girls!

Back at the house, Katja has no hesitation in following me through to my bedroom. I'm delighted, of course, to have the opportunity to share a bed with her, but I've no expectations of sex. After all, like Lisa a few weeks back, she's a nice girl who has a boyfriend and I feel I should show some respect for that. But why does she have to be so stubborn about removing her top?

The therapeutic effect of being reacquainted with a female body lying close to mine all night is hard to quantify. I wake in the morning with an overwhelming feeling of self-confidence. It's as if someone has injected me with a powerful, mind-altering drug.

On the dot of 9.00, a plumber arrives with a couple of assistants to begin the installation of central heating. I've had to take out a loan of three thousand pounds to pay for it, but it should make the house more saleable in the future, not to mention a tad warmer. Katja and I stay in all day so that I can make a series of phone calls on her behalf to various social service departments in and around London. Once again, there are no positions available for the foreseeable future. By late afternoon, Katja accepts rather disconsolately that she'll have to review her plans to be a social worker in London.

About teatime, Rupert Stanley rings to ask if the two of us fancy joining him and a friend at … *Opportunity Knox*. Katja appears more than happy at the prospect of clubbing two nights in a row, so I accept his kind offer. Considering that my guest and I are now much closer, I feel less threatened by the lecherous Rupert.

Just before 10.00, Rupert's friend, Barry Whiley, a tall, balding, bear-like man in his early twenties, ferries us to the club. I'm surprised to see how busy it is for a Tuesday. Then again, it is half term. Inevitably, Rupert picks up where he left off on Saturday night, trying every trick in the book to charm Katja. Confident that she'll repel any proper advances, I leave him to it and head to the circular bar in the middle of the club for more drinks.

Whilst I'm waiting to be served, I notice that Katja has taken a step closer to Rupert. Before I have chance to blink, their heads have moved together in search of a maiden kiss. Overcome by jealousy, I abandon my position at the bar and race across to intercept. I arrive just as their lips are about to touch.

"Hey, what the hell's going on?" I ask angrily.

Both parties are shocked by the ferocity of my question and stand bolt upright in military fashion.

I address Katja first, perhaps rather harshly: "Jetzt weiß ich, was für eine Frau du bist." [Now I know what sort of woman you are.] Tears instantly fill her eyes and she runs off to the Ladies, leaving me to confront Rupert.

"What d'you think you're playing at?" I ask, slightly more calmly. "She's involved with me."

"How was I sposed to know that?" he replies. "I'm not a mind reader." "You mean, she didn't tell you?"

"No, she didn't. So don't go blaming me, all right?" There's more than a hint of recrimination in his voice. "It's all her fault, the bitch."

It occurs to me that I'm the one who's supposed to be livid and in need of appeasement, yet here I am trying to pacify one of the guilty parties. Before long, Rupert's voice returns to its normal volume and the profuse apologies start to flow.

"I'm sorry, okay," he says with apparent sincerity. "I'd never've done that to a mate. You've got to believe me."

At the end of the evening, as we're collecting our jackets from the cloakroom, Katja speaks to me for the first time since the incident with Rupert.

"I'm so sorry," she says timidly. "I can move to a hotel, if you like." "Don't be silly," I reply. "My spare room's still available."

Needless to say, the atmosphere on the way home is a little strained. Back at the house, Katja wants to talk, but I've had enough drama for one evening and disappear into my bedroom, closing the door firmly behind me. Safely under the duvet, I realise that whatever drug I was injected with twenty-four hours ago has well and truly lost its effect.

The following morning, Katja is full of contrition. Since I have no intention of spoiling the last full day of her visit, we make up. We have an enjoyable lunch together at a restaurant recommended by the plumber and then a quiet drink at *Alfredo's* in the evening. Being such a reasonable bloke, I allow the young lady to access my bedroom once again. As a sign of remorse, Katja removes her top. Nothing more, but one has to be grateful for small mercies.

One of my worse qualities is my timekeeping. On the Thursday morning, I completely underestimate how long it'll take to reach Heathrow in the mid-week traffic. With only twenty minutes remaining until her plane is due to take off, I dump a tearful Katja at Terminal 2 amidst hurried goodbyes. I park the car and return to the terminal to check that she made the flight. She did – by the skin of her teeth.

As I make my way home along the busy M25, it strikes me how much I'll miss my little German friend. Although her behaviour on Tuesday night reinforced my belief that Rupert Stanley is more attractive to the opposite sex than I am and compounded my current self-image problem, I did enjoy her company enormously. Her stay has helped to dispel the fear I sometimes have that, through living alone for such a long time, I've become too self-centred to share my life with anyone.

By the end of the day, the plumber gets the central heating going. The house is transformed within minutes into a tropical greenhouse. Luxury, at long last!

Back at work after half term, Ruth Sutton finally hands over the fifteen pounds she borrowed from me a few weeks back. Somewhat reluctantly, I'm obliged to return her stylish leather jacket. Oh well, I suppose it didn't entirely perform the miracles that I'd hoped. Was worth a try, though.

At the end of the first week in March, I take my mini-bus test. I then drive my colleague, Thelma Parker, the current German assistant and nine second-year German students to my old university to see a production of a German play they've been studying. Lisa Thomas is the prompt and receives us cordially.

A few days later, interviews are held for the position of Head of Modern Languages vacated by Desmond Willis last summer. There are four short-listed candidates, including our very own Marilyn Butcher who's been doing the job since Desmond's departure. The selection process lasts all day and it's not until the close of play that Marilyn emerges, triumphant, from Avril's office. There are congratulatory hugs and kisses all round the top end of the Staff Room. As mum always says: "Better the devil you know".

Rumour has it that an advert will appear shortly in the *TES* – *Times Educational Supplement* – for a permanent Head of German for September. Thelma Parker is keen to put herself forward as a candidate. My proposed switch to part-time would rule me out of contention.

Clive Moss, the Vice-Principal, catches me on my way out and confirms that he's perfectly happy for me to reduce my hours next year, provided that I resign formally from my full-time position before the usual May 31st deadline. At least I'll have a bit of time to chew over my plan before taking the plunge.

The following lunchtime, I head into town, wearing my Student Activities' hat, in the pursuit of sponges for Red Nose Day. Apparently, certain members of staff will be making an appearance in the stocks. I wonder why *Woolworths* and *Halfords* are so willing to make a contribution.

In the evening, I make the usual trip to my private gym to set up the equipment.

Afterwards, I catch the end of a leaving party organised for Patricia Bates, a popular member of the College Main Office team. We always got on well and she was kind enough to come along to support me in *Adrian Mole* a couple of years ago. With speeches out of the way and the leaving present handed over, someone announces that today is the thirty-third birthday of Charles Spackman's immediate IT boss, David Harding. All those present join in with Happy Birthday.

After Patricia's bash, I accept David's offer to join him, Charles and a few others at what is now officially my second home – *Opportunity Knox*. As was the case over half term, Steve Whately, the Door Manager, grants my guests and me free entry. What it is to be treated like royalty!

It doesn't take long to establish that the ravishing Maria is present with Natasha. After a fair few drinks, I find myself pouring my heart out to David, a father of four.

"But does she like *you*?" he asks.

"I'm not sure," I reply with a shrug. "There've been positive signs over the last eighteen months. Then again, there've been some negative ones too. Anyway, I'm hopeless at reading women."

"Okay, then it's quite simple. You've got to tell her how you feel."

"But how can I? She's a student and I'm a teacher. It'd be unprofessional, wouldn't it, even in these enlightened times?"

"So what? She'll be gone in a couple of months and you'll spend the rest of your life wondering what could've happened."

"But what if she grasses on me to the Principal? It really wouldn't look good if …"

"Then you just deny it. It's not as if you'll have done anything really terrible, anyway."

Somehow, when David speaks, everything seems so incredibly straightforward all of a sudden.

"Believe me," he says finally. "Life's too short to just sit back and do nothing."

The following morning, I go for an eye test at the opticians near College. It's owned by the husband of the Chemistry technician who I sometimes sit next to over lunch. It's years since I last had a test and she promised special rates for colleagues.

Afterwards, I run into Rachel and Amanda. We have lunch together on the top floor of a small café in the High Street. They both confess that they're not looking forward to their time at College coming to an end.

"Apart from anything else, we'll miss the gym and trampolining," Rachel says rather sombrely.

With a grin, I say: "But not the gym and trampolining coach, of course." Rachel smiles bashfully.

"So will you miss *us*?" Amanda asks.

"Yes, of course I will. You'll be impossible to replace."

"I'm scared I'm going to fail all my exams," Rachel says, changing the subject.

"Hey, come on, you're an excellent student. You'll be fine."

From her expression, it's apparent that Amanda doesn't share Rachel's fear of exams. But then she's always been the more confident of the two.

On our way out, I thank the girls for their company and suggest that we could perhaps meet again for lunch sometime. Both nod enthusiastically.

In its effort to keep abreast of modern technological developments, the College recently installed a swipe card system for registering staff and student attendance. As well as swiping at the beginning and end of the day, we're required to use our cards at the start of each lesson. Certain members of staff have refused to embrace this new system, on the grounds that they're unwilling for the management to have access to their exact arrival and departure times. Consequently, they have to manually sign an in-and-out book by Reception. Is there a difference? I don't object in principle to the new system, although it's far from perfect. In fact, it broke down so frequently in the beginning that David Harding and the Bursar had to completely re-write the programme. Then there's the small issue of students swiping in for each other or simply forgetting to bring their card with them to College. As a back up, we're expected to continue to keep manual registers. What was all this talk of technology saving time?

At Hannah Murray's request, I agree on Red Nose Day to be timed running round the campus, swiping at all the posts. I set a time that other volunteers then have to beat. Needless to say, there are several strapping eighteen-year-old PE students who annihilate my effort. The adrenaline rush and the fact that I'm off to Poitiers tomorrow for the French Exchange convince me that now is the time to approach Maria.

I catch her at the beginning of lunch coming out of 'Bomber' Lancaster's History lesson.

"Hi, Maria," I say. "Can I have a brief word?"

There's a look of unease on her face.

"What have I done?" she says.

"Er, nothing. Nothing at all."

I open my classroom door and signal inside it with an outstretched arm. Maria pauses momentarily before complying with my request. I follow her, feeling increasingly anxious, yet incredibly determined at the same time. I take a very deep breath.

"Maria, there's no easy way of saying this," I begin with a nervous cough.

"Have I done something wrong?" she asks, a look of trepidation all over her face.

"Er … no – you haven't. It's just that …" I pause and gaze out the window in search of divine intervention, my heart racing almost uncontrollably. I look back at her. "It's just …" It's no good. The speech that I'd rehearsed so carefully beforehand has all but deserted me and I'm forced to improvise. "Okay. You … you know it was me who sent you that thing … erm … tape on … on Valentine's Day. Well, it … it wasn't a joke or anything."

My heart is beating faster than ever now, with every nerve in my body desperate for this encounter to be over. As for my conscience, why does it have to return right at this very moment? I imagine Avril or Marilyn with an ear up to the door, and the embarrassment and humiliation that'd follow. Throughout my torment, Maria just stands there, staring at me as if she hasn't the foggiest what all the fuss is about. If only she knew and could help me out.

I brace myself once again. "Erm, what I'm trying to say is that I … I'm crazy about you and I … I've never felt like this before."

Maria shakes her head vigorously several times. Before I have chance to continue, she opens her mouth to speak, her demeanour as cool as a cucumber: "You'll soon forget about me when I've left."

"No, Maria, that's just it – I won't."

She shakes her head even more forcefully than before and moves hastily towards the door. I follow her, desperate to finish my spiel, to utter all those romantic words that came together so easily earlier today. But it's pointless. Her body language has completely broken my spirit. Okay, I may be hopeless when it comes to reading the signs, but on this occasion even a blind man would have little difficulty concluding that the young woman in front of me has only one thing on her mind – escaping as rapidly as possible. I bow my head in defeat, all my hopes torn to shreds. I feel my bum collapse onto the corner of a desk.

"Goodbye, then," Maria says without the slightest trace of emotion and disappears hurriedly out onto the landing.

I sit motionless for what seems like an eternity, my entire body stripped of the desire to move. Then, all of a sudden, it hits me. Not humiliation or guilt, but an overwhelming feeling of emptiness as if someone close to me has just died.

Eventually, I haul my lifeless frame off the desk and move across to the window. Below, there's a buzz of activity, hungry bodies striding purposefully towards the canteen, each one oblivious of the reckless farce that's just unfolded on the top floor of the *Grosvenor*.

"Well, that's that, then," I mutter to myself with resignation and head off wearily to lunch.

Following ten relaxing but relatively uneventful days in France and the daily sight of François back to his serious, unadventurous old self, I return to England to see out the last couple of weeks of term. This year, the holiday won't be quite as long for me as usual as I've agreed to help out with the College's latest money-spinner, a three-day Easter Revision Course. It's open to students from other educational establishments as well as our own and it'll involve four hour and a half sessions per day. I'll be responsible for teaching A level German, although so far only a couple of girls from Thelma Parker's Upper Sixth group have enrolled. It promises to be a hard slog, but will be exceptionally kind to my bank balance. Whilst I have it on good authority that money can't buy love, I feel certain that it can help to compensate for a lack of it.

SUMMER TERM

In some ways, car dealers present as a big a problem for me as do the fairer sex, for the simple reason that they're masters at pulling the wool over my eyes. My love affair with the rally-bred Lancia Delta underwent a severe setback recently after a conversation with the previous Scottish owner revealed that it was a rust bucket when he relinquished it to the Italian car specialist who subsequently sold it on to me. Despite being marketed as totally original, it seems that extensive restoration work had been carried out. I complained profusely to the manager, but he explained that the term 'original' usually only applies to the mechanical condition of a car. Hm!

With bubbles already reappearing on the bottom of the front doors, I decided to move the car on over Easter. A Scottish bloke and his mate – not the original owner – travelled down to view it and liked what they saw. Unfortunately, the money transfer failed to go through before the close of play at *NatWest*, so I found myself offering the two Jocks accommodation for the night in my spare room. Appreciating their eagerness for a bevvy or two before hitting the sack, I took the lads pubbing in town. Both were convinced they'd be able to show me a trick or two about charming the ladies. But they were mistaken.

"Ah dinnie believe the birds doon here," both commented with incredulity when we arrived back at the house after closing time. "They're mere up for it at hame."

Despite the lads' undoubted friendliness, I decided to sleep with the keys to the Lancia under my pillow – just to be on the safe side. However, the transfer went through without a hitch in the morning and the new owner and his mate departed northwards in good spirits.

With the Lancia gone and summer approaching, I'm now the proud owner of a gleaming red 1976 Fiat 124 Spider with a lusty twin-cam engine and twin 40 carburettors. The money I earned for the eighteen-hour Easter Revision Course easily covered the insurance premium. The sheer exhilaration of open-top motoring aboard a classic created by the same Italian design house that penned almost all of the Ferraris can't be overstated. In fact, it goes some way to atone for my total inability to find a girlfriend and for making a complete fool of myself in front of Maria at the end of last term.

Whilst I can appreciate why I agreed with David Harding's advice to offload my feelings before it was too late, surely I should've chosen a more opportune moment out of College with the support of alcohol to loosen my tongue. What did I expect when, sober, I have a history of cracking even in the company of women I find half as delectable as Maria Grey? And how could I've thought that my conscience wouldn't intervene whilst attempting to play Romeo in a professional environment? Sometimes, my enthusiasm outweighs all perception of my limitations.

I can't pretend that I'm not apprehensive about bumping into Maria during her remaining six weeks as a *Mardall's* student, but at least it'll only be in the corridor or covered way and not on the trampoline.

On the Saturday of the first week back, Rupert's friend, Barry, calls round to the house unexpectedly and asks if I fancy accompanying him on a trip to *Opportunity Knox* without 'manly Stanley'. I've nothing else planned, so I join him willingly. We're early, so call into *The Barley Mow* first for a swift pint.

On our way out, we pass a couple of girls who I vaguely recognise, but Barry knows.

"We're off clubbing," he tells them and does a small jig in the doorway.

The eldest of the two girls chuckles.

"You mean, off to pull some hot chicks," she says.

I'm quick to point out that I've never pulled a 'chick' in a nightclub in my life, hot or otherwise.

"Come off it, you must've done," the other girl says kindly.

I shake my head in confirmation that I'm not bluffing. With this, we bid the girls goodbye and hit the road. In the car, I'm reminded what a decent bloke Barry seems to be – genuine and good company.

On our arrival at *OK*, Steve on the door waves us in without troubling the tills. Halfway up the stairs to the first floor, I all but fall over a girl curled up on one of the steps, sobbing her heart out.

"I thought nightclubs were for having a laugh," I say spontaneously.

She looks up at me and, before I have chance to see her face properly, springs to her feet, wrapping her arms around my midriff in the process. Her head sinks onto my left shoulder.

"Why don't you come upstairs and I'll get you a drink?" I say, aware that we're blocking access to the club.

The girl releases her grip, wipes her eyes with the back of her hand, then follows me up into the main arena. I lead her directly to the circular bar. Already, the sobs have become more intermittent.

With a large swig of vodka and lemonade, the girl, not dissimilar in appearance to Juliette from *Clifford's* with her long, straight blonde hair and pallid complexion, starts to explain, hesitantly at first: "I came here … with … my boyfriend, but he … he's gone off with … another girl."

"That's not very nice," I reply, placing a gentle hand on her shoulder. "Have you been together long?"

"Over a … a year. I'm sorry, I haven't told you my name. I'm Fran."

I introduce myself and Fran shakes my hand firmly. Her eyes are now dry and her face considerably brighter.

"Thanks for being so kind to me," she says, leaning forward to give me an enormous bear hug.

Before I have chance to contemplate any further questions, Fran transfers her hands from around my torso to behind my neck and pulls my head towards hers. She then plants her mouth firmly onto mine, her tongue forcing its way through my astonished lips. There's an unmistakably strong taste of garlic, but with her slender frame now glued against my appreciably bulkier one I'm hardly in a position to protest. I find myself responding instinctively.

After about a minute, I pause for breath, my whole body numb from the intensity of her tongue-dominated kisses. Over her right shoulder, I catch a glimpse of Barry in the distance, his eyebrows half way up his forehead and his mouth wide open. I bury my tongue into Fran's mouth once again, eager for more of this mind-blowing therapy.

About ten minutes later, the two of us return to the bar for more drinks.

"So is your boyfriend still here?" I ask, suspicious of her motives.

"No, he's gone," she replies. "So, Al, what d'you do for a living?"

"I … I'm a gymnastics and trampolining coach."

As soon as the words have left my mouth, it occurs to me that this is the first time in six years that the word 'teacher' hasn't featured in my answer. But then this is hardly a usual encounter and I'm enjoying myself far too much to risk putting a damper on it.

"What about you, then?" I ask.

"Oh, I'm still doing my A levels."

"Really? What subjects are you taking?"

"English, French and German."

I choke on my drink, but am quick to disguise it as a cough. Having established that her Sixth Form is many miles away from mine, I decide that it should be safe to continue with my ego boosting adventure.

"After all, it's not as if it's going to go any further," I tell myself.

I finally introduce Fran to Barry. After a brief exchange of formalities, he tactfully leaves us alone for the remainder of the evening. We talk a lot and there are frequent interludes for more kissing.

All too quickly, the fun comes to an end. Fran has already arranged a lift home, so declines Barry's generous offer. On the way out, she gives me an elaborate farewell kiss before slipping a scrap of paper into my hand.

"Promise you'll ring me," she says. "I'd really like to see you again."

"Er ... yes – okay, " I reply and we part.

"You lucky bastard, Mr Bond!" Barry says on the way back to the car. "She was a bit of all right, she was."

"Mr Bond", eh? Looks like someone has been spending too much time with Rupert.

Over the next few days, I decide that it's probably not worth making contact with Fran, on the grounds that she'll have almost certainly made up with her errant boyfriend.

On Thursday evening, however, I find myself dialling Fran's number anyway – just on the off-chance. She seems pleased to hear my voice.

"You forgiven your bloke yet?" I ask.

"Nope, we're completely finished," she tells me with a flourish.

"Oh, right. Er ..."

"I hope you're not having second thoughts about me cos I've been looking forward to your call all week. I've even told my mum about you."

"Your *mum*?"

"Yeah, why not? My parents are quite laid-back."

"I see."

"Mind you, they'll want to meet you briefly before we go out. So where you taking me, gorgeous?"

My reply is rather on the faltering side. After all, I was so sure she wouldn't want to see me again that I hadn't got as far as deciding what to do. "Erm ... I ... er ... don't know. I could pick you up and we ... er ... we could go out for dinner somewhere, maybe."

"Sounds good to me," Fran says, her manner refreshingly upbeat. "I'm busy on Friday, but I could do Saturday."

"Er, yes – that'll be fine. I'll pick you up at about 7.30, then. What's your address?"

On Saturday, I make the thirty-minute journey to Fran's house, wondering exactly what I've let myself into. It's a warm, dry evening, so I take the hood down on the Spider.

"Nice car!" Fran calls out from the front door as I reach the end of the long, shingle drive.

"Thanks," I reply, climbing purposefully out of the driver's seat in an attempt to mask my apprehension.

She greets me with a kiss, then grabs my hand. "My dad's not here, so you'll only have to meet my mum and she's lovely."

I breathe a sigh of relief.

Fran's mum turns out to be every bit as friendly and easy-going as her daughter described her and betrays no obvious reservations about Fran dating an older man. Her sole stipulation is that she'd like her back by midnight.

At *Ten Tenths*, we're shown to a table upstairs next to the one that François and I shared a year ago.

"Fran," I say awkwardly before she has chance to view the menu, "I've got a couple of confessions to make."

"Really?" she says, mirroring my unease. "Go on, I'm intrigued."

"Okay, here goes. Well, first of all, how old d'you reckon I am?"

"I dunno. 'Bout thirty?"

"Oh, right – good guess. I'm twenty-nine, actually."

"I haven't got a problem with your age, if that's what you're worried about."

"Really? Oh, that's okay, then." One down, one to go.

"So ... what's the other confession?" Fran asks, placing the menu back down on the table.

"Er ... well, you know that I told you I was a gym and trampolining coach?"

"Yeah."

"Well, that ... that wasn't the whole truth."

"No? C'mon, then, spit it out. I'm dying of anticipation here."

"Okay. Well, I ... I'm also a ..."

"A *what*?"

"A ... an A level French and German teacher."

"Oh, thank God for that! I thought you were gonna tell me you were married or something," she says with a visible sigh of relief. "Now, let's have a look at the menu. I'm starving."

At my guest's request, I order a large bottle of red wine with the meal, even though I'll only be able to drink a single glass.

The food is as delicious as ever. Just as we're about to tuck into our huge desserts, a familiar voice calls out my name. I look up from my dish to see a couple of *Mardall's* colleagues from the Psychology Department standing by the edge of our table, giving my dining partner the once-over. I'm embarrassed, realising that they probably think she's from the College. I endeavour, however, to behave as naturally as possible. After an exchange of formalities, they wish us a pleasant evening and move across to their table in the far corner of the room.

"I don't believe it," I mutter to myself. "All the times I've been here and I've never set eyes on anyone from work before. Great timing once again, Al!"

With the desserts devoured, Fran polishes off the remainder of the bottle of wine. I pay the bill.

"So what d'you fancy doing now?" I ask, glancing at my watch. It's already 10.00. "We could move downstairs for more drinks. Or would you prefer to go somewhere else?"

"I'd quite like to go back to your place for coffee," she says decisively, leaning forward across the table and placing her hands on one of mine.

Back on my settee, Fran and I indulge in another bout of sensuous kissing. Only, on this occasion, without the added flavour of garlic. After a few minutes, she takes hold of my right hand and guides it slowly up the inside of her skirt. She raises her brows and pouts her lips seductively.

"I haven't got any knickers on," she says.

Somehow, the sobbing girl on the stairs of *Opportunity Knox* seems a million miles away. Feeling increasingly out of my depth, I allow my junior partner to direct operations and a serious degree of heavy petting ensues.

"Can't we go somewhere a bit more comfortable?" Fran asks finally.

I glance at my watch once more. It's almost 11.00. Sensing that there simply won't be time for us to reach the stage where I have to face another battle with my moral conscience, I agree to show Fran upstairs to my bedroom. After all, it would be good to be a bit more comfortable for the last ten minutes or so.

Scarcely have we got through the bedroom door when Fran sheds all her clothes right before my very eyes. She then sets about stripping me. I'm shocked again by the forwardness of her approach, but at the same time overcome by the sight of her sexy, disrobed body.

Before I know it, I'm naked too and she's pulled me into bed on top of her, the nipples on her pert breasts visibly erect. She fondles my body, sensitively at first, then more aggressively as the level of her arousal increases. Suddenly, I feel her drag her razor sharp nails down the length of my back, inducing an audible wince.

"Sorry, darling!" she whispers into my ear.

There's more kissing and heavy petting, leaving me with the feeling that I'm approaching the point of no return.

"Fran, we have to stop," I protest, my conscience kicking in. "We haven't got time."

"We'll just have to be very quick," she replies, easing my hips closer to hers.

"But I'm not very experienced. I'd hate to disappoint you."

But I'm wasting my breath. Another minute passes and I have to acknowledge that there's no going back. I reach across into the drawer of my bedside table for protection. With the condom firmly in place, there follows a frenzied lovemaking session between the master – or, more appropriately, the *mistress* – and the apprentice that's over in the bat of an eyelid.

"Don't know what you were worried about," Fran says, gasping for air. "You weren't bad at all."

"You can talk," I say, exhausted. "I didn't realise A level students were so handy between the sheets."

"Ah, but then I have been sexually active since I was fourteen and had quite a few partners."

"Really? How many?"

"Oh, nine or ten."

I should be shocked or appalled or perhaps both by Fran's revelation, yet nothing about this girl surprises me any more. Only one thought enters my head: "Maybe I should've slipped on a second rubber for good measure."

"Fran, we need to get a move on." I say, suddenly aware that it's approaching 11.20.

As I throw on my T-shirt, I notice in the large mirror in the corner of the room by the window that my back is adorned with an array of full-length, vertical scratches.

"Whoops!" Fran says with an apologetic grimace. "Got a bit carried away there."

The mild, tranquil April night compliments perfectly my sense of calm and self-satisfaction as the Spider meanders its way spiritedly across country to return Cinderella before the parental curfew.

"Thank you, darling. I've had a lovely evening," Fran says with a parting kiss. "I'll speak to you tomorrow, yeah?"

Back in my bedroom, I have to pinch myself, not once but several times, to believe this evening's extraordinary events. I always thought stories like this were just made up by blokes down the pub wanting to impress their mates. I climb into bed with a bizarre feeling that, at the age of almost thirty, this teacher has just been given a sex education lesson by a College student some twelve years his junior. And what's even more remarkable, she seems to really like me and want further contact.

"I spose I shouldn't feel guilty about sleeping with her if we end up having a relationship," I tell myself. "I just wish she hadn't let on about her sexual history."

The following Saturday, Fran invites me to the theatre.

"My parents were given some tickets they don't want," she says excitedly.

Throughout the performance, she holds my hand and, at regular intervals, leans across to kiss me affectionately.

"Is everything okay?" Fran asks as the curtain comes down. "You seem a little stand-offish tonight."

"Do I?"

"Yeah, a bit. Look, I really like you, Al."

"I know you do. It's just that ..."

"Just *what*?"

"Oh, you know."

"No. C'mon, tell me."

"Well, you have only just split up with a long-term boyfriend and ..."

"And ...?"

"And maybe you're ... you're on the rebound, that's all."

"No, definitely not, darling. You're so much nicer than my ex. There's simply no comparison."

"Oh, really?"

"Really!"

Placated by Fran's kind words of reassurance, we return to my place and make love once again. This time, it's less frenetic than before and I'm spared any elaborate artwork down my spine. At this particular juncture in my life, it appears that romance comes not only when you least expect it but also with the least likely person. But hey, after the last few years, I'm hardly in a position to complain.

"You've been really chirpy this week," Rachel says on the way home from gym the following Friday.

"You mean, I haven't been my usual, miserable self?" I reply.

"No, you're always Mr Happy. It's just that you seem extra bouncy, that's all."

"I like the trampolining analogy. Well, you never know, it might have something to do with the new woman in my life."

Through the rear-view mirror, I see Rachel flash a rapid glance at Amanda in the front seat.

"Oh, right," they say in unison.

The remainder of the journey is completed in relative silence.

"That's odd," I ponder later as Rachel walks away from the car. "I thought they would've been happier for me."

On the last Sunday in April, I'm treated to a hugely scary experience. On the way back from my weekly food shop in the Spider, I suddenly become aware of a strong smell of burning. At first, I assume that it's coming from outside, but as it fails to disappear I begin to realise that it's much closer to home. Since I'm only a few hundred yards from my road, I decide to press on.

Back in the drive, I switch off the ignition and jump out. Only, for some bizarre reason, the engine continues to tick over. At this point, I notice smoke rising gently from under the carpet covering the nearside inner sill. I take a close look and see the wiring smouldering away slowly. I jump back well away from the car and grab onto my hair with both hands. I'm in a mad panic. Instead of racing to disconnect the battery, I stand frozen to the spot, terrified that my pride and joy will ignite before my very eyes, possibly taking the house with it.

Before I have chance to allow my vivid imagination to take me any further, the engine dies suddenly. I move towards the car cautiously and take another look. Closer inspection reveals that the 'fire' has burnt through the ignition wire.

A few mornings later before work, an old friend, Gareth Sunderland, an aircraft engineer with BA and a whizz with cars, arrives to repair the wiring on the Spider.

"You were very lucky," he says, resurfacing from inside the boot. "The wheel brace must've touched up against the fuel pump and shorted out the cable. It's smouldered the wiring along almost the full length of the car."

Just before leaving for College in my cheap Vauxhall Astra runabout, I catch Gareth eyeing up some of the shrubs in my exotic rockery – the previous owners' doing, not mine.

"Would you mind if I take some cuttings?" he asks.

"Be my guest."

"Thanks. I should finish here in about an hour, so you'll be able to use the Spider again tomorrow."

I thank Gareth profusely, slip him a few quid and set off for work.

During the first few weeks of May, the U6 are exposed to a wide variety of past papers as a final preparation for their exams. It's not necessarily the most exciting part of the course, but an essential one that's sometimes overlooked by teachers. I continue to be extra 'bouncy' as a result of my blossoming romance with Fran.

On the 18th, after receiving the news that Fran has failed her driving test, I head back to College early in the evening to collect my old friend, François. Oh yes, believe it or not, the French are here again. However, on my arrival in the front car park, I discover that their coach has been delayed at Dover. I sit and wait with Marilyn and the host families until it finally appears at 11.30.

On the way home, I inform François that I'm no longer single. His ears prick up.

"I will … euh … maybe meet 'er?" he asks.

"Yes, definitely," I nod confidently, "although she's out with friends this weekend."

On Saturday, I reacquaint François with his old haunts and he's delighted to bump into some of his lady friends from last year. Although undoubtedly more outgoing than he was in France before Easter, I sense that he's given himself a good talking to in the light of what happened on his previous visit. It seems that the local girls won't have to equip themselves with condoms, after all.

By Tuesday, I haven't heard anything from Fran. I decide to call her to arrange to meet. As soon as she picks up, I detect an anxious note in her voice.

"What's up?" I ask.

There's a pregnant pause before she speaks, her tone somewhat more sombre than usual.

"I'm really sorry," she says. "You were right about me being on the rebound. When I went out at the weekend, I met this American bloke and it made me realise that I want to be single at the moment and have some fun."

With these disappointing words, my month-long relationship with Fran bites the dust. I relate my bad news to François, then take him with me to the gym for training where I let off some steam.

Afterwards, we go to *Alfredo's* for a drink. My little French friend bends over backwards to cheer me up. In my opinion, it doesn't matter how long you've been going out with someone or how strong your feelings are towards them, being dumped is an upsetting experience in itself. None of us, if we're truly honest, cares much for rejection. However, I have to admit that the cynic in me is surprised that Fran and I lasted as long as we did. Deep down, I always felt her sexual history didn't inspire confidence in a lasting relationship. I'm sad, of course, but then this has been a largely positive adventure and not one I would've believed possible six weeks ago. What's more, it's helped to combat Emily's depressing theory that I'm completely x-factorless.

Towards the end of May, just before the start of the dreaded A level exams, I have lunch again with Rachel and Amanda.

"Will it be okay for Rachel and me to carry on coming in for gym and trampolining during the exam period?" Amanda asks.

"Yes, of course," I reply. "Mind you, both the Hall and Drama Studio are being used for exams this year, so we might have to go outside."

Both girls look at each other excitedly. Then Amanda speaks again: "How's it going with your new girlfriend?"

"Ah, it's not going that well at all, actually. In fact, we've split up."

"When did that happen?" Rachel asks in an offended tone of voice.

"Oh, I dunno. A few days ago."

"You didn't tell us."

I bow my head and give the top of my left hand a castigatory slap.

"So how's *your* romance developing?" I ask Rachel.

She exchanges glances with her friend before replying: "Mm, not that well, really."

"Why's that, then?"

"Oh, we're more like just friends now."

"You don't seem too bothered."

She smiles convincingly. "No, I'm not, as it happens."

After a spot of negotiation with Avril and Marilyn, I manage to rearrange some of my Lower Sixth lessons at the beginning of June so that I can have a long weekend in Germany with my Past Masters gym team. One of our more senior members, a former British international, was posted in the country years ago during his time in the army and built up some useful contacts. The club where he trained is hosting a huge gym display and has invited five of us Brits – accompanied by a wife, a girlfriend and a daughter – to take part. Should be a laugh.

I'm just back from an enthralling three and a half days in Germany. Our hosts welcomed us with open arms and provided a level of hospitality that's hard to imagine. I don't think I've ever come across so much gratuitous food and beer in my life. Being able to speak the lingo was a bonus and I found several of the female gymnasts warming to me. Amongst them was the eighteen-year-old daughter of one of the coaches. After an evening of booze and merriment, we enjoyed a brief kiss in the moonlight. I say 'brief' because the girl suddenly remembered she had a boyfriend and tore herself away with cries of "Ich bin eine Kuh, ich bin eine Kuh!" [I'm a cow, I'm a cow!] I have to confess, I wasn't aware of any horns, although I was more than happy to milk the situation. Haha!

It really is hard to believe that I could've felt so unattractive just a few weeks ago because at the moment, I'm buzzing with confidence. I think I have Fran to thank for this.

Back at College, Rachel, Amanda and I have a highly enjoyable tramp session on the patch of grass outside the Library/IT building. Charles is busy and unable to join in, but manages to watch for a few minutes from the window on the top floor.

At the end, the two girls hand over an amusing card, thanking me for all the time and energy I've put into helping them with gym and trampolining. To go with it, there's a joke book – what, they think I need one? – a T-shirt with a picture of Mr Silly on it and a gigantic packet of wine gums.

"We know this isn't the last session," Amanda says, "but we couldn't wait any longer."

Flattered, I can't thank the two girls enough for their kindness.

The following weekend, I find myself at *Opportunity Knox* with Rupert and Charles. Soon after our arrival, we bump into my two star trampolinists. Rupert's eyes almost jump out of their sockets when he sees Rachel's size ten figure in a flowery summer dress. He doesn't waste a second before launching into that now familiar spiel that would've won over Katja's affections before Easter had I not intervened. Charles doesn't look too impressed and I find myself going into protective mode, on the grounds that Rachel is far too good for the philandering Rupert.

After a while, it appears that Rachel is successfully repelling Rupert's advances, so I leave them to it.

"I spose she'll have to get used to blokes like him at uni," I tell myself.

About ten minutes later, however, Charles comes rushing across towards me in a bit of a state.

"Your mate's pulled Rachel!" he says, gasping for breath.

I follow him back to the spot where we left her and find the pair close together but not kissing. At the sight of me, Rachel frees herself from Rupert's clutches.

"Your friend tried to kiss me," she whispers into my ear a little later on.

I tut in disapproval. "Now why doesn't that surprise me?"

As if trying to escape a teacher's sanction, she then says: "I didn't kiss him, though."

For the remainder of the evening, Rachel avoids Rupert and there's no repeat of the earlier incident.

"She did kiss me," Rupert insists in the car on the way home. "I promise you."

A few days later, after another of our outdoor tramp sessions, I drop Amanda off outside her house. As we're pulling away, Rachel starts to whinge about a lack of entertainment at home at the moment.

"I'm sick and tired of just sitting around listening to my mum and sister arguing," she says.

"Well, I could always meet up with you for a drink or something." I say. "After all, you have officially left College now."

"Okay."

"Just let me know when you're free."

"I'm not doing anything tonight."

"Oh, right. Well … er … nor am I, actually. We could always go for a bite to eat first, then … er … have a drink afterwards."

Rachel nods enthusiastically.

After a meal at *Ten Tenths*, Rachel comes back to the house. Sitting together on the settee, I can't fail to notice her flirtatious glances as she speaks. Her face is more radiant than ever tonight and I can't honestly recollect a time when she looked prettier. With the assistance of alcohol, words start to pour out of her beautifully formed lips like never before. In the twenty-odd months that we've been acquainted, I never realised how full of conversation she is.

"I was so jealous when you had a girlfriend," she says suddenly.

"Really?" I say, raising my brows.

She nods feverishly before continuing: "And then there were the holidays. You've no idea how it tore me apart being separated from you for so long."

I'm gobsmacked. "Rachel, I don't know what to say. I … I'd no idea."

Overwhelmed by the strength of her feelings, I take Rachel in my arms and hold her close to my chest, my fingers instinctively caressing her waist-length, almost satin, hair. She grips on to me as if her life depended on it, passion steaming out of her ears.

I feel her smile into my right cheek. "I think you're the only reason why my attendance at College was so good. There were days when I really couldn't face going in, and then … then I remembered I wouldn't see you."

For a man so heavily crushed by female rejection over so many years, her words are like music to my ears, uttered with a degree of force and sincerity that belies her previously shy image. For once, it seems, here is a young woman who really does know her own mind. I'm flattered more than ever before. I turn my head to face hers. Our eyes meet. Then our lips come together for an inaugural kiss.

In a trance-like state, we eventually retire to my bedroom. Fully clothed, we lie on my bed in the dark, holding on to each other and talking incessantly.

"You must've realised how I felt about you," Rachel says emphatically. "I made it so obvious."

"I'm afraid I've never been much good at picking up signals," I say. "I mean, I knew you liked me – Amanda too – but … but not to this extent."

"Then you're a very silly boy!"

"But even if I had known, I wouldn't have been able to do anything about it whilst you were still at College."

"Not even after I was eighteen?"

"That doesn't seem to make a lot of difference. Teacher-student relationships are regarded as unprofessional, full-stop."

"I would've been discreet."

"So discreet that you wouldn't have mentioned it to Amanda?"

"I don't tell her everything, you know."

We talk a bit about her relationship with the lad from her trampolining club and I'm surprised to discover that, although they were together for a few months, Rachel has no proper sexual experience. I'm consoled by the thought that even in these modern, enlightened times not all Sixth Form girls are as sexually active as Fran. I can't speak for other men, but I must admit that I've always found chastity an endearing quality. Whether this has something to do with my own background or the fact that I'd feel more secure with a chaste woman is hard to say.

After midnight, I drop Rachel home. Back in my bathroom, I scrutinise myself in the mirror and wonder what it is exactly that's brought about such a dramatic turn-around in my fortune over the last few months. After all, I really haven't changed much physically since I was at university.

I go to bed, aware that never before in my adult life have I felt such a high level of self-esteem in a romantic context. How ironic, though, that I should spend so much time fantasising about someone who, by all accounts, wasn't the remotest bit interested in me when all the time there was a little diamond by the name of Rachel Hill right under my nose. I wonder why I didn't notice. Maybe part of Maria's appeal was the fact that, unlike with Rachel, her academic future didn't depend on me. And considering she only flirted in a relatively innocent fashion, I suppose it was always a pretty safe fantasy. I was never going to initiate anything whilst she was still at College and, if she didn't either, my professionalism wasn't going to be severely challenged. Okay, there was the highly tempting encounter on New Year's Eve eighteen months ago, but at the end of the day my conscience still intervened.

With my brain working overtime, I decide that my inability to read the signs probably did me a favour in Rachel's case. It might've made things rather awkward between us.

Two days later, I find myself coming out of a florist's near College carrying a rather large bouquet of red roses.

"What on earth did I do that for?" I ask myself. "I must be off my rocker."

In reality, I know exactly why I did it. Earlier today, I caught sight of Maria after her final Spanish exam.

"I wrote an essay from the wrong section," she informed me almost tearfully.

I'd never seen her looking so crestfallen before and I found it rather touching – hence my spontaneous decision to splash out on an eighteenth birthday present. It's tomorrow. Given that I'm meeting up with Rachel again tonight, I suppose I shouldn't have bought flowers for another woman, but I just suffered a moment's weakness. I think it was more of a parting gesture, anyway, rather than a further attempt to win the affections of someone who's blatantly not interested. For almost two years, Maria did help relieve the misery of unsuccessful romance in the real world and I always have had a sentimental streak.

Rachel and I spend another romantic evening together. By the time I'm ready to drive her home, it's official – we're now boyfriend and girlfriend. The fact that she knows what I'm like outside the classroom has helped convince me that her feelings are one hundred per cent genuine. I'm sure it's not a case of a student just having a crush on a teacher. It's at times like this when I do wonder whether everything in life has a purpose. Maybe my 'suffering' at the hands of Petra, Emily, Eva, Lauren, Katja, Fran and co was just a preparation for my romance with Rachel. Okay, I'm probably talking out of my backside, but everything seems to have turned out just perfectly.

During the following week, I introduce Rachel to the gang – including Emily – and the two Dutch girls. There are raised eyebrows all round and the bouncer look-alike, Gary, as tactful as ever, asks what the hell such a beautiful woman could possibly see in me. Even Rupert Stanley is impressed, but careful to keep his hands off, although, of course, he can't resist the temptation to stress once again that Rachel did kiss him on that night at *Opportunity Knox*.

A week later, Rachel and I decide to tell the rest of the world about our relationship. My parents and her mum are first on our list. To our relief, the response from both seems positive. My sister, Jayne, and her husband also have the pleasure of meeting my new girlfriend. Even baby Chloë gives a whimper of approval from her cot.

Next up is Marilyn. I'm slightly taken aback by the lack of shock in her reaction.

"Oh really, young man, that doesn't surprise me at all," she says prosaically as if I've just informed her that one of the booths in the Language Lab has given up the ghost.

"How come?" I ask.

"Well, it was pretty obvious to all of us with eyes that Rachel had a huge crush on you."

"Was it?"

"Oh dear! You really are a typical man, aren't you?" she chuckles. "Walk around all day with your eyes shut."

"So you don't disapprove, then?"

"Why should I? Rachel's no longer a student here. I would be careful if I were you, though."

"Careful? In what respect?"

"Rachel is a very attractive young lady and she'll be off to university shortly. I'd hate to see you get hurt."

"Thanks for your concern, but I don't intend to get too involved."

"Very wise, young man, very wise."

During the last few weeks of term, I continue to walk on water, with every aspect of my life functioning impeccably. I now understand what people mean when they say that being in a loving relationship helps you to see everything else in a favourable light. Even a rather unfortunate encounter with Maria at *Opportunity Knox* couldn't induce the bubble to burst.

"How dare you send me flowers!" she erupted on catching sight of me. "What did I ever do to make you think I fancied you?"

A few days later, Louise told me on the quiet that Maria really liked the roses. Surely she's not envious of my relationship with Rachel. I mean, if you don't want somebody yourself, you can't exactly feel miffed about them dating someone else, can you?

Anyway, Rachel is the only girl for me now and I can't wait for us to do loads of exciting things together over the summer holidays. I'm not forgetting Marilyn's words of caution, but, hey, October is a long way off and a lot can happen before then.

I'm a Loser

(Year 4)

Although I laugh and I act like a clown,
Beneath this mask I am wearing a frown.
My tears are falling like rain from the sky,
Is it for her or myself that I cry?

AUTUMN TERM

"Sss…so how many ddd…days of the www…week will we be blessed with your ppp…presence?" Michael 'Bomber' Lancaster asks with apparent interest as our paths cross under the covered way.

It's now the beginning of September, and I'm back at work in my new capacity as a part-time French and German teacher and peripatetic gymnastic coach.

"Oh, just Tuesdays, Wednesday mornings and Thursdays," I reply. "So don't worry, you'll get a couple of days' respite. Well, that's unless you're unfortunate enough to run into me on a Monday evening when I'm here for my adult class."

He gives a characteristic nod with a half smile. "I as…as…as…assume it's just language teaching you'll be ddd…doing here nnn…now?"

"Not at all. I'll also be coaching a group of Upper Sixth PE students – the ones who've opted to do gym as part of their A level practical assessment."

"Bbb…but I thought the whole point of you ggg…going part time was to enable you to offer a gym coaching service to local schools."

"You're right, it was."

"So when are you going to squeeze that in, then?" The stuttering has now ceased and he's in full flow.

"Well, on Wednesday afternoons, I'll be coaching gym and trampolining as part of an activities programme at King George's."

"Oh yes."

"Then on Fridays, I'll be employed by a Convent school in my old town to run a lunchtime gym club. Whilst there, I'll also be teaching four Sixth Formers two academic units of their A level PE course."

"I thought your degree was solely in Modern Languages."

"It is, but the school sent me on a course over the summer. Seems they're not so insistent on degree-level qualifications in the private sector."

Now fully enlightened, 'Bomber' nods once again, ducks his head and shoulders, and storms off down the covered 'runway' as if late for an important engagement.

The location of the Convent is ideal since it's only a stone's throw from my private gym club where I'll once again be in charge of the coaching on a Friday evening. There should even be a couple of hours between jobs to call in on mum, dad and Auntie Flo, and grab a bite to eat. I have to say that I'm chuffed about the prospect of such a varied working week. I've made a few rough calculations and, if I'm not mistaken, I shouldn't be any worse off financially. Well, that's provided I take a lodger to compensate for the fact that the gym coaching won't pay during the holidays. I've submitted an advert at the Accommodation Office of the local Art College and cleared out the middle bedroom in anticipation.

Shortly after my conversation with 'Bomber', I have a similar one with Tom Black, the rather shy, unassuming Head of Design Technology, who shares my passion for Italian cars. Like me, he's been unlucky with the ladies. Unlike me, however, Tom actually knows how to fix them when they go wrong – the cars, that is – and has come to my rescue on numerous occasions.

With my track record, it may come as a huge surprise to learn that my relationship with ex-student Rachel Hill actually survived the summer holiday period. In fact, we've just celebrated our three-month anniversary, which is a personal record for me. In order to mark this historic achievement, the two of us went for an Indian, with Rachel footing the bill.

"You're always forking out for me," she'd said, "so now it's my turn."

Ah, the joys of sexual equality!

Despite this thoughtful gesture, however, I'd be lying if I claimed our romance has been anything other than a roller-coaster ride. Admittedly, the initial phase was heavenly, but then the A level results came out and Rachel discovered that she'd underachieved in Science and, more significantly, in French. Marilyn and I had confidently predicted a B, but she only scraped a D, which scuppered her plans to study the language at university. It seems that she was overcome by nerves in the oral exam. She did get an A for the literature paper, which was an option I taught, but this wasn't enough to tip the balance. I tried my utmost to stem the flow of tears, but Rachel was virtually inconsolable and it was a far from easy task. After persistent cajoling, I did eventually manage to persuade her to reconsider her choice of course and contact the university clearing service. There were possible places for Architecture at universities on the south coast and in the Midlands, so I drove her along to both to take a closer look.

When the deadline for a decision arrived, I wasn't the first man in Rachel's life to be told which of the two universities she'd plumped for. This honour fell to her ex-boyfriend from the trampolining club, Pete. For some reason, she'd arranged to spend the evening in his company, watching videos on his bed. Already nervous about her motives for continuing to see her ex, I flew off the handle. We had a slanging match on the phone, which ended with me slamming down the receiver. I wonder how she'd have reacted if the shoe had been on the other foot. It took some serious grovelling the following morning for me to be forgiven.

"You don't know how close you came to losing me," Rachel scolded. Obviously all my fault, then!

Since the exam result bombshell, it hasn't escaped my attention that Rachel has been considerably more temperamental than usual and has sometimes appeared indifferent about meeting up. In a way, I think my business-like attempt to help her organise an alternative academic future in time for October has been construed as a lack of sympathy for the extent of her disappointment. It's also possible that she holds me partly responsible for her poor showing in French. After all, I was one of her teachers. In my defence, however, the results for the rest of the group comfortably lived up to expectations.

Whilst Rachel's timely declaration of love back in June was hugely flattering and a great morale-booster, it's now left me in a position where I feel I'm continually skating on thin ice. So intense were her feelings towards me at the outset that I can't stop wondering whether there's anywhere for them to go other than down 'Hill' – if you can excuse the pun. I'm sure this was what fuelled my outburst a couple of weeks back, along with the fact that she now seems to be a magnet for serious male attention wherever we go. I only have to turn my back for five seconds and, hey presto, there's a Mr Smoothie trying to muscle in on her.

There was an incident over the summer when I took Rachel to *Clifford's*, my old stamping ground. Another bloke tried several times to crack onto her right under my nose. Since she made it perfectly clear she was with me, I refrained from intervening, but couldn't believe my ears when the geezer asked for her phone number as we were leaving.

"I felt really mean not letting him have it," Rachel said once we were back at the car. I assume – make that *hope* – she was referring solely to her number.

On the journey home, I began to wonder what'll happen when the university term starts and I'm no longer around. Keeping up a long-distance relationship with a beauty queen like Rachel Hill won't be plain sailing, that's for sure. Now I fully understand the significance of the song *When you're in love with a beautiful woman*.

I suppose it was naive of me to expect that my past insecurities wouldn't return to haunt me at some stage in our relationship. Naturally, we've talked at length about the imposed separation, with Rachel insisting that she wants us to stay together regardless of the distance. It's just that … well, you know, I'm a bit of a sceptic when it comes to trusting the convictions of the fairer sex. I have to confess, though, that I'm completely smitten and determined to hang on to my new woman, mood swings 'n' all. What was all that talk of not getting too involved? Maybe Marilyn knows me better than I know myself.

Another downside to my relationship with Rachel is the detrimental effect it's had on my friendship with Charles Spackman. Quite understandably, he's miffed that I've ended up dating his dream woman, particularly in view of my long-standing infatuation with Maria. I do feel a bit guilty, of course, but then Rachel did confirm the other day that she's never been interested in Charles romantically. Why is it we often have to lose in order to gain?

On the Friday of the first week back, Rachel is entrusted with the all-important job of handing out enrolment forms at the relaunch of my evening gym club. Howard Parish puts in an appearance and kindly lends a hand with the coaching – just like old times. The turn-out of previous and possible future members is impressive, and I leave on a highly optimistic note. The days of a hundred plus gymnasts on the register could well be on the cards once again.

Shortly afterwards, I receive a letter from my Swedish friend, Erika Peterson, announcing that she's accepted an *au pair* position in the West Country. She expresses an interest in welcoming visitors and includes a number for me to call. Since I'm keen to see Rachel at every available opportunity in the time that's left, I think I'll arrange to meet up with Erika after my 'nearest and dearest' has gone to university in early October.

I remember mentioning earlier in the year that part-ownership houses were being built on the piece of land next to my pad. Well, they've been finished for a while now and my immediate neighbours are an unmarried pair of bikers, Greg and Tina. They've got a baby son called Harley. Tina is particularly friendly and has spoken to me on several occasions down at *The Barley Mow*. Greg, it seems, is the full-time babysitter at weekends.

Next door to this young couple lives a rather rotund redhead with a lazy eye called Maude. She's a single mum, with two young sons, who's also keen to chat. In fact, she's bent my ear more often than once about her rather unfortunate marriage to a soldier who abandoned her and the boys. Apparently, he's become an expert at shirking maintenance contributions. As a prospective dad (hopefully), this is a situation I find impossible to comprehend.

Late one sunny afternoon during the second week in September, when Rachel and I are canoodling on the settee, there's the sound of ferocious hammering on the front door. We both jump out of our skin. I head off to investigate the source of the commotion. Barely have I turned the latch when the door flies open in my face and Maude surges through into the hallway.

"My little Billy's kicked his ball into your garden," she wheezes through a set of crooked, gapped teeth.

Before I have chance to stall her, she hustles past me and makes a beeline for the lounge. On her arrival, she comes face to face with Rachel, sprawled out on the sofa in her bikini looking like a Miss World contestant.

"Oh, I ... I'm sorry, dear," Maude says awkwardly and backtracks into the hall.

Rachel smiles bashfully.

"I'll just go and retrieve Billy's ball for you," I say, mildly amused.

Out in the garden, I spot the offending article at once, nestled by a weed in the middle of the lawn. I look up at the towering ten-foot hedge and wonder how on earth a six-year-old boy managed to clear such a height as well as the entire width of Greg and Tina's garden. Gazza beware!

Maude is grateful to be reunited with her son's ball and scurries out of my front door as rapidly as she came through it.

Rachel chuckles.

"Looks like I've got some serious competition," she says.

"I think you may well be right," I reply. "Oh well, you'll just have to make an effort to be a hugely attentive girlfriend from now on to prevent my mind from wandering."

In the middle of September, Rachel and I spend an evening at *James Dean's*, a nightclub just up the road from *Razz*. Amanda and some of her other College friends are there too. We have a fun time, although I'm rather surprised to catch the six-foot brother of motor racing enthusiast Merv Fitzgerald trailing me round the club. Merv is also present, so I question him about his brother's rather peculiar conduct.

"He's obsessed with your girlfriend," he says, "and thinks you snatched her away from him."

I raise my eyebrows. "You're not serious?"

"Fraid so. He also reckons you stole her innocence. Hates your guts for it, in fact."

"I don't like the sound of this, Merv."

"Don't worry. He may be a big bloke, but he won't try anything. Just ignore him."

I flash a glance over my shoulder and pray that Merv knows his brother as well as he claims.

"We were good friends at College, but I never gave any indication that I fancied him," Rachel assures me when I ask later about Fitzgerald junior.

It seems that not all the lads at College were oblivious of her presence, after all, and that I'm not the only hopeless sign reader on the planet.

With the start of the university term drawing ever nearer, Rachel makes a bizarre comment early one evening that flies in the face of my need for reassurance.

"Wouldn't it be great if it was possible to sleep with all the men in the world?" she says randomly.

In view of the fact that I'm the only man she's ever slept with, my natural interpretation is that she's anxious for more sexual experience. And what better place to find it than a university campus with the boyfriend conveniently out of the way?

The following Saturday, I've made plans for the two of us, only to discover that Rachel has arranged to catch up with some of her friends instead. Against my better judgement, I allow my disappointment to show, which sparks off another row.

"Why d'you always try to make me feel guilty when I want to go out with my friends rather than you?" she fumes.

"Do I?" I reply with an air of innocence.

"Yes, all the time. And it's the same when I don't feel like staying over too."

"It's only cos I love spending time with you and … well, you know."

"Know *what*?"

"Er … well, we're not exactly going to be living on each other's doorstep for much longer, are we?"

There's a pregnant pause before Rachel opens her mouth again and says: "But I'll still get to see you more often than my friends."

I suppose this final remark should be enough to put my mind at rest, but somehow it misses the mark. Defeated, I bring the conversation to a close and wish Rachel an enjoyable evening out with her mates.

I head off wearily to *The Barley Mow*, trying to convince myself that it's just the age gap that's responsible for the imbalance in our levels of interest. Then I remember the enormous affection she held for me when we first got together and sink progressively into depression. I share my concerns with Gary, the bouncer look-alike, over a few pints. He recently got engaged to his long-term girlfriend, Kathy.

"Doesn't sound good to me," he says with a slow shake of his head.

What hasn't helped my situation is the recent discovery that a tall, good-looking lad from Rachel's trampolining club is going to the same university. Guess what – he's also called Al. Bloody marvellous, isn't it?

"At least I'll have someone to hang out with," Rachel told me. Trouble is, I've seen the way he looks at her.

On our final trip to a nightclub before the big day, Rachel and I are joined by Rupert, Barry and the two Dutch girls, whose stay in England is almost over. It's a relaxing, enjoyable evening. On our return to the multi-storey in the early hours, I find myself walking alongside Eva.

"Everything okay?" I ask. "You seem a little quiet tonight."

She stares at the pavement in front of her.

"Maybe a bit, yes," she says.

"You sad about going home?"

"Yes, I am. And I have some regrets too." She glances across at Rachel, then back at me dolefully.

"What, not about *me*?"

"Yes, I think so."

I'm flattered by her unexpected confession, of course, although I've never quite understood how someone who's not good enough when single can suddenly fit the bill when unavailable. When I was single, I was always over the moon to discover a girl I got on well with wasn't attached.

On our last night in bed together before her departure, Rachel suddenly breaks into a sob.

"Hey, what's up darling?" I ask, rolling over to face her. I place my right hand on her left shoulder.

She wipes away the tears before replying almost inaudibly: "Not what you think."

"And … what exactly am I thinking?"

"That I'm crying because … you know." She sniffs several times.

"Actually, I haven't got a clue why you're crying."

She looks up at me before launching into a rather incoherent explanation: "Knowing you, you probably think I'm upset cos … cos I think it's the last time we'll, you know …"

I sit upright and pause briefly to reflect. "You mean, because it's the last time we'll sleep together?"

"Yes." There follows a couple of slow-motion nods of her head. "But it's not that."

"Well, I wasn't thinking it was, anyway. So what *are* you crying about, then?"

"It's too hard to explain," she says finally with a defeated shrug. She then rolls over away from me, burying her face deep into the pillow.

I lay still in the silence, none the wiser. What is it they say: Men are from Mars and women are from Venus?

It's now the first Sunday in October and the dreaded day of Rachel's departure is here. It's a windy but surprisingly mild morning, so I decide to take the Spider. Equipped with my beloved's favourite beverage – a bottle of Malibu (and some cans of coke) – I head over to her mum's house. Her parents are divorced.

On my arrival, I notice at once that Rachel has cut her beautiful waist-length hair and now sports a trendy, shoulder-length bob. I comment favourably, even though I prefer the old style. I'm introduced to Mr Hill whose Honda is piled high with his daughter's possessions.

"I hope you don't mind, but I've told dad I'll go with him," Rachel says. "I don't see him that often."

Following tearful goodbyes to her mum and younger sister, we leave in convoy for the south coast.

Just over an hour later, we find the house where Rachel will be lodging. The middle-aged lady owner is there to receive us. With all the luggage unloaded, the three of us then amble off in the direction of the university campus to take a look around. Rachel's dad shows obvious concern for his daughter's welfare and seems almost as much on edge as she does.

"Is this just a natural parental reaction to an offspring leaving home for the first time?" I ask myself. "Or, like me, has he picked up on her blatantly nervous demeanour and apparent vulnerability?"

Sensing no doubt that Rachel and I would like to spend some time alone together, Mr Hill tactfully makes his excuses after lunch, giving his daughter an emotional farewell hug before setting off.

"I promised Al from trampolining that I'd call in on him sometime this afternoon," Rachel says, the minute her dad is out of sight. "I've got the address of his student house in my pocket."

Al 'junior' gives us a warm welcome. Although determined not to communicate any feelings of insecurity I may harbour about the threat he poses to my relationship, I find myself involuntarily monitoring his body language as he addresses Rachel. Even a sign-blind old fool like me can't fail to spot his interest in her. The eyes of the other lads in the house also light up when she speaks.

Once we've left Al and co, Rachel becomes strangely detached. She remains this way for the rest of the afternoon and early evening.

"I'm sorry, I'm just really nervous," she says when I ask what's up.

"What, about living away from home or about the course?"

"Everything. What if nobody likes me and I don't make any friends?"

I give her a hug and whisper some words of reassurance. A little voice in my head tells me that making friends will be the least of this fresher's worries in the coming weeks, particularly on a course where all but four of the hundred-odd students are male. If anyone should be uptight at the moment, surely it should be the twenty-nine-year-old teacher, not his stunning eighteen-year-old girlfriend. Since tomorrow is Monday and I won't have to work until the evening, I offer to stay the night. Rachel declines, on the grounds that it wouldn't be fair on her landlady so soon.

After a meal together in a local restaurant, it's late, so I decide to make tracks. Rachel clings onto me as if her life depended on it, her whole body overcome by a perpetual tremor.

"I'll ring you tomorrow before your Evening Class," she says, "and let you know how my first day went."

"Great," I say in parting. "I'll look forward to your call. Good luck, darling!"

Pulling away in the Spider, I feel a huge lump in my throat as I look up to see Rachel's glum face and forlorn wave through the tiny upstairs landing window. On the one hand, I'm desperate for her to be happy in her new life. Yet on the other, I'm aware that this may well come at the expense of our relationship. I shed a few private tears on the journey home.

"It's strange," I reflect. "I was lonely for so many years without a girlfriend and now I've got one I still feel a bit lonely. I wonder if it's because I sense she no longer cares for me as much as I do for her."

Rachel phones the following afternoon as promised. She sounds really upbeat.

"It wasn't as bad as I'd thought," she says. "And I've made a friend."

I'm relieved to hear it.

"Good. A little boy or a little girl?" I ask.

"A little boy. He's a bit boring, but easy to talk to."

All of a sudden, I find boring people peculiarly endearing – particularly male ones. "So you don't feel too unhappy, then?"

"Nope, I'm fine."

"Great! I'm really pleased for you."

A few days later, the report from Rachel is even more enthusiastic: "We went to a brilliant club last night and I had the best time of my life. I don't think I've ever felt so confident."

"Excellent!" I say slightly nervously. "Who did you go with? Your new friend?"

"He was there, but was a real pain and wouldn't stop following me around. But it was okay because I had Al to keep an eye on me. The club was so packed, he held my hand all evening so we wouldn't lose each other."

I refrain from commenting, reasoning that she probably wouldn't have mentioned Al if anything untoward had happened between them.

Nevertheless, my night's sleep is somewhat more restless than usual. I start to wonder how I could've allowed myself to become so emotionally attached to Rachel with university beckoning. It's not as if I was oblivious of the odds against our relationship surviving such a split. Mind you, there were several girls I fancied during my time at university who wouldn't give fellow students a second look because they were madly in love with a boyfriend back home. Oh well, que sera, sera!

At the weekend, Rachel is keen for me to visit. After a successful gym display as part of the Convent's annual Open Day, I head southwards on Saturday afternoon. Given the highs of the earlier part of the week, I'm surprised to find her deeply upset.

"I'm missing home and I'm really unsure about the course," she sobs onto my shoulder, her arms gripped firmly around my torso.

I try to revert to teacher mode in an effort to be as objective as possible. You know, harping on about sticking it out and how things are bound to improve. Whilst the romantic in me would love her to give up and come home, my head knows that this is far from the best option for Rachel.

In the middle of my spiel, she suddenly becomes queasy. It transpires that she hasn't eaten anything all day, so we pop into town and grab a late lunch. She perks up noticeably afterwards.

On the recommendation of her landlady's daughter, Rachel and I go for dinner in the evening at an excellent Indian restaurant where we celebrate our four-month anniversary. We become as close as we've been since she left home.

On settling up – my shout this time – we then adjourn to the back seat of my latest run-around, another old Fiat. The Spider has been put away for hibernation, which is just as well since it has the tiniest of rear seats. With steamed windows and an array of bizarre bodily positions – thank God I took up gym as a child and not tiddlywinks – Rachel and I reconfirm our feelings for one another.

I set off just after midnight in a happier, more secure frame of mind. Maybe, just maybe, she does love me, after all.

Monday is a perfect autumn day. Rachel agrees to meet up again after her afternoon lecture and accompany me to the beach. I wait as planned outside the theatre. As she comes out, I catch her flirting overtly with a tallish, broad shouldered lad with long, unkempt blonde hair. I move across to join her and detect at once a hint of embarrassment.

"Oh, Luke – this is Al, my … er … old French teacher," she says. "Al, this is Luke. He's on my course."

There's an awkward silence.

"You mean *former* teacher," I say in an attempt to break it. Luke and I then shake hands.

"Luke's a competitive swimmer," Rachel adds, for want of something better to say.

"Oh, really?" I say, for want of a better answer.

As soon as we've set off to make the twenty-minute journey to the coast, it's apparent that Rachel isn't in a particularly good mood. After the euphoria of Saturday night, my confidence is hit once again. Fighting to retain my composure, I find myself saying: "You seem to get on well with Luke."

Rachel bites my head off: "What are you suggesting?"

"Er, nothing."

"Doesn't sound like it to me."

"Well, you did seem to be flirting with him when you came out of the lecture." Oh, bugger! I really wanted to avoid any signs of jealousy today, but it just slipped out.

"Yeah, well I have to flirt with the blokes on my course, otherwise they wouldn't talk to me and I wouldn't have any friends."

"Then, surely they're not worth knowing."

"I don't really care. I just want people to like me."

"So you don't fancy him, then?" God, what happened to playing it cool?

"Who? Luke? He'd be all right if somebody cut his head off."

At this point, we arrive at the beach and I'm grateful for a natural break in the conversation. Walking along the shoreline sucking an ice-lolly, Rachel apologises for her unfavourable mood.

"So what's new since Saturday?" I ask.

"Not much. Oh, I was ill last night at Al's house."

"Really? What was wrong?"

Rachel shrugs her shoulders. "I just felt really funny. And before you make some wise-crack about it, no, I wasn't pissed."

"I wonder what it was, then."

She shrugs once more and, with an embarrassed laugh, says: "I wasn't well enough to go home, so Al let me lie on his bed."

"What, all night?"

"No. I felt better later on, so Al called a taxi at about 4.00 in the morning."

"Oh, right. So poor old Al had to kip on the floor for the first part of the night?"

"No."

"So ... where did he sleep?"

There's a lull in the conversation before Rachel says collectedly: "On the bed too."

From the moment I fetched her from the campus and witnessed her flirting, I've been fighting a furious inner battle to contain myself. With these alarming words, the battle is well and truly lost.

"Rachel, if you're trying to tell me that you slept with the other Al last night," I erupt, "then please spare me the torture and ..."

"I knew you'd jump to conclusions. I shouldn't have said anything."

"Too right you shouldn't."

"Don't you trust me?"

Great, that age-old tactic – switching the blame.

"No. I mean, yes, of course I do. I'm just confused, that's all. I've seen the way Al looks at you and I can't believe he wouldn't misread the signs and try to ..."

"Try to *what*?"

"Well, you know – touch you."

"Yeah, well, I spose he might've done a few times. After all, it was only a single bed."

At this juncture, I take a seat on the shingle and gaze forlornly at the waves pounding the shoreline just a few feet away from us. After a brief hesitation, Rachel sits down next to me. There follows a protracted silence before I take several deep inhalations of sea air and utter some very difficult words: "Rachel, I really like you – I think you know that by now – and I'm desperate to make this work. But at the same time, I haven't forgotten that you're eleven years younger than I am and in an exciting new environment with lots of good-looking blokes around you."

"What you trying to say?"

"Just that ... if you want to break things off with me, then ... then I will understand."

She sits motionless for a few seconds, her head in her hands, then looks up and across at me. "I don't want us to split up. I'm just in a weird mood, that's all."

"Sure?"

"Sure."

We walk for about another half an hour, then it starts to get chilly, so I drive us back to Rachel's lodgings. There, I produce a paperback recipe book for students. She smiles sweetly at the sight of it.

"And if you can't motivate yourself to cook some proper meals from here, then you can pig out on this," I say, handing over a giant, two-pound bar of Cadbury's chocolate. "I can't bear the thought of you not eating."

The smile broadens. "Thank you, sweetie."

Before I leave for home, we kiss on Rachel's bed. I'm anxious to take things further in an attempt to scale the heights of Saturday night in the car, but my advances are repelled.

"Not with my landlady in the house," she says.

Over the next few days at work, I feel unusually distracted. I just can't stop myself fretting about how far Rachel is prepared to go in the pursuit of friendship. Although hugely inexperienced when it comes to relationships, I'm well aware that I should back off and give her some space. After all, you don't see someone like Rupert Stanley pining when his Austrian girlfriend isn't around. He just gets on with his life in the knowledge that if she loves him, she'll come back, and if she doesn't, there are plenty of other fish in the sea. If only I could be so laid-back and philosophical.

By Wednesday afternoon, I've worried myself into a frenzy. After my two-hour gym coaching session at the private school, I decide to drop in on Rachel unannounced. Given that a couple of the thirteen-year-old girls tried their utmost to undermine my authority today, I'm not in the best of moods. On the dual carriageway, I find it impossible to dismiss the thought of catching Rachel together with Al 'junior'.

"Why am I so paranoid?" I ask myself. "After all, she did say quite categorically that she didn't want to split up with me."

On my arrival, however, my concerns are borne out big time – Rachel is indeed up in her room with no other than ... Al 'junior'. There's embarrassment all round. Very wisely, my namesake makes a hasty exit.

"It's not what you think," Rachel says. "Honestly! Why are you here, anyway?"

"I was missing you," I confess, "and just came down on the spur of the moment."

Sensing that she's eager to clear up the 'Al' misunderstanding, I take a pew on the end of her bed. I'm all ears.

"There really is nothing going on between us. Okay, you were right, he does fancy me. But I promise you that it's totally one-sided."

"All right, I believe you. But don't you think you should tell him? It's not really fair to lead him on."

"I have been meaning to. But it's not easy."

The last thing I want at the moment is another row and it appears that Rachel is feeling the same way. Over the next hour, we talk in depth about our situation – in an adult fashion, for the most part. Rachel finally admits that she's confused and struggling to motivate herself.

"To be honest, Al," she says wearily, "I really don't know whether I want us to carry on or not."

"I see."

"Sometimes, I think I only need you when I'm lonely. But I promise you it's got nothing to do with the other Al or anyone else. I had doubts even before I came here."

"I spose I've sort of sensed that you weren't completely sure."

"This probably sounds arrogant, but all the blokes I try to be friends with here end up fancying me. And it's doing my head in. I really need to get to know some girls."

I nod in wholehearted agreement.

After further discussion, we decide to carry on as we are, although Rachel suggests I refrain from visiting for a while to enable her to get her head straight and build some platonic friendships.

During the course of the next few days, my initial relief that Rachel has finally spoken from the heart is soon replaced by a strong sense of impending gloom. The arrival in England of Rupert's pretty Austrian girlfriend for a short stay and the sight of her swooning all over her man as if he were the best thing since sliced bread only adds salt to my already gaping wounds. I wonder if she would let him off the hook this time if she knew how many other women he'd cracked onto during her absence.

As a means of distraction, I make contact with Erika, my Swedish friend. When she proposes that I pay her a visit at the weekend, I jump at the chance.

"My South African family will be on holiday, so you can help me look after their many pets," she says vibrantly.

I'm on the verge of leaving for the West Country on the middle Saturday in October when Rachel calls.

"Where've you been?" she asks, a note of recrimination in her voice. "I've been trying to call you all morning."

"Oh, nowhere special," I reply. "Just in town grabbing one or two things for my trip to Somerset."

"*Somerset?*"

"Yup. I'm off in a minute to visit that Swedish girl I told you about."

"Oh, okay. Well, don't do anything I would."

"Don't do anything I would," I repeat in my head once I've put the receiver down. I'm not sure why, but Rachel has this irritating knack of making cryptic comments that trigger off the analyst in me.

"Was she subtly urging me to remain faithful or attempting to let on that she hasn't been?" I ask myself as I cruise down the A303. "Or was it simply a random observation with no rhyme or reason behind it?"

It's great to see Erika again. It doesn't take long to establish that she wasn't exaggerating about the number of pets she's been left to keep an eye on. In fact, I'd say that one sheep, three pigs, sixteen ducks, a cockerel, an army of hens, two cats and a dog amount to nothing short of a smallholding. It strikes me at once that the owners have seriously exploited Erika's position of *au pair* by expecting her, a nineteen-year-old foreigner, to hold the fort single-handed whilst they soak up the sun on some Mediterranean beach.

My host gives me a guided tour of the large house and grounds before requesting some help to herd the ducks into their overnight enclosure. It takes the two of us almost half an hour, so I can't imagine how Erika will cope alone.

"Don't worry," she reassures me. "I'll ask one of the neighbours to help when you've gone."

In the evening, we tuck into a delicious leek and onion pie that Erika has prepared. Afterwards, we share a bottle of wine on the sofa. Hector, the dog, reveals a jealous streak, barking repeatedly and rather threateningly each time the two of us sit too close together. This proves to be a particular problem when we attempt to view some photos. Erika sighs.

"I can't put him in another room," she says, "because he'll scratch all the paint off the door."

Despite the dog's menacing presence, I can't help feeling attracted to my diminutive friend, although the more I drink, the more my thoughts return to Rachel. If only I could be spontaneous like Rupert and just go with the flow. Then Rachel would have to chase me or lose me. It's at this point that I remember that we haven't officially split up and that I've always been averse to cheating. I'd never forgive myself if we do manage to stay together.

"Have you got a girlfriend?" Erika asks, interrupting my thoughts.

I screw up my face and mumble: "Well, I think I have."

"You're not sure?"

Over the next half an hour, I find myself relating a story that I was anxious to avoid when I first arrived. I describe in detail how Rachel and I got to know each other as student and teacher, and how I've come to develop such strong feelings for her. Erika listens attentively, but doesn't comment.

Later, in one of the spare rooms, I lay awake, convinced that I've sabotaged any chance of anything between us in the immediate future should Rachel decide to dump me.

"Why couldn't I have played everything down?" I mutter under the duvet. "It really wasn't necessary to provide a blow-by-blow account. My big mouth!"

Whether Erika actually fancies me or not seems immaterial at this stage. True to form, I've absolutely no idea what she thinks of me.

The following day, I drive the two of us into Taunton. We're on a mission to track down the whereabouts of Erika's long-lost father who was last heard of in the area. The vicar at the local church is unable to assist, but advises us to visit the County's Records Office. Not surprisingly, it's closed on a Sunday.

We have lunch in a Carvery, go for a drive in the country, then return to the house for a nap on the settee once the blessed ducks are safely away for the night. Hector ensures that we both sleep at opposing ends and won't stop fussing over his substitute mistress.

Later, Erika shows me some rather touching letters her dad wrote to her mum shortly after absconding.

"He'll be fifty years old on Wednesday and it would have been so nice to have found him before then," she says with a tear in her eye. "But I think it's too late now."

I place a sympathetic hand on her shoulder.

"I think you're probably right," I say. "Still, better late than never, eh?"

I detect a profound sense of sadness in Erika and wonder how any father could've done this to his daughter.

I leave early on Sunday evening with a promise to return over half term to lend a hand with the ducks.

"Thank you," Erika says with a wave as I reverse out of the drive. "I'd like that very much."

Back home, I can't resist the temptation to give Rachel a quick call. She's in and we have a calm, friendly chat.

"I feel a lot happier now," she tells me. "I'd like you to visit soon. Maybe next weekend. I'll ring on Saturday morning to let you know for sure."

I head for bed, relieved that I managed to resist the temptation to do a Rupert impersonation last night.

A couple of days later, Alfie Moorhouse, an eighteen-year-old Yorkshireman who's studying at the nearby Art College, comes to take a look at my spare room. It meets with his approval and he agrees to move in immediately at the bargain rate of fifty pounds per week inclusive. He reminds me very much of a six foot six giant from Scarborough who was one of the four lads I shared a house with in my second year at university. The others were a mere six foot four, six foot one and five foot nine.

I wonder whether this rather than my gym career is responsible for my recurrent stiff neck. In a bizarre way, my new lodger's resemblance to my old friend is enough to convince me that he's trustworthy. Not very scientific, I know.

At *The Barley Mow* on Friday evening after gym, several members of the gang ask whether I'm still going out with Rachel. As usual, I provide too much information, which prompts each one in turn to comment on how precarious my situation has become. In my capacity as the world's greatest doubter, I leave the pub on a bit of a downer, wondering what I'd do without such supportive friends.

A phone call in the morning, however, challenges their negative assessment.

"Hi, sweetie," Rachel says buoyantly. "How d'you fancy coming to see me today?"

Not wanting to appear too eager, I hesitate for a few seconds before saying: "Er ... yes. That ... that should be okay."

"You wouldn't be able to do me a favour and collect my art box from home, would you? It'll mean meeting mum during her lunch hour, but I'd be really grateful."

"Don't see why not."

Just before setting off, Rachel calls again. "You wouldn't also be able to bring the portable TV from my bedroom, would you, sweetie? I've managed to contact mum at work, so she knows you're on your way."

With Rachel's art equipment and TV safely on board, I leave her mum's house as if it were the first day of spring.

"There's no way a nice girl like Rachel would've asked me to do this if she'd been planning to give me the elbow," I tell myself, my smile as broad as my optimism.

Rachel is delighted to be reunited with her art box and TV. Once she's found a home for them in her immaculately tidy bedroom, we sprint along the coast to Southampton to buy some essentials for her imminent trip to Paris with the Architecture Department.

Following Rachel around the shops in my old uni town, which has undergone considerable development in the last six years, it strikes me how self-assured she's suddenly become, almost to the extent of being bossy. This is a side to her personality that I'm unfamiliar with and it unsettles me.

With a holdall, purse and an umbrella on the counter of a medium-sized store, Rachel fumbles around in her pockets like an old lady.

"I've forgotten my debit card," she says suddenly, turning to me for support. "Could you ...? I'll pay you back later."

"What's that one you've got in your hand?" I ask, frowning.

"Oh, that's Luke's credit card. You know, the swimmer that you met outside the lecture theatre."

With the goods paid for on my credit card, we head back to the car.

"It may seem a silly question, but how come you've got Luke's card?"

"Oh, it must've fallen out of his pocket after he'd walked me home from a club the other night." She giggles nervously. "It was too late for him to catch a taxi back, so he stayed over."

"Really? Was your landlady out?"

"Nope."

"So where did he sleep?"

"In my bed."

"You let him have your bed?"

"No, we shared it."

At this point, I have visions of an ecstatic eighteen-year-old lad ripping his jeans off uncontrollably, his credit card falling out of one of the pockets and disappearing under the bed. My blood boils at the thought.

"Hang on a minute," I say angrily. "You refuse to allow your boyfriend to sleep over cos … cos you're concerned about your precious landlady and yet you … you don't think twice about letting some random bloke off your course …" I pause for breath, my hands shaking with fury. "So c'mon, then. You might as well break the bad news to me now."

"What d'you mean?"

"For God's sake, Rachel, I wasn't born yesterday. If you've had sex with this Luke guy, at least have the decency to admit it."

She eyeballs me fiercely. "Two people can sleep in the same bed without anything happening."

Back in Portsmouth, we pop into Sainsbury's for Rachel's maiden food shop as a university student. She hops up and down like a small child.

"Now my grant cheque's come through," she says, "I can buy some things to do my own cooking."

"Not without your debit card," I reply light-heartedly. My manner stems purely from the belief that humour often has a calming influence. Rachel looks at me like a begging dog. I relent: "Go on."

With a basket in her hand, Rachel charges round the store as if released from her reigns for the first time. In the checkout queue, she then maliciously imitates one of my facial expressions without the slightest provocation. Still uncomfortable from her earlier revelation, I feel a strong urge to abandon her on the spot with her groceries and no means of payment. Then I remember that I'm supposed to be the mature party in this relationship and beyond tantrums, so I hold my ground. She doesn't half know how to wind a bloke up, though.

On our way out of the supermarket car park, Rachel breaks the silence: "Would you be able to drive round to Luke's place so I can drop his card back?"

Does she want blood? Convincing myself that no guilty party would dare to make such a request, I oblige.

"I'm sure it was down here," Rachel says for the umpteenth time in the space of some forty-five minutes.

Once again, I carry out a three-point turn.

"This is ridiculous!" I snap finally. "I'm going to stop and ask somebody."

Up in Luke's room on the second floor of a Victorian house, the card-returning mission proves to be a rather awkward affair. Unable to read Rachel's body language, I have little difficulty interpreting Luke's – he fancies the pants off her. The cynic in me can't begin to imagine this testosterone-pumped hunk settling for an innocent night's kip in a single bed. My heart stings at the thought of the two of them wrapped round each other – in a bed that I've been denied the pleasure of sharing. How could she do this to me?

Back in Rachel's room, I'm anxious for a reassuring hug and kiss, yet she proceeds to unload and rearrange her art box as slowly and methodically as possible. My patience is running thin.

"Can't you do that when I've gone?" I ask.

She mutters something incomprehensible and carries on in the same vein.

It takes a good half an hour in all and with the box neatly back in its new home, Rachel pulls out a large art pad from one of her drawers. Sitting side by side on her bed, she shows me some of her sketches. They're most impressive, so I make some appropriate complimentary remarks.

About half way through the viewing, I decide I've had enough. I remove the pad carefully from Rachel's lap, then lean forward assertively to kiss her on the lips. My assertiveness stems from years of performing on stage and in the classroom, and has absolutely nothing to do with my current state of mind. To my initial relief, she doesn't back away, yet the kisses that follow immediately evoke memories of those shared with Mrs Panda, my sister's giant cuddly toy, who was the unfortunate recipient of my early teenage romantic rehearsals. God, what a confession!

"Rachel, what's up?" I ask. "It … it doesn't feel the same."

Tears stream down her cheeks.

"I'm so sorry, Al," she says. "It's not me coming here that's done this. It would've happened anyway."

In a flash, more than a decade of insecurities return to cripple my already tortured soul and tears fill my eyes like never before. For what seems like an eternity, we sit cradled in each other's arms, sobbing our hearts out like two small children. And then we talk, openly and sincerely like we used to. Rachel's hugely confident exterior of earlier is replaced by the vulnerable, self-doubting one that has been her trait over the last two years – characteristics of a young woman who I've come to fall in love with.

"This is the hardest decision I've ever had to make," she says, weeping almost uncontrollably.

Many more tears are shed and gentle, sentimental words uttered before we finally pull ourselves together and head into town for a swansong Indian.

I decide to make tracks shortly after we've eaten. As I turn to go, Rachel pulls me towards her, taking me in her arms for what'll surely be the last time. We kiss almost instinctively for a few seconds before she withdraws in order to whisper some bizarre words into my ear: "Please don't tell anyone about our sex life."

My journey home is full of unprecedented emotion, every word, every phrase relived a thousand times. And there are questions, many questions. Why would it have ended even if she hadn't gone to university? Has she fallen for Luke, even with his head intact? What was the significance of her parting comment – did I make her feel inadequate in bed? And why, why did she ask me to bring stuff from home if she knew she was going to dump me? Nice people don't do things like that, do they?

Back home in bed, the final question keeps me awake. A sudden recollection from the distant past helps me decide that insensitivity is probably an age thing. In Austria at the start of the third year of my degree, I pulled an English girl on the introductory course for new foreign language assistants. She was keen to go out with me, but was posted a good two-hour train journey away. After serious consideration, I decided that I didn't want to spend my year abroad in the company of an English girl as it would almost certainly jeopardise my progress in German. Anyway, she invited me for the weekend and I accepted, on the grounds that it would provide a perfect opportunity to gently relay my decision. I took the train westwards, accompanied by a large sack of dirty laundry. I'd been mistakenly led to believe that, unlike me, she had use of a washing machine.

Having broken the poor girl's heart, I then stood by and watched her hand wash my soiled clothes. Okay, she did offer, but … really! Sensitivity, it seems, is a quality acquired with age. In order for my clothes to dry, she insisted I stayed overnight and virtually begged me to make love to her. As a highly moral virgin, I climbed into bed with all my clothes on out of fear that instinct would lead me to do something I'd regret. How my life has changed since that innocent Austrian adventure almost a decade ago.

I eventually fall asleep in the early hours, under no illusions that I'll bounce back quickly from my split with Rachel. It may well have been an impossible romance right from the outset, but I feel sure the pain will last a long time. With my thirtieth birthday only a fortnight away, the timing couldn't have been worse.

Towards the end of the following week, I'm awoken one morning by the sun pouring magnificently into my bedroom via a minuscule crack in the curtains. As I slowly come round, I'm struck by an overwhelming sense of happiness, initiated I'm sure by a special dream that I can't quite remember. And then reality hits me like a bolt from the blue and my heart turns to lead. My gorgeous 'Damon' has outgrown me and moved on and there's nothing in the world I can do about it.

For most of the day, just like every other this week, it feels as if I'm completely alone in my grief – that no-one in the universe understands the extent of my anguish. How can they when all the sympathy I've received – and there's been plenty of it – is followed by the customary "Don't worry, you'll get over her", "There are plenty more fish in the sea" or "Well, she probably was a bit young for you. You should go for someone your own age". I know they're only trying to be kind, but at this juncture in my life, I don't want to move on. I want to hang on to all those precious moments when I genuinely believed that I'd finally discovered the secret ingredient of lasting romance.

To her credit, Rachel has phoned on several occasions, ostensibly to check I'm okay, but also to stress that her parting kiss was purely a sentimental gesture and of no lasting significance. Thanks! Her trip to Paris was a success, although she claims to have developed a taste for excessive amounts of alcohol.

"I can't understand why I'm drinking so much," she tells me.

Even if I wanted to move on, it wouldn't be easy with constant reminders of Rachel all around me. I see her in every room of the house, in all the pubs and bars we used to frequent, not to mention at her desk in my classroom and at her booth in the Language Lab. Then there's the spot by the covered way that she and Amanda made their own and, of course, a trampoline that seems so desolate without her. All these places leave me with an immeasurable sense of loss. Even a trip to the Motor Show with dad and the sight of a plethora of stunning girls adorning the gleaming new models fails to provoke the slightest hint of arousal.

In an effort to ease my suffering, I've tried turning back the clock to remember how I felt when Rachel was nothing more than a pretty student that I, the supremely confident teacher, got on well with. However, it's proved impossible to erase what's happened since. Although it feels that I'm in love with Rachel and merely displaying the symptoms of a broken heart, it's crossed my mind that I may also be ruing the end of the happiest period in my professional life. It doesn't feel quite the same now that so many of the great characters have left *Mardall's*.

I've been longing to ring Mario Campbell and pour my heart out, yet we seem to have drifted apart over the past year. My last three calls were all cut short, with a promise to ring back at the weekend, which never materialised. I'm not sure what I've done to upset him, but there's no way I'm prepared right now to expose myself to any further rejection by braving another call. I just couldn't take it.

Through preoccupation with my private life, I acknowledge that I've made few references to work since the start of this academic year. However, I wouldn't like anyone to assume that my failed romance has allowed my standards of professionalism to diminish. In fact, most of my surplus energy has been channelled into putting on a brave face in order to teach and coach to the best of my ability. Admittedly, this has proved particularly difficult at the co-ed private school where three of the girl gymnasts have regularly been a real handful. I discovered recently that gymnastics was not one of their first or second choice activities, which perhaps explains their reluctance to cooperate. Anyone who believes that teaching in the independent sector is, without exception, a piece of cake should think again. Fortunately, the Convent girls have been beyond reproach.

As regards my evening gym club, the numbers have continued to grow steadily. Moreover, I've been successful in assembling a reliable team of coaching assistants. One of these is Sally O'Neill who I had a brief relationship with when I first took over the club on my return from university. She's older than I am and divorced with two kids. Her daughter, Daisy, used to creep up behind me when I was busy coaching and bite my bum. She was only three at the time. To Sally's great amusement, two new precocious thirteen-year-old girls in the advanced group have been flirting with me outrageously. Almost thirty and single and only appealing to thirteen-year-olds. What's happened to my life? I don't think I've ever felt more down in the dumps.

With his Austrian girlfriend conveniently out of the way again, Rupert has resumed his lecherous ways of old. I bump into him in town late Saturday morning and relay my bad news about Rachel. After roughly three seconds of commiseration, he switches the topic of conversation to a tall redhead who works in *Dorothy Perkins*.

"She's hotter than any other bird I've ever seen," he says excitedly.

When have I heard this before? He then suggests we follow her on her lunch break. Too weary to protest, I comply with his request. With my misery plain to see, I conclude that this apparent insensitivity is simply his way of helping me to deflect thoughts of Rachel. After all, the great Rupert Stanley would never be guilty of egotism.

At the start of half term, I'm all ready to pay Erika another visit, but she stalls me at the last minute.

"I'm sorry, I have a friend coming to stay and I forgot when we spoke yesterday," she tells me over the phone.

Perhaps sensing my disappointment, she goes on to mention her forthcoming trip to London. "I'll come and see you then. Oh, and happy birthday for the week after next!"

Soon after talking to Erika, I receive a surprise call from Amanda Redpath, Rachel's best friend from College. She seems to have adapted well to university life and I'm pleased to hear that she's joined a trampolining club. Inevitably, we get onto the subject of the big break-up.

"I always thought you were the more vulnerable of the two," she says.

What? Considering Rachel's blatant vulnerability during her first few weeks at university, I find Amanda's comment rather depressing.

However, my mood is lifted slightly by her subsequent words: "I don't know if I should be telling you this, but there were times in the summer when Rachel was happier than I've ever seen her."

Having been stood up by Erika, my sister, Jayne, persuades me to spend a few days in Wales with her, Joe and baby Chloë.

"You're looking really gaunt," she tells me when I arrive.

I step onto her bathroom scales and am shocked to discover that I'm three quarters of a stone below my normal weight. Although my appetite over the last few weeks hasn't been quite what it was, I haven't exactly been on hunger strike either.

"That's what worry and stress do to you," Jayne says.

We talk a lot about my situation and she's careful to avoid any clichéd observations. In many ways, Jayne probably has a clearer understanding of how my brain works than anyone else. Chloë proves to be a perfect distraction, entertaining us all with her attempts to walk unaided. She really is a sweetheart.

Before leaving Cardiff, I call at one of the university halls of residence where a former French student, Claire Matthews, is residing. Unlike her contemporaries Cara Mitchell, Mandy 'Mandarin' Bailey and my one-time cleaner, Alicia Burns, Claire has remained in regular contact since leaving *Mardall's*. Unfortunately, there's no answer when I bang on her door, so I slip a brief message under it containing Jayne's number.

It's not until I'm back home that Claire rings and apologises for the delay in responding to my message.

"At first, I thought you were another Al on my course who I'm trying to avoid," she says.

God, not another one! She seems genuinely disappointed to have missed me, but announces that she's arranged to meet up with a few other ex-students at *James Dean's* on the evening before my birthday.

"It'd be great if you could come along too," she adds, as ebullient as ever.

To celebrate my thirtieth, I invite about fifteen members of my family to the house for tea on the preceding Sunday. This is the first time that I've entertained in my own place, which is a statistic I'm not particularly proud of. With mum and Auntie Flo helping out with the catering, the day proves to be a real success.

I feel in good spirits until after dark when the blues make an unwelcome return and I have to slip into acting mode. If only Rachel had been here to join in with the fun. Never in my wildest dreams had I envisaged that I'd reach this milestone as a single man.

As planned, I spend the eve of my birthday at *James Dean's* in the cordial company of Claire Matthews, Ian Thompson, Jonathon Freeman-Hardy and Lititia Jones-Thomas, a cute blonde from Cara and Mandy's French group. Aware of the recent upheaval in my life, they bend over backwards to ensure that I see in the dreaded three zero in style. Claire even insists on driving me home afterwards so I can down a bevvy or six. To my profound relief, there are no signs of my stalker all evening. Moreover, I feel on top form with scarcely a thought spared for Rachel.

When I wake the following morning, I open the various presents that my guests left on Sunday, along with a stack of cards brought by the postman. I'm pleased to discover that Rachel hasn't forgotten me. *I'll ring you later* is written at the bottom of her card. After the excesses of last night, I'm relieved to remember that normal teaching at *Mardall's* has been suspended for the whole day to enable staff to meet individually with underperforming students. This is usually a biannual occurrence and is known as Consultation Day.

There are only six students on my list and I 'consult' with them at varying intervals throughout the morning. I use the time in between to catch up on some admin.

At 1.00, I meet Claire Matthews for lunch as agreed last night. She has some bad news of her own – her boyfriend of two and a half years, a

College Rep who I liked, dumped her this morning. The look in Claire's piercing blue eyes is one of bewilderment rather than misery.

"Well, I spose we haven't been as close since we left College and went to uni," she says philosophically.

At this point, I wonder how I'd feel in her shoes, given that the end of a meagre four and a half-month relationship has thrown me into the depths of despair. If only I could be of an equally philosophical disposition.

Whilst we're eating, it suddenly occurs to me that my run-around is still in the multi-storey near *Opportunity Knox*, where I left it last night, and liable for a parking fine. Claire kindly offers to put a ticket on it after lunch. I'm grateful for her generosity once again.

"So you'll definitely give me a call next time you visit your sister," she says as I hand over some loose change for the meter.

"Definitely," I reply. "My niece's christening's sometime in the middle of December, so I'll look you up then."

Claire smiles warmly, then scurries off to her car, her long, wavy, mousey brown hair flapping on the shoulders of her slim frame.

With Consultation Day over, I return home. Scarcely have I turned the key when my new lodger, Alfie, emerges from his room with an urgent message for me from Rachel. I ring her back immediately. She's in a favourable mood, reiterating her birthday wishes. Without really thinking it through, I find myself proposing that I visit so we can have a celebratory meal together.

"I've got nothing else planned," I tell her, perhaps over-eagerly. "I can be with you by about 9.00."

"Well, okay," she replies. "As long as you realise that nothing's changed."

Bouncer look-alike Gary kindly agrees to drop me over to the multi-storey to collect my car. Before I know it, I'm heading for Rachel land just two weeks after vowing never to set foot in the gale-ridden, godforsaken place ever again.

As I step into Rachel's bedroom, I find her busy at work on her drawing board.

"Oh, hi," she says brightly. "I won't be long. Just got to finish off this sketch. You can have a look at my Paris photos whilst you're waiting, if you like." She gestures towards the top of an immaculately arranged bookcase.

I flick slowly through the pictures and notice at once that they have a common element – Luke.

"So you going out with Luke now, then?" I ask calmly.

"No, 'course not," she replies with equal tranquillity.

I flash her an incredulous look.

"What?"

I knit my brows.

"Well, I might do one day."

In spite of myself, my heart freezes. I take a few deep breaths. "I bet you've pulled each other, though."

Her eyes remain glued to the drawing broad in front of her. "No."

"Rachel, I haven't come all this way for a birthday meal just to be fed a pack of lies."

There's a seemingly endless pause followed by a rather timid confession: "We ... we have a few times."

With every sensible sinew in my body urging me to abandon this suicidal interrogation, I take a step closer and ask with mock composure: "So have you slept together as well?"

"No!" she says vociferously as if I've just accused her of plotting to blow up the Union building.

"I'm sorry, but you're lying. Please just be straight with me. I need to know."

Rachel places her pencil and slide rule meticulously onto the bed beside her, then contemplates me for the first time. Well, the area of floor around my feet, to be more precise. "Yes, we have. A few times."

"What, here in this bed?"

She takes hold of the pencil and slide rule once again and feigns an essential alteration to her sketch. On this occasion, there's absolutely no need for a verbal response.

"Great!" I say, collapsing in agony onto the end of her bed, my face buried deep into my palms. "So much for showing concern for your bloody landlady."

"But I'm not going out with him," my torturess adds as if convinced this'll provide instant relief from my suffering. "That's the truth."

What follows defies all logic and common sense. Instead of cutting and running, I escort Rachel to the restaurant where we celebrated our four-month anniversary and ply her with further questions in the absurd belief that nothing can possibly get any worse.

"So how come you're not going out with him?" I ask, using a fork to prod the starter.

Rachel prods her dish in identical fashion. "I think he's got a girlfriend back home."

"And you're happy to sleep with a bloke who's got another woman on the go?"

"Yes."

"Can't you see he's just using you? You can do so much better."

"I spose he is, but I don't care."

"Why not?"

"Cos he's friends with most of the other blokes I know on the course and they'll all hate me if I stop seeing him."

With this final, pitiful confession, my heart is all but smashed to smithereens. Never before in my life have I been more aware of my capacity for tears than at this particular moment. After all, I'm a typical man, moulded by the world around me into a tough, resilient individual who never cries. Whether my torment stems from overwhelming self-pity or from the revelation that the woman I love has totally lost her self-respect is impossible to gauge. All I know is that this is the worst birthday party I've ever had and that I've plummeted to depths that, throughout my previous thirty years, I never knew existed.

Drying my eyes every few seconds, I try to reason with Rachel, make her see sense. Yet, through the mist of my tears, all I can behold is a pair of eyeballs bereft of emotion. Even in the midst of our most heated exchanges or on the evening of our break-up, there was something there – something that convinced me she still cared. But now, I detect absolutely nothing. Just emptiness.

I settle up with the waiter and, having ensured that Rachel is home safely, leave this southern sea port for what, on this occasion, is unquestionably the last time. The road ahead is obscured by a thick fog reminiscent of the mental state of a sad, lonely teacher.

"How on earth have I got to this?" I ask myself.

I had a blissfully happy childhood. I was good academically. I had a successful sporting career that's still not over. I've performed on stage on countless occasions. I have jobs that I can excel in most of the time. And yet here I am at thirty with my life feeling so loveless and empty, with little prospect of improvement. All my past achievements came about through determination and perseverance, but these are qualities that now appear largely redundant in the perplexing world of human relationships where that certain x-factor reigns supreme. A factor that, at the end of the day, this teacher simply doesn't possess.

I know for sure that whilst of sound mind I'd never take my own life, but as I battle my way through the fog on this cold, lifeless November evening, I understand for the first time why some people are driven to such a drastic measure. Maybe one day in the distant future, I'll look back on this whole dark episode with shame and wonder how, at such an advanced age, I could've been such a pathetic, hopeless case. Surely no other teacher in history can have endured such pain at the hands of one of his former students. After all, teachers are serene professionals, superhuman beings perpetually in charge of their emotions, aren't they?

On the Saturday evening before little Chloë's christening, I call in on Claire Matthews as promised. She invites me to join her, Jonathon

Freeman-Hardy, his girlfriend, plus half a dozen other Cardiff University students for a meal in town.

Afterwards, we all drift back to Claire's flat and indulge in a spot of casual drinking. Little by little, the number diminishes and by midnight, Claire and I are alone in her room, playing computer games.

"Well, I'd better make a move," I say, not wanting to outstay my welcome.

"If you don't fancy walking back in the dark, you're more than welcome to sleep here," she says. "There are some pretty dodgy people about late at night."

As per usual, I haven't a clue whether Claire is just being her kind, considerate self or hinting at something of a more intimate nature. After all, there's only a single bed and hardly any room on the floor. Why am I always so uncertain? In view of the fact that I'm far from over Rachel, I decide that it would be unfair to stay and risk embroiling Claire in a rebound situation, even though I'm definitely attracted to her. It could potentially jeopardise our friendship.

The christening runs like clockwork, although poor Chloë is under the weather all day and uncharacteristically grizzly. As her proud godfather, I have to take vows relating to her future upbringing.

Six days before Christmas, I drive Rupert Stanley and me to *Opportunity Knox*. Once inside, we bump into Rachel and Luke who are now officially girlfriend and boyfriend. Rachel bends over backwards to be civil, yet I can't help noticing how uncomfortable Luke is about my presence at the club. The sight of such an extreme role reversal cheers up the less altruistic side of my nature.

I'm the master of my emotions until later in the evening when Rachel and Luke suddenly break into a passionate kiss right under my nose. As if by magic, that familiar stabbing pain in my chest returns.

"How come it's okay for her to kiss him in front of me," I ask myself, "when she always refused to show any signs of affection with me when her ex, Pete, was around?"

As if to force the dagger in deeper, Rupert pulls one of my best German students from last year and they head for her car in the multi-storey for a bit of privacy.

"She gave me a wicked blow job on the back seat," Rupert gloats on the way home. Cackle, cackle, cackle.

The last thing I need in the early hours after another soul-destroying evening is a lengthy discussion about his macho antics, yet he leaves me with little choice. For almost an hour, we sit in the car outside his house and he subjects me to a protracted justification of his infidelity, just a few days before he's due to fly to Austria to spend Christmas with his devoted girlfriend.

"Maybe I should ask her to marry me when I'm out there," he says. "What d'you reckon?"

Sometimes, I wonder if I'd be no worse off in a lunatic asylum.

After a lunchtime family gathering on New Year's Eve, I return to the house at 8.00 to find an unexpected message from Rachel on the answer machine. *Luke's gone back home to see in the New Year with his mates and I just wondered what you were up to* it says. Reasoning that she's probably already made alternative plans by now, I decide not to return her call. Instead, I wander down to *The Barley Mow*.

There are many familiar faces there and, during the course of the evening, I have an interesting discussion with a self-confessed nineteen-year-old bisexual called Nicky Baker. As far as I know, this is the first time in my life that I've been in the company of an openly non-heterosexual woman.

During our time in Austria, Mario and I befriended a gay male teacher called Friedrich – or 'Freda' to some – who had no inhibitions whatsoever about his sexuality. He even warded me off one of my younger male Austrian friends, on the grounds that he was certain the latter batted for the opposing team.

"I don't think so," I said. "I've known him for months and he's never tried anything on."

Freda then lent forward, squeezed my leg under the table and said, with a grin the size of Vienna: "But nor have I ... yet."

Back in the present, I ask Nicky if she has a preference.

"No, not really," she says. "I just have double the chance of seeing someone I fancy when I go out."

Her frankness reminds me very much of good old Friedrich and I enjoy our little chat. She lives locally, so I'm sure we'll be seeing more of each other.

Just after midnight, when all the couples around me are lost in a passionate embrace and I'm alone dreaming of happier times, my next door neighbour, Tina, approaches me, looking the worse for wear.

"Would you be able to walk me back, Al?" she asks rather flirtatiously.

With her skinny, jet black-haired figure draped over me, the two of us set off for home. About half way there, Tina stops and swivels me round to face her. Grabbing hold of both my hands, she then moves her lips towards mine.

"Tina, I don't think that's a good idea," I say, withdrawing to a safe distance.

She nods feverishly.

"It's okay," she says. "Greg and I aren't together any more."

"Really? I could've sworn his bike's been outside your house all week."

"Yeah, that's cos he's got nowhere else to go and I've agreed he can stay on for the time being."

She clasps my hands once again and tugs me towards her, her lips pursing as they reach mine. I find myself responding for a few brief seconds before backing off uncomfortably. I retrieve one of my hands, coaxing her gently forward with the other.

"Come on," I say firmly. "It's cold and I'm knackered."

We're soon back home. I give Tina a hurried kiss on the cheek before striding hastily up the drive. She follows me to the front door.

"Aren't you going to invite me in for a cup of coffee?" she asks.

"Erm ... er ... I ..."

My tortured efforts at conjuring up a valid excuse are interrupted by a sudden excruciating wail, emanating from the other side of the fence. And it's getting closer. Tina and I both swing round instinctively to confront the deafening racket and spot Greg charging towards us ferociously, an empty bottle of vodka brandished above his head.

"No, no, no!" he yells.

At this point, I see my whole life flash before me and feel certain that I'm on the verge of becoming a second murder victim in my road almost a year to the day after the first. As Greg draws nearer, my body stiffens in preparation for battle. Just as he's within arms-length of the two of us, Tina dances forward deftly and seizes hold of her ex's shoulder-length mop of curly black hair. With a series of aggressive tugs, she successfully halts his advance. After what seems like an eternity, the commotion ceases and Greg sinks disconsolately onto one of the larger stones in my rockery, the vodka bottle slipping out of his grasp and rolling a few feet down the drive. He then sobs lamentably.

"I think you two need to go next door and have a chat," I say, at the risk of stating the obvious.

Greg slowly hauls himself to his feet. He collects the escaped bottle and, with Tina in tow, makes his way home, his head hung low. With a huge sigh of relief, I let myself in and climb the stairs to my bedroom.

No sooner have I pulled the duvet over my trembling body, however, than there's a loud thud on the door. I trundle wearily back down the stairs to investigate. Opening up cautiously, I find Tina on the doorstep.

"Right, where's that cup of coffee?" she asks, as fresh as a daisy.

With the New Year barely an hour old, it seems certain that the madness of my life is set to continue.

SPRING TERM

With a sore head, I surface at lunchtime on New Year's Day, aware that the start of the spring term is just a couple of days away. My popularity of the earlier hours continues with another visitor at the door. The sight of Greg twitching menacingly on the drive as I open up sends involuntary shivers down my spine. I'm far too hung over to face his wrath right now. I soon discover, however, that he's in an apologetic rather than a confrontational frame of mind.

"I'm sorry, mate, about last night," he says humbly. "I'm not dealing with our break-up very well. Can't bear to see Tina with anyone else."

I assure him that I know exactly how he's feeling and stress that I have no interest whatsoever in his ex. The relief on his face couldn't be more evident. He retreats next door after a further apology.

Back inside, two thoughts cross my mind. One: why do I always assume that bikers are hard nuts? And two: why have I grown up believing that men are predominantly the initiators of heartbreak? On this note, I think of Rachel and decide to return her unexpected call from yesterday.

"With Luke not here, I just thought you might've wanted to meet up," she says affably.

I try to play it cool by pretending I'd made New Year plans a while back, but then soften when she suggests I visit later. Apparently, her mum and sister are out all afternoon. Considering that I have a belated birthday card and small present for her – she was nineteen just after Christmas – I agree to pop round.

At Rachel's, the two of us sit together on a small settee in the lounge and watch a video. After a while, she makes herself more comfortable by draping her legs across my lap – just like she used to. This surprises me. We chat a bit at intervals during the film and she tells me that although she gets on really well with Luke, she's definitely not in love with him … yet.

"He's got topless pictures of Pamela Anderson plastered across his bedroom wall," she says somewhat bitterly. "I don't know what he sees in her."

I'm on the verge of stating the obvious when I recall Rachel's previous insecurity about the size of her own breasts. I decide to hold my tongue. The extreme optimist in me wonders whether all this talk is a kind of signal and I find myself sorely tempted to come on to her. But then I remember her one-time comment that she only really needs me when she's lonely and my pride steps in. The more I think about this, the more irritated I become.

I give Rachel a rather formal kiss on the cheek before parting at six o'clockish. On the way home, my frustration at feeling used is at its height. Or am I actually just annoyed with myself for starting the New Year as I ended the last, still at the mercy of a former student some eleven years my junior? Why am I finding it so hard to let go?

In an attempt to regenerate my life, I decided before Christmas to start singing lessons and join a competitive trampolining club. Sessions for both start soon after I've gone back to work and, in the case of the singing, not all goes according to plan. Having instructed me to stand upright in her front room and sing a familiar tune with both hands by my side, the middle-aged female teacher assesses my embarrassed effort.

"I'm afraid to say, you may well be tone deaf," she tells me after a series of follow-up activities. "Do you want to bash on or knock it on the head now?"

"I'm not going to give up that easily," I retort. "When can I come again?"

During the second week in January, Jayne and Joe bring Chloë up to visit her grandparents. I call in after work one evening and find that she can now walk a few paces on her own without toppling over. She insists on sitting next to me at dinner and, after every mouthful or so, puts her arm round me, resting her head on my shoulder in the process. Aw!

I leave mum and dad's in a reflective frame of mind. I wonder if there's a reasonably attractive, compatible woman out there who'd like to have a family with me one day. At present, I'm not sure I'd want to gamble my life's savings on it.

Having finally secured a room in the student village, my lodger, Alfie Moorhouse, packs his bags and moves out. Whilst appreciating his wish to live amongst other students of his own age, I'm sorry to see him go. Finding an equally trouble-free replacement may not be easy. I place an ad in the local paper.

During the first couple of weeks in February, I begin to feel like an estate agent as I show one potential lodger after another my spare room. Eventually, a rather strange lad in his mid-twenties called Max agrees to take it from 1st March. In response to my question about the nature of his employment, he informs me that he's a chef at a private school and a copper at the local nick. It's only after he's gone that I begin to question the possibility of someone holding down two such major jobs.

I ring the school and they confirm that Max does indeed work in their kitchen. However, my enquiries at the local police station are not so fruitful – no-one has ever heard of him.

When Max returns a few days later to drop off a deposit, I tackle him about the police job.

"They won't admit to you that I work there for security reasons," he says confidently.

Soon after he's gone, I receive a call from a friendly, loquacious New Zealander called Dylan who's seeking accommodation. Disappointed to discover that the room is soon to be taken, he asks if he can stay for a couple of weeks until Max moves in. Unwilling to turn down extra cash, I agree.

A further visit to the police station reveals that there are no top security agents on the payroll.

"We wouldn't have a problem admitting your friend worked here if he did," the officer on the front desk says.

"So what d'you advise me to do?" I ask.

"Give the geezer his deposit back and tell him to get lost."

By chance, I run into Max a day or two later in town. Not wishing to delay any further, I have the unpleasant task of informing him that I've changed my mind on account of advice from his colleagues in the Force.

"I only work there now and again," he says as I hand back his deposit. I'm intrigued.

"So why did you mention it in the first place?" I ask.

"Cos I didn't want you getting worried if someone in uniform called at the door looking for me."

Nice one, Max! Have I really got 'mug' etched across my forehead? Back at the house, I offer Dylan the room on a more permanent basis. He accepts gladly.

Since our amusing chat on New Year's Eve, Nicky, the bisexual, has become a good friend, offering herself as a sounding board whenever I've needed to offload my feelings about the opposite sex.

On the Saturday after Valentine's Day – no cards, once again – I drive Nicky, her French *au pair* friend, Natalie, and a male friend to *Opportunity Knox*. The plan is for the four of us to catch a taxi home should I fail to lay off the booze.

Any hopes of an abstention are immediately quashed by the arrival at the club shortly after us of Rachel and her younger sister. With Nicky's encouragement, I've been trying really hard since our last meeting to put her out of my mind and move on. Her presence, therefore, comes as a bit of a blow. Apart from a nod of acknowledgement, I manage to steer clear for almost an hour before my defences crack and I drift towards her. I ask how she's been.

"Okay, thanks," she replies. "But why did you phone Pete about me?"

At the beginning of January, a male friend of Rachel's had approached me one evening and announced that she'd been carrying on with her ex from the trampolining club whilst we were together. I tried to dismiss the suggestion, but it started to bug me. In pursuit of the truth, I rang Pete and requested an honest answer, but he refused to get involved. I explain this to Rachel. She looks gobsmacked.

"How could you believe such rubbish?" she says. "I've always been totally honest with you about Pete."

One brief glance into her eyes is enough to convince me, although I'm left wondering whether someone, somewhere has been paid a lot of money to finish off what remains of my self-esteem. Mind you, if it had been true, moving on would be a hell of a lot easier than it is now.

Predictably, the two of us find ourselves going over old ground once again. Only, this time, Rachel introduces concrete reasons for dumping me.

"You never understood how devastated I was when the A level results came out," she says. "And then you didn't support me properly when I first went to uni."

What? Is she serious? Initially, I try to defend myself, but soon realise that I'm wasting my breath. Rachel leaves shortly afterwards without the hint of a goodbye.

Just to cap a 'perfect' evening, Nicky's male friend hitches a lift home with a mate and, faced with a larger taxi bill than we can afford, the two girls and I have little option but to 'crash' in my car – them in the back, me across the front seats. It's cold and uncomfortable and we barely sleep a wink. What's more, I have several unfortunate nocturnal clashes with the handbrake.

We return home at dawn. After dropping off my two comatose passengers, I manage to grab half an hour's kip before leaving for my now regular Sunday morning trampolining session. The club is one of the best in the country with numerous international performers. The chief coach, Lynne, a Psychology teacher by profession, quite rightly doesn't rate a hangover as a valid excuse for skipping training. Needless to say, my efforts on this particular morning resemble those of a pregnant hippopotamus.

Back home, I'm surprised by a call from Rachel, wishing to apologise for leaving last night without saying goodbye.

"Mum has strongly advised that I put the past behind me and sever all contact with you," she whispers down the line. "So I'm phoning behind her back."

We have a friendly chat and, in my heavily fatigued state, I find myself promising to keep in touch. Whilst part of me agrees with Mrs Hill, the other part still hankers after those memorable summer days together and doesn't want to erase the slim possibility they could be recaptured sometime in the future when Rachel is older and more mature.

I know I should have more self-respect, but I haven't noticed any other pebbles queuing up on the beach so far in '96. My Swedish friend, Erika, hasn't made any further contact and I think I'd be crazy to consider a long-distance relationship with Claire at Cardiff University. It'd be a case of 'out of the frying pan and into the fire'.

On the first Monday in March, I receive a long, detailed letter from Rachel, attempting to clear her conscience and put the record straight, although she expresses doubts about the wisdom of doing so. To begin with, I'm touched that she still cares about me enough to want to explain her feelings, but as I read on, it hits home that the truth, however honourable, isn't always what we want to hear.

> *I feel terrible about the way I've hurt you*
> *and have tried to deny how you feel about*
> *me in an attempt to mask my guilt. I*
> *deliberately tried to change when I went*
> *to uni because I thought it'd make it easier*
> *to believe we'd grown apart. But really I*
> *haven't changed. I hope you believe me about*
> *Pete. He actually treated me very badly and*
> *the only reason I continued to be friends with*
> *him after we split up is that I couldn't accept*
> *that someone could be so horrid to me.*

"Sounds familiar," I mutter within the confines of my bedroom.

And so when all is said and done, her only motive for wanting to stay in touch is that she feels guilty. Okay, that's it. Time to move on now.

At the weekend, an old school friend called Malcolm Thorpe – aka Mr Bean – pays me a visit. Now a civil servant, he's always impressed with his encyclopaedic knowledge of British politics and cricket. In fact, he stayed with me for a week during my year in Austria and woke me one night whilst in the middle of a highly vocal 'wet' dream – he was commentating orgasmically (if that's a word) on the results of a past general election. I seem to remember his namesake, Jeremy, receiving a particular mention. Moreover, if it hadn't been for Malcolm, I doubt if I'd have ever become such an avid cricket fan and I'd almost certainly have missed Ian Botham's heroic feats throughout the 1981 Ashes series, surely one of the highlights of this country's sporting history. Although rather shy in unfamiliar circles, Malcolm comes into his own in the company of those he knows well. He is a first-class writer and penned a large proportion of the scripts I used as a teenager to impersonate various members of staff at our secondary school's end-of-term concerts. These were held in the hall where I now run my private gym club and propelled me to celebrity status at this four hundred strong comprehensive. I've always felt Malcolm never received the acclaim he deserved.

Shortly after Malcolm's arrival at the house, the two of us set off on a pub crawl around some of my locals. Given that it's a while since we've seen each other, there's plenty of cricket and political news to catch up on.

We end up at *Alfredo's* at about 10.00 where we bump into Gary from the gang and his fiancée, Kathy. They strike up conversation with Malcolm and, after a few minutes and another pint, he soon sheds his inhibitions. This provides me with a perfect opportunity to chat up a pretty brunette that I've caught sight of standing at the bar. She's a lovely girl and particularly easy to talk to. Moreover, she's in no hurry to return to her friends. Whilst I'm in full flow, I suddenly spot Malcolm out of the corner of my eye lose his footing and slide down the wall he's been leaning on. Gary gives me the sign that he's had one too many before hoisting my rag doll-like guest to his feet. I step away from the bar and am relieved to discover that Malcolm is conscious and unhurt.

This distraction coincides with 'time at the bar'. Overcome by cold feet, I find myself lost for words as my new friend prepares to leave. In a panic, I scribble my phone number down on a scrap of paper and press it into her hand as she and her friends are on their way out.

"You bloody idiot!" I reproach myself once she's left. "Why the hell didn't you ask for *her* number?"

Gary shakes his head slowly as if to suggest that I really am beyond redemption.

I walk home disconsolately with an uncharacteristically tipsy Malcolm. Normally, he exercises extreme caution when drinking alcohol. Any hopes that his condition may have dampened his enthusiasm for a late night political debate fade fast. Oh well, it was good to catch up and see him chat so confidently to people he didn't know.

Each time the phone rings during the following week, I pick up in the vague hope of hearing the voice of my *Alfredo's* friend at the other end of the line. But I'm clutching at straws. There's no way a nice girl like her is going to make the first move, is there? I blew it, simple as that. The only positive thing to be derived from my missed opportunity is that it seems to confirm that I really have moved on. Hallelujah!

With impeccable timing once again, Rachel calls and complains that she's feeling really down, a lack of money and motivation to study being the source of her blues. Apparently, Luke hasn't been very sympathetic. The irony of her revelation amuses me. Somehow, though, I can't envisage 'lack of support' signalling the end of her relationship with him. Cool guys like Luke and Rupert always do seem to get away with murder. It's just a depressing fact of life.

At the beginning of April, I'm driving through town in the Spider when I pass Alice, an attractive Zimbabwean who's started working behind the bar at *Alfredo's*. She waves excitedly and spoils me with an enormous smile, revealing a set of resplendent snow-white teeth. Actually, judging from the animated Disney production, Alice is exactly how I imagine a real-life version of Snow White to look. Along with the balmy spring air blowing in my face, I feel a sudden rush of optimism, as if to confirm that the dark, dispiriting winter months are well and truly behind me.

On Good Friday at *Alfredo's*, Alice leans across the bar and, placing her hands on one of mine, asks if I'd mind entertaining her friend from back home who's staying for a few weeks. I have no objections, so she introduces me to the girl. The two of us then spend the remainder of the evening in conversation.

At closing time, Alice joins us once she's finished tidying the bar.

"Have you got a tennis racket?" she asks me rather unexpectedly.

"Yes, I have," I reply, my eyes lighting up. Terrific! She wants to have a knock up with me.

"Good. How d'you fancy playing with Josie and me on Easter Sunday?"

My heart sinks. "Oh, I'm really sorry, I can't make it on Sunday. I've promised my parents that I'll spend the day with them. My little niece'll be there and she'd be ever so dis…"

"Never mind!" Alice says, cutting me short.

"Maybe we can play another time?"

Alice nods, but with little conviction. Timing, once again.

I discover on Easter Sunday that Chloë can now run at a fair old pace. Still pint-sized, she looks sweeter than ever. Her latest trick involves sprinting up to family members, stopping, pursing her lips exaggeratedly, then kissing them affectionately. I know I'm heavily biased, but it's the cutest thing I've ever seen. Well worth missing a frolic on the tennis court with Snow White for.

The following day, I call into *Opportunity Knox* with a bottle of whiskey for Steve Whately, the Door Manager. Having saved me a fortune in entry fees over the past year or so, I wanted to express my gratitude. Whilst there, it occurs to me that I haven't heard from Rachel in a while. I conclude that she must be pretty happy at the moment and no longer in need of a sounding board. Recognition that I'm only of use to her when she's lonely or down in the dumps has, I'm sure, helped to heal my broken heart.

Later in the week at *The Barley Mow*, I announce to Nicky and Natalie that I'm officially completely over my ex. Out of monumental relief, they hold up their glasses to toast the momentous news.

SUMMER TERM

The new term is already underway by the time I next see Alice.

"I went away during the last part of the Easter holidays," she says when I ask why she hasn't been at work.

Having resolved to chance my arm with her, I ask twice during the course of the evening whether she'd like to play tennis at the weekend. She ignores my question the first time, then bustles away awkwardly when I repeat it. This leaves me with little doubt that I've misread the signs once again and that I was only useful to her when her friend was around. Maybe I have got 'mug' stamped across my forehead, after all. Sensing my wrath, Alice avoids me for the rest of the evening.

By pure coincidence, I bump into Alice in town the following day and she greets me as if last night hadn't happened. I know the score – I've heard it often enough: "You're a lovely bloke and all that, but ..."

Not for the first time, poor old Dylan is subjected to my ranting and raving about the fairer sex. As usual, he just offers a sympathetic smile. He's planning to do a spot of travelling around Europe in May and, aside from the regular additional income, I'll miss his companionship. Nicky and Natalie get on well with him too. In fact, the latter even shared his bed one night.

By the end of May, one thing is clear – most women don't fancy the prospect of sharing a house with a single male owner, even a friendly, innocuous one like me. The familiar dialogue goes something like this:

Woman:	"It's a nice size room and I like the idea of having free run of the whole house. Who else lives here?"
Me:	"Oh, just me at the moment."
Woman	(*after awkward hesitation*): "Okay, well I ... I've got a few other rooms to see first, so ... um ... I'll let you know ... er ... soon."
Outcome:	woman doesn't let me know, room stays empty and my finances suffer.

Just into June, I get a call from a female FE College teacher seeking accommodation. I decide not to beat about the bush.

"I'm the only other person in the house," I tell her, "so if you've got a problem with that, then there's no point in you coming to look at the room."

"That doesn't bother me," she says in a matron-like fashion. "I'm more than capable of handling myself."

She comes round to view the room and, after careful consideration, decides that she'll take it. She is, however, obliged to give three weeks' notice at her present lodgings.

"I'll ring you a couple of days before moving in," she says on her way out of the door.

In view of the inherent mutual respect professionals in the public sector hold for each other, I consider it inappropriate to request a deposit. After all, everyone knows you can always rely on a teacher.

With the summer holidays fast approaching and the prospect of six weeks with no income from my regular gym coaching jobs, I head along to the local Sports Centre to discuss my plans to run a holiday gymnastic course for kids. The manager likes the idea and gives me the thumbs up. Now I'll need to design a snazzy poster on the computer to help advertise the course.

I haven't really mentioned this before, but when I started at *Mardall's* I had virtually no IT skills at all. Whilst I've always been rather slow to embrace modern technology, I have to admit that *Windows* is a wonderful resource for helping teachers prepare transparencies for use on the overhead projector – as well as worksheets, of course. I use it all the time now.

The day for my new lodger to move in has now arrived, yet she's failed to make contact as promised. I ring her college several times. On the third attempt, I manage to catch her in between lessons.

"Oh, I've been trying to get hold of you," she says timidly. What happened to matron? "I'm afraid I've moved in with a friend."

Concerned that I'm about to unleash a barrage of expletives, I bring the conversation to a premature conclusion. Since there's absolutely nothing wrong with my answer machine, I have to acknowledge that she's simply buried her head in the sand. So much for trusting a fellow teacher.

Anxious that I've lost a further three weeks' rental income, I place another advert in the local paper, stating unambiguously that there's a room to let in a house near the town centre with the owner who is MALE.

A few days later, a tall man with a beard, dressed in a smart suit, comes to view the room. He announces in a distinctly plummy voice that his name is Clement Byers. At a guess, I'd say he's approaching fifty.

"Splendid, I'll take it," he says after a fleeting guided tour of the house. "I'll move in this afternoon if that'll be acceptable to you."

Sensing an immediate solution to my mounting overdraft problem, I shake on it.

Before I have chance to reflect on my hasty decision, Clement has returned, unpacked his suitcase and taken up residence.

"I forgot to ask earlier if you could provide a reference," I mention once he's changed into shorts, a T-shirt and flip-flops, and collapsed onto the settee.

"Oh dear, that could be rather tricky," he says. "You see, I've spent the last three years in America."

"Really? How come?"

"Well, I suppose now is as good a time as any to tell you." He sits bolt-upright, then leans forward with a grave expression written all over his face, his hands clasped together on his lap. "I used to run an antiques shop in London in the King's Road. But one morning, I awoke to the sight of my partner dead on the floor. I was devastated, so I sold up and moved to the States."

"Oh, no!"

"Yes, it was a ghastly experience. Anyway, if it's a reference you're after, I suppose you could always speak to my mother. She lives just outside town."

Convinced beyond any shadow of doubt that I'm inadvertently sheltering a homicidal madman on the run from the police, I place several hefty chairs firmly up against my bedroom door before turning in.

I survive the night.

In the morning, I take a call from an elderly lady wanting to have "a brief word with Clement".

"Oh, mother, hellooo. How aaare you?" he says when I hand over the receiver.

Without wishing to eavesdrop, I can't help overhearing the ensuing conversation, which reassures me that the woman at the other end of the line is in fact Mrs Byers and not some ageing female accomplice. I decide that the chairs probably were a bit over the top.

"So your partner that died," I ask, once 'mother' has completed her 'brief' chat. "Was it a man or a woman?"

"His name was Gerald," he says. "We were lovers."

Having assumed rather naively that Clement had used the word 'partner' to refer to a business associate, I'm initially lost for words.

"I think you should know that Gerald died from AIDS," Clement adds. "But don't be alarmed. I've been tested and I'm free of HIV."

"Oh, right."

Clement then treats me to a protracted account of his love affair with Gerald. It proves to be a real tearjerker, leaving me feeling rather guilty that I could've considered the sensitive, passionate man in front of me capable of murder.

"I'm actually bisexual," he says after a period of reflection. "There've been loads of women in the past."

Contemplating whether bisexuality has become the latest craze, I head for bed on this second night, wondering if I should barricade myself in, after all. Although I am in no way homophobic, actually sharing a house with someone who fancies men is a totally new experience for me and I can't help feeling a little uneasy.

My fears are compounded towards the end of June when I return from the pub one evening to find Clement sprawled across the settee in a drunken stupor. Whilst it hasn't escaped my attention that his full-time occupation involves sampling the finest malt – usually commencing at breakfast – this is the first time I've witnessed any undue effects.

"Oh, hellooo. C...come and j...join me," he says as I enter the lounge. "I w...want to t...talk."

I pause briefly to assess his condition, then ease myself nervously into the armchair opposite.

"I w...want to t...tell you why I t...took the r...room," he continues before emptying the last dribble of whiskey out of the bottle and into his glass. He then slowly and meticulously raises it to his lips, a task requiring particular skill in his current state. The contents are consumed in one fell swoop. "As I w...was saying, the r...reason I t...took the r...room is th...that I ..."

"That you *what*?" I ask, wondering what gibberish is about to follow.

"Th...that I ... I f...fancied your th...thighs and your bbb...butt!"

He stretches forward in one violent movement as if to stress the final syllable, his eyes as large and dilated as a full moon.

Visions of Clement eyeing me up on the stairs on that first day as I led him up to the room send a nauseous shiver through my transfixed body. I utter an awkward, involuntary laugh. Without further ado, Clement hauls himself out of the settee with one aggressive shove.

"It's n...no g...good," he says, surging forward.

Before I have chance to escape, he's reached me and placed his hands firmly on my shoulders. At first, I'm frozen with shock. Then I find myself rising instinctively to my feet and swinging my unwanted admirer round in one deft movement until he collapses into the chair that I've just vacated. Clement shakes his head vigorously, as if attempting to eradicate the effects of the booze, before hoisting himself up once again.

"Oh d...dear," he mumbles. "I th...think I had b...better turn in."

With this, he staggers out of the room and crawls up the stairs to bed.

The following day at *Mardall's*, I decide to give Clement his marching orders. But then one of my colleagues asks whether I'd resort to such a drastic measure if a female lodger I didn't fancy had thrown herself at me in a similar fashion. I have to concede that I wouldn't.

By the time I've got home, I settle for an informal warning. Clement has sobered up completely and makes light of the previous evening's escapade. However, he promises there won't be a recurrence.

A few days later, I return from work to find Clement grinning like a cat that's just got the cream.

"What's happened?" I ask.

"I've just seen someone in town who's rather scrumptious," he says.

I ply him with further questions in the hope he'll divulge the identity of his new fancy man (or woman) – anyone to divert his attention from me.

He's unwilling at first, but sensing that I won't let up, he eventually comes clean: "Oh, if you must know, it's the fruit and veg barrow boy at the market."

Oh dear!

On the first Saturday in July, it's Nicky's twentieth birthday. I'm invited to a party at her friend Elisabeth's parents' house. Elisabeth is training to be a primary school teacher. On our previous few meetings, we've had interesting discussions about various aspects of the teaching profession.

The house turns out to be a large five-bedroom property in the heart of the country, complete with swimming pool and tennis court. I soon discover that Elisabeth's parents and siblings are away and that we have exclusive use of the facilities. Well, that's after we've danced the night away at *Opportunity Knox*.

I manage to hitch a lift to the club with Nicky, Elisabeth and two of their other friends. Before entering, we meet a couple of N's old school chums at the station. They've travelled down from London. N whispers in my ear that the smaller of the two, Hazel, is also bisexual.

All the girls pull men at the club, although Elisabeth is the only one to invite hers back to the house. For once, I didn't feel too nostalgic at *OK*, but didn't see anyone that particularly caught my eye. However, in the taxi on the way back to the 'mansion', Hazel places her hand on my knee, then eases it progressively up my leg towards my groin. It turns me on, as does the sight of her naked body jumping into the swimming pool soon after we arrive. Nicky joins her and reveals a similarly curvy frame with firm boobs. As they splash about in the water together, only Nicky's dark bob distinguishes her from her short blonde-haired school friend as I watch from my vantage point on the patio. All of a sudden, I'm seeing both girls in a totally different light.

"Is it the effect of alcohol or nudity pure and simple?" I ask myself.

Back in clothes, Hazel joins me inside on the settee. We kiss for a good half an hour, her hair still moist. I'm feeling on top form. At this point, Nicky decides to intervene.

"It's my turn now," she says, dragging Hazel off me and into her own arms. "After all, it is *my* birthday."

What follows is something that I've only caught a glimpse of a couple of times on a German satellite TV channel – inadvertently, of course – never in real life. Without the slightest inhibitions, the two girls indulge in an extended bout of kissing and petting right in front of my very eyes. I'm fascinated at first, as are the other guests close enough to witness this unprecedented event. However, it's not just a temporary exhibition and, after a few minutes have elapsed, I begin to feel neglected. I know that for many men, this spectacle would be a dream come true, but it's Al Bentley we're talking about here – the teacher with a paper-thin ego.

In spite of myself, I feel an unwelcome stab of rejection. Huffing and puffing, I abandon the scene and disappear into the bedroom the host has kindly put aside for me. Any vague hopes that Hazel may come looking for me fade fast. I fall asleep with my pride dented once more.

Fortunately, I'm back in good spirits when I wake in the morning. Alcohol, it really does have the effect of exaggerating one's emotions. On my way down to breakfast, I pass Nicky on the stairs.

"What happened to you last night, Al?" she asks. "Hazel and I were hoping you were going to join us. Elisabeth let us sleep in her parents' double bed."

On the way home just after lunch, I can't help reflecting what a crazy year this has been. When I started back to work last September, I had a beautiful girlfriend, which made me the envy of men for miles around. Ten months later, here I am single again and apparently only attractive to bisexuals of both gender. Has the world gone completely mad?

After the bizarre events of the last month, the College year drifts to a rather dull, unremarkable conclusion. Whilst I can't deny that my part-time status has considerably reduced the amount of time I have to devote to lesson preparation and marking, it has left me feeling more isolated from College life than I used to. I'm sure having to give up my Student Activities job hasn't helped either.

Since it's too late to contemplate a return to a full-time position, which would probably involve leaving *Mardall's*, given our dire financial situation, I've decided to persevere in my current role for at least another year. Fortunately, the co-ed private school and Convent have both renewed my contract for September. Moreover, my private gym club is going from strength to strength. Sadly, the take-up for my proposed holiday gym course has been poor and I've had to cancel.

To compensate for the loss of earnings, I've turned my office at home into another bedroom and offered it to a heterosexual friend of Nicky's who's a keeper at the nearby wildlife park. She's a giant of a girl with a mop of striking long, red, curly hair. Rather fittingly, her name is Sandy. Although shy and somewhat introverted, she seems to be settling in okay and gets on fine with Clement.

The final day of the *Mardall's* academic year is a Friday in mid-July. With the Convent having broken up a fortnight ago, I decide to show my face at the end-of-year staff meeting. There are presentations for colleagues who are leaving or retiring plus piles of gratuitous food on offer. Definitely not to be missed. Before we are able to tuck in, however, the staff have to endure more bad news about finances.

"Next year, we shall be offering more senior colleagues the opportunity to take early retirement," Avril informs us gravely. "Failing that, redundancies are, I'm afraid, inevitable."

Let It Be

(Year 5)

And when the night is cloudy,
There is still a light that shines on me.

AUTUMN TERM

"All this talk of redundancies has set off alarm bells," I confess to Marilyn on the first day back at *Mardall's*.

She chuckles dismissively before replying: "Oh, I wouldn't be overly concerned if I were you, young man. I'm sure Avril has every intention of hanging on to enthusiastic, able young teachers like yourself."

I screw up my face. "Even though I'm only part-time?"

"I can't foresee that being an issue. Don't forget, you've got age and flexibility on your side, not to mention your willingness to assist with Evening Classes, extra-curricular activities and holiday courses."

Her words reassure me. As the Head of Department, I feel certain that she'd be the first to know if I were in line for the chop. Whether her choice of the word 'flexible' is a reference to my capacity to teach both French and German to A level standard or my ability to do the splits, I've no idea.

"Oh, by the way," Marilyn says. "On the subject of holiday courses, how was your trip to France?"

She's referring to a course I attended in Annecy during the first week of the summer. A French-speaking colleague who teaches Leisure and Tourism was signed up to go, but withdrew at the last minute on discovering that it wasn't taking place during term time.

"You haven't got any family ties, Al. Surely you could step in and represent the College," Marilyn had proposed. "It'll look good on your CV and prevent us losing the two-hundred-pound enrolment fee."

I fill her in on what was a largely worthwhile venture.

"Excellent!" she says as soon as I've completed my brief account. "Maybe you could provide some detailed feedback for the whole department at our next meeting."

I nod in agreement. My mind then drifts back to my sun-soaked week in Annecy, an idyllic tourist attraction on the Swiss border with breathtaking mountains and vast lakes warm enough to swim in. The town centre itself was almost Venice-like in appearance with its intricate network of artificial waterways and stylish architecture. I revelled in the opportunity to mix with language teachers from other schools and colleges, although I found the oral incompetence of one or two of the more seasoned campaigners rather alarming. Then again, before the mid-eighties, modern languages were generally taught through the medium of English, with scant regard for the training of oral skills. For some reason, reading, writing and listening were always considered more important. Whilst not all the changes in education in recent years are to be applauded, this is one area where I feel progress has definitely been made.

I got on particularly well with a similarly aged Brummie. The two of us grabbed every opportunity to experience the local nightlife. A combination of sun, delicious food and cheap beer fuelled my courage, and I managed to break the ice with a striking local brunette in her early twenties by the name of Emmanuelle. By pure coincidence, she happens to be spending four months in England early next year on a work experience project. What's more, the chemical company that'll be employing her is only about an hour's drive from my house and she suggested paying me a visit without the slightest hesitation. Maybe there is a God, after all.

"Oh, before I forget," Marilyn says, interrupting my reverie. "Val in the Adult Education Office wants to see you. She's had instructions from Finance to amalgamate this year's French and German GCSE Evening Classes."

"What, they want me to teach both languages at the same time?"

"Looks like it."

"Another one of Avril's cost-saving exercises, no doubt?"

"Yes, I'm afraid so. Apparently, the numbers are simply not high enough to justify the employment of two teachers. I know it's not an ideal scenario, but it would provide a perfect opportunity to incorporate our new software programmes into your teaching."

A week later, it's Induction Day for the new students and I'm drafted in to cover for a Set Tutor who's otherwise engaged. I enjoy the proceedings enormously and it reminds me how much I've missed this aspect of the job since becoming a part-time member of staff. It may well generate mounds of additional paperwork, but I find the extra contact with students and their day-to-day problems stimulating.

On the Friday afternoon, I arrive at mum and dad's before gym to the sight of Chloë charging around the garden kicking a football. At the sound of my voice, she abandons her game and sprints towards me, her stubby little legs moving furiously.

"Owl!" she cries out and jumps up into my arms.

After a protracted, bear-like embrace, she lowers herself to the ground, takes my hand and leads me onto the lawn in search of her new toy.

"Owl play," she says, recovering the ball from under a bush and rolling it in my direction.

Together, we enjoy a lengthy kick around until 'owl', obviously overcome by the excitement, inadvertently breaks wind.

"Pooh!" Chloë says, pinching her nose with her right thumb and middle finger and pointing at my backside with the index from her other hand. She doesn't miss a trick, this one.

Dad tells me later that she pointed in similar fashion at a Lotus Elise featured on a recording of *Top Gear* he was watching.

"Owl's car," she said.

Okay, 'owl's' car is a Fiat and twenty years older, but he was, nevertheless, impressed by her ability to recognise a roadster, particularly considering that she was only eighteen months when she last saw mine. She may still be knee-high to a grasshopper, but is as sharp as a blade.

Later on at the gym, Annette Enquist, our former Swedish member, puts in a now rare appearance to complete a survey on sports injuries for her physiotherapy course. Her manner is unmistakably flirtatious, which helps me appreciate how I misread the signs before. Mind you, maybe this is where I've been going wrong in the past – interpreting overt flirting as a positive signal. Perhaps a degree of coyness is a clearer indication of genuine female romantic interest. It certainly was the case with Rachel before she left College. I think the misunderstanding may stem from the fact that, in my opinion, men don't generally bother flirting with women they're not attracted to. I can see why I got the wrong end of the stick.

Based on my experiences of three educational establishments, I'd say that one of the most common disagreements amongst teachers from different curriculum areas concerns the ideal length of teaching periods. Naturally, those responsible for predominantly practical subjects like Art, Design Technology and PE prefer longer sessions whereas those in charge of more theoretical courses usually request ones of shorter duration. As a general rule, language teachers fall into the latter category with the old adage 'little, but often' proving highly applicable.

After much debate, the management here at *Mardall's* has come down on the side of departments seeking extended teaching sessions and devised a new timetable for this current academic year. Double periods of forty-five minutes each will be the norm with the odd triple thrown in for good measure. This means effectively that some members of staff will have no option but to take certain classes for two and a quarter hours in one go – no mean feat when you consider the average attention span of an adult, let alone a teenager. Fortunately, the restrictions imposed by my part-time status, along with my involvement in the PE Department, spare me this torture. One of the new Lower Sixth French groups is scheduled for a triple, with my colleague, Diana Llewelyn, down to replace me after the second period. Looks like the term 'variety of task' will take on a whole new meaning. I don't envy her.

The first Evening Class of the new term kicks off on the middle Thursday in September. Like last year, it's a two-hour session, but there's a difference this time round – I am indeed required to teach both the French and German classes together.

I start off by demonstrating the *Vektor* software to both groups in the small adjoining computer room, then leave the three Germanists to practise on their own whilst I teach the six Francophiles in a more conventional fashion in the main classroom. Fortunately, my task is simplified to a degree by the lack of complete beginners in either group.

After a short coffee break at 8.30, the classes swap over. Whilst the arrangement is far from ideal, it actually works better than I'd feared. Anyway, the priority at the moment is to save the College money.

At the Convent the following day, the lunchtime gym club continues to thrive, although the four-strong group of girls who started out on the A level PE course last year has been whittled down to two. One decided As weren't for her and left the school, the other was withdrawn by her parents so she could attend a clinic to support her struggle against bulimia. According to the Head of Department, eating disorders are now a common problem at the Convent. It appears that the desire for the 'perfect' figure has become a major preoccupation amongst teenage girls in the late nineties. The sad thing is, I'm not convinced that most men, Rupert Stanley apart, prefer the stick insect types that dominate the catwalks and the pages of glossy magazines. Surely there's nothing sexier than a few curves.

By chance, I bumped into the two remaining girls, who are twins, on a couple of occasions during the holidays at *Opportunity Knox*. I was shocked to catch one of them kissing another girl on the dance floor in full view. It really does seem that sexual experimentation is all the rage at the moment.

On the last weekend of the month, a wedding in Scotland provides a further stark reminder of the celibate nature of my existence. The lucky man is Stuart, a former member of the gym club from the days when I was at university and dad was the chief coach. He's a super lad and, although seven years my junior, has found a lovely bride who adores him. It's great to see them at the reception looking so happy, even if I can't deny feeling a tinge of envy.

"Still, at least this proves that it's not always the hard nut, macho types that get the cream," I reflect. "Maybe there's hope for me yet."

In true Scottish tradition, the food is barely enough to fit onto a small coffee table and doesn't appear until 10.45 in the evening. Having made do with a minuscule snack on the coach almost twelve hours ago, I'm famished and bereft of enough energy to consider hitting the dance floor in pursuit of the few apparently single WOMEN. You won't catch me jumping on the sexual diversion bandwagon. As is now customary on many a social outing, there's a teaching connection. The parents of one of my former secondary school pupils are among the guests.

With their honeymoon delayed for a couple of days, the newlyweds kindly put me up for the night. Excessive alcohol and an empty stomach really don't go well together.

At breakfast, my hosts pose the now all too familiar question: when do I intend to get my act together and find a nice young lady with whom to tie the knot? In time for their silver wedding anniversary, perhaps. Why is it everyone assumes it's simply a case of snapping my fingers?

I arrive back home just before 11.00 on Sunday evening and have little choice but to dip immediately into a whole wad of marking and lesson preparation for the week ahead.

"How come so many people view teaching as a part-time occupation?" I ask myself as I extract the relevant files from my school bag and place them on the settee beside me.

No sooner have I picked up a pen than I'm interrupted by the familiar slap of Clement's flip-flops entering the lounge.

"Oh, you're back. Hellooo," he says. "Did you enjoy yourself?"

I answer in the affirmative as he lowers himself into the armchair opposite, a half-empty bottle of Scotch in one hand, a glass in the other.

"Have a drink with me," he says. "I need to talk."

Too weary to put my foot down, I find myself listening to my lodger's latest romantic encounter with a man of a similar age. The marking and preparation are completed, but take twice as long as I'd hoped. Another late night.

It's now the end of October and half term is with us once again. Although all my jobs have been ticking over quite nicely, I have to admit there's been very little excitement on the social front. I suppose I should be grateful for a bit of peace and quiet after the various dramas of the last twelve months.

The trouble is, I've begun to slip into that unpleasantly familiar rut where confidence on my evening excursions to the pubs in town is nowhere to be found. It seems to highlight how dependent I've become on female attention to keep my fragile ego intact. Not for the first time, the only let-up in this area has been provided by a couple of girls in my College trampolining group – Amelia, a lanky six-footer, and Gillian, an averagely-sized brunette with an almost ghost-like complexion.

Whilst I wouldn't want to draw too many comparisons with Cara and Mandy or Rachel and Amanda at this stage, they're both very friendly, if a little cheeky. On discovering by chance that my weekly singing lesson takes place near where they both live, Amelia asked rather boldly during one of the trampolining sessions a couple of weeks ago if I'd mind dropping them home en route. Apparently, the train service isn't very reliable. I couldn't think of a valid reason to decline, so obliged.

The singing lessons themselves have been going really well. Whilst Pavarotti doesn't need to quake in his boots just yet, the teacher has confirmed that her initial fears that I may be tone deaf were unfounded. It just goes to show that, with the possible exception of human relationships, perseverance does have its rewards in the long run.

Over the first weekend of half term, I make a rather nervous appearance in a team trampolining competition in South Wales. I manage to stay on the bed and complete my two ten-bounce routines. I have to acknowledge that it's proving harder than anticipated at the ripe old age of almost thirty-one adapting over two decades of gymnastic technique to competitive trampolining. However, as with the singing, I'm getting there slowly but surely. I stay overnight with my sister and her husband.

In the morning, I learn the all-important art of changing a nappy. When asked if she's done a pooh, Chloë responds by lying down on her back on the floor with her legs in the air. She then waits patiently for her nappy to be inspected. It's a party piece that impresses her uncle enormously as does the fact that she correctly pronounces my name on several occasions. Looks like I won't be the wise old 'owl' for much longer.

Back home, I drive to College on Tuesday morning to use one of the computers. On my arrival, I find that the proposed revamp of the staff car park at the front has already begun. The grass island in the middle and surrounding verges have been dug up and are in the process of being replaced by smart, all-over brick paving. It won't be long before half the cricket field to the right of the main building receives similar treatment as part of Avril and the Governors' latest expansion programme. When challenged at a recent staff meeting to justify such a substantial financial outlay in times of poverty, our esteemed leader claimed that the money was "ring-fenced" and could under no circumstances be used to ease the looming teacher redundancy crisis.

"What's more, an extension to the College parking facilities is a must if we are to expand as an institution and, by so doing, ensure our long-term survival in these difficult times," she insisted. "As you are all now aware, the more students we can accommodate on site, the larger our slice of the cake from the Further Education Funding Council."

I must admit, I haven't a clue about the origins of the term ring-fencing. The authors of my Collins dictionary don't seem to be familiar with it either.

I take a long, melancholic look at the cricket pavilion at the far side of the field and wonder how many student as well as staff matches it's hosted over the years. Since one of the two alternative fields is to be sold off for development and the other is used exclusively for football and rugby, it appears that cricket at *Mardall's Sixth Form College* is soon to become a thing of the past. If Avril's priorities mirror those prevalent throughout the country, it's hardly surprising that in the Test Match arena we've struggled for years as a nation.

On Thursday, Nicky and I meet for lunch and catch up, which doesn't exactly take long on my side. I'm surprised to learn that one of her breasts is naturally smaller than the other and that she'll soon be undergoing surgery for the insertion of a silicone implant. It occurs to me that had I not been so sensitive and straitlaced at her birthday party back in the summer, I may well have witnessed or even felt this size discrepancy myself. The thought remains with me all afternoon.

In the evening at *The Hogshead* – a relatively new addition to the town and renowned for an impressive selection of strong Belgian beers – I overhear a conversation at the bar whilst waiting to be served.

"I definitely recognise you," the barman tells the dark-haired lad standing in front of me. "You sure you didn't go to *Riverside Comp* about … er … seven years ago?"

The lad shakes his head before shifting his position to the left to allow me access to the bar.

"Thanks," I say with a nod. "It's odd, isn't it, when you get mistaken for someone else? I used to get Mark Hammill thrown at me all the time when I was younger. You know, Luke Skywalker."

My use of the word 'thrown' is more literal than it may seem. Whilst on teaching practice, a fourteen-year-old lad hurled a two-inch model of the Star Wars hero in my direction.

"Well, funny you should say that," he replies, turning to face me, "but I am actually a little bit famous."

I take a closer look and realise that the bloke I'm attempting to make polite conversation with is none other than the actor who plays Tiffany's gay brother, Simon, in EastEnders.

"But I'm not … er … you know – my girlfriend's sitting over there," he says hastily, pointing at the far side of the pub.

We exchange a few further formalities before he picks up his drinks from the bar and heads off. Surely he didn't think I was trying to come on to him.

The following morning, I make my usual trip to the Convent on account of the fact that half term there is next week. As soon as I arrive, the Head of PE informs me that she's booked a physiotherapy appointment during the period that falls between lunchtime and my A level PE theory class. I generally use this time for marking and preparation.

"Would you be able to do me an enormous favour and watch over a few of my Year 11 girls on the trampoline?" she asks.

The temperature in the Sports Hall seems lower than usual, so I'm not surprised to see most of the group appear wearing their extra-large school sweatshirts. About ten minutes into the session, a shy girl of oriental appearance climbs onto the bed and begins bouncing with little hint of arm movement.

"Try and get your arms up," I say.

The girl ignores me and continues in the same fashion. I repeat my instructions several times over, but to no avail.

"Come on," I urge again, this time with greater force. "Lift your arms above your head on the upward bounce. Or haven't you got any arms?"

At this point, the girl spotting to my left taps my shoulder to attract attention. I half turn my head to face her without losing sight of my apparently obstinate performer. First with her left, then with her right hand, she proceeds to imitate a sawing motion against the opposite elbow. Never before in my capacity as a teacher or coach have I felt a more intense desire for the floor to open up beneath my feet and swallow me. Rather ignorantly, I'd assumed that the girl on the bed was hiding her hands inside the arms of her baggy sweatshirt as protection from the cold. In reality, it seems that she doesn't have any hands or forearms. Blushing heavily, I make the necessary apologies.

"You could've warned me!" I castigate my superior colleague on her return from the physio.

"Sorry about that," she says. "It completely slipped my mind. But don't beat yourself up over it. She's not a particularly sensitive girl."

Back at *Mardall's* shortly after my seemingly harmless – or should I say 'armless' – comment at the Convent, Hannah Murray, the Head of

Student Activities, asks if I'd be willing to help out with this year's Rag Ball at the beginning of November, even though I'm officially no longer a member of the team.

"It'd be great to have an experienced hand present," she says.

With no girlfriend or exciting social life to deter me, I'm happy to accept.

On the eve of the Ball, my replacement as the Events Organiser rings me at home to warn that she won't be arriving at the club until 9.00, a couple of hours after the doors are due to open. I tell her not to worry as I'll be there at the start. However, after I've hung up, it occurs to me that she's now being paid to do this job and should really make herself available all evening.

Even without the lure of alcohol, the function proves as popular as ever. Just as I'm about to make tracks shortly after midnight, Gillian, from my trampolining group, approaches me with a friend.

"Al," she says, swaying from side to side as if about to ask an awkward question or even a favour. "We've missed the last train. I don't suppose you'd be able to …"

Having established that there are no further strays, I set off with the two girls.

"I hope you appreciate this," I say, glancing at the clock on the dash. "You know, going out of my way on my birthday."

"It's your birthday? Well, in that case, you should be honoured that we're here to celebrate it with you," Gill remarks with a mischievous grin.

It's another late night for me, but I'm not particularly bothered since the buzz of the occasion and the fact that I was able to make myself useful have helped lift my spirits once again.

Following a curtailed night's sleep and a full day at *Mardall's*, I spend the evening of my thirty-first birthday teaching my two adult classes. Despite weeks of trouble-free operation, the computers choose this of all nights to crash. Differentiation with a mixed ability group in one language is challenging enough, but in two languages … Fortunately, they're a patient, understanding crowd and we survive without great trauma. With a class of thirteen-year-olds, it would've been a different ball game, I'm sure. Anyway, anything to save the College money.

"Oh, Al, it can't possibly be rent day again," Clement says wearily on the Saturday after my birthday. "You're bleeding me dry, you know."

He then proceeds to appeal to my good nature by proposing a spot of gardening in lieu of this week's payment.

"Bleeding you dry?" I mutter under my breath. "I haven't noticed a reduction in the crates of JD entering the house. Funny that."

To his credit, Clement works like a slave all afternoon, mowing, trimming and pruning. After three trips to the tip, we're both pretty thirsty and head for *Alfredo's*.

By about 10.00, Clement has knocked back an impressive number of shorts and become somewhat tipsy. To my surprise, he suddenly decides to try his charm on some of the local totty. After a brief exchange of words, each girl in turn makes a hasty retreat.

"No wonder you can't find yourself a girlfriend in this town," he says once we're back at the house. "The women here are quite simply dreadful. What you need is a nice young man."

"But aren't you forgetting something?" I reply good-humouredly.

"Oh, am I? What's that, then?"

"That I wasn't born with a predilection for *young men*."

"Oh, Al, that doesn't matter in the slightest. You only have to look at what happened during the war."

"The *war*?"

"Of course. Everyone knows that homosexuality was rife amongst soldiers deprived of female company. And look what goes on in prisons."

"Mm, perhaps, but I haven't completely lost hope of finding a nice young lady. Not yet, anyway."

"It's a terrible shame, you know. You'd get far less grief from a man."

I head for bed, pondering the roots of non-heterosexual tendencies. Is it nature or nurture? And what about self-esteem? Where does that come from?

Later in the month in *The Hogshead*, I bump into a pair of nineteen-year-olds called Robyn and Natasha who Rupert and I befriended a while back. I hardly need to add that Rupert pulled one of them whilst it was made perfectly clear that neither was the remotest bit turned on by me. Yawn, yawn! They invite me to sit with them.

"Just for a matter of interest," I ask Robyn when her friend is in the loo. "What is it that's so special about Rupert?"

Her reply is immediate: "I think *he's* really good-looking."

"Meaning that I'm not?" I surmise, but refrain from verbalizing.

God, how I despise Rupert sometimes. I wouldn't mind so much if I could actually see what's so amazing about his looks, but I can't. He is over six foot, though.

Just before closing time, I return to our table with a final round of drinks. There's an awkward silence.

"Talking about me again?" I ask.

Robyn bites on her lower lip. "Oh dear, please say you didn't overhear what I just said."

"No, I didn't, but you made it pretty obvious that it was me you were discussing. So, come on, then. What nice things were you saying?"

The girls make such a performance out of trying to dodge the subject that I probe further out of curiosity. Maybe tonight has forced them to see me in a whole new light. And what I'd give right now for a few complimentary remarks.

"All right, then," Robyn yields finally. "I just said to Natasha that I thought you were gormless, that's all."

My heart sinks. Unattractive and gormless at the same time. Terrific! I really don't know why I bother getting up in the morning. Perhaps my neighbour did murder me with his empty whiskey bottle on the first day of the year and I've been living on the outer fringes of hell ever since.

It occurs to me on the way home that had Robyn said something flattering, I'd be off to bed in a totally different frame of mind. At this particular point in my life, it appears that a few simple words can either lift or crush me as easily as a major event.

The following Tuesday, I'm cheered up considerably by the friendly, respectful banter of Amelia and Gillian in the car on the way to my singing lesson. Although only a couple of years younger than Robyn and Natasha, they seem to view me in a completely different light from women I encounter outside teaching, as has frequently been the case with students in my charge. I'm led to wonder whether it's purely my status as a teacher that ensures this or my superior confidence in a work situation. Whatever the case, it's a hugely frustrating state of affairs.

After dropping Amelia home, I turn into a side road on the way to Gillian's house. Suddenly, the latter reaches across from the passenger seat and grabs the wheel, her hand resting on mine in the process.

"Let me steer," she says confidently.

"Er, I don't think so, somehow," I reply.

"Oh, go on, you loser. I can drive really well."

I'm stunned by Gillian's audacity. No previous student has ever spoken to me so brashly whilst still at College. I decline once again.

"Your problem is that you're so unadventurous," she says, her hand still in contact with mine on the wheel. "No wonder you haven't got a woman in your life."

"It's all very well for you to say that, but you're forgetting that I'm a teacher and you're a student, and that there are certain responsibilities that go with the job."

"Yeah, but you only coach me for trampolining. You need to lighten up and get a life."

As I pull away from the front of her house, I begin to wonder whether Gillian was actually hinting at more than just operating the steering wheel of my car. God, I'm hopeless, I know. Anyway, I reckon I made my position clear enough.

Over the next few days, I find myself reflecting on Gillian's hard-hitting words. Maybe she has got a point. Maybe I am simply too conservative and, therefore, boring by definition.

With immaculate timing, a letter arrives shortly afterwards from Emmanuelle, the French girl I met in Annecy in the summer. In it, she confirms in French that her four-month work placement will begin in Swindon in January and expresses the desire to meet up as soon as possible – if I'm still game. You bet I am! She asks if it'll be okay to ring to arrange something once she's arrived in England. I send her a Christmas card with a brief note endorsing her suggestion.

Towards the end of November, the management finally agrees to fork out a bit of extra cash to pay a French assistant from a local school to assist with my Evening Class. Although the French group has found the software useful, several of the less confident members have requested proper teaching for the full two hours. To be honest, I don't blame them. The Germanists, on the other hand, appear satisfied with an hour of me and an hour of the computers. Despite the additional financial outlay, it'll still prove considerably cheaper than employing a couple of qualified teachers for the full two hours.

On the last Wednesday of the month, I arrive at the co-ed private school for my weekly gym session, only to be informed by one of the older lads that there'll be no more gymnastics after next week. Apparently, the school has exhausted its budget for remunerating external coaches.

I track down the activities organiser before leaving and he confirms the abrupt termination of my contract for financial reasons. He apologises for any inconvenience caused, but not for the unfortunate way I found out.

Now that schools and colleges have begun to mimic the world of business in terms of the way they operate, 'appraisal' has become a major buzzword. The management at *Mardall's* has arranged for each member of the teaching staff to be observed and appraised internally by a more senior colleague before the end of the summer term.

The day after the unfortunate news about my coaching job, Marilyn sits in on one of my A level French classes.

"Very good, young man," she says once the last student has filtered out of the room. "I was particularly impressed with your use of the target language and your rapport with the group."

"Oh, thanks very much," I reply.

"And your objectives remained clear throughout. However, I do feel that you could've upped your pace at times."

What is it with women? When you've got them in bed – if my memory isn't betraying me – they're constantly on at you to slow down. Yet out of it, they seem desperate for you to speed up. Are they never satisfied?

On a more serious note, I have to say that Marilyn's predominantly complimentary assessment of my teaching has given me a timely boost. Anyone who's ever stood up in front of others and attempted to teach them day-in, day-out over a protracted period will understand what a thankless task it can be. Open praise is not something frequently encountered in the teaching profession.

In my opinion, it doesn't matter what you do for a living, a few occasional compliments can do wonders for motivation levels and self-esteem. I'm sure this is a basic human requirement that often gets overlooked in this country. You only have to look at our leading sportsmen and sportswomen to see how adept at criticism we are as a nation at the expense of praise and encouragement. Mm, maybe staff appraisal ain't such a bad thing, after all.

On my final visit to the co-ed private school in early December, I find the group surprisingly subdued, not to mention well-behaved. Almost every member of the class thanks me for my efforts and two of the three difficult girls stay behind at the end to express their disappointment.

"It's the best activity we've ever had," one of them states with genuine regret. Her friend nods.

Somewhat taken aback, I set off for the last time, aware that I'm even incapable of seeing through a pair of thirteen-year-old girls. For the best part of fourteen months, I was convinced that they abhorred my gym lessons. Considering that I've been receiving a more than generous fifty-five pounds a week for two hours' work here since going part-time at *Mardall's*, I'll definitely feel the pinch financially.

During the last week before Christmas, two former students from Rachel and Amanda's trampolining group appear out of the blue one lunchtime and ask if they can have a bounce. In the middle of the session, one of them lands awkwardly and twists her neck. Fortunately, there's no major damage, but the sudden recognition that neither girl would be covered by the College insurance policy unsettles me. An ex-student with a broken neck under my supervision is just what I need at the moment.

Christmas at mum and dad's comes and goes in a flash. Before we know it, it's Chloë's second birthday party. Slightly reluctantly, I nip away from the celebrations early in order to attend what has become an extremely rare event – a lunch date with a woman. The lucky lady is Denise, a university French student who works at *Alfredo's* during the holidays. I first got to know her back in the summer, but only recently plucked up the courage to ask her out on a date.

As agreed, I catch up with Denise in the *Virgin Megastore* at 1.00 – her other holiday job. I soon discover that her shift for the day isn't over as I was led to believe and that we'll only have an hour for lunch.

"How are you, then?" I ask cheerfully.

"Really knackered," she grumbles. "I was up half the night talking to my ex."

She emits a heavy, audible sigh before gathering her things and following me reluctantly out of the shop.

"This is gonna be a bundle of laughs," I mutter to myself.

As soon as we're seated at the bistro up the road, my plans to turn on the charm and cheer her up are stalled for a good ten minutes as Denise indulges in a spirited in-depth chat with the waiter who she appears to know and find attractive.

Eventually, the latter brings the discussion to an abrupt close as if suddenly aware of a look of disapproval from his boss. He extracts a notepad from his shirt pocket.

"I'll just have a coffee," Denise says decisively whilst clasping hold of her brown ponytail with both hands, her cheeks more flushed than usual. "Don't feel like food after the night I've had."

I look at her with an air of disappointment. "Oh, go on. I don't want to be eating on my own."

She shakes her head furiously. "Sorry, I just don't fancy anything." She checks her watch before adding: "Anyway, I can't stay long."

Once the waiter has retreated to the kitchen, Denise's face darkens further. I try my utmost to animate her, but am confronted by an endless barrage of protests about the extent of her fatigue. I don't have to be brain of Britain to acknowledge that a lunch date with Alan Bentley is the last thing she'd choose to engage in at this particular juncture in her life.

"I just don't understand it," I whinge to the toilet mirror. "She's always been so friendly towards me in the past and she seemed really enthusiastic when I suggested lunch."

My food arrives just as I'm beginning to run out of conversation starters and there follows a long period of awkward silences whilst I eat.

"So when d'you go back to uni?" I ask finally in a desperate attempt to break the deadlock.

"Not for a couple of weeks," Denise mumbles, peering over her shoulder in the direction of the waiter.

She then removes some loose change from the pocket of her jeans and places it on the table in front of me.

"Here, that should cover my coffee," she says, rising to her feet. "I'll have to get back to the shop now."

I glance at my watch and register at once that we've only been seated here for about forty minutes. With my mouth full, I look on in amazement as Denise retrieves her coat from the back of her chair, picks up her handbag and makes for the exit with a virtually inaudible "See ya".

"There must be something wrong with me," I mutter under my breath. "Otherwise, why would a nice girl like that treat me with such contempt?"

As if taking pity on me, the waiter fails to include Denise's coffee on the bill when I ask to settle up. I query it, but he waves me away. I pocket her change and return hurriedly to Chloë's party where I'm appreciated once again. What would I do without the sanity of my family?

The following evening back at home, I play host to three of my cousins and their other halves. At *Alfredo's*, Denise bounds over to our table and demands to be reimbursed the few quid she left at the bistro for her drink.

With knitted brows, I say: "I beg your pardon?"

"My friend," she says. "He told me he didn't charge you for it."

I chuckle. "Oh, and there I was thinking he fancied me."

She sniggers unkindly. "Huh! D'you really think *you're* attractive to men?"

For once, I'm lost for words. It's at this point that my cousin, Toby, now eighteen, comes to the rescue. Leaning forwards towards Denise, he asks, with a perfect deadpan expression: "D'you think *you're* attractive to men?"

Ignoring his comment, she snatches the money from my outstretched hand, turns on her heels and storms off back to her position behind the bar.

"Nice one, Toby!" his sister, Susannah, says.

I pat him on the back out of appreciation for his timely, face-saving interception.

The remainder of the evening proves highly enjoyable. We all return to the house at closing time to arrange the pile of pillows and duvets amassed on the lounge floor. I go to bed, wondering how all three of my younger cousins have managed to find such lovely, compatible partners so easily.

"Perhaps they're just nicer, more interesting people than I am," I sigh as I turn out the light.

SPRING TERM

Two days into '97 and I'm just beginning to sober up properly after seeing in the New Year at *Opportunity Knox* in the company of a friendly giant called Jamie, whose older brother employs Nicky, and some of his friends. Contrary to recent form and expectations, I managed to pull three times. Well, that's if you can count the fact that it was the same girl on three separate occasions during the course of the evening.

The girl's name is Rhiannon Smith. I've known her for over fifteen years since her parents lived just round the corner from mine and her older brother and sister both came to the gym club many years ago. To boot, the whole family has turned out in force for my old amateur dramatics group for as long as anyone in the town can remember. It was Rhiannon who was responsible for my one and only experience of illegal substances, sitting in the lane outside *The Combine Harvester* one night after a show. We walked home together afterwards and kissed a bit on our way through the churchyard, although to be fair Rhiannon seemed less up for it than I was. Given her lack of enthusiasm on this previous encounter, I was rather surprised to find her coming on to me the other night – three times. But naturally, there had to be a fly in the ointment. After each bout of kissing, she told me in no uncertain terms that she didn't fancy me.

"Why would a woman repeatedly kiss a bloke she didn't fancy?" I ask myself as I chew over the events of thirty-six hours ago. "Was she just drunk or was I the only mug who'd responded to her advances?"

Watching EastEnders in the evening, I find myself identifying with Grant's friend, Nigel, who attracts a significant amount of female interest, but never really makes much headway. At the end of the day, he's just a nice bloke, the sort many women would love to have as a big brother. God, how I detest that label! I suppose I should be grateful for the fact that I have had some entertaining romantic encounters in the past – even if they were short-lived – when there are men out there who never pull. Mind you, I do wonder whether the frustration is less intense when you've no idea what you're missing.

Clement returns from Cornwall later in the day, having spent Christmas and New Year with Darren, his latest boyfriend.

"Oh, we had a ghastly time," he sneezes into an embroidered handkerchief. "Spent the entire week laid up in bed together with flu."

Perish the thought!

My Annecy girl, Emmanuelle, rings late on Saturday afternoon to announce that she was confused by the one-way system in town and has ended up in Sainsbury's car park. I head out to rescue her. After offering her hand rather formally, she follows me back to the house.

My initial attempts at conducting a conversation in English are largely unproductive as Emmanuelle's confidence in the language proves rather shaky. Once I've switched to French, however, her mood brightens dramatically, and we talk openly and effortlessly for a good couple of hours. Her intelligence and air of maturity inspire me with confidence.

By the time we've taken our seats at *Ten Tenths* and are ready to order, my disastrous pre-New Year date with Denise is well and truly forgotten. When the waitress appears with our starters, it does cross my mind briefly that dinner here with the opposite sex has never turned out to be a good omen in the past, but then I've never been particularly superstitious, and the food and ambience are hard to beat locally. Nevertheless, there is one important lesson I've learnt as a result of my previous first dates here in town – avoid Rupert Stanley at all costs.

Emmanuelle proves delightful company during our three-course meal and I can't help feeling a rush of excitement, which I have to fight to contain. In addition to her appealing personality, I find myself hugely attracted to her gorgeous brown eyes, matching hair and olive skin. It also hasn't escaped my attention that her bodily proportions are exactly to my taste – curvy yet well toned. In my mind's eye, I see Basil Fawlty dancing a merry jig on the spot and kissing the heavens out of thanks for God's life-saving intervention.

With dinner successfully behind us, my sexy date and I move on to *The Hogshead* where I feel confident of dodging the likes of Rupert. No sooner have the doorman waved us through into the crowded bar than I'm accosted by an eighteen-year-old girl who spoke to me at length a while back, but has barely bothered to acknowledge me since. There follows an enormous bear hug and a smacker of a kiss on my right cheek.

"What the hell's going on here?" I ask myself. "Oh well, I spose it won't do any harm to appear popular in front of my attractive guest. On past experience, it should even improve my chances with her."

Whilst in the queue for drinks, another eighteen-year-old who I hardly know – or is she seventeen? – approaches me in similar fashion, repeating the hug and kiss-on-the-cheek routine. Like the first, she gives Emmanuelle the once-over before asking where I met my lady friend. I explain briefly. As soon as she's on her way, I turn to Emmanuelle and smile confidently. To my surprise, she returns an expression of total disapproval, her eyes full of fire and ears exuding large puffs of smoke.

"Qu'est-ce qu'il y a?" I ask, somewhat bemused.

She snorts before glancing in the opposite direction. Mystified by her seemingly exaggerated reaction, I decide to focus my attention on accessing the bar.

It soon becomes apparent, however, that it's going to take considerably more than a few additional glasses of wine to appease Emmanuelle. For the remainder of the evening, she acts out the role of the offended girlfriend, and the flowing conversation and good humour of earlier cease. My confidence nosedives as a result, allowing the familiar self-doubts of old to return with a vengeance.

"Someone up there must really have it in for me," I mutter wearily.

At this point, I see Basil shaking his fist furiously at the heavens with the accompanying words of sarcasm: "Thank you, God! Thank you so bloody much!"

Back at the house, Emmanuelle surprises me once again. Instead of sloping off to bed to continue her sulk, she insists on staying up to watch TV. I offer her more wine, but she declines in favour of a soft drink. With her eyes glued to the screen, conversation proves even more torturous than in the pub.

"Oh, bugger! I'm really out of my depth here," I tell myself. "I just don't have enough experience of relationships to know how to salvage the situation. If it is salvageable, that is."

After about an hour, Emmanuelle rises to her feet with a wide yawn.

"You are certain I can have your room?" she says. "You do not mind the sofa?"

Not for the first time, it strikes me how atypical her French accent and pronunciation are. Maybe it's because Annecy is so close to Switzerland.

"No, I'll be fine down here," I reply, although in truth I'd give my right arm to join her upstairs in my bed. If only I had the bottle to suggest it. Then again, it'd almost certainly go down like a lead balloon in her current frame of mind. Memories of Fran ripping her clothes off in front of me on our first date seem a million miles away.

When my visitor surfaces in the morning, I'm surprised to discover that she's not in a desperate hurry to leave. I drive her to the City where we spend several hours drifting around the town window-shopping. Emmanuelle insists on paying for lunch. The atmosphere is marginally better than it was last night after our arrival at *The Hogshead*, but still a far cry from scaling the heights of dinner and the few hours before.

Back home, Emmanuelle decides to make tracks late afternoon. She expresses concern that she may struggle to find the M4 in the fading light, so I offer to lead her there. She accepts.

At the motorway junction, she thanks me rather formally for letting her stay, her unaffectionate kiss goodbye leaving little doubt that our meeting was not a success.

"I just don't know what I did wrong," I whinge to Clement on my return.

"Sounds as if you behaved quite charmingly," he says. "I'm sure everything will be just fine."

Later in bed, it occurs to me that my sinking self-esteem may well be clouding my perception of other people's reactions to an even greater extent than usual.

"Maybe Clement's right," I concede. "Maybe she just wanted to slow things down."

Eager to put my mind at rest, I call Emmanuelle a couple of days later. I ask first about her job. She tells me that it's started well and that everyone has been very friendly towards her. However, when I suggest we meet up again soon, there's a protracted silence.

"Perhaps," she says finally, just as I'm beginning to wonder if we've been cut off. "But I think not for quite a while."

"Quite a while." What's that supposed to mean? A week? A month? Ten years? Certain that this is Emmanuelle's way of declining tactfully, I wish her well and hang up disconsolately. I guess I'll never discover now exactly how those two girls managed to turn the course of our date.

Talk about kicking a man when he's down. Shortly after my soul-destroying phone call, I find a gaping split on one side of my circumcision scar. A rather sore one at that.

"Bloody hell!" I curse aloud. "How can this've happened when I haven't had sex for over a year? Whatever next?"

For the remainder of the week, I apply regular smidgens of Savlon first thing in the morning and last thing at night, but to no avail.

Anxious that I may've developed an infection, I drop into the health centre on Saturday morning on the off-chance of getting my war wound checked over. It transpires that my designated GP is on holiday, but there's an appointment available with a locum. To my initial shock, this turns out to be a young Asian woman barely out of medical school.

"So what can I do for you, Mr Bentley?" she asks, looking directly at me, her face beaming with youthful exuberance.

After several faltering, unsuccessful attempts to describe the exact nature of my ailment, I decide I have little option but to reveal it in the flesh. I unzip my jeans and carefully extract my tool. I then hold it up to the light for the young doctor to scrutinise.

"Oh, yes, it's definitely infected," she says almost squeamishly, withdrawing her eyes sharply from the scene of her examination. She searches for a pad on her desk and picks up a pen. "I'll prescribe you a special cream."

She hands over the prescription hurriedly and sends me on my way without any further eye contact.

"Poor girl," I chortle as I close the door behind me. "Hope I haven't given her second thoughts about her chosen career."

Since making it clear to Gillian before Christmas that I have no intention whatsoever of being led astray by one of my students, she seems to have calmed down. This may also have something to do with the fact that her brother is, apparently, about to undergo an operation to remove a cancerous lump.

"Now that my parents are divorced, I hardly ever see my mum," she discloses on the penultimate Tuesday of the month, "and I'm terrified of losing my brother too."

At first, I wonder whether this is an attention-seeking ploy. Then, fearing that I'm in danger of becoming an old cynic, I offer myself as a sounding board.

Over the next few days, Gillian stops me in the corridor at regular intervals with the latest news on her brother. Her mood on each occasion is uncharacteristically sombre, so I try my best to cheer her up.

On the day after her brother's scheduled operation, Gillian tells me rather vaguely that everything went fine. She then slips into the conversation the fact that her ex-boyfriend is keen to go out with her again and that she'll probably accept.

On the subsequent two Tuesdays, both Gillian and Amelia find alternative means of returning home after trampolining. Whilst I'm not ashamed to admit that I'll miss their company, I think it'll be safer and, therefore, less stressful for me if they continue to keep their distance.

For the first time in three years, I receive a Valentine's card on 14th Feb – a beautiful handmade one, in fact. The inside is decorated with the words *I love you, Al*, followed by about thirty spidery kisses. There's no disguising the writing – it's from dear little Chloë, my gorgeous niece.

In the evening, Clement returns late to the house in a highly drunken and confused state. He appears desperate to talk. Not for the first time, I listen patiently to what he has to say.

"You know, Al, I would've taken my life years ago if it weren't for my mother," he says rather alarmingly.

"But I thought things had really taken off with you and Darren," I reply.

"So did I. At New Year, we even talked about getting a flat together in London."

"Well, there you are, then."

"Only, now he says he's having second thoughts."

He lowers his bearded chin dejectedly and stares into a half empty glass of cider – his other tipple.

I try to reassure him: "Moving in with someone's a big step. He's probably just got the jitters."

But my efforts are in vain. Over the next twenty minutes or so I have to endure further talk of suicide.

"You see, Al, I've lost my *joie de vivre*," he says finally.

"And I'll lose mine if you decide to slash your wrists in my lovely house," I think, but refrain from voicing.

In stark contrast to Clement, who actively seeks my company, my other lodger, Sandy, appears to actively evade it. Since taking my box room last summer, she's turned into a proper little hermit, so much so that she even eats her meals up in the confines of her bedroom. It hasn't escaped my attention that a selection of four-legged creatures from her job at the nearby wildlife sanctuary have spent the night in her company, among them a pigmy goat, a chinchilla and various breeds of rat. In fact, it was only the other day that she raised the issue of breeding chinchillas in the shed at the bottom of the garden. Apparently, babies market for several hundred quid each. I promised to chew over the idea.

To be honest, I'd be more enthusiastic about Sandy's suggestion if she made a little more effort to be civil towards Clement and me. A week or so ago, at about 9.00 in the evening, I knocked on her door and requested politely that we swap cars round in the drive so I wouldn't have to do it first thing in the morning when she left for work. Considering I didn't have to be at the Convent until midday, it seemed a sensible proposal. However, Sandy claimed to be in bed, then bit my head off when I offered to move the car myself. The outcome: I had to get up at 7.00. Once again, I haven't a clue what it is I do to command so little respect from some – make that *most* – of the women I know outside my family and job.

Towards the end of the month, there's an INSET day at work. With all the teachers gathered together in the Library, Avril seizes the opportunity to announce an update on the current staffing crisis. For the first time, she conveys precise details of the departments most heavily overstaffed and, therefore, most likely to be hit by redundancies before the May 31st deadline. History and Modern Languages are revealed as the two largest curriculum areas under imminent threat. By Avril's reckoning, there are one and a half language teachers too many. Rather frustratingly, she refuses to provide any indication of which colleagues are in line for the chop until after the next Governors' meeting in late March.

A time management session is scheduled for the afternoon. Marilyn and I are spared the flip charts and tedious brainstorming in order to meet a rep from a satellite TV company. Marilyn is keen to replace our existing system in the Language Lab. The new equipment on offer proves to be vastly superior and the prospect of acquiring it for next year to compliment our teaching excites both of us.

"Have you been given any idea which of us Avril intends to get rid of?" I ask informally once the rep has made tracks.

"No, not at all. I'm as much in the dark as you are, young man," she replies. "Still, I suppose it won't be long before I'm granted that pleasure."

On the way home, I conclude that my senior colleague's decision to involve me in her future plans for the Language Lab must be a positive sign. It also occurs to me that the management is probably waiting for the OfSTED Inspection in mid March to be over before committing itself to specific redundancies. After all, it couldn't possibly risk disgruntled members of staff rocking the boat.

Just before the start of the Inspection, my sister gives birth to a five-pound baby boy – James. Although exceptionally tiny, he's given a full bill of health. By all accounts, Chloë is over the moon about having a little brother.

When the dreaded week of reckoning arrives, there's an unmistakable cloud of unease hanging over each individual member of the Modern Language Department. Okay, Inspections send a shiver down the spine of most teachers at the best of times. Under normal circumstances, however, there isn't the accompanying threat of redundancy looming large on the horizon. It's as if we all feel that our performance during the round of lesson observations could help to influence a decision on our immediate professional futures.

I arrive at College early on Tuesday morning to discover that both staff photocopiers are out of order, preventing me from copying an answer sheet onto an overhead projector transparency. Typically, the lady inspector appears at my period one Upper Sixth French lesson and takes a seat at the back. With speaking exams just round the corner, I continue with my recent policy of insisting that one lesson a week begins with an oral presentation by one of the group on a chosen topic – all part of the final run-in. On this particular occasion, the honour befalls Adrian Major, arguably the brightest male language student I've ever taught. He presents an impressive exposé on the Channel Tunnel, which kick-starts the lesson superbly. I then take over and lead a discussion on various key aspects of a French novel we've been studying. The students then embark on a series of follow-up written exercises, which I just have enough time to go over at the end.

"It was an excellent lesson," the inspector says kindly. "You've certainly got some very able students, particularly the boy who gave the presentation. The only point I'd make is that it might've been helpful to put up the answers to the exercises on the overhead projector."

Sodding photocopiers!

By Wednesday afternoon, all members of the department have been observed teaching. The inspector summons us all to Marilyn's room for the initial feedback. To our unanimous relief, she informs us that the positives easily outweigh the negatives in every area and that we've earned a grade two as a department.

The following day, Kelly Thompson, a pretty half English, half Caribbean girl from Adrian Major's group, who I've been helping with grammar in one of my frees following a poor showing in the mocks, asks if I'll miss her when she's gone.

"Of course I will," I reply instinctively.

"I'll miss you too," she says in a somewhat lugubrious manner.

I'm flattered by her confession, although I can't help wondering for the umpteenth time what it is I do to impress the ladies in the classroom yet manage to screw up so consistently with those I meet in the outside world. Am I really a different person? It's strange because that's what I like so much about teaching in a Sixth Form College – the fact that I don't feel I have to put on a front in order to teach successfully.

The term ends with the assessment of nine PE students who elected back in September to offer gymnastics as part of their practical component. The club where I trained for my Past Masters competitions provides the venue. The students are impressed by the facilities, which are far superior to the modest ones they've been used to at *Mardall's* over the last year. All the preparation pays off, with each one putting on a good show for the assessor, a certain Alan Bentley.

Complete with a list of carefully recorded marks to send off to the Exam Board, I leave the club at about 7.00, relieved at the prospect of eighteen days without the worry of Inspection and free from redundancy-related gossip.

At the beginning of the Easter holidays, I'm summoned to mum and dad's for a few days to keep an eye on Auntie Flo whilst they're away. The latter encourages me to go out in the evening. I decide to turn back the clock and visit *Clifford's*, my old haunt. Since my parents and Auntie moved to a nearby village last year, it's no longer on the doorstep. Too stingy to call a taxi for the four and a half-mile trek, I resolve to making the journey by foot.

It's now the following morning and I'm reflecting on my bizarre excursion to *Clifford's*, which resulted in a trip in a police car and a night all but spent in bed with an eighty-three-year-old woman. Taking pity on a poor lad staggering home after a night on the tiles, a couple of local cops stopped their patrol car in the early hours and offered me a lift home. With a further three miles to complete, I was only too happy to take advantage of their generosity. Back at mum and dad's, I nipped to the bathroom in the middle of the night to relieve myself. In my semi-conscious state, I then returned to the first bedroom on the left rather than the second. I was just about to climb back into bed when Auntie woke with an enormous start. Her cry was enough to bring me round fully. We both had a good laugh, particularly once I realised the likely reason for my blunder – in my own house, first on the left from the bathroom is my bedroom whereas second on the left is Clement's.

A few days later, I have dinner at *Ten Tenths* in the company of a woman in her early twenties called Sandra Priest who I met years ago at Easter when her boyfriend was working as a barman at *Clifford's*. Only, at the time, I didn't know he was her boyfriend, hence my decision to try out a corny chat-up line on her in an attempt to impress my friend and colleague, Simon Lennon.

"Is it okay if I chat you up?" I asked. "You see, my friend over there's boring me."

Fully expecting a slap, I was surprised to find the girl oblige. Before the evening was out, she slipped me her number when her boyfriend wasn't looking.

I rang the next day and agreed to Sandra's suggestion that we go out for Sunday afternoon tea. Following this, she invited me back to meet her parents and brother who I joined in a game of Scrabble. Whilst we were playing, Sandra insisted on hand-feeding me bits of Easter egg in between frequent calls to her boyfriend. I concluded that I wasn't really in with a shout and didn't contact her again, although we have bumped into each other two or three times since. On our last meeting, Sandra invited herself over.

"So why did you give me your number that night at *Clifford's* and suggest we meet up when you had a boyfriend?" I ask once the starters have arrived.

"I wasn't very happy in the relationship," she says, "and was hoping you'd provide a way out."

Through the main course, she proceeds to talk about life forces and conversations with trees, which I find a bit odd.

By the time we've made it to the *Six Chickens* pub just along from *The Hogshead*, I've decided that we really aren't compatible. I approach the bar for a round of drinks.

"Just a glass of water for me, please," Sandra says.

"I'm sorry, we only serve tap water to regular customers," the middle-aged landlady replies. What?

We take the nearest available seat, only to discover that there's a bit of a draft, which prompts Sandra to shiver. I close the offending window.

"Who shut this window?" the landlady roars a few minutes later.

"I did," I say, raising a tentative palm. "My friend here was cold."

"Well, sit somewhere else, then. This is my pub and when I open a window, I expect it to stay open."

Incensed by such unnecessary rudeness, I open my mouth to protest, but think the better of it. I'm not sure exactly what's going on in this town at the moment. The landlady in *The Barley Mow* frequently tells the punters to "fuck off" at closing time. She also turned on a group of French students recently on a Thursday night for being too rowdy. I commented in their defence that the noise level was far inferior to that made on a typical Friday or Saturday evening.

"That may well be the case, Mr Know-all Teacher," she snapped, "but on a Thursday, my baby sleeps in the room directly above the bar and there's no way I'm having him woken up."

"And at weekends?" I asked.

"At weekends, he's in the back bedroom."

It seems that good public relations are no longer a priority among some of the local pub owners. I may make myself unpopular by saying this, but I do wonder sometimes whether the push for sexual equality is having an adverse effect on traditional femininity.

Back at the house, Sandra makes no bones about revealing her interest in me. Unable to resist a long-awaited boost to my self-confidence, I allow her to kiss me on the settee. All right, it was me who made the first move. Before I have chance to think it through, we've climbed the stairs and jumped into my bed half-naked.

"I'm not going to let you make love to me," Sandra says firmly. What's left of my fast-fading conscience is relieved to hear it.

"You wouldn't want to go too far and lead her to believe a relationship could follow," it advises me.

Despite her rather weird declarations at *Ten Tenths*, Sandra is a genuine girl with a good figure and I find the kisses and cuddles that follow undeniably pleasurable.

"Oh, you've got such a gorgeous body," Sandra says suddenly. "I want you to really turn me on."

"But ... but I thought you said...," I half reply.

Now I've got a dilemma on my hands. Talk about head and heart – this is much more a case of pure self-control.

Unable to resist the strong urges from down below and egged on by a rapidly swelling ego, I step up the foreplay.

"Hey, what you doing?" Sandra asks. "I told you nothing's going to happen."

Miffed that I've allowed myself to get carried away, I back off. A few minutes later, however, history repeats itself. Sandra reiterates her desire for me to "seriously turn her on", so I respond instinctively, only to be reminded quite firmly that "nothing's going to happen".

Over the course of the next thirty minutes or so, the charade continues, both of us fighting a desperate battle to keep our physical impulses in check. With the effects of the wine and beer from earlier gradually diminishing, my head finally takes control and I put a stop to the farce. I get dressed. Sandra follows suit.

Shortly after 1.00, she heads off in her parents' classic Mercedes, safe in the knowledge that nothing untoward happened.

"Phew!" I sigh as her car disappears out of site. "That was a close one."

More than ever before, I have to acknowledge how vulnerable I am at this stage in my life to even unwanted female interest. Why are mutual feelings of attraction so hard to come by?

SUMMER TERM

During the first week back at *Mardall's*, I pass Cynthia Burrows, one of the History teachers, on the *Grosvenor* stairs. A diminutive, rather frail-looking woman in her late forties, Cynthia devoted many years of her adult life to caring for an elderly mother until the latter's recent death. It's no exaggeration to say that she's one of the most genuine, sweet-natured people you could possibly meet.

"Hello, Al," she says, greeting me warmly. "I don't know whether you've heard, but rumour has it that the management has decided to pursue a policy of 'last in, first out'."

"No, I haven't," I reply. "But surely that would leave Michael Lancaster in the frame in your department."

"Not at all. Michael arrived the year before I did."

"Oh, Cynthia, I'm really sorry. Let's hope it's just a rumour."

"Well, with any luck, we might hear more at tomorrow's staff meeting."

She smiles bravely before clasping hold of the banister and continuing down the stairs, one cautious step at a time.

I stand motionless for a few seconds, trying to figure out the exact implications of a 'last in, first out' policy in the Language Department. In theory, this would target Pamela Robertson, Desmond Willis' replacement as Head of German, but surely it'd reflect badly on the management and its future planning strategy if she were dismissed just over a year after her appointment.

At the staff meeting the following day in the Library, Avril confirms to a full house that a joint decision has been reached by the management and Governors to the effect that redundancies will be determined through the adoption of a 'last in, first out' policy.

"However, this will not apply to any colleague in a managerial position," she says.

There's a buzz of unease amongst those present. It doesn't take long for me to register the fact that this would save Pamela Robertson's skin at the expense of my own. I feel a heavy, painful blow to the back of my skull.

"We believe this to be the fairest method in the most trying and unpleasant of circumstances," our leader says rather uncomfortably.

She then hands over to the Bursar who, with the aid of an overhead projector and a plethora of figures and statistics, attempts to prove that a trimming of certain departments is financially unavoidable. He's replaced by Economics teacher and Union Rep, Dennis Waterton, a tall, slim man in his early thirties with snow white hair. He presents alternative figures, which counter the claim that redundancies are inevitable. His calculations are based on the fact that there's still a considerable amount of money in the College contingency fund – easily enough to postpone any decisions on redundancy for another year. And with a General Election at the beginning of next month ...

After Dennis has retired to his seat to unanimous applause, Avril takes centre stage once again.

"I'm afraid that the money Dennis was referring to is ring-fenced for essential maintenance repairs and updates on certain classrooms," she says. "In other words, our hands are tied and it remains unreleasable for other purposes."

'Ring-fenced', eh? How I've come to loathe that expression.

Still with a sore head and rather numb from Avril's disclosure, I encounter a furious Marilyn on my way out of the meeting.

"I'm so sorry, Al!" she seethes. "I just can't believe that the management has had the audacity to arrive at such cutting decisions without first consulting the relevant Heads of Department."

My mood on the way home is one of deep despondency. My job at *Mardall's* has formed the cornerstone of my existence for almost five years. It's helped me rediscover the magic of my childhood after more mundane, less inspiring times as a university student and secondary school teacher.

"Thirty-one years old and without a girlfriend," I tell myself. "And soon, I'll be without a job too. Is there no end to this misery?"

My observation is, admittedly, rather melodramatic. Not that anyone could blame me for such a kneejerk reaction, I suppose.

On the first day in May, Labour wins a landslide victory in the General Election, bringing to a close almost twenty years of Conservative rule. Tony Blair takes up residence at number ten as one of the youngest Prime Ministers in history. The wave of optimism sweeping the country is echoed in the Staff Room at *Mardall's* where there's a firm belief that the new government will deliver its promise to invest considerable sums of additional cash into the education system.

"Just not in time to save the likes of me," I ponder rather gloomily.

Whilst I can't deny that I feel incredibly sorry for myself at the moment, I have to spare a thought for my German-teaching colleague, Thelma Parker, who will almost certainly join me on the scrap heap after twelve years of loyal service. What's more, she actually applied for the vacant Head of German position, only to be passed over in favour of Pamela Robertson, an outsider. Having helped the College out by running the department with my assistance for over a year prior to Pamela's appointment – and very successfully too – she has every reason to feel severely aggrieved. In the circumstances, you really do have to question the wisdom of Pamela's employment, given that the threat of redundancies has been with us for the best part of three years.

Just to cheer me up, both Clement and Sandy announce almost simultaneously that they'll be moving out shortly. Clement's boyfriend, Darren, has definitely agreed to share a flat in London and Sandy has found a larger room for similar money, presumably with a shed in the garden substantial enough for the breeding of chinchillas.

As if this isn't enough to threaten my finances, I discovered the other day that the three-year fixed rate on my mortgage has expired, leaving me tied in to a much higher rate of interest for a further two years. This will mean an increase in my monthly premium of eighty-five pounds. It never rains …

A few days after the election, I arrange to see Avril in her office.

"When am I likely to receive official confirmation of my redundancy?" I ask. "It's just that I need to start making decisions about my future."

"I'm afraid I'm not as yet in a position to say for certain," she replies. "But probably next week."

"So there is still an element of doubt?" I add, clutching at straws. "I mean, my job could be safe?"

Avril places her head on one shoulder in a now familiar display of sympathy. "Sadly, that is an unlikely state of affairs, Al."

In a final act of desperation, I seize the opportunity to remind her of my dedication to the College. I mention my extra-curricular contributions, my willingness to assist with Exchanges and take on board Evening Class and Easter Revision Course responsibilities.

"But you were well remunerated for the latter two," she says, with little hint of diplomacy.

I feel the urge to point out that none of my language colleagues was prepared to offer his or her services, but instead, I opt to slip in the fact that I haven't missed a single day through illness in the five years since my appointment.

Avril's left ear moves a notch closer to her shoulder. "I deeply regret the situation that we find ourselves in and would like to emphasize once again how grateful myself and the Governors are for all the sterling work you've done for the College. We had hoped that some of your more senior colleagues would snap up the more than generous early retirement package on offer, thus avoiding the need for redundancies. Unfortunately, not one of them has been tempted."

"Okay," I cede finally, "but you do understand my impatience to receive official confirmation so that I can begin to look for another job."

"Absolutely! I shall endeavour to get a letter out to you by the middle of next week."

"Thank you. I'd appreciate that."

"By the way, I think you should be aware that if you are successful in finding alternative employment in education for September, you will not be entitled to redundancy pay."

Ouch! I storm out of the Principal's office, biting hard on my lower lip. Surely this has to be the lowest point in my professional life to date.

I make a rapid call to the local external Union Rep and explain my situation. He reassures me that it should be possible to engineer a break in service and advises that I crack on with searching for another position.

On Friday morning, I scan the recruitment pages of the *Times Education Supplement* (*TES*) and find two vacancies in the area for language teachers – one in a Further Education College, the other in a boys' private school. I phone both and request further details and an application form. On account of the fact that house prices are reported to be on the up, I also arrange for an estate agent to come round to value my property.

On Monday of the third week in May, Avril confirms that notice of my redundancy will arrive in my pigeonhole by midweek.

When I check my pigeonhole at the close of play on Wednesday, there's no sign of my redundancy letter. The Principal is nowhere to be found, so I seek out her deputy, Clive Moss, whose daughter I taught for French during my first two years at *Mardall's*. She got an A. Unaware of Avril's whereabouts, he assures me that the letter will appear tomorrow.

On my arrival at College in the morning, I discover that Avril is out for the day. Clive seems genuinely upset after his promise of yesterday and charges into his superior's office where he retrieves a letter off the large oak desk. As he runs through the contents with me, I can't fail to notice tomorrow's date at the top – when I'm scheduled to be at the Convent.

"Nice to see the Principal's got her priorities right," I mutter, with a slow shake of my head. "You wouldn't believe a professional's livelihood was at stake."

With furrowed brows, Clive apologises profusely for what's happened. I sense genuine regret in his tone of voice.

"I'm pleased to say, though," he announces, with a tactfully restrained smile and a tickle of his greying moustache, "that the Governors have agreed to grant you your full redundancy entitlement of two thousand pounds with or without a break in service."

Clive places the letter in an envelope and hands it over. He then shakes my right hand firmly with the accompanying words: "Many thanks for everything you've done here, Al. Our loss is another college's gain."

Despite being kept on tenterhooks for most of the week, I leave on Thursday afternoon, fully aware that the events of the last month were not just a bad dream and that my demise is now reality. By the middle of July, my dream job at *Mardall's Sixth Form College* will be consigned to history. Two thousand pounds for eight years' commitment to the county. Doesn't seem a lot to show for my efforts.

Thelma and Cynthia also receive confirmation of their redundancy, along with a handful of other colleagues in smaller departments.

Every black cloud has a silver lining say some and, despite my current mood of misery, I have to admit that there may well be some truth in the old proverb. Two separate estate agents have valued my house at seventeen thousand pounds more than I paid for it, and I've been called for interview at the FE College and the private school.

My interview at the private school – *Royal David's* – comes first on the middle Tuesday in May. I find myself immediately warming to the incoming Head of Department, Brian Woolly, a balding, highly enthusiastic family man in his mid-forties. The sporting facilities are superb and, with the promise of a significant amount of A level teaching in the mixed Sixth Form, I enter the Head's office in the afternoon in an optimistic frame of mind.

As I stand ready to leave about half an hour later, however, the bubble has all but burst. Although an extremely likeable man, talk of upholding the Catholic faith and leading boys in prayer has put serious doubts in my mind. Whilst I may have no fundamental objections to religion, I'm hardly a practising Christian.

"It's been most interesting talking to you, Mr Bentley," he says, offering me a long, bony hand. "You should be hearing from me in a couple of days."

Back home in the evening, I'm surprised by a phone call from the Head at *Royal David's*.

"We thought you were an ideal candidate," he says with almost exaggerated enthusiasm, "and would be delighted if you would agree to join the staff."

Caught on the hop, I decide quickly that I have no option but to lay my cards on the table. I convey my reservations about teaching in a Catholic school and betray the fact that I have another interview on Thursday.

"Fair enough," he says phlegmatically. "I appreciate your honesty. I'm fully prepared to wait until Thursday evening for a decision."

"Oh, congratulations!" Clement beams when I return to the kitchen. "At least you've got something to fall back on. Mainly boys, is it? I don't suppose there's a vacancy for a master in charge of wielding the cane?"

Randy old sod!

My interview at the FE College proves to be rather more conventional in nature due to the fact that I'm introduced to the other short-listed candidates. This was not the case on Tuesday at *Royal David's*. We're shown around the campus in the morning by a group of students and it doesn't take me long to realise that the working environment is largely reminiscent of *Mardall's*, if arguably more modern.

By mid-afternoon, I find myself sitting expectantly in the Principal's office, confronted by the four-strong interview panel. At this point,

I harbour no doubts whatsoever that this is the job for me. The excitement stirs me into action and I give a performance that I'm more than satisfied with. Then again, interviews have seldom fazed me.

"Having taken a good look at the College this morning, Mr Bentley," the Principal says finally, "may I ask if you'd be willing to accept the post if we were to offer it to you?"

"To be honest, I've been very impressed by everything I've seen and would love to work here," I reply. "Only, I do need to ask about my salary before committing myself to an answer. You see, my mortgage has just gone up and ..."

"Yes, yes, very wise." He sifts through a pile of papers on the desk in front of him. "Let me see. You'd be earning something ... erm ... something in the region of ... er ... sixteen thousand pounds."

My lower jaw sinks towards my lap. Whilst I was aware that FE College salaries fall short of those existing in Sixth Form Colleges, I had no idea the difference would amount to a humungous six thousand quid. With the private school offering me slightly more than my *Mardall's* salary, it doesn't take long to decide that I'd be crazy to take a job that would seriously impinge on my current standard of living. All of a sudden, the thought of leading boys in prayer doesn't seem quite so daunting, after all. With regret, I politely disclose to the panel that I'd not be in a position financially to incur such a heavy drop in salary. They seem to understand.

Later, back at home, I receive a courtesy call from the Principal.

"It's always a pleasure to meet bright, young teachers like yourself," he says benevolently. "If there'd been any way I could've offered you a more attractive pay package, I would've done, I promise. I wish you all the best for the future."

Without further ado, I ring through to *Royal David's* and accept the job. The Head seems delighted. Given that the school is situated in a traffic hotspot some thirty miles away, I make a second call to *The Halifax* in town and give permission for my house to be released onto the market. Whilst there's no denying the appeal of this quaint market town, the three years I've spent here have played havoc with my self-confidence.

"A new start all round," I tell myself positively. "Yes, I'm going to make this redundancy work in my favour."

Yesterday

(Year 6)

Why she had to go, I don't know, she wouldn't say.
I said something wrong, now I long for yesterday.

AUTUMN TERM

It's now the first day in September and it scarcely seems possible that three months have elapsed since I received formal confirmation of my marching orders from *Mardall's Sixth Form College*, then secured a full-time position at *Royal David's Independent School*. Having said this, an awful lot has happened during the interim period, what with seeing out my contract at *Mardall's*, selling my old house for the asking price and finding an alternative property closer to my new job.

After much rigmarole, I'm now the proud owner of a spacious 1930s ex-council house on the fringes of the City. Somehow, I managed to wangle a mortgage amounting to four times my new salary plus Friday evening gym-coaching wage, which means effectively a monthly repayment figure of seven hundred and fifty pounds – over half my monthly income. In order to obtain this loan, I was obliged to redeem my old mortgage and change lender. The redemption penalty came to a depressing two thousand quid – exactly the figure I was awarded as a redundancy settlement. My new property, however, comes equipped with three bedrooms, two bathrooms – one en-suite – double glazing, central heating, a decent size garden, double garage and parking for about four cars. What's more, its location is ideal – just a stone's throw from the town centre, mainline train station and major road network.

To help with my finances, I've taken in a lodger – one of my former secondary school French pupils, Mark Bowles. Now twenty-three, he's studying at the Art College close to my old house. The original plan was for him to have Clement's room when he moved out, but then, of course, I decided to sell up, so he joined me here in the City instead. After a series of painful break-ups, Mark is now back together with his childhood sweetheart, Julia Francis, who I also taught for GCSE French. She used to live round the corner from me and, for almost a year, relied on my two-hundred-quid, bright yellow Alfa Sud to ferry her to and from school. Given that she resided just outside the catchment area and didn't qualify for a bus pass, the Deputy Head had requested my assistance. To show her gratitude, Julia chose to use me as a live model for her GCSE Art portfolio. A fully-clothed one, naturally. Her teacher was none other than my old mate Simon Lennon who no doubt suggested me as a practical joke.

As for Clement, his boyfriend, Darren, did the dirty on him by chickening out at the last minute of their plans to share a flat in London. I'm relieved to report that he resisted the temptation to top himself and, by all accounts, is happily knocking back crates of JD in a sizeable flat not far from my old place.

My bisexual friend, Nicky, is now in an exclusively heterosexual relationship with a bloke who cracked on to her a while back whilst she was enjoying a quiet drink with me at *Alfredo's*. He's a golfing instructor on a good salary and the pair are already cohabiting.

Whilst there have been many changes in the last few months, all of these pale into insignificance when compared with the tragic events of yesterday – the sudden death of Diana, the much-loved Princess of Wales, in a car crash in Paris. Tragedy, it seems, is no greater respecter of royalty than it is of any other mortal being. The whole country is in mourning.

With my new job about to get underway tomorrow, Diana's premature death serves as a stark reminder of the importance of seizing opportunities when we can and making the most of them. It may well be a cliché, but none of us can be sure what lies in wait around the next corner.

By the end of the second week at *Royal David's*, I find my latest *carpe diem* policy under serious threat. Already, I'm missing my *Mardall's* job more than I could've ever imagined. This is in no way a reflection of the quality of the school. In fact, it's a well-run establishment, blessed with as friendly a teaching and administrative staff as you could possibly hope to find. It's just that I'm having difficulty readapting to a secondary school ethos.

First and foremost, it's a noticeably stricter, more formal environment than I've become accustomed to over the last five years, demanding on my behalf a less natural persona in the classroom. I find this tough. All male teachers are expected to wear a suit and although jackets may be removed when teaching, they must be replaced for excursions to the canteen, Staff Room or toilet. Even the Sixth Form have to follow a formal dress code. Moreover, there's little evidence so far to suggest they're treated like young adults to the extent they were at *Mardall's*.

Every Tuesday morning, there's a Catholic service in the small on-site chapel, led by one of the three Fathers dressed in a cassock-like robe. All in all, it's a highly ceremonial affair.

Whereas at *Mardall's* free periods were guaranteed for lesson preparation, marking and other administrative duties, the odds here of being collared to cover another absent teacher's lesson are fairly steep. On top of this, there's a detention rota, which will mean coming in on a Saturday morning when my turn arrives. My new Head of Department, Brian Woolly, has also come from the Sixth Form College sector. Unlike me, however, he made a conscious decision to return to secondary teaching. Nevertheless, he can relate to the huge transition gap.

On a more positive note, all members of staff are entitled to a gratuitous lunch and a brand new trampoline has been purchased to enable me to pursue my extra-curricular interests.

My mood of nostalgia is heightened on Friday evening after gym when I meet for a drink with a crowd of former *Mardall's* students, among them Mandy 'Mandarin' Bailey, Cara Mitchell, Ian Thompson, Claire Matthews and Lititia Jones-Thomas. At closing time, we move on to *James Dean's* where Lititia, a bright blue-eyed blonde, surprises me with a suggestion.

"I think it'd be really nice if we went out for dinner sometime, Al," she says, playing with her ponytail. "Would you be up for it?"

"Er ... yes," I reply. "Why not?"

"Good. I'll give you my number and perhaps you can call me over the weekend to arrange something."

The evening is a great success and reminds me how fortunate I was at *Mardall's* to have the opportunity to work with such terrific young people who obviously value me enough to want to continue meeting up some three years after leaving the College. And maybe, just maybe, there'll be romance on the near horizon with one of them. Al, you're an incorrigible old sod!

"Hi, Lititia, it's Al here," my phone conversation begins late on Sunday morning.

"Oh, hi," Lititia says somewhat timidly. Then again, she's always been softly spoken. "How're you?"

"I'm fine, thanks. I had a really good time on Friday. How 'bout you?"

"Yes, me too. It was a really fun evening."

It may well have been Lititia's proposal in the first place, but the prospect of bringing up the subject of dinner suddenly sends a shiver down my spine. What if it was the drink that was talking and she's changed her mind? Besides, I've never been particularly comfortable trying to secure a date on the phone. I cover the receiver with my left hand and take a large inhalation of air.

"Just thought I'd ring to see if you were still up for dinner," I say eventually.

"Yeah, sure. When did you have in mind?

"Erm ... how about ... er ... next Saturday?"

"Sounds good to me."

We agree on a time and venue.

I'm about to hang up when Lititia says somewhat hastily: "Oh, one more thing. I hope you don't mind, but I've asked Ian to come along as well."

I slowly replace the receiver, disappointed that I'm to be denied the pleasure of wining and dining Lititia on her own. On reflection, I suppose it was simply too good to be true. I have it on the best authority that the average man thinks about sex every six minutes. Whilst I have to admit that I've never actually timed myself, there's little to suggest that this statistic is far off the mark in my case.

"You shouldn't be so single-minded," I lambaste myself later. "Ian's a really decent lad and I'm sure we'll have a great time. After all, I do need to establish a friendship circle here."

Dinner out with Ian and Lititia proves a success – so much so, in fact, that I find myself suggesting I cook for both of them back at the house next weekend. They appear flattered to be asked and accept.

When Saturday comes round, my culinary skills pass the test, although I have to excuse the rather unpleasant odour emanating from the lounge/dining room carpet. Whilst I don't like jumping to conclusions, I've got a feeling the previous owners' ageing Labrador may well have been caught short on the odd occasion. I'll have to get hold of some carpet cleaner as I can't afford to replace it just now.

Generally speaking, the house is in a good state of repair considering its age, even though the décor is not exactly to my taste. Mark hasn't wasted any time stripping his room of the Snoopy wallpaper. In its place are several coats of magnolia, covered by an intricate pattern of musical notes, courtesy of his artistic girlfriend. Thankfully, she resisted the temptation to adorn the walls with an array of miniature Al portraits.

By the beginning of October, it begins to hit home how few people I actually know here in the City. It's true that I've seen the odd familiar face since moving, but most of these belonged to occasional visitors, not permanent residents. Of course, I should be trying to make new friends, but it isn't that straightforward, given that the crowds seem to be different every weekend.

My overall mood of pessimism isn't helped by the discovery of further drawbacks to my job. Firstly, the traffic in the morning is horrendous. Sometimes, it can take up to an hour of crawling to complete the fifteen-mile journey. I've never been a particularly patient driver and I frequently find myself arriving at work completely stressed out. This doesn't put me in a favourable frame of mind to deal with some of the under sixteen lads who appear more unenthusiastic about learning languages than many I encountered in the state sector. Any thoughts I may've entertained about private school pupils being models of virtue in terms of motivation and conduct have proved seriously unfounded. But then I should've known this after my gym-coaching experience last year. They're not malicious in any way, just silly and non-cooperative. Reflecting on my previous experiences of teaching this age group, I'd have to say that the presence of girls had a positive influence on all but a few of the lads.

There are, of course, girls here in the Sixth Form and, so far, my A level teaching is proving the highlight of the week. The students are every bit as conscientious as those I taught at *Mardall's* and, on the whole, seem more able. There's little doubt in my mind that Sixth Form teaching is where my strengths lie. Still, I'm just going to have to pull myself together and grin and bear it for the rest of this academic year. Leaving mid-year is just not my style. Anyhow, where would I go?

Holidays in the independent sector are renowned for being more generous than those in the state system. On the surface, this is a plus point. The only thing is, the terms are shorter as a consequence, which means less time to cover the course content. With so much to get through and over two hundred pupils and students in my charge, I'm finding the workload rather heavy. Faced with two sets of internal exams and reports for each year group before the end of the summer term, there's little hope of respite at any stage in the coming year.

"I really must try to sort out my social life," I tell myself. "If I led less of a lonesome existence in the evenings and at weekends, maybe I wouldn't miss *Mardall's* as much as I do at present."

I have to say, there are a lot of very attractive women around in the various pubs and clubs. Surely they can't all be taken.

Towards the end of the first week in October, I make another of my solitary excursions into town and discover that a new pub belonging to the *Hogshead* group – *The William Pitt* – has opened up by the river. With the taste of dark Belgian beer already on my lips, I step inside to check it out.

The wooden décor conjures up memories of *The Combine Harvester*, although the beams are surely not as antiquated. Behind the bar, I find Coral James, a former elite gymnast from the club where I used to train for my Past Masters competitions. She recognises me immediately.

Realising that the rest of the pub is deserted, I plonk myself onto a barstool and catch up on her news. We talk until closing time.

On the way home, it occurs to me that with the exception of my *Mardall's* reunion, subsequent dinner dates with Ian and Lititia, and a visit from my old school friend, Phillip Thatcher, tonight was the first time I've felt at ease here in the City since my move at the end of July. I head off to bed in a more positive frame of mind. With a familiar face behind one of the bars, suddenly it doesn't seem such a lonely place, after all.

One Tuesday about ten days later, only a handful of my Fifth Year French group turn up for my period two lesson.

"The others are having their bags and lockers searched for drugs, sir," one of the more sensible members of the class informs me. "So they might not be here for a while."

Determined not to be outdone by the pupils, Brian offers his colleagues a different kind of drug at the lunchtime departmental meeting, be it a licit one. With a couple of glasses of Liebfraumilch willingly consumed by all, the meeting proves somewhat more animated than anticipated and the prospect of afternoon lessons less daunting.

I'm still in good spirits by the time the final bell rings. It's not until I switch on my car radio on the way home and hear of the tragic death in a plane crash of the country singer, John Denver, that my mood changes. Although perhaps too slushy for some, Denver's emotive, melodic ballads about love and nature have always appealed to the romantic in me. I first discovered him in my time at university and found that classics like *Annie's Song, Follow Me, Sunshine On My Shoulders* and *Leaving on a Jet Plane* went some way to compensate for the lack of romance in my own life. RIP, John!

At the weekend, I receive a visit from mum, auntie and Chloë. Despite my protests, the two ladies set to work at once on cleaning the kitchen and downstairs bathroom. With a few extra ingredients required for lunch, I nip to the local shop, accompanied by my adorable little niece. Her road manners prove most impressive – at least ten exaggerated looks to the left and right before crossing. How she's growing up!

In the evening, we're all invited over to mum's brother's house for a family dinner. With lots of people to talk to, I feel much more like my old self. With half term fast-approaching, I'm more determined than ever to hit the town in the evenings and make myself known.

At the start of half term, I make a conscious effort to chat up one of Coral's fellow barmaids at *The William Pitt*, a pretty blonde in her early twenties. She tells me her name is Brigitte. Detecting at once that she's got an accent, it doesn't take long to establish that she's from Germany. Confident that my ability to speak her language will give me extra brownie points, I decide to switch to her mother tongue.

"I didn't think there were any English people who spoke German," she says with obvious surprise.

Our conversation soon reveals that she's a sensible, easy-going young woman with a mature outlook on life.

At the end of the evening, I'm eager to stick my neck out by suggesting we meet for a drink sometime. Unfortunately, I lose my bottle at the crucial moment and miss my chance. What am I like?

My old amateur dramatics friend, Martin Studd, pays me a lunchtime visit a couple of days later. He is now a qualified teacher and claimed to be revelling in the challenge when we last spoke. On top of this, he married his long-term girlfriend last year and they recently moved into their own property. Enough reasons to expect him to be in high spirits. However, this proves not to be the case. Throughout his stay, Martin proceeds to talk rather gloomily about growing old and not fulfilling his ambitions. Not exactly what I need right now. He even refuses to stay for a night on the town, which is most out of character.

"How'd you fancy joining me on holiday for a week in the summer?" he asks before leaving.

"What, just the two of us?" I reply, wondering about his other half.

"Yes, that's right."

I tell him I'd be more than happy to accompany him in principle, but that I haven't really thought that far ahead.

"There's no hurry," he says, climbing into his car. "I was thinking of getting something at the last minute."

As he pulls away, it crosses my mind that I should've perhaps enquired about the state of his marriage. Poor old Martin. I hope everything's okay.

Phillip Thatcher makes his second appearance at my new house in the evening, complete with a couple of cheap rail tickets to France for the following day.

"Hopefully, we'll meet some desirable ladies on board the ferry," he enthuses.

Philip and I start out at 5.30 in the morning and catch the first train to Portsmouth. Standing in the harbour waiting for the ferry connection, my mind travels back to my last visit to this gale-ridden town on my thirtieth birthday and the heartbreak surrounding my split with Rachel Hill. I smile sentimentally at the reflection and wonder whether Rachel is still persevering with her Architecture course. And her macho swimmer – I wonder if he's still on the scene. With my thirty-second birthday just over a week away, this means I've been single for almost two whole years. God, what a depressing thought!

Although undeniably an enjoyable break, the trip brings Phillip and me into contact with almost exclusively married or middle-aged booze cruisers. It seems that on this particular day single women on both sides of the Channel are busy at home washing their hair.

It's not dark yet, but it's getting there sings Bob Dylan on one of the tracks of his latest album *Time Out Of Mind*. It's Sunday and the final day of the half term holiday. I pause from my attempt at varnishing the patio-like doors that separate the kitchen from the lounge and reflect on the significance of these words to my own life situation. I recall my determination to use this week of freedom to put myself on the map in the City and feel a sense of disappointment that I've failed to do so. If only I'd taken the bull by the horns and asked Brigitte, the German barmaid, out for a drink.

On the Wednesday after my birthday, there's an unexpected phone call for me at *Royal David's*.

"Hello, Al," says a vaguely familiar female voice. "It's Val Winterbourne here from the Adult Education Office at *Mardall's*. How are you and how's your new job going?"

I exaggerate about the current state of my happiness and, intrigued as to why she'd want to call me at work, await an explanation.

"I hope you don't mind me ringing you like this out of the blue, but I need your help. It's just that your old colleague, Mary Castle, is struggling to combine the French and Italian Evening Classes, and I was wondering whether we might be able to lure you back here to take over the French group. It'd be on a Thursday."

The prospect of returning to the scene of such an uplifting period in my life appeals immediately. However, I manage to contain myself and tell Val I ought to sleep on her proposal before making a commitment. She's happy for me to do so. It's only after I've put back the receiver that it occurs to me that her request was actually a bloody cheek after my ruthless dismissal last summer. Then again, I suppose it wasn't Val's decision to lay me off.

Unable to resist a return to my old College, be it in a tiny capacity, I ring Val when I'm back home and accept her offer. She expresses delight. Or is it relief?

With another year under my belt, I excel myself on Friday evening after gym by inviting the lovely Brigitte out for a drink.

Brigitte and I meet the following afternoon after her shift at a bistro in town. I ask about her life in Germany and she informs me, amongst other things, that her father is Hungarian. The conversation flows as naturally as it did with a bar between us, prompting me to wonder whether the two of us might actually hit it off.

"Al, I wanted to ask you," Brigitte says suddenly. "How old are you exactly?"

"I'm thirty-two," I reply unashamedly.

There's an unmistakable look of disappointment in her eyes. "Oh, I thought you were ... maybe ... twenty-four or twenty-five."

At this point, I think of Rupert Stanley who'll unscrupulously shave eight to ten years off his real age if he believes it'll increase his chances of getting his leg over.

"Once they've fallen for me, they don't usually care about a white lie," I've heard him say in defence of his actions.

It strikes me that whilst a seasoned charmer like Rupert may be able to pull it off, I'd almost certainly be ditched at once on account of my dishonesty.

Brigitte continues to chat freely for the remainder of our date, but leaves me in little doubt that she considers me too old for a relationship.

In the evening, I join my lodger, Mark, his girlfriend, Julia, and a couple of their mutual friends – one male, one female – for a few drinks in town. Whilst at one of the bars, we're offered free entry tickets for *James Dean's*. Unfortunately, the others aren't keen and suggest we return to the house instead to open a bottle of wine.

I chat extensively to the female friend on the way home and find that I quite like her. However, once back at my front gate, she has a quiet word with Mark, then jumps into her car and speeds off without the hint of a goodbye. Before I have chance to establish her motives for leaving so hurriedly, Mark and Julia have retired to the former's bedroom, closing the door firmly behind them. I glance around for the male friend, but he's nowhere to be seen. Somewhat offended, I return into town and join the queue outside *James Dean's*. Needless to say, there are no free entry tickets to be found. But all is not lost. On the door of the club, I spot the familiarly rotund figure of Steve Whately.

"I left *Opportunity Knox* in the summer to take a break from door work," he explains. "Now I'm back working here. I'm afraid I haven't got the authority to let you in for nothing like before, but I will sign you in tonight as my guest."

The sight of Steve back in his rightful place cheers me up. How I relish familiarity.

To my disappointment, there are no familiar faces in the club and none of the women there gives me a second look. After one drink, I decide to call it a night.

Given the events of this evening, I jump under the duvet, wondering exactly why it was I was so convinced a move to the City would change my fortune on the romantic front.

On the following Thursday, I return to *Mardall's* to resume my old job as an Evening Class tutor. Stepping into the once so familiar building feels almost like a homecoming. From what Val had told me, I'd assumed that the numbers in the French group would be vast. But I was wrong. In fact, it's a class of just four. It strikes me as ironic that the money saved from my redundancy has probably helped to fund the luxury of one teacher per language for Evening Classes. And one of those teachers happens to be me. Oh well, it's great to be back and the extra money will come in handy.

My renewed contact with the College soon lands me additional work – regular private tuition with one of Marilyn's A level French students and a couple of gym-coaching sessions on site with three girls who've chosen gymnastics as part of their PE practical and need help constructing floor routines.

The latter takes place in mid-December after I've broken up from *Royal David's*. Whilst there, I bump into my old colleague, Michael 'Bomber' Lancaster, in the toilet.

"You mmm...must be gutted about Avril's recent ann...ann... announcement," he says after I've explained the reason behind my unexpected presence.

"What announcement's that?" I ask.

"Oh, sss...sorry! So you haven't heard? Well, apparently, the mmm... maintenance costs weren't as steep as her ladyship had ppp...projected last year and there's now a surplus in the kitty of sixty-five ggg...grand."

"You're pulling my leg?"

"Fraid not. She ttt...told us about it at the last staff meeting. None of the redundancies was necessary, after all."

Coupled with the recent discovery that the professional scrubbing of the brickwork on the main building and cleaning of its many windows that took place prior to my departure in the summer had cost in the region of ten grand, this latest revelation leaves me feeling as sick as a parrot.

A few days into the Christmas holidays, I'm supping contentedly on a Leffe Blonde on a busy night in *The William Pitt* when one of the door men, a Michelin man of mixed race who they call BJ, suddenly approaches me.

"Excuse me, mate. There's a young lady outside who's keen to get to know you," he says affably. "Thing is, I reckon she's a bit on the shy side."

Convinced that I'm the innocent target of a practical joke, I sit motionless for a couple of seconds digesting his words. BJ then nods in the direction of a female figure standing outside with her back to the large window. Intrigued, I follow him out of the pub and notice at once that the girl in question is rather tall with distinctive short, blonde hair. BJ tactfully leaves me alone with her.

"Hi," I say cheerfully. "The bouncer said you wanted to talk to me."

The girl looks up with a start and there's no mistaking the apprehension in her sky-blue eyes.

"Hello," she mumbles nervously, forcing a half-smile.

It's at this point that it registers – we've actually met before. I screw up my forehead in an effort to remember where. Then it comes to me. She was a member of the girls' recreational gym squad that used to train on the same night as my Past Masters team some three or four years ago. Not that I remember her as such, but I do recall running into her and a friend a while back when I came into the City with Nicky and some of her mates. I didn't recognise the pair, but they explained how they knew me.

"I'm sorry," I continue, in as friendly a tone as I can muster, "but I've forgotten your name."

She glances back down at the pavement. "Samantha Woodfield."

"Well, it's … er … it's good to see you again, Samantha. You not coming inside?"

She raises her head slightly before replying, her body twitching uncomfortably: "No, I … I'm … er … waiting to give some of my friends a lift back." Several exaggerated nods of her head follow.

Sensing that I've been set up and that my presence is embarrassing the poor girl, I decide to return into the pub.

"Well, I guess I'll see you again … er … sometime," I say in parting. "Bye now."

Her reply is noticeably more audible than her previous words: "Yes, bye. See you soon."

Returning to the smoky haze, I come face to face in the doorway with a tall, solidly built girl of Greek appearance.

"So you spoke to Sam, then?" she says confidently.

"Yes, I did, but I don't think she was that eager to talk to me. Was it a wind up or something?"

"No, not at all. She really likes you. Has done for ages."

"But …"

"She's quite shy, so you probably embarrassed her. Oh, I'm Teresa, by the way. Sam's best friend."

"Pleased to meet you, Teresa. I'm Al."

"Yeah, I know. Sam told me. So d'you come here often, Al?"

"It is one of my favourite pubs in town. So … yes, I guess I do."

Teresa smiles, then heads off back to her other friends.

As I'm making my way home, I can't help feeling mildly uplifted by the evening's bizarre events. Life really is full of surprises sometimes. I try to calculate Sam's age and conclude that she can't possibly be any older than eighteen.

"Oh well, a wee bit too young for you, Mr Bentley," I tell myself as I turn the latch on my front door. "There's no chance you're going to expose yourself to the indecision of another teenager like Rachel."

The final Friday gym session of the term brings with it a bounty of wine and chocolate for the chief coach, courtesy of the little gymnasts and their grateful parents – one of the perks of the job. Afterwards, one of the mums and my youngest coaching assistant, Kayleigh Yearwood, persuade me to join them at *Clifford's*. Unbeknown to me, they've been friends for a while. On the way there, they inform me that the building is scheduled to be bulldozed in January to make way for new houses.

Once inside, I find myself reliving some of the more memorable evenings spent at the club when I used to live just a few hundred yards away. It saddens me to think that this will almost certainly be my last visit.

The following evening, I unwrap one of my bottles of wine and down the entire contents before making a beeline for *James Dean's*. There's a ridiculously long queue outside, but the booze has had a mellow, calming effect and I willingly take my place at the back of the line. An hour and a half later, I make it through the doors into the crowded club.

Shortly after my arrival, I stumble across Helen Forward, one of my trampolinists from Rachel and Amanda's era. She was the girl who visited College last year and hurt her neck on the trampoline whilst having a sentimental bounce. I'm pleased to discover that she's experiencing no lasting effects from her injury – quite the opposite, in fact, as she manoeuvres her head and upper body close to mine in an overtly flirtatious display. Even in my intoxicated state, I have little difficulty deducing that Helen fancies me – something I was oblivious of when she was at College.

"Why is it I can read a woman's body language when she's drunk," I ponder, "but be completely thrown by it when she's sober?"

Before I have chance to reflect any further, I find myself kissing Helen in a surprisingly confident fashion. The sense of relief that I haven't forgotten what to do is colossal. I'm disappointed when her lift drags her away early, but no sooner has she gone than a replacement steps in – Libby Lawrence, a former pupil from my state secondary school days over six years ago. She's now studying Art at university and this is reflected in her colourful choice of clothes and purple-streaked hair. Like Helen before her, she kisses me with wholehearted enthusiasm, helping to plug the many holes in my ravaged ego.

With the demons of the last two years already in retreat, I return home at 2.15 on the proverbial cloud nine. Anyone who's doubted his or her attractiveness to the opposite sex for as long as I have will understand what a hugely therapeutic experience tonight was.

There's an extra spring in my step when I arrive at mum and dad's on Christmas Eve. Jayne, Joe and the two children are already there, and I soon discover that I'll be sharing a room with my little niece at her request.

When I turn in, I find that Chloë is still awake.

"Go to sleep!" she says as soon as my head hits the pillow.

As obedient as ever, I squeeze my eyes shut in exaggerated fashion. No sooner have I done so, however, than I feel the full force of Chloë's weight on top of me – she's jumped from her bed across onto mine. I open my eyes and sit up.

"Go to sleep!" she repeats, pushing me back into a prone position and returning to her bed.

I obey immediately, only to be jumped on once again.

The game continues for a good ten minutes until I decide it's time for both of us to get some kip. The mere threat that Father Christmas only calls on little girls who've had a good night's sleep has the desired effect.

Christmas Day and Boxing Day turn out to be sublime, with Chloë and James' excitement helping to recapture the magic of Jayne's and my childhood. Sometimes, I hanker after those heady days when the world was there to be conquered and everything – and I mean *everything* – seemed possible. Were they really that long ago?

Between Christmas and New Year, I run into Helen Forward again in town and we spend the afternoon in each other's company.

In the evening, we join Mark out for a drink with one of his Art College friends. Helen remains rather subdued throughout our time together, which I attribute to shyness.

"So what you up to on New Year's Eve?" I ask before we part.

"I've got tickets for a pub near *Mardall's*," she replies. "How 'bout you?"

"Oh, nothing definite yet. I'll probably go out in the City."

"Well, you're more than welcome to join me and my friends. I've got a spare ticket."

"You sure? I wouldn't want to cramp your style."

"No, it'll be fine. The only thing is, I'm not sure what time we're meeting up. I'll call you early evening and let you know."

It's now 8.00 pm on New Year's Eve and I'm striding impatiently around the living room, waiting for the promised call from Helen.

"There's no way she'd stand me up," I try to convince myself. "We've known each other for too long."

I contemplate ringing her, but decide she's probably left the house already. Anyway, I've never been the sort of person to go where I'm not wanted.

As the minutes tick by, I start to feel increasingly dejected. If Helen doesn't want to spend New Year with me, that's no big deal. What I can't stomach, however, is the fact that she's left me in the lurch on such an important date on the social calendar. With most of the pubs insisting on a 'ticket only' policy, I could be facing a night in on my own – a prospect of disastrous proportions.

By 8.30, I've given up the ghost.

"What heinous crime did I commit in the past?" I ask myself despairingly.

Smarting from my latest taste of female rejection, I prepare to settle in front of the telly. Then, all of a sudden, I'm overcome by a strong desire from within to fight my misfortune and make my own luck.

"There's got to be a pub somewhere in the City that'll let me in," I blurt out in exasperation. "I'm not going to be defeated that easily."

I tart myself up and march into town with a bit between my teeth. I pass *The William Pitt* and curse myself for not purchasing a standby ticket when I had the chance. It occurs to me that I may be allowed in as a regular customer, but I dismiss the idea at once as wishful thinking. I then proceed to do a large circuit of the City Centre, passing all the popular watering holes. As I'd feared, each one bears a large sign on the door or in the window: *Ticket only.*

Back outside *The William Pitt*, I'm on the verge of abandoning my quest. Then, quite by surprise, a male voice cries out to me from the doorway. I take a few steps closer and spot BJ, the Michelin man, a gentle giant if ever there was one.

"You not coming in, then?" he asks.

"I'd love to," I reply, "but I haven't got a ticket."

He produces a huge ivory smile. "No worries, mate. I've saved you one."

"You serious?"

"Yeah, no problem. C'mon, get yourself inside. Your young lady's here."

He waves me through into the pub. With profuse thanks, I step over the threshold into the crowd.

"My pleasure," he says with a wink and another broad smile. What a super bloke!

Within seconds of accessing the bar, I feel a tall female figure breathing down my neck. I turn to catch Samantha Woodfield's friend, Teresa, hovering over my right shoulder.

"Hi, Al," she says affably. "Sam's here. I wanna see you two get it on tonight, no messing."

Rather taken aback by her frankness, I find myself humorously playing down the possibility.

"At least come over and talk to her," Teresa says forcefully, tossing her head towards the rear of the pub. "She's a really lovely person."

"All right, I'll be over in a minute," I say finally, if only to get her off my back.

With a Leffe Triple in my right hand, I move away from the bar and come face to face with Romana Lopez, a young woman of Mediterranean appearance who I taught for German at *Mardall's* three years ago. She wasn't a natural linguist, but secured a good grade through a beaver-like approach to her studies. I stop for a chat, and am delighted to hear that she's now doing the language at university and in the middle of her year abroad in Austria. We compare notes on the country. Already, I'm feeling more upbeat.

After wishing Romana all the best for the future, I decide that, out of politeness, I ought to seek out Sam Woodfield and her friend. I find them easily enough and am relieved to discover that Sam, although still a little reticent, is more at ease than on our last meeting. My attempts to break the ice reveal that she's in her second year of A levels at a single sex independent school near *Mardall's*. Furthermore, she's doing languages and PE. This common ground paves the way for further discussion and, with the conversation starting to flow smoothly, I make up my mind to stay put. After all, it has to be an improvement on drinking on my own. Anyway, Teresa was spot on in her assessment of her best friend – she is indeed a lovely girl.

As Sam begins to relax in my company, it soon becomes clear that she's more mature than the majority of girls of her age that I've met in either a professional or social capacity. What's more, she's got an excellent sense of humour. As the evening progresses, I find myself increasingly mesmerized by the warmth of her smile and the sparkle in her sky-blue eyes.

Before I know it, it's ten to midnight. At Teresa and Sam's request, I follow the two girls out of the pub, passing BJ's raised thumbs and triumphant smile. We cross over the river bridge and road, and climb the cobbled High Street towards the famous clock. As in previous years when I accompanied Simon Lennon here, we encounter a huge, expectant crowd, excitedly awaiting a new dawn.

Teresa disappears off to find other friends, leaving Sam and me to take refuge in a supermarket doorway just a stone's throw from the clock. With the woes of the earlier part of the evening behind me and now overflowing with confidence, I lean forward to kiss my young companion on the stroke of midnight. As if waiting all evening for such a move, she thrusts her head towards mine in eager anticipation. I feel an instant shudder of excitement as our lips come together. Rather strangely, perhaps, my alcohol-distorted brain tells me that from this moment on my life will never be quite the same again.

SPRING TERM

When I wake late morning, it takes a few seconds to establish that the events of last night weren't just a pleasant dream. A small scrap of paper on the bedside cabinet displaying the name 'Sam' and a telephone number dispels any lingering doubts.

All afternoon, I toy with the idea of giving Sam a call as I promised I would when we parted shortly after midnight. The problem is, with a clearing head, I'm reminded of the fact that she's still in the Sixth Form and some fourteen years my junior. Okay, there's no law against a teacher dating a student from another school any more than there is against one dating a former student, but it'd certainly be frowned upon by some, particularly now that I'm over thirty. Then again, I've spent most of my life worrying about what other people think and it's a burden I'd love to shift. It's not as if toeing the line and doing the 'right' thing have brought me much joy romantically in the past.

Mind you, now that she's 'pulled' me, Sam's interest will have probably waned – just like it seems to have done with Helen Forward. On the subject of Helen, it occurs to me that her failure to ring last night was rather fortuitous, given that I couldn't possibly have had a more enjoyable evening. Maybe there's such a thing as fate, after all.

Won over by my emerging rebellious streak – if you can call it that – I make up my mind to phone Sam at around teatime. She's pleased to hear from me, but can't talk long as her dinner is on the table. We agree to meet at *The William Pitt* tomorrow night.

My meeting with Sam on the second day in '98 proves to be an overwhelming success. Even without the support of alcohol, we chat like old friends and kiss passionately and with remarkable fluidity – as if our lips too are life-long acquaintances.

"It feels so right," Sam says with another of her heart-warming smiles. And in spite of myself, I find it hard to disagree.

However, by the time we meet for lunch the following day at a remote restaurant in the country, my head has had time to catch up with my racing heart.

"What's up?" Sam asks, detecting at once a change in my mood.

Although anxious not to harp on too much about the past, I proceed to tell her about Rachel and how I made a firm promise after our split never again to be sucked in by the charms of a teenage girl.

"Al, I really like being with you," she says calmly, resting her hand on mine in reassurance. "And not all girls of my age are the same."

I lighten up. "Mm, I suppose you're right. But if we're still together when the time comes for you to go to university, then that's the end of it, okay?"

There's a glow of delight in Sam's eyes. "So does that mean we're officially going out?"

"Er, well, erm … yes. I spose so. See how it goes."

Out in town in the evening, Teresa has a quiet word in my ear: "Sam told me about your reservations, but don't worry, she won't let you down."

Another friend, Hannah, echoes Teresa's words of encouragement. In the light of their comments, I decide that it'd be criminal to put a stop to what has been a remarkably happy start to the New Year, purely because I'm a teacher and Sam is a few months off completing her A levels. Of course, in an ideal world, she'd be older, but hey, beggars can't be choosers.

It soon comes to my attention that, like Rachel when we got together, Sam has no previous sexual experience.

"I got very close to a German bloke I met on holiday in Lanzerote," she tells me, "but decided I wasn't ready to go all the way."

"I admire you for that," I reply. "And I want you to know that just because I'm older, it doesn't mean that I'll push you into anything you're not ready for."

Sam beams. "Thanks. It's reassuring to hear that you're not just after me for my body."

"Absolutely not! It's your mind that I'm after one hundred per cent."

With my social life flourishing, I return to work with renewed optimism. Excited by the prospect of further meetings with Sam, the days seem to pass less stressfully than before Christmas.

My Swedish friend, Annette Enqvist, rings during the second week in January. She delights in informing me that she's passed her physiotherapy course and already landed a position in a large hospital.

"And I've started seeing one of the doctors," she says. "He's an amazing guy."

I've lost count of the number of 'amazing guys' she's dated in the past, only to discover a short while after that they weren't that amazing, after all.

It used to nark me that, despite our excellent camaraderie and her excessive flirting, she never considered me to be that 'amazing'. On this occasion, however, I'm just pleased for her.

"Oh, by the way, I've met this amazing girl," I can't resist slipping into the end of our conversation.

Naturally, Annette warns me of the dangers of dating someone so young.

Annette's comment is reiterated by Martin Studd and Phillip Thatcher after they've met Sam at the pub on the following Saturday. As if I need reminding.

I suppose I can forgive Martin's cynicism on account of the fact that his girlfriend of five years and wife of one and a half has decided she doesn't wanted to be married any more and packed her bags. This explains his eagerness to partake in a lads' holiday on his last visit.

"We hadn't broken up when I mentioned it," he says, "but I could sense a split was on the cards."

I offer my sincere commiserations, yet how can I possibly say anything that'll make him feel better about his situation? The poor bugger. I almost feel guilty about having a girlfriend.

"So what do your friends think of me?" Sam asks with Martin and Phillip out of earshot.

"They like you," I reply.

"But they don't approve, do they?"

"Oh, they're just looking out for me, that's all. Don't worry about it."

"What, because of my age?"

"Well, yes, I guess so."

"I hate that!" Sam snaps in an uncharacteristic display of anger. "Why does everyone have to be so negative all the time?"

On the penultimate Saturday in January, my old friend, Nicky, joins me at *The William Pitt* with Sam and a few of her friends.

"So how's it going with your golfing pro?" I ask.

"Well, we're still living together," she says, "but the bastard's been cheating on me."

"You're joking. I thought he was crazy about you."

"So did I. But fear not, I've been getting my own back."

"Really? How've you managed that, then?"

"By peeing on his toothbrush first thing in the morning."

"You little devil, you! And he hasn't realised?"

"Well, he hasn't mentioned anything and still uses it quite happily, so I guess not."

Nice one, Nicky! However, this turns out to be only a small part of her reprisal. She joins me at *OK* after Sam and her friends have gone home and pulls four times, obtaining on each occasion the phone number of her conquest. Revenge, how sweet it can be. Despite the fact that I've got a trampolining competition tomorrow – or, rather, later today – I don't make it to bed until 3.45.

With only a few hours' sleep under my belt, I bounce like a maestro in the afternoon – well, almost – and, at the fourth attempt in two years, pass my first major grading. At this point in his life, it seems that Alan Bentley can walk on water.

Shortly after my trampolining achievement, I'm granted the pleasure of meeting Sam's parents and younger sister, Claire. It's a fairly low-key encounter with no indication whatsoever that they disapprove of the age gap.

"Al, I think I'm ready to … you know," Sam says later, interrupting a bout of passionate kissing back at my place. We're lying on top of my bed.

"You sure?" I ask sceptically. "As I said before, I'm more than happy to wait."

"Yes, completely sure. I feel closer to you than anyone I've ever met in my life and that includes my family."

With these words, Sam and I consummate our relationship. With additional flattering comments emerging from her lips, I allow my defences to drop and confess exactly how strong my feelings for her have become. What happened to playing it cool?

On the last day of the month, I join Sam, Teresa and Hannah at *Paddy's*, the Irish bar just along the river from *The William Pitt*. I introduce the ladies to the barman, Adrian Salmon, a former *Mardall's* student. Although I never had the satisfaction of teaching him, he recognised me on a recent trip to the bar.

"Most of the blokes at College were envious of you coaching all those fit girls on the trampoline," he disclosed with a laugh.

We chatted at length whilst I sipped my pint and it didn't take long to establish that Adrian is a genuine, friendly lad with not an ounce of malice in his body. He suggested we had a lads' night out sometime and I was more than willing to accept. And to think it was only about six weeks ago that I was bemoaning my solitary, loveless existence here in the City. How things have changed.

Sam and I, as close as ever, get a kick out of attempting to find suitable partners for Teresa and Hannah. Adrian joins in with the fun. I don't think I've ever felt happier or more confident in a social context.

In early February, my cousin, Susannah, and her boyfriend, Richard, visit at the weekend. Down at *The William Pitt*, they become acquainted with Sam. As a conscientious student, the latter declines the chance to go clubbing afterwards in favour of homework assignments, leaving Susi, Rich and me to brave *James Dean's* on our own. To my relief, the queue is decidedly more inviting than it was during the Christmas holidays.

Once inside, my popularity of recent weeks continues when I'm approached by a tipsy ex-*Mardall's* student by the name of Holly Cook who I taught for French. At the time, she was head over heels in love with one of her tall, hunky classmates. I lost count of the number of times I had to step over the pair in the corridors of the *Grosvenor Building*.

"You still with Gary?" I ask.

"No way!" she replies directly into my ear, her cheek in intimate contact with mine. "We split up years ago."

"Oh, you surprise me. I thought you two made the perfect couple."

"Me too. At least until he started beating me up."

"No...?"

"Fraid so. He got really jealous when I spoke to other blokes and tried to control me."

"I'm very sorry to hear that, Holly. Anyone else on the scene?"

Her right thigh is now pressed firmly against my left one.

"No, not really. How 'bout you?"

I tell her briefly about my New Year encounter with Sam and subsequent relationship. Surprisingly, this only intensifies her flirting.

"I'd milk the situation if I were you," Susi and Rich advise when Holly nips to the loo.

Their suggestion astonishes me and I begin to wonder whether they're anxious for me to hit it off with someone a few years older than Sam.

Back by my side, Holly resumes her overt flirting. Whilst I can't deny that I'm flattered by the attention, there's no chance of me cheating on the lovely Sam. I've always been a one-man woman. Or is it the other way round?

On the 14th, Sam receives roses and a card by special delivery. On my return from work, I spot a red envelope resting against the patio doors at the rear of the house. On opening it, I'm confronted by the large, bold French words *Je t'aime* (I love you) inscribed across the front of a cute, lovey-dovey card. Inside, hand-written, is the word *Forever.* Although after such a short time, it'd be crazy to read too much into this remark, the romantic in me can't help but feel touched.

On Saturday, there's a Valentine's party at Hannah's mother's flat, which, according to Sam, is just round the corner from *The William Pitt*. With permission from her parents to stay over, the two of us plan our first full night together.

The evening gets off to a bad start when Sam arrives to pick me up an hour later than agreed. As the world's lousiest timekeeper, it's perhaps hypocritical of me to feel peeved, yet I fail to conceal my annoyance in the car on the way to Hannah's.

Once at the party, Sam places her arms around my neck and, with what has become a ritual bend of her knees to bring her mouth in line with mine, kisses me warmly on the lips.

"I'm really sorry, Al," she says affectionately.

It doesn't take long to win me round and the smile produced for Teresa's camera as I pose with my arm around Sam is one hundred per cent genuine.

It's a well-attended party with people coming and going as they please. Sam indulges in alcohol for the first time since we met. In the company of many of her school friends, she abandons her usually shy exterior.

"I love Miss Ford!" she cries out suddenly about half way through the evening, brandishing a bottle of Reef above her head.

Astounded by such a bizarre declaration, I half expect stunned silence to break out among her friends, but not a single one bats an eyelid.

"So who exactly is Miss Ford?" I enquire later when Sam and I are sprawled out on top of Hannah's bed, enjoying an intimate kiss.

"Oh, she's our PE teacher at school," she says dispassionately. "Everyone loves her."

"Oh, I see."

Sam then bites her bottom lip and says rather tentatively: "Al, I need to tell you something."

"Really? What's that, then?"

"It's a bit awkward. Look, I'm sorry, but I ... I can't stay with you tonight."

With these simple words, a wave of panic sweeps over me. "Why not?"

"Er, it's a bit embarrassing."

"Well, I'm listening."

"Erm, it's my ... period. It's ... er ... come early."

I feel an overwhelming sense of relief. "That's okay, we don't have to do anything. It'll just be great to have you lying beside me for more than a couple of hours."

"Mm, I'll have to see."

With this, we return to the sitting room.

By 2.00, I'm knackered and ready to leave the party. Sam, however, is torn between staying over in the flat with Hannah and a few other friends, and coming home with me. After much deliberation, she opts to accompany me back to the house, along with her friend Tanya, a diminutive girl of Colombian extraction.

Tanya takes the sofa bed in the lounge whilst Sam, complete with T-shirt and tracky bottoms, joins me upstairs.

"Be honest with me, Sam," I say before closing my eyes. "Do you regret having sex with me? I mean, was it too soon?"

"No, not at all," she says at once. "I really have got a problem with my periods. I've been to the doctor about it and it should be sorted soon."

A few days later, Sam produces a photo from her jacket pocket.

"Here, this is Miss Ford," she says, handing it to me. "As you can see, you've got nothing to worry about."

I take a closer look and notice a plain woman in her mid-thirties of slightly butch appearance. Surprised that Sam felt the need to play down her announcement at the party, I return the photo.

During half term, I accompany Sam and her mum to an Open Day at my old university in Southampton. We have lunch at a pub I assure them is merely a five-minute walk away from the language block. But I'm wrong.

We arrive just before the French Professor's introductory talk is due to get underway and discover that a new Language Centre has recently been constructed on the far side of the campus. With profuse apologies to the two ladies, I lead a sprint across to the impressive new building.

By the time we've located the correct room, the Professor is already in full flow. Sam's mum opts to remain outside, leaving the two lovebirds to interrupt the meeting. To my surprise, it's the same Professor that took over half way through my degree and there's an unmistakable look of recognition as he pauses for me and my young lady partner to find a seat. All rather embarrassing.

Later, on one of the guided tours, we bump into a former *Mardall's* student who was the star of her German group and left with a much-coveted grade A. Now taking a degree in the subject, she enthuses about her course. As with my New Year encounter with an ex-student, it's hugely reassuring for me as a teacher to discover that two years under my wing in the classroom didn't sap her enthusiasm for the language.

The rest of the visit runs like clockwork, although by the time I've got back to the house, I feel a little down in the dumps. Whether this is out of acknowledgement that I didn't really make the most of social opportunities whilst at Southampton myself or because the visit reminded me that my days as Sam's boyfriend are numbered, I'm not sure.

However, I soon perk up the following day when Sam arrives at the house unannounced to meet my parents. Earlier on the phone, she protested that she was too shy to put in an appearance and I'd given up hope.

"She's a pretty girl," mum says later. "And so tall!"

It strikes me as ironic, given Howard Parish's insistence back in '93 that my height was a disadvantage in the highly competitive world of dating, that I should end up four and a half years down the line with a girlfriend several inches taller. I suppose it just goes to show that when it comes to human attraction – thank God – there are no hard and fast rules. Nothing is set in stone.

For a change, Sam and I spend the evening at *Razzmattaz* and enjoy some of our most intimate moments to date, barring our handful of sexual encounters, that is. There's a level of intensity to our relationship that I've never felt before, even during my time with Rachel Hill. Although experience tells me otherwise, it seems impossible at this point to conceive of a time when we won't want to be together. Is this love? If so, why has it taken me so long to find?

On the penultimate Saturday of the month, I tweak a muscle in my lower back whilst trampolining, which leaves me barely able to walk out to the car park at the end of the training session. As for driving home, well, that's not much fun either.

In the evening, Sam fetches me from the house and ferries me to *The William Pitt*. Once seated inside, she looks after me superbly, running off to the bar whenever I'm in need of a top-up. What a woman!

When I wake on Sunday, I find that I'm hardly able to move and end up spending the whole day in a prone position. I ring Brian Woolly in the afternoon and warn that I may not be fit enough to carry out my duties in the morning.

There's no improvement overnight, so I do indeed have to take only my second absence in almost nine years of teaching and the first for six years. This miffs me considerably. As is customary in secondary schools, I'm obliged to phone through the work for my classes first thing – rather a laborious task.

After a spot of manipulation at the Sports Injuries Clinic in town, my mobility returns miraculously. On Reception is the mother of a boy and girl I taught for French in my very first job over eight years ago. She recognises me from my previous visits to the clinic and provides the latest instalment of her offspring's progress.

I return to work on Tuesday, feeling like a new man.

By Saturday, I feel severely under the weather – a rare occurrence, given that teachers usually build up immunity to common bugs. But it's my shout for detention duty, so I drag myself into work. If only the traffic were as friendly during the week. For two hours, I sit supervising three miscreants who, by all accounts, put in regular appearances on a Saturday morning. So much for the theory that detention serves as a deterrent.

The first day in March is a Sunday. With a hint of spring in the air, Sam and I enjoy our most intimate love-making session yet. Afterwards, we go for a stroll around the City Centre. Normally shy about daylight displays of affection, Sam takes hold of my hand.

"It was really lovely," she whispers into my ear, tightening her grip. "You know, back at the house. All I need to do now is get my problem sorted."

By this, I assume she's referring to her confused menstrual cycles.

Midweek, Sam flies off to Manchester to attend another Open Day, with the firm promise that she'll ring in the evening to report back. But she doesn't call until the next day.

"I'm afraid I won't be out this weekend," she tells me in a rather detached manner after extolling the virtues of Manchester.

I ask if everything's okay and receive an unconvincing reply in the affirmative.

On Saturday, my services are required once again at *Royal David's*, along with those of the other teaching staff. It's the annual Open Day. The event is well attended, confirming the continued popularity of the school in the area. It seems that for many local parents money is no object when it comes to their children's education.

Just to make sure that she really is okay, I call on Sam unannounced on the way home in the afternoon. I find her in an uncharacteristically distant mood. Rather bizarrely, she openly praises the physical attributes of a male singer displayed on a poster on her bedroom wall.

"I think he's so gorgeous," she says.

Under normal circumstances, I wouldn't feel threatened by a celebrity, yet the bloke in question couldn't possibly be of more contrasting appearance to me – tall, dark and excessively skinny. Almost puny, in fact. Coupled with Sam's inability to look me in the eye, insecurities of old return. An intense conversation ensues with Sam expressing doubts about the future of our relationship. Apparently, her trip to Manchester on Wednesday got her thinking.

"We've been kidding ourselves," she says almost tearfully.

Her use of the word 'we' surprises me, given that I've never harboured any illusions about our long-term future together despite Sam's reassurances. Unsettled by her obvious grief and horrified by the prospect of a premature split, I find myself fighting our cause.

"October's over sixth months away," I say buoyantly. "Anyway, if two people love each other enough, then distance shouldn't be a problem."

Despite my experiences with Rachel, it seems that at this particular moment I have wholehearted faith in the words I'm uttering, so strong is my desire not to lose the happiness I've found since New Year. Perched on the edge of her bed, Sam buries her head deep into her hands. There's a protracted silence.

"I need time to think," she says finally, removing her face from the sanctuary of her palms. "I'll call you in a day or two."

I comply with Sam's wishes and return home, remembering what it's like to be overcome by a strong feeling of vulnerability.

A few hours later, the phone rings. It's Sam.

"Al, I just want to say that … that I love you," she says with total conviction. "And I mean it."

"And I love you too," I tell her, wiping the perspiration from my brow.

With this, it appears that Sam and I are back on course after our first major wobble. What a close shave!

Home from work on the following Tuesday, I just make it into town in time to collect a reprint of Teresa's photo of Sam and me from the Valentine's party. Back at the house, I proudly show it to Mark before finding a frame and putting it on display in a prime position in the lounge.

At about 6.00, there's a ring on the doorbell. I open up to the sight of Sam's friend, Hannah, holding an envelope in an outstretched hand. I take it from her.

"I'm really sorry, Al," she says before turning abruptly on her heels and scampering down the road.

I return to the lounge to read the hand-written contents – a note from Sam.

> *Dear Al,*
> *This is the hardest thing I've ever had to do,*
> *but I'm afraid it's over! Our relationship has*
> *given me some of the happiest moments of*
> *my life, but I now feel that you're tying me*
> *down by being too serious. I liked this in the*
> *beginning, but not any more.*
> *This is so difficult because I really do love*
> *you – it's just come at the wrong stage in my*

life. Please don't try to contact me, I need
some time alone.

Love Sam.

Both surprised and deflated by the words before me, I sink down onto the sofa bed. Mark emerges from upstairs, wondering who was at the door. I show him the letter.

"I'm really sorry, mate," he says, scratching his head. "You two looked so solid."

"I spose everyone was right all along – she was just too young," I say almost mechanically. "More the fool me for not listening."

"Yeah, but you have to stick your neck out sometimes or you'd spend all your life wondering 'what if?'"

Whilst his observation concurs exactly with my philosophy of life, it brings little solace at this disappointing moment. What does offer temporary relief, however, is the reminder that Mark's relationship has known many splits over the years and is now thriving. Then I remember that second chances are not a privilege I've been accustomed to in the past and my heart stings once again.

For the rest of the week, I fail to rediscover that aura of magic that's cast such a positive spell on my time at *Royal David's* since Christmas. Never before have I been more aware of the uplifting influence of my private life on my attitude at work. Then again, at *Mardall's*, the opposite was always the case with my teaching compensating for the shortcomings outside the job.

I return from gym at about 10.30 on Friday, emotionally drained. Not wanting to be alone and desperate for a beer to drown my sorrows, I shower, change and head off to *James Dean's*. Inside the club, I see Teresa and another of Sam's friends, Stephanie, an ex-gymnast who's interested in joining my coaching team on a Friday evening. Both reveal that Sam has been really down in the dumps since Tuesday and is anxious to talk to me.

Back from trampolining late the following morning, I decide to brave a call to Sam. She's relieved to hear my voice.

"I'm so sorry, Al," she says. "I never wanted to send you that letter."

"Really? Why did you, then?" I ask. "Was it your parents?"

"No, it wasn't them. It's … it's really hard to explain."

"Sounds to me as if you don't know what you want."

"Oh, but I *do*."

"So what is it, then?"

"It's you. I want *you*. It's just that … it's not that simple."

I try various approaches in the hope that she'll shed some light on her cryptic remarks, but I'm wasting my breath. If it were any girl other than Sam, I'd deduce that she was deliberately playing mind games. But I know her too well for that, don't I? In the end, we agree to meet later at *The William Pitt*.

My firm intentions to tread carefully on my reunion with Sam go right out the window the second I clap eyes on her. Within minutes, we're back where we were and I'm left wondering why I took her letter so seriously in the first place.

"She was just panicking, that's all," I tell myself, as happy as punch.

We have a great evening together and part with the decision to give our romance another try.

Sam drops in briefly on Wednesday night to invite me to a friend's birthday celebrations on Saturday at *Paddy's*.

"I should be at *The William Pitt* on Friday as well," she says. "Will you be calling in after gym?"

When Friday comes round, I make it to the pub for 10.30. It's as crowded as ever, but I soon spot Sam sitting at a table with four of her friends. Judging by the downcast look on her face and the lack of enthusiasm in her greeting, you'd think that someone had died.

"Can I get you a drink?" I ask cheerfully.

Sam shakes her head slowly and mumbles almost incomprehensibly: "I'm not staying much longer."

I get in a pint for myself. On my return to the table, I find that Sam has already vanished.

"I'm sorry," Hannah says, "she's just left. But if you're quick, you might catch her. Her car's parked outside *The Ram*."

I hand Hannah my drink and storm out of the pub in pursuit of my increasingly wearing girlfriend. As I sprint up the road, I can feel the saliva draining from my mouth – something I used to experience just before gym competitions.

Five minutes later, I'm back in *The Pitt* having missed Sam by a whisker.

"I can't believe she's done this to me again," I rage, on retrieving my pint from Hannah, my self-confidence in tatters once more. "Tell her that … that if she doesn't ring me by … by midnight, then … then I'll never speak to her again."

It's a pathetic threat made by a man caught up in a pathetic situation.

"Isn't this the sort of adolescent rubbish I should've gone through fifteen years ago?" I ask myself despairingly. More than ever, I feel hopelessly exposed by my late-starter status.

Before the bell rings to signal time, I manage to down a further three pints, which only serve to heighten my fury. How could anyone dare to treat me with such disdain?

Instead of staggering back to the house to await a possible call from Sam, I agree to join Dave, one of the barmen, at *James Dean's*. Stephanie is there again.

"I'm so pleased to hear that you and Sam are back together," she says kindly.

I inform her of the latest development.

She looks dumbfounded. "I'm really surprised. She seemed so happy at school this week."

"I don't understand it either. But I know one thing – she's driving me insane."

"Give her a call in the morning, Al. I'm sure you'll be able to sort it out."

I shake my head slowly. "Oh, what's the point?"

"She *really* likes you. You can't leave it like this."

"She's at a lacrosse tournament all day tomorrow, but we were supposed to be meeting at *Paddy's* in the evening for Sylvia's birthday."

"Go along, anyway, and talk to her."

"Er ... okay. If you insist. I spose there's no harm in trying."

"Promise?"

"All right, I promise."

"Oh, by the way, I'd definitely like to accept that gym-coaching job if it's still going."

Back home, there are four bleeps on the answer machine with no messages. Dialling 1471 reveals that the last caller was Sam.

With a firm conviction to bring my relationship with Sam to an amicable conclusion, I make my way to *Paddy's* on Saturday evening. I find her in the company of a lad in his early twenties called Kelvin and notice at once that he's the spitting image of the pop star in her poster. In spite of myself, I'm overcome by a wave of jealousy.

My efforts to communicate with Sam prove largely unsuccessful. She's furious about my threat from last night and the fact that I wasn't at home to take her calls. Her manner is cold and ruthless, a side to her personality that I've not witnessed before.

She begins to lighten up towards closing time and finally admits what's become blatantly obvious to even a dork like me – she doesn't have a clue what she wants.

"How could I have been so wrong about her?" I ask myself. "No-one could've appeared more certain of their desires than Sam did in the first two months of our relationship."

It occurs to me that had I started playing the dating game as a teenager like everyone else, I might've learnt by now how to spot a woman who doesn't know her own mind.

Before she leaves, Sam invites me to join her, Teresa and Kelvin at *Razzmattaz*. Determined not to be a slave to her capriciousness, I decline on the pretence that I'm meeting someone in *OK*.

Typically, the queue outside *OK* is rather daunting. Ten minutes or so into my wait, Sam breezes past with Teresa and Kelvin in tow, having presumably parked her car in the multi-storey round the corner. They catch sight of me immediately.

"Come with us," Teresa says. "You'll be waiting for hours to go in there."

Too weary to contemplate for even a split second what's become of my self-respect, I follow the trio almost magnetically to *Razz*. Kelvin shows off by producing a huge wad of ten-pound notes from his wallet and pays both girls' entrance into the club. Flashy git!

Once inside, Sam and Kelvin make straight for the edge of the dance floor, and resume their conversation of earlier. The latter's body language leaves little doubt in my mind that he's a man on a mission.

"What the hell am I doing here?" I ask myself.

"How you doing, mate?" asks a voice from behind, interrupting my thoughts. "Is everything okay?"

I turn to see an ex-*Mardall's* student called Mike standing behind me. We shake hands and I explain briefly the reason for my blatant anxiety.

"Don't worry," he says. "I don't think she's interested in him in that way."

"No? How can you be so sure?"

"Body language, mate."

There's a relaxation of my stance.

Five minutes later, however, Kelvin lunges forward and sticks his tongue down Sam's throat. And as far as I can see, she's more than willing to return the compliment. Before I have chance to restrain him, Mike, a keen visitor to the gym, skips down the steps onto the dance floor and has a word in Kelvin's ear. As a result, the latter retreats and makes himself scarce. Hot on Mike's heels, I come face to face with Sam.

"How could you do that to me?" I ask. "Right under my nose as well."

"You've got no claim on me any more!" she retorts almost viciously.

I turn to go and pass Teresa on the periphery of the dance floor.

"I can't believe anyone can change their mind so easily about someone," I protest.

"I can," she says. "I've done it myself. Sam does still love you, but more like a brother."

Back home in the warm sanctuary of my bed, I fail to sleep a wink all night, my stomach retching incessantly. Somehow, I just can't dismiss the thought of Sam enjoying steamy sex with her pop star irrespective of her 'problem' and it really hurts. Who would believe that emotions could have such a profound physical effect on the body?

"Maybe it's just as well I didn't fully discover the agony of failed romance as a teenager," I console myself. "I may not have survived through to adulthood."

On Tuesday, the Head observes me teaching one of my A level French classes as part of the school's appraisal process. The lesson runs like a dream, and he leaves at the end with a broad smile and the promise to provide detailed feedback in the morning.

In the evening, Mark shares a bottle of wine with me in the lounge and announces that he'll shortly be moving out in order to take up residence with Julia. She's expecting. In view of my lodger's obvious delight, I congratulate him on his excellent news. At least someone's life is looking up.

My meeting with the Head on the last day of term is a richly positive one. He's full of praise for my teaching abilities.

"The pupils and students think very highly of you too," he says congenially.

Whilst I'm delighted to hear this, it doesn't make it particularly easy for me to broach the awkward subject of my possible resignation in the summer term. However, I feel it my duty to keep him in the picture. I inform him of my love of A level teaching and my reservations about the lower school.

"I understand entirely what you're saying," he says when I've finished my spiel. "You must do whatever's best for you. That said, I would appreciate it if you could arrive at a decision as soon as possible after Easter so that I have time to find a replacement."

He hauls his tall, skinny frame out of his armchair and offers me a hand. "Have a very Happy Easter, Alan!"

After work, I receive a surprise visit from Sam. She's after some photo negatives she lent me.

"I'm really, really sorry about Saturday," she says on her way out.

"Why did you do it?" I ask calmly.

"I don't know. I'm afraid I just can't explain it. As I said, I'm sorry."

I nod in acknowledgement. With little else that needs saying, Sam heads off. At least for once I managed to keep my emotions in check and play it cool.

Mark joins me for a drink at *Paddy's* in the evening. Right on cue, Sam and Teresa appear with Kelvin. I greet them politely, but make no attempt at conversation.

"Good lad!" Mark says. "You played that very well."

"It wasn't easy," I tell him. "My stomach churns at the mere sight of her with him."

"God knows what she sees in him. Looks like a puny little runt to me." How I'll miss Mark's emotional support.

A few days into the holiday, one of Sam's friends approaches me at *James Dean's*.

"I see Sam's completely over you now." she says, almost gloating. "She's got a new boyfriend."

I'm sure there's a word for such kind, tactful individuals.

Soon afterwards, I come across Sam and her friends at *The William Pitt*. Although there's no sign of the puny runt, I decide anyway to persevere with my air of friendly detachment. By chance, I spot an ex-pupil at the bar who's now twenty-one. She's pleased to see me and, what's more, she seems keen to chat.

We're still deep in conversation when the landlord calls time. Finishing off the last drop of my pint, I hear a female voice from behind say: "Excuse me."

I turn to catch Sam towering over us.

"Al, I really need to talk to you," she says. "Is it okay if I pop round and see you sometime?"

Jealousy, what a powerful emotion it can be.

SUMMER TERM

All bad things come in threes says one proverb, *Third time lucky* says another. It's now the end of the Easter holidays and I'm reflecting on a bizarre string of events that resulted in Sam Woodfield worming her way back into my affections once again. Oh yes, 'sucker of the century' is a title I can now claim as my very own. "Al, I need to talk to you" turned out to be a desire on Sam's behalf to clarify her position. Contrary to popular belief, she hadn't started a relationship with Kelvin, for the simple reason that she wasn't ready to move on so rapidly after such a 'special' romance with me. A week in Lanzerote with her parents, sister, friend Tanya and a photo of a certain language teacher helped her decide that, in reality, she didn't want to move on at all. With Kelvin eagerly awaiting her return down at *The William Pitt*, Sam gave the cold shoulder and threw herself into the arms of a gobsmacked Alan Bentley who just happened to be sitting at a nearby table. Kelvin's threat to assemble an army of mates in the pub car park to 'get me' didn't materialise.

Sam's explanation of her few weeks of insanity was so convincing and her apologies so genuine that I found myself agreeing to have a final stab at our relationship – on the condition that it wouldn't get in the way of her exams.

"That's just it," she said. "I want us to be together during them cos it'll help me focus."

No previous girlfriend has ever finished with me and fully realised her mistake once, let alone twice, and I can't help feeling that this must mean something. And as the older party, surely it'd be insensitive not to make allowances for her age and the turbulent stage of her life. Over and above all this, though, I'm more certain than ever that I'm actually in love with Sam and I've been told that the course of true love never runs smooth.

With lodger Mark's departure to play happy families with his girlfriend, I've cleared out his old room and decorated the middle bedroom with a view to taking on two replacements. I've placed an ad on the staff notice board at the General Hospital up the road in the hope of enticing a couple of young doctors. Or, better still, a pair of nurses to look after me should Sam decide to ditch me for a third time.

Back at work in mid-April, I take the plunge and hand in my notice without another post to go to. With the deadline for resignation in the independent sector falling a month earlier than in the state system – on 30th April – I've decided that, if push came to shove, I'd rather sell my house than struggle on in the wrong job for what would effectively be another year. It's simply not in my nature to abandon exam classes at Christmas or Easter. The Head expresses his disappointment, but promises a good reference.

A few days later, I spot an advertisement in the *TES* for a Curriculum Manager for German at *Lower Valley Sixth Form College*, one of *Mardall's* competitors. It's only a twenty-five minute drive from the City.

"D'you think I'd be capable of running my own department?" I ask Brian Woolly, the current Head of Languages. I give him the low-down on the job.

"Absolutely!" he replies. "If you think about it, you've more or less been in charge of Upper Sixth French here since Christmas, anyway. You'd be a fool not to apply."

On reflection, he's right. With Sandrine, my French-teaching colleague, on sick leave through stress, I've had to take sole responsibility for the two second-year French A level groups for the whole of the last term. Considering that classes were shared at *Mardall's*, this has been a new experience for me, yet hardly one that's proved much of an issue. I decide to submit an application for the *Lower Valley* job.

On the second Monday after Easter, Sam is keen to call round after an early evening swimming practice at school. I'm just about to leave for my trampolining training, so I have to put her off.

Sam pops round on Wednesday in a hot and flushed state after staying on for tennis. Everything seems fine, although I reckon it'll be some time before I feel completely at ease with her again. I keep this insecurity to myself, of course.

On Saturday, Sam reappears with the notes she's made in preparation for her French oral presentation and asks me to check them through. She's a bright girl and there's very little to correct. I suggest giving her a full mock oral, but she declines politely.

Sam is tied up with exam revision in the evening, so I head off to *The Pitt* on my own. Whilst there, I get talking to an exceptionally pretty French-Canadian girl called Celine who's been employed by the landlord and his wife to be a nanny for their two young children.

The following Thursday, there's a note from Sam in the letterbox, informing me that she's off to the theatre tonight, but that she'll ring tomorrow.

It's now Saturday and it appears that Sam is up to her old trick of not phoning when she says she will. I hate this whoever it is. I give her a quick call in the evening to see if she's okay and receive an answer that's far from convincing. She's also unusually taciturn. Here we go again.

At the pub later on, I bump into her friend, Tanya.

"Is everything more stable now with you and Sam?" she asks.

"I thought it was," I reply, "but ..."

"But *what*? Go on, you can tell me."

I hesitate first before proceeding to inform Tanya about the phone call.

"Al, it's not on," she says insistently. "You mustn't let her treat you like this."

"I know I shouldn't, but I'm worried about putting her under too much pressure with the exams so close."

"You don't need to be. Sam is really brainy and will fly through her A levels whatever happens. You're being too nice."

"D'you reckon?"

"Yes, definitely! Look, I'm seeing her tomorrow. I'll get her to call you so you can sort this out."

After an hour's private tuition in the morning, I return to an angry answer machine message from Sam, accusing me of not trusting her. I call back immediately and it isn't long before she drops her hostile front.

"I'm so sorry, Al," she says wearily. "It's not your fault. It's me ... and my problem."

"What, your period problem?" I ask.

"No, it's ... it's more complicated than that."

"Well, if you'd just tell me what it is, maybe I could ..."

"No, I ... I just can't. I'm sorry. But ... but you do need to know that what's happened between us will never happen again."

How I loathe the word 'never'. It always seems so final. Totally bamboozled and without an ounce of fight left in my body, I bring the conversation to an abrupt close.

"I will explain one day, Al," Sam says as a parting comment. "I promise."

As if the pain of losing someone I love for the third time isn't bad enough, the look of 'I told you so' on the faces of those close to me only serves to heighten my mood of despondency. Yet, however naive and stupid I've been since the beginning of the year, I'm finding it impossible to dismiss the role fate played in bringing Sam and me together in the first place. My shock redundancy. An imposed house move to another town. Months of solitude. Helen Forward's stand up on New Year's Eve. Doorman BJ's kind intervention at *The William Pitt*. And finally, Sam's timely presence at the pub. Somehow, the Fatalist in me felt that this peculiar train of events had to point in the direction of something significant. But, with the benefit of hindsight, all these seemingly related incidents amounted to little more than a series of coincidences and the only significant factor was the exposure once again of a vulnerable romantic hell-bent on finding true love.

I've already lost count of the number of times I've been told to remember how mixed up I probably was at eighteen. Yet in spite of my undoubted faults and lack of experience of love at that age, I always knew what I wanted. Indecision is not a condition I've ever been able to relate to easily. What I can relate to, however, is the truth and, as much as it hurts me to admit it, I have to accept that Sam Woodfield obviously isn't THE ONE any more than Rachel Hill was, irrespective of her 'problem'. I have to move on. It's as simple as that. It would be interesting to know what the problem is, though. I still can't believe that Sam made it up to get her off the hook.

Just as I'm in the process of exploring pastures new one night at *The Pitt* with Celine, the French-Canadian *au pair*, Barney Underwood, a former

French student from Cara and Mandy 'Mandarin's' year at *Mardall's*, descends on our table in Rupert Stanley fashion.

"You gonna introduce me to this gorgeous young lady, then, Al?" he asks in a typically confident, almost arrogant, manner.

He takes a seat. Now a tree surgeon, Barney's appearance has changed little since his college days – long, wavy, somewhat greasy hair, prominent stubble on his face and dirt under his fingernails. Celine beams at the sight of him. Within five minutes, the clean-cut language teacher, trying his best to heal a broken heart, is cast aside in favour of a rough and ready ex-student some ten years his junior.

A few days later, Barney announces with glee that he's bedded Celine and that he may or may not start to date her properly, depending on how he feels. If only I could've been blessed with such supreme confidence. I think I'll cancel that hairdresser's appointment and search for an evening job in a chippy. Maybe a skim through *Lady Chatterley's Lover* wouldn't go amiss either.

On the penultimate Wednesday in May, I attend an interview for the Head of German position at *Lower Valley Sixth Form College*. On my arrival, I'm introduced to the other three short-listed candidates, two of which are German native speakers. The third is a young English woman with only a couple of years' teaching experience. The eldest of the two Germans displays an extremely confident manner and discloses that he's been an A level oral examiner for one of the Boards for many years. His fellow countryman is a rather shy man with a beard, glasses and an unfortunate blink – less of a threat, on the surface.

The interview process proves to be the most demanding I've ever encountered. Each candidate is required to teach a twenty-minute German lesson to a group of Lower Sixth students, conduct conversations in German and French – the latter with a native speaker – and undergo a literary assessment. And all this happens before the formal interview in the afternoon with the Vice-Principal, a Mr Kevin Gough. Apparently, the Principal, a certain Dr Robert Faulkner, is in London attending an important meeting.

With all the interviews completed, there's a long, nervous wait in Reception until Kevin, a highly enthusiastic, witty man in his mid-forties, reappears.

"Al," he says with a flourish. "Would you mind stepping into my office one more time?"

Before I have chance to take a seat, he thrusts his hand into mine.

"Congratulations!" he says with a broad grin. "You were the best candidate and I'm delighted to be able to offer you the job. Everyone

involved in the selection process came down on your side, including the
students. Very well done!"

I thank him for his kind words.

"I gather you were very happy at *Mardall's College* before a last-in,
first-out redundancy. Well, I can say with hand on heart that we've got an
even better set-up here."

Breathing a huge sigh of relief, I drive away from the College with the
professional side of my life firmly back on track.

As if to emphasize the upturn in my fortune, a pair of Spanish girls, who
are employed at the hospital as cleaners, respond to my ad for lodgers and
take up residence at the end of May. Their names are Victoria and
Arancha. Both are in their early twenties. After some negotiation, it's
agreed that they'll share the larger bedroom from the beginning of August
to allow a third Spanish friend, Natalia, to join them. Nurses they may not
be, but hey, am I complaining?

The final day at *Royal David's* for the Upper Sixth is an emotional affair.
Some of the lads have been at the school for twelve years. There's a
concert in the chapel at lunchtime and I help my form sing a cleverly
rejigged version of *Imagine*:

> *Imagine no Royal David's,*
> *It's really hard to do* etc etc

Whilst it may not have been the right job for me, that doesn't mean to say
that I haven't met some great people here over the last year and enjoyed
some special moments.

Shortly afterwards at *The William Pitt*, I make friends with a single man
in his mid-thirties called Colin Stringfellow. He works for a high-powered
computer company and is the spitting image of Oliver Hardy with the
addition of a rosy complexion and a thick West Country accent. Moreover,
he's as keen as I am to meet the lady of his dreams. We have another
point in common – he too seems to have developed a strong affinity for
The Pitt.

On a visit to the pub in early June, I find BJ back on the door after a long
absence. He's pleased to see me and asks after Sam. I fill him in.

"I'm very sorry to hear that, mate," he says. "You two made such a
great couple. If it's any consolation, you'll probably be the best man she
ever meets in her life."

"Thanks a lot," I say. "It's really kind of you to say that."

"You never know. Sometime in the future you could be walking through town on a miserable, wet afternoon and you'll come across a forlorn figure wrapped up in an anorak. The face'll look down at you and you'll recognise it at once as Sam's. She'll smile and you'll know for sure that this time she really is ready for you."

What a better place the world would be if there were more BJs in it.

A couple of days later, I run into Sam. She apologises once more for her recent behaviour. I ask one last time about her 'problem', but she just shakes her head.

"There's no way I can tell you," she says. "It's far too risky. Anyway, I think you've got a reasonable idea what it is."

Have I like hell!

One evening back at the house, I'm alone with Arancha, one of my Spanish lodgers, who's ditched her cleaning job at the hospital for a better paid position at *Opportunity Knox*. She's fractionally shorter than I am with brown eyes, jet-black hair and a curvy body – typically Mediterranean, I suppose. We chat in depth over a bottle of wine and I discover that she postponed the chance to go to university in Spain to come over to England to improve her English. With the bottle virtually empty, I end up relating my adventure with Sam and expressing my continued love for her. To my surprise, Arancha edges closer to me along the sofa bed. We exchange a few kisses.

"I do not mind that you are still in love with your girlfriend," she says. "I do not want to be serious with an English man."

I've never been a rebound person in the past, but I decide that it's a new experience I should perhaps try as a form of therapy.

The following week, Arancha returns from *OK* at 2.30 in the morning and sneaks into my bedroom, waking me in the process.

"I not want sex," she says assertively, climbing under the duvet.

With the alarm set for 6.30, I'm relieved to hear it and roll over. Arancha, however, sees this as a challenge and sets about trying to turn me on. The result – I don't get back to sleep until 4.00.

"Why did you tease me like that?" I ask in the morning.

"I wanted to see if you have self-control."

"Oh dear, that's another test I've well and truly failed."

Needless to say, keeping my eyes open at work proves a far from straightforward task. With reports to write and end-of-year exams to mark for my own classes as well as some of Sandrine's, my nocturnal adventure couldn't have come at a worse time. Some people, eh – they're never satisfied.

In the middle of June, I run into yet another former French student from *Mardall's* who gave me a lift home from *Razz* one night last year soon after I'd moved to the City. She expressed an interest in corresponding with me on her return to university, so I popped into the house and scribbled down my address on a scrap of paper. After that, I never heard a word.

"I'm sorry I didn't ever get in touch, Al," she says, "but the black guy who was in the car with us when I dropped you back ate your address."

Was he hungry or just out to obliterate all opposition?

I spend the following day at *Lower Valley Sixth Form* in preparation for next year. Just as I'm about to head off after a constructive and highly informative induction, the departing Curriculum Manager for German has a quiet word in my ear.

"I think there's something you should know about Yvonne, the Head of Languages," she says somewhat diffidently.

Concerned that she's about to burst the bubble by telling me that the woman is impossible to work under, I brace myself for the worst.

"It's just that she's … well, she's a lesbian," she says. "And she's having a relationship with one of the English teachers. It shouldn't be a problem, but I wouldn't want you to put your foot in it like I did when I first arrived."

With Nicky and Clement in mind, I assure her that I'm now an old hand on the subject of sexual deviation.

On the penultimate Sunday of the month, Arancha cooks an impressive-looking paella. She explains that her parents are the proprietors of a restaurant back in Spain and that she's used their secret recipe. The taste is simply sublime. I have to admit that, whilst her attentions have helped to keep my ego intact, it really is too soon for me to erase Sam's memory. In fact, I've begun to realise why dating someone on the rebound rarely works – it only serves to intensify the sense of longing for what has been lost. I feel guilty about this, particularly as Arancha seems to have become more attached to me recently. She's heading off to Majorca for a three-week holiday in a few days and I'm looking forward to some time alone to get my head straight.

Back at work, my replacement, Natalie Giordinelli, comes in for the afternoon. She's a pretty, half-Italian girl in her mid-twenties. Given the school's rugby tradition, Brian asks at lunch if she has any interest in the sport. Natalie goes on to describe with apparent glee an occasion at university when she joined the rugby players in their training.

"At one point, I actually managed to get hold of the ball and run a few yards with it," she says. "Then all of a sudden, I felt the whole team go down on me."

With Brian and I in hysterics, Natalie looks on innocently. We manage eventually to stem the flow of laughter and finish our desserts. Conscious of the time, Brian rises to his feet.

"Right, young lady," he says to the new recruit. "It's time you and I cracked on. Would you like to follow me upstairs?"

My final day at *Royal David's* arrives on 3rd July. On every staircase and in every corridor, I seem to run into a colleague who's awaiting my leaving speech with bated breath.

"I'm expecting a lot of laughs," each one declares.

With nothing prepared in advance, I take advantage of a free period to make some notes.

There's a final service in the chapel at noon. With all the pupils and students dismissed, the teachers then assemble in the small, cosy Staff Room. Downing a huge swig of wine for Dutch courage, I take the floor nervously after Brian has given a generous 'epitaph'. I make the necessary thank-yous, then launch into the main part of my speech, a fictional story.

"So, after Phil, our beloved Head of PE, had requested that I find a replacement trampolining coach amongst the current staff, I drew up a shortlist of four," I begin. "Firstly, there was Susan, our delightful Head of Sixth Form. She tried on a series of brightly-coloured Lycra leotards, but none of them looked quite right, so I turned my attentions to Tommy, my diminutive friend in the Maths Department." Tommy looks up from an armchair nearby and smiles. "But, unfortunately, each time he attempted to bounce on the trampoline, he disappeared through one of the tiny holes in the webbing and ended up in a pile on the floor below."

There's moderate laughter, although not from Tommy whose smile has miraculously disappeared. I take a deep breath before resuming.

"So this left me with Harry, my drill sergeant colleague from the Language Department, and his ravishing fiancée, Lucianna Thompson, our resident expert on the History of Art." Harry is away on a course, but Lucianna is present in her full glory and beams bashfully. "As I'm sure you're all aware, these two lovebirds came together as a result of each renting one of the small on-site chalets. Anyway, since I've found it impossible to set this couple apart, I've made up my mind that they should share the job of trampolining coach."

I pause for breath once more and notice an array of faces eagerly awaiting the punch line.

"So, instead of bouncing together in the privacy of one or the other's chalet," I conclude, "I thought they could give regular public displays on the trampoline over in the Sports Hall."

There's laughter and warm applause on all sides. Relieved that my gamble seems to have paid off even in the presence of the three men of the cloth, I thank everyone once more and step down. The Head takes my hand and shakes it firmly.

"Excellent speech, Alan!" he says sportingly.

As we all make our way over to the canteen for the final meal, there are further handshakes and generous praise for my 'performance'. High on adrenaline, I take a seat alongside Brian, with the firm belief that I've just experienced the perfect send-off. But I'm counting my chickens. No sooner have I started to tuck into the first course than I'm accosted by an irate Lucianna Thompson, a strict Catholic.

"How could you be so cruel about us?" she seethes. "In front of all the staff as well. I'll never forgive you for this!"

"I'm sorry – it was only a joke," I say, holding up both hands. "I ... I think everyone was aware of that."

"But that's just it. I don't think they were. What's more, Father Malcolm's the curate who's agreed to marry Harry and me in the summer. What must he have thought? I've never felt so embarrassed in all my life."

Brian takes a large intake of breath through clenched teeth as I try in vain to dig myself out of a sizeable hole. Unwilling to be appeased, Lucianna storms off back to her table. Brian coughs awkwardly.

"Don't worry," he says. "She'll come round."

Aware that my attempts at humour have overstepped the mark, I decide not to hang around after lunch. As I make my final exit from the school grounds, it occurs to me that for the second time in the space of a year a whole new chapter in my teaching career is soon to unfold. Only, this time, I'll be rejoining rather than leaving my favourite sector.

The Long
and Winding Road

(Year 7)

Many times I've been alone and many times I've cried.
Anyway you've always known the many ways I've tried,
But still they lead me back to the long, winding road.

AUTUMN TERM

With its maiden French A level lesson under the direction of yours truly successfully negotiated, the twelve-strong group of young hopefuls spills out into the corridor, leaving a lone straggler hovering over my right shoulder. I look up from my desk and notice a slightly older-looking, dark-featured girl with smiling eyes waiting to address me.

"Erm, excuse me, Mr Bentley – er, sorry, *Al*," she says. "Could I have a word, please?"

Impressed by the young lady's impeccable manners, I smile warmly and say: "Of course you can."

"Er ... it's just that I think you should know that I haven't done any French for ... well, almost a year now."

"Really? How come?"

"Well, I started my A levels last year in the Sixth Form of my school. But then I went down with glandular fever and had to take time off."

"Oh, bad luck!"

"Mm. I felt a lot better after a couple of months, but I was so far behind I decided to get a job for the rest of the year and start somewhere else this September."

"And here you are."

"Yes."

"Okay, fair enough." I glance down at the makeshift register in front of me. "So what's your name?"

"I'm Charlotte. Charlotte Rhys-Jones."

"Er, oh yes. Here you are near the bottom. Hello Charlotte."

"Hi ya," she says with a cheesy grin. "I wanted you to know cos I'll probably be a bit rusty and need some extra help, particularly with grammar."

"That won't be a problem. There's some excellent support material here in the department that you're more than welcome to make use of."

"Cool."

"And don't be afraid to ask for any other assistance you may need. That's what I'm here for."

"Okay, thanks."

The conversation seems to have run its course, but Charlotte is in no hurry to leave.

"I taught myself Spanish at home last year and managed to pass a GCSE in it," she says.

"Well done!"

"Mm, I don't know. But I am taking it for A level as well as French."

"Good. Sounds like you're a talented linguist."

For the first time, Charlotte's composed, confident exterior falters as she bows her head coyly.

"I'm not sure about that," she murmurs. After a momentary pause, she looks up at me again and says in her normal volume: "I am very keen, though."

With a broad, ivory smile complementing a prolonged focus of her sparkling hazel eyes, she then thanks me, says "See ya" and marches off.

"What a sweet, friendly young woman," I say to myself. "Really enthusiastic too."

It's amazing what a change of setting can do to lift one's morale. I'm just over a week into my new job at *Lower Valley Sixth Form* and already it feels like a breath of fresh air. In fact, I'm starting to buzz very much like I used to at *Mardall's*. Gone is that constant fear of being undermined in the classroom by bolshie eleven- to sixteen-year-olds. There's no escaping the fact that I'm simply not ruthless enough to deal effectively with the most challenging offenders. Rather frustratingly, they seem to end up liking me at the expense of respecting my authority. A bit of a character flaw on my part, I guess. As the unmistakable clip-clop of Charlotte Rhys-Jones' boots disappearing down the corridor fades, it really strikes home how lucky I am to be back in the more adult Sixth Form set-up.

So far I haven't noticed any drastic differences from *Mardall's*. The population of the College is roughly the same – about fifteen hundred students – with the majority taking A level or GNVQ courses. With the Principal, Dr Robert Faulkner, insisting on first name terms between staff and students, it promises to be an even more informal working environment. I'm told he places a strong emphasis on running the College along business lines, with the students regarded as our highly valued customers – ones whose demands must be satisfied at all costs. In return, the students are expected to take responsibility for their studies and behave in a mature fashion. It all sounds impressive on paper.

For the first time in my full-time teaching career, I won't be required to take charge of a form for registration. This is down to the fact that there are sixteen members of staff who are employed to teach their subject for half a timetable and share pastoral duties for the other half. They're known as Personal Tutors here. It's a dimension to the job I'll miss every bit as much as I did as a part-timer, but then I am expecting to have my work cut out managing and teaching the German students single-handed. Whilst I'm settling in, I think I'll hold fire before volunteering to run gym and trampolining clubs. It'd be crazy to overburden myself with commitments at this early stage.

I know I'm incorrigible, but it hasn't escaped my attention that one of the Personal Tutors – a shorthaired brunette from Liverpool in her mid to late twenties – is rather cute. I first noticed her on the day of my interview and we exchanged a few brief words. I think she remembers because on the handful of occasions we've passed in the corridor so far this week, she's treated me to a warm, almost flirtatious, smile. Things are definitely looking up.

As far as the summer holidays are concerned, Arancha returned from Majorca in early August determined to end our liaison and back it up with the silent treatment. I assumed this was in response to my admission before her departure that I still felt unable to commit to a relationship. In my defence, she did know the score right from the outset. To be honest, though, it's more than just a question of a broken heart on my side. Despite Sam's horrendous indecision and ultimate lack of respect for my feelings, we did share many common interests – sport, languages, taste in music and humour – and this isn't the case with my Spanish lodger. I've never subscribed to the 'opposites attract' theory. A further angle to Arancha's protest has involved her deliberately rearranging objects in the house to her own liking without consulting the landlord. I'm all for an amicable truce, but this is impossible to achieve when one of the parties refuses to communicate. Why is life always so complicated? I guess, with hindsight, that it was unwise to indulge in a rebound romance with someone so close to home.

There were a couple of possible romantic opportunities over the summer, which I think are worth mentioning. The first kicked off when I returned to *Royal David's* mid-August on the day the A level results were released. I was proud to discover that all but one of my twelve French students had passed – there were five As, two Bs and two Cs – and that there were two As and two Cs in the four-strong German group I shared with Brian Woolly. My buoyant mood prompted me to ask my replacement – twenty-six-year-old Natalie Giordinelli – out for dinner. We met up a few days later and she spent what seemed like the entire duration of the meal explaining why she didn't believe in sex before marriage. On top of this, her dad called her twice on her mobile to check she was all right. The bizarre thing is, had our paths crossed about ten years ago when I was still Mr Innocent, I'd have almost certainly found her attitude endearing. But now, the thought of sexless dating at the age of almost thirty-three after so many years of abstention has seriously lost its appeal.

My second adventure began one Friday evening towards the end of August when I bumped into a striking twenty-year-old brunette called Laura Nicholson who was propping up the bar at *The William Pitt*. She used to do German at *Mardall's* and, although I didn't teach her, recognised me at once. She then spent over an hour chatting to me in a flatteringly flirtatious fashion. I didn't read too much into this at first since she'd told me she had a serious boyfriend. However, when the bell rang to signal time, she confidently asked if I'd mind walking her home.

"I'm actually engaged to my boyfriend," she said, as she led me down one of the dark back streets. "I do love him and I'm sure we'll get married one day, but … but sometimes I think it'd be nice to have a bit more fun first. D'you know what I mean?"

Uncertain as to whether it was me she was lining up as a possible playmate, I just kept walking. Anyway, I had to spare a thought for her poor fiancé. Five minutes later, we arrived at her front door and she paused for reflection.

"Would you like to come in?" she then asked decisively, flicking her long, mahogany hair out of her face to reveal a warm, seductive smile.

"What about your … er … boyfriend?" I asked back. "I thought you mentioned earlier that he lived with you and your mum?"

"He does, but he's away at the moment and mum'll be in bed. C'mon."

Laura then turned the key and I followed her into the hallway, somewhat intrigued.

"Would it really matter if something happened?" I asked myself, deciding to go with the flow. "After all, I'm not the one who's engaged and … well, she is pretty 'fit'."

Just as my conscience had settled the moral dilemma unanimously in my favour, I spotted a female figure, clad in a baggy dressing gown, drifting in an almost ghost-like manner down the stairs.

"Laura, is that you?" she called out, seconds before arriving face to face with me, standing in the obscurity of the kitchen door.

There was an embarrassed silence before Laura finally spoke up, her manner unmistakably hesitant: "Oh, mum, this is … er … Al. He used to be one of the … er … German teachers at *Mardall's College.*"

"Hello, Al," Mrs Nicholson replied, taking my hand. "Laura, there's a bottle of wine in the fridge. I'll join you and Al for a glass."

Laura's mother's untimely appearance meant that I never did get to find out what Laura had in store for me, if anything. We did meet for lunch the following week, but she was completely sober then and the topic of conversation revolved almost exclusively around her fiancé.

With my social life languishing once again, I found myself making contact with Rupert Stanley and inviting him over for a night out on the town. Having finally decided to ditch his long-term Austrian girlfriend rather than lead her down the isle – or should I say 'up the garden path?' – he jumped at the opportunity to hit one of the City's clubs in search of another devoted partner. At *James Dean's*, he targeted a seventeen-year-old *Mardall's* student called Amber who, after an earful of Rupert charm, was only too happy to give the green light. Back at my place, he kept me up drinking until 4.00 in the morning, reiterating his good fortune. And this after I'd poured my heart out over my failed romance with Sam. If I hadn't known him better, I'd have thought he was deliberately ramming his success down my throat.

"Was going out on my own really such a big deal?" I remember thinking when I finally managed to convince him it was time to turn in.

Since then, Rupert and Amber have become an established item. Needless to say, she thinks the sun shines out of his backside. If I were a betting man, I'd wager that he'll be the first to lose interest, not her. And you can be sure there'll be no unmentionable problems tormenting his young lady. Things like that just don't happen to the Ruperts of this world. Jammy old bugger!

In addition to Alan Bentley, the Language Department at *Lower Valley* is composed of three permanent female teachers, all over the age of forty. At the helm is Yvonne Lambert, the lesbian, whose shyness frequently prevents her from making eye contact. This can be a bit disconcerting at first, but I like her. She's taken charge of all the Upper Sixth French A level classes, leaving me to share responsibility for the three Lower Sixth groups with a native speaker by the name of Simone. She's a lady who pulls no punches. Although some may interpret her manner as bordering on the rude, I'd just describe it as 'direct', which means there are seldom misunderstandings when she's around. My ideal woman, in this respect. Margaret Becker, the Head of Spanish, is also a Personal Tutor. She's a tall, imposing woman who at meetings leaves no-one in any doubt that her workload exceeds that of any other colleague. Whilst there's a different

French and German language assistant from abroad each year – this year's ones will arrive in early October – the Spanish Department employs a local Spanish lady called Begonia to come in and take conversation classes. On appearance, I'd say she's only marginally older than I am.

All in all, I've been made to feel very welcome in the Language Department during my first month here. What is slightly disappointing, however, is that the new Staff Room isn't quite finished. Consequently, getting to know colleagues in other curriculum areas is limited to lunchtimes in the canteen, which are generally a mad rush.

On the penultimate Sunday of the month, I pop over to Sam's to collect some French books I lent her months ago.

"They've been in my car for weeks," she says. "I'm sorry, Al. I thought I was bound to bump into you before I went away."

One evening during the following week, I'm busy preparing lessons on a computer my new drinking partner, Colin, salvaged from the scrap heap at work when I receive a surprise visitor. It's Sam.

"I couldn't remember your number," she says sprightly. "And I wanted to invite you to *OK* on Saturday for Tanya's birthday. It'll also be a farewell party before we all go off to uni."

Presuming that this is a goodwill gesture on Sam's behalf, I agree to look in.

At the club on Saturday, I barely have chance to say hello to Sam when she leaves to catch up with another group of friends who are drinking somewhere else in town.

"I'll be back later," she says over her shoulder.

However, by 1.00 there's no sign of her, so I finish my drink and head off home.

"How is it," I ask myself, "that Sam manages to let me down just as much when we're friends as when we were together?"

In many ways, I think I'll be happier when she's at university and I won't bump into her other than during the holidays.

Incidentally, Sam's friend, Teresa, has begun to reveal a darker side. On several occasions recently, she's passed me in town and muttered "paedo" under her breath. And to think she was instrumental in bringing Sam and me together in the first place. I know I should be thicker skinned, but I find her manner rather upsetting.

As one of the most popular pubs in the City, *The William Pitt* has started to attract some of my former students from *Royal David's*. They always seem pleased to see me and most are keen to hear about my new job. I'm aware that many of them are still seventeen, but my attitude towards this is the same as it's always been: it's not my responsibility as a teacher to police under-age drinking in my free time. For this purpose, the pub always employs bouncers on the door like BJ who are supposed to check ID. One of the students, Siobhan O'Donohue, a member of the school's trampolining club, has been helping out at my private gym club on a Friday night.

On the first Saturday in October, I'm at the bar in *The Pitt*, chatting to Siobhan, when Colin approaches us with a child-like smirk and pushes two one-pound coins into my palm.

"That's the money you lost in the condom machine on your last visit to the loo," he says with an Oliver Hardy grin and moves hastily along the bar.

Siobhan's eyes jump out of their sockets. Out of the corner of my eye, I can see Colin milking his joke with the landlord, Stu. Colin has become particularly pally with him and his wife, Lynne, and often helps out with glass collecting. What's more, he frequently treats the couple and some of the other bar staff to doughnuts on a Saturday lunchtime. I wonder what he's after.

The weekend after his prank, Colin asks me to accompany him on a trip to Plymouth to clear out his recently deceased mother's house. We go pubbing in the evening and Colin introduces me to one of his former girlfriends who he insists is a perfect match for me. Whilst I'm not entirely convinced, we do, nevertheless, share a drunken kiss in the taxi on the way back to the house.

Back at *The Pitt* the following Friday, Colin can't wait to inform Stu, Lynne, the bar staff and anyone else present that Al has actually pulled someone older than one of his students. For some reason, he finds the whole situation highly amusing.

On Saturday, Martin Studd joins me at the pub. Before it gets busy, a man with a seven- or eight-year-old daughter comes in collecting for charity. Martin and I make a donation as do Colin and the few others present.

"Why don't you run after her?" Colin shouts out once the man and young girl have left the premises. "She's about the right age for you!"

He then emits a hearty roar from the base of his large lungs. Some of the bar staff join in with the laughter, among them a twenty-two-year-old called Andrew who was a pupil in my first job almost ten years ago. The landlady, however, retains a deadpan expression. With a sporting smile, I shake my head slowly.

"You shouldn't let him do that to you," Martin whispers into my ear once the commotion has died down.

I screw up my forehead and say: "Oh, but he's only having a laugh."

"Mm, maybe, but I don't think it was that funny. There are people in here who don't know you and may've got the wrong impression."

Confident that Martin is worrying unnecessarily, I end the conversation with a shrug.

In his first few weeks at the College, the new German language assistant, Hans Schneider, has made a positive impression. He's a highly sociable individual in his mid-twenties with a taste for hand-made clothes, which compliment perfectly his hippie appearance. A lengthy discussion one afternoon reveals that he has an ulterior motive for spending a year in England – to be closer to an English girl he met on a trip to India. She lives in Cambridge. He tells me that she's visiting later in the month and suggests I join them for dinner at an Indian restaurant he's booked. I accept.

A few days later over lunch, Paul Redhead, the phlegmatic Curriculum Manager for RE and Philosophy, invites Hans and me to a party at the house he rents with a couple of other teaching colleagues. By chance, it clashes with our proposed dinner date, so Hans declines the invitation politely.

"Well, it's an all-night party with lots of people planning to stay over, so you're more than welcome to come along after your meal out," Paul says kindly.

"Yes, that would be very nice. Thank you," Hans says after receiving a nod of approval from me, the driver.

Just out of interest, I ask Paul which other members of staff will be turning out and am happy to hear that my Scouser friend, Penny, has received an invite.

A German assistant friend joins Hans, his girlfriend and me at the Indian on the Saturday of the party. The restaurant is packed and the service painfully slow, which means we don't arrive at Paul's place until about 11.30. Everything appears ominously quiet, although from the doorstep it's possible to see through the gaps in the Venetian blind that there's a small group chatting in the kitchen.

The door is opened cautiously by a striking young woman who I've never seen before. I explain who we are. Without a word, she leads us with obvious reluctance through to the kitchen where there are two male teachers and – wait for it – Penny. Yes! My initial excitement is held in check by the sudden recognition that we've probably walked in on two imminent or even present couples, hence the blatantly unfriendly welcome.

At this point, Paul enters the kitchen in shorts and a T-shirt, followed by his teenage girlfriend. He greets us warmly and introduces his other half – an attractive brunette from the Eastern bloc. He then apologises for the fact that most people have already crashed for the night. Before returning upstairs to the bedroom, he invites us to help ourselves to booze.

In an attempt to ease the tension, I strike up conversation with one of the blokes – an English teacher from *Lower Valley* called Carl. Hans and his girlfriend follow suit with Penny and the other woman.

"So ... erm ... which of the ... er ... young ladies here is your other half?" I ask with an exaggerated air of nonchalance.

Carl chuckles.

"None of them," he says. "Phil and I are gay. But not together, of course."

Excellent! So I could still be in with a chance with the lovely Penny. The fact that she's closer to my age would definitely help to silence Colin and the rest of *The Pitt* gang.

"And Penny and Colette," Carl adds. "Well, they're ... er ... partners."

Stunned by an announcement that I'd have never predicted in a million years despite my wide experience of sexual deviation – if you know what I mean – I open my mouth to speak. But nothing comes out. The words in my head, however, are loud and clear – someone, somewhere is splitting their sides at my expense.

Hans, his girlfriend and I stick around for about an hour, making polite conversation. The atmosphere in the kitchen improves considerably, although my desire for partying wanes somewhat after my shock discovery. How could I have got it so wrong? I could've sworn Penny's smiles in the corridor were more than just a friendly gesture. Oh well, back to the drawing board, I guess.

Towards the end of October, I enter *The William Pitt* to find Heather, one of the barmaids, celebrating her thirtieth birthday with Lynne and various other members of the bar staff. Unbeknown to me, Colin has had his eye on her for a while and lets on that he sent her a large bouquet of roses via *Interflora*.

"Al, we're off into town for an Indian in a few minutes," Heather says. "Why don't you join us?"

I glance across at Colin.

"Not me. I'm off home," he says. "Been feeling under the weather all day."

Whether the flowers didn't quite trigger off the reaction he'd hoped or he is genuinely unwell is hard to say. I turn back to Heather.

"Well, it's kind of you to ask me," I say, "but I'm sure you'd prefer to just have your work mates with you."

"Don't be silly. The more, the merrier."

Ten minutes or so later, I find myself walking towards the City Centre with Heather, seven *Pitt* employees and the landlady, Lynne. The latter indicates that she wants to have a word in my ear and hangs back slightly from the others.

"So tell me, Al. Are you happy with your life?" she asks rather bluntly.

"Er, how d'you mean?" I reply, thrown by the random nature of her question.

"Well, take a look at yourself. You're in your thirties and most men at that age are married with kids. But not you. Instead, you choose to get your kicks out of preying on innocent young girls down the pub. And from what I gather, some of them are biologically young enough to be your daughters. For a teacher, I think that's disgraceful, even sick."

The vehemence of her assault catches me off-guard and I find myself completely tongue-tied. Gradually, however, I manage to pull myself together enough to denounce her predatory accusations. I explain that I was a late starter in the dating game, that I never meet childless, unattached women of my age and that I've ended up going out with younger women because they fell for me. But my words fall on deaf ears. Lynne makes it perfectly clear that she has already made up her mind what sort of scum bag I am and isn't, under any circumstances, prepared to change it.

Bruised and offended by Lynne's harsh character assessment, I grab a seat at the restaurant well away from her, opposite a twenty-year-old university student called Steph who works part-time at the pub. In the relatively short time that I've known her, we've got on well. In fact, she requested my assistance recently when her best friend needed someone to check a French essay.

Despite the somewhat inauspicious start, the evening proves to be good fun, with even Lynne joining in with the general laughter and clowning around. At one point, she challenges me, as a gymnast, to walk the length of the restaurant on my hands. I oblige and receive tumultuous applause.

I'm still full of party spirit when we set off back to *The Pitt* just after 10.30. Suddenly, however, Lynne turns on me again.

"You were seriously out of order tonight," she scolds. "In fact, I ought to bar you from the pub."

I stop dead in my tracks. "I beg your pardon?"

"Undermining me by discussing my sex life in front of my staff. How dare you!"

"Lynne, I don't know what you're talking about. I think you're confusing me with someone else."

"Well, you've obviously had too much to drink to remember."

I'm intrigued. "So what ... er ... what is it exactly I'm supposed to have said?"

"You know full well."

"Erm, I'm afraid I don't. C'mon, tell me."

"You mentioned to the others that Stu had told you I need three glasses of wine to get going in bed."

Lynne's words bear so little resemblance to any conversation I had throughout the meal that I have to conclude that she's winding me up. Yet the expression on her face leaves little doubt that she's left every ounce of her humour back at the restaurant. Totally confused by these fresh allegations and annoyed that my new-found critic has put a damper on an otherwise enjoyable evening, I wish her a hasty goodnight and head off in the direction of home.

"You'd better come in tomorrow and apologise or you won't be allowed back in!" she yells after me.

The following evening, I approach the bar at *The Pitt*, only to be told by the landlord, Stu, that his beloved wants a quiet word with me upstairs in their flat. Assuming that she's eager to apologise for her ridiculous accusations whilst under the influence, I put my money back in my pocket and head up the stairs.

On entering the flat, Lynne greets me routinely and offers me a seat.

"Right, I'm not going to beat about the bush," she says. "Your behaviour at the restaurant yesterday evening was unacceptable. Basically, I'm going to give you two choices. Either you apologise to me now and I'll forget about the incident or, alternatively, you can refuse to do so and you'll be barred from the pub indefinitely."

Feeling like a school kid wrongly accused by a tyrant of a teacher, I profess my innocence once again, suggesting that with all the wine that was consumed she probably misheard or has got the wrong man.

Lynne shakes her head slowly. "Alcohol never affects my memory. So I'm afraid you're going to have to accept you're in the wrong or find somewhere else to drink."

Incensed, I open my mouth to select the latter option, but then a voice in my head tells me I'd be cutting off my nose to spite my own face. *The Pitt* is, after all, the liveliest pub in town at the moment and I do enjoy Colin's company as well as the Belgian beers. I cross my fingers. "All right, then. I'm sorry Lynne for whatever it was I said that offended you."

"I accept," she says. "As far as I'm concerned, the matter's closed and you can continue to drink here as before."

So it's official at last – I'm gay. At least, this is the opinion of Jen, one of *The Pitt* barmaids who didn't attend Heather's meal last week. She's only a couple of years younger than I am.

"You're always smartly turned out," she says on Friday after gym, "and you never fail to say please and thank-you for your drinks, so I assumed you batted for the other team."

"Is that it?" I ask, mildly amused.

"Well, I'd say that you're also a bit of a pretty boy. You know, with your blonde hair and blue eyes."

Uncertain as to whether I should be flattered or offended by Jen's remarks, I let the subject drop.

Later on in the evening, I start to wonder if other women have also misread my 'orientation'.

"Oh, sod it!" I say to myself. "Why can't other people keep their opinions to themselves? I'm paranoid enough as it is at the moment."

At closing time, Colin suggests I stick around since he's sending for a pizza with Heather and some of the other bar staff once the pub is empty. Apparently, it's all part of Heather's continued birthday celebrations. It hasn't escaped my attention that, off-duty, the birthday girl has spent the evening at the bar, downing spirits and cocktails like there's no tomorrow.

With the final punters sent packing, Colin takes orders for pizza and phones them through on his mobile.

"Wh...wh...what's that ww...wanker, Al, doing here?" Heather screeches suddenly, almost falling off her barstool in the process.

A gobsmacked Colin steps in to appease her as she lowers herself clumsily to her feet, but his efforts are in vain.

"Y...you up...upset my fr...friend," she says falteringly, pointing an accusing finger in my direction. "I d...don't w...want you here, you ... you ..."

Baffled by Heather's unprovoked outburst, I'm left to assume that by 'friend', she's referring to Lynne. I take a step forward towards Colin.

"Look, mate, I think it's better if I go," I whisper into his ear and make for the exit.

Colin follows me to the door.

"She's pissed," he says, sounding more West Country than ever. "Don't worry, I'll have a word with her when she's sobered up and sort it all out."

Rather mystified, I head off home to bed.

Colin rings on Saturday afternoon to inform me that Heather has expressed shame at her comments and is anxious to apologise. I suggest that I should perhaps steer clear of *The Pitt* for a while, but he convinces me that it really won't be necessary.

"Come in tonight so the poor girl can make her apologies," he says.

Always keen to avoid unpleasantness, I call into *The Pitt* in the evening. To my relief, Heather does indeed bend over backwards to excuse her unprovoked verbal assault. She claims to be highly embarrassed and blames excessive quantities of alcohol for the blip. I try to persuade Colin to join me at *Opportunity Knox* after a few drinks at the pub, but he declines on the grounds of fatigue.

Whilst in the queue for *OK*, a tall, burly lad who I don't recognise brushes past me, heading in the opposite direction.

"Paedophile!" he says with an aggressive stare over his left shoulder, then continues on his way.

I step temporarily out of the line to take a closer look at him as he disappears down the pavement towards the car park. But once again, he seems unfamiliar.

"Just some random person prating around," I mutter to myself.

Still, this is yet another comment I could do without right now. A gay male paedophile who's obsessed with teenage girls. Is this humanly possible? I think someone up there must really have it in for me.

On the last day in October, I bump into Sam, back from uni. She seems seriously down in the dumps and is eager to talk. Sitting in her car, she explains how unhappy she's been away from home. I spend the next half an hour trying to reassure her as best I can. I recall my early days at university and disclose how desperately homesick I was.

"But it will get a lot better," I tell her. "I promise."

"I'm not so sure it will," she says disconsolately. "It's the people there, Al. I just can't relate to them."

In spite of myself, I can't help feeling flattered that, after all we've been through, I'm still the one she turns to for advice. I should probably hate her for the way she's treated me in the past, yet every time we meet the only emotion I'm capable of feeling is one of enduring affection – with a touch of exasperation thrown in for good measure. If only she'd let on what it is that's really troubling her.

On the first Saturday in November, Colin returns from a business trip to Amsterdam with a souvenir for his drinking partner.

"I thought this'd be perfect for you," he chortles and hands over a teen porn magazine in full view of some of the bar staff and nearby customers.

I remember Martin Studd's words of warning, not to mention the rather offensive remark outside *OK*, and feel a strong desire to shove the magazine down Colin's throat whilst giving him a piece of my mind. Yet my attempts are thwarted by a combination of the good-natured laughter from those nearby and their blatant interest in the somewhat disgusting photos.

As predictably as night becomes day, Rupert has come to the conclusion
that Amber isn't irrefutably THE ONE, after all.

"So what's the problem?" I ask. "Is it the age gap?"

"No, not at all," he replies. "We get on brilliantly. It's just that every
time I go out, I see other fit girls."

"Oh, right. So it's just looks you're interested in, then?"

"No, don't be silly. I really do love her. And you know I treat her well.
But there's just so much talent out there."

"A few months ago, she was your perfect woman."

"Yeah, all right. Fair point. But I've seen other birds since then that
I could possibly be happy with for the rest of my life."

"Ones that you've spoken to?"

"No, not necessarily."

"Then how can you be so sure?" I ask, weary of a conversation
reminiscent of many we've had before.

"I dunno. I just am."

Rupert has two degrees and an above average IQ. He also earns
more than three times what I do for a nine to five, five-day-a-week job.
Sometimes, I wonder whether the two of us are living on the same planet.
Before changing the subject, I suggest that if he cares about Amber as much
as he claims, he should do the honourable thing and break up with her.

"You're right," he says. "But she's really loved-up and I don't want to
hurt her."

"The longer you leave it, the more painful it'll be," I advise in my new
role of marriage guidance counsellor.

"Okay, I'll do it this week."

Anyone for a sweepstake?

Shortly after my chat with Rupert about his besotted teenage girlfriend,
I run into Jerome Howard, one of my former secondary school teaching
colleagues, coming out of *The Pitt* with a young woman on his arm.
A highly respected Head of English, Jerome rose rapidly up the ranks
to the much-coveted position of Head of Sixth Form. He was also a
good friend of Simon Lennon's. In fact, the two of us were both invited
back to Jerome's place one evening years ago to meet his stunning Czech
bride. My former lodger, Mark, informed me a while ago of a scandalous
rumour he'd heard about Jerome ditching his wife and changing schools
to be with a pupil called Kat who we both taught when she was thirteen.
With initial greetings out of the way, it doesn't take long for me to
recognise his lady friend, now twenty, and for Jerome to confirm the
rumours.

"We've both been through hell and high water to be together," he
says. "But it's been worth it every inch of the way."

He turns to his young partner who nods in whole-hearted agreement. Once they've moved on, I pause for a second just inside the pub door and wonder why Jerome and Rupert, both older than I am, have been able to hold on to much younger girlfriends when I haven't. What qualities do they possess that I lack?

By the end of November, my confidence is at rock bottom once again. On a routine weekend visit to *The William Pitt*, Heather stalls me at the entrance and announces that I'm barred.

"What the hell for?" I ask, totally dumbfounded.

"I'm afraid I'm not at liberty to tell you," she says in a military tone. "Now please leave."

"Can't I speak to Stu or Lynne first?"

"No, you can't. They'd tell you the same thing. Now go."

Out of the corner of my eye, I spot Colin with his double chin almost on his chest. So sombre is his expression that any resemblance to Oliver Hardy is no longer apparent.

"All right. I'll just have a quick word with Colin, then I'll leave," I say in resignation.

Heather takes a step back and allows me to pass.

"Search me what's going on," Colin shrugs. The red of his cheeks has now spread to the rest of his face. "I had no idea they wanted you out."

"But as a sign of your loyalty, you'll leave with me, won't you?" The lack of response and further droop of his chin tells me all I need to know. I'm wounded by his choice. "Thanks very much! You're a really good mate. I hope you realise that if it were you they were barring, I wouldn't think twice about walking out in protest."

With my frustration at a peak, I storm out of the building, a place where I've spent hundreds of pounds over the last year. Walking dejectedly across the City towards one of the clubs, it occurs to me that this is the first time in my life that I've felt obliged out of self-respect to turn my back on a friend. Although I can't believe that Colin is in league with Lynne and Stu, he obviously values them and their lousy pub more than he does my friendship. He may well have sorted me out with a computer and shown huge generosity when buying rounds, but sometimes material things just aren't enough. What's more, I'm in no doubt that his constant wisecracks in public about my supposed fixation with young girls have done my reputation no favours whatsoever. If only I'd listened to Martin Studd and nipped them in the bud when I had the chance. Mind you, I can't help feeling that had I not been a teacher, no-one would've batted an eyelid. I would've just been deemed a typical, red-hot male.

Soon after my 'dismissal' from *The Pitt*, I bump into Steph, the barmaid who sat opposite me at the Indian restaurant on the evening of Heather's birthday. I decide to put her on the spot with a question, more out of curiosity than anything else: "Be honest with me, Steph. Did I insult Lynne at the meal? You were close enough to hear everything I said."

"Al, I really don't want to get involved," she says. "I value my job too much."

"Oh, c'mon. Please, just tell me. I need to know. I won't mention it to anyone else, I promise."

Steph hesitates for a few seconds before opening her mouth and saying rather tentatively: "I ... I think it's terrible what they did to you. That's all I'm prepared to say."

When the final day of the autumn term at *Lower Valley Sixth Form* arrives, I have to acknowledge that, socially, the last month or so have been as demoralising as any I can remember. I could never have predicted this during the earlier part of the year when everything seemed so rosy. Once again, what has saved my self-esteem from the gutter has been my job. Apart from an obsession with IT and league tables, *Lower Valley* has indeed proved to be a carbon copy of *Mardall's*. The students are friendly and, for the most part, hard-working. The few lazy ones – and there are always some – are well aware that they need to pull their finger out. I only have to remind them of the contract they signed on entering the College.

Charlotte Rhys-Jones, the student who missed a year through glandular fever, has been a delight to teach, her maturity, enthusiasm and sweet nature reminding me that there are some lovely young women out there. She often stops behind at break for an amiable chat and even gave me a birthday card with the postscript *I want you to push me hard, cos I'm aiming really high* written clearly inside.

Christmas is spent with my sister and her family in Wales. Mum and dad are there too. After a few glasses of bubbly with the turkey, I find myself relating my unfortunate adventures at *The Pitt*, so incensed as I still am by the injustice of the situation. Mum reminds me that I can be rather good at speaking out of turn and that pubs and nightclubs are possibly not the best environment for making close friends, let alone for meeting a future wife.

Like last year, Chloë insists on sharing a room with her uncle. At 6.00 in the morning of the 27th, she wakes me with feverish excitement.

"Al, I'm four!" she says. "Three's gone away for ever now, hasn't it?"

A whole crowd of her play school chums arrives in the afternoon for a party and, infected by the uninhibited exuberance of the youngsters around me, I manage to temporarily forget my woes of recent times. What a shame we have to grow up.

On my way home after the party, I recall with fondness the events of a year ago and how I found romance quite unexpectedly on New Year's Eve.

"With '99 just a few days away, it's time to look forwards, not backwards," I tell myself with mock confidence.

SPRING TERM

Whilst New Year's Eve didn't in any way scale the heady heights of last year, it was, nevertheless, an enjoyable night out, which ended with a kiss under the large clock with a girl who was probably as drunk as I was.

Back at the house, I've had to make some changes to curb the Spanish lodgers' predilection for greenhouse temperatures and for giving the washing machine too many punishing workouts. Whilst I was away in Wales, Natalia sneaked into my bedroom and turned up the central heating thermostat to maximum. Overwhelmed by the excessive heat emanating from the radiators, the three girls then proceeded to open half the windows in the house. The solution – a lock on my bedroom door. On the laundry front, Natalia has been repeatedly putting two or three clothes items into the machine – sometimes knickers only – and running a full cycle. The solution – a note by the start button reminding her of ecological issues and Al's increasingly unhealthy bank balance.

To my relief, Arancha has found herself a serious boyfriend – a really nice Spanish lad who works at the nearby *Tesco Superstore*. I say 'relief' because it now means that she's prepared to have civilised conversations with me and refrains from rearranging the house to her own taste.

One morning in early January, Vicky, by far the largest framed of the Spaniards, bellows up the stairs: "Al! Al! Greaseball on the telephone."

On the way down to the lounge, my brain is working overtime, trying to figure out who I know who'd refer to themselves as 'Greaseball'. I draw a blank. I pick up the receiver with intrigue. "Hello, Al speaking."

"Oh, hi, Al," a familiar voice says at the other end of the line. "It's Chris Paull here. I've got some Fiat spares I think you might be interested in."

On the second Friday of the year, I'm forced to postpone the first gym session of the term due to a lack of coaches. Sam's old school friend, Stephanie, is ill and Siobhan out celebrating her eighteenth.

I go clubbing at *James Dean's* earlier than usual and am approached by a mother of four who leaves me with little doubt that she'd welcome some additional practice honing her baby-making technique. She's not really my type, yet the situation leads me to question whether I could ever fall for someone with a ready-made family. Let's face it, if I were to follow the advice of those close to me and 'go for someone my own age', this is what I'd probably have to come to terms with. As I tried to explain to Lynne before Christmas, it's not as if desirable, single, baggage-free thirty plus women are in abundant supply.

"Is it unnatural for a single man with no dependants to want to meet a female equivalent?" I ask myself after politely evading the advances of my new admirer.

I go on to wonder about the whole age thing. I'm not exactly the only man on the planet to have dated much younger women. Take Paul Readhead, Rupert and Jerome, for example, not to mention a host of celebrities from the world of show business and sport.

With my brain working overtime, I recall Jerome's description of the hostility he encountered as a teacher in his late thirties abandoning his wife for one of his former pupils. With divorce now a sadly common part of everyday life, I can't help feeling that the teacher-pupil relationship would've ruffled more feathers than the break-up of his marriage. It's worth pointing out that I haven't to date heard a single unfavourable comment about Rupert going out with a seventeen-year-old at the age of thirty-five. In our society, it seems, there are many who feel that when it comes to the dating game, there are extra rules for teachers that simply don't apply to most other members of the workforce.

Whilst I'm privately bemoaning the lot of teachers, a former *Mardall's* student called Ali, who was a stalwart of my gym and trampolining clubs for three years, comes over for a chat. Instantly recognisable by her almost Heidi-like blonde hair, Ali reached a good recreational standard in both sports. She was always bubbly and good-humoured, and contributed to the positive atmosphere of the two extra-curricular groups. I liked her a lot. Previously unlucky in love, she delights in showing me her engagement ring.

"I'd really like you to come to the wedding," she says with a grin the width of the dance floor. "So when we've fixed a date, I'll let you know."

At *James Dean's* on a Saturday in early February, I bump into an ex-*Royal David's* student called Rose, a skinny brunette who's had Rupert's eyes jumping out of their sockets on more than one occasion in the past. Whilst we're in the middle of a friendly chat, I notice a tall, broad shouldered lad standing nearby, watching over us like a hawk. He appears familiar. Although definitely not my 'stalker', he's locked in the same angry expression that I became accustomed to with the latter when Rachel and I were together. Rose catches my gaze.

"That's my boyfriend," she says. "Scott Dixon. He remembers you from *Mardall's*. I'm afraid you weren't one of his favourite teachers."

"Really?" I reply. "But I'm sure he wasn't in any of my classes."

"He wasn't, but he reckons you abused your position by going out with some girl in his year."

"What, Rachel Hill?"

"I've no idea what her name was. Anyway, just ignore him."

Later in the evening, as I'm standing alone with my drink, minding my own business, Scott sidles up to me.

"How d'you have the nerve to show your face here?" he says somewhat aggressively. "You pervert!"

"I beg your pardon?" I say, now realising that he's the bloke who insulted me outside *OK* before Christmas, not some drunken stranger as I first thought.

"You heard."

"Look, I've no idea what your problem is, but I can assure you that you've got your wires crossed."

All I want is for him to move on and leave me in peace.

Scott takes a step closer. "Don't give me that shit. Everyone knows you got sacked from *Mardall's* for shagging students."

"That's ridiculous! D'you honestly think I'd have managed to get another job in education if it were true? The previous Head or Principal is always called on as a referee."

"Fuck off! I know for a fact that you've screwed under-age girls as well."

In spite of mounting anger in the light of such an outrageous accusation, I find myself uttering an involuntary laugh. Surely he must be winding me up. I challenge him to name names, but he just mutters something inaudible, presumably another expletive, and turns to walk away. I call after him, demanding details, but he ignores me.

With my anger now at its height, not just as a result of his slanderous remarks but also out of recollection of what happened at *The William Pitt*, I direct my right foot towards the back of his thigh to attract attention. Unfortunately, I mistime my swing and catch him bang smack on his coccyx. He swivels round on impact, then surges forward, his six-foot rugger-player frame towering over me.

"You wanna go outside?" he asks, his upper body tensing ready for battle.

"C'mon, then," I reply ludicrously, my common sense suddenly taken over by aliens. "Let's go."

I take a step in the direction of the exit. Scott shakes his head twice before tossing it backwards and emitting a loud, derisory sneer, as if to say:

"I'd only have to breathe on you mate and you'd be dead." He turns once more and moves off at a slow, measured pace.

A few minutes later, Rose comes rushing over.

"I'm really sorry about Scott," she says. "I told you you should just ignore him."

"That's not easy," I reply, "when someone accuses you in public of sleeping with under-age girls."

"Oh, shit! I didn't realise he'd said that. Sorry! Unfortunately, Scott's got a bad back and you got him right in the spot where it hurts."

"Whoops! It wasn't intentional. I was only trying to stop him walking off mid-conversation."

Rose manages a warm, forgiving smile, which I find myself reciprocating.

"Don't worry, I'll have a word with him when he's calmed down," she says in parting. "Tell him that he's got his facts wrong."

Whilst I appreciate her eagerness to smooth things over with her boyfriend and me, I don't believe for one second that he'll take a blind bit of notice.

Rather shaken by the unpleasant nature of the evening's events, I lie awake in bed afterwards, wondering how I've managed to instil such hatred in others. I've always been such a passive, non-violent person, yet there was a moment tonight when I really would've taken on Scott Dixon had he not walked away, a contest of David versus Goliath proportions. It was as if my dignity and self-respect depended on it. I just can't comprehend why I'm suddenly being exposed to the darker consequences of being a single teacher who enjoys pubbing and clubbing when for years my encounters with ex-pupils and students were always so positive. As if the misery I experienced at the hands of Rachel and Sam wasn't enough at the time. Now I'm having to relive it through the disapproval of others.

Highlighting perfectly the contrast between the level of respect I can command at work and in my private life, all twenty of my Upper Sixth German group meet the internal deadline for the submission of written coursework without the slightest fuss, even the four or five less organised members. I'm pleasantly surprised. At *Mardall's*, my colleagues and I almost always ended up frantically chasing up unreliable students for coursework at the last minute. Yvonne isn't so fortunate with all her French charges and is quite impressed with my achievement.

Later in the week, Dr Faulkner, the Principal, stops me in the corridor.

"I'm hearing good things about you, Al, from some of your students," he says generously. "Particularly in German. It seems that you've already transformed the Department. Um ... er ... well done!"

He nods two or three times, one hand stroking his bearded chin, before continuing on his way. I pause for a few seconds and chuckle at the thought of an imaginary postscript to the boss' words of praise: "However, rumour has it that you're not much cop at wooing the ladies. I'll see if there's a course we can enrol you on as part of your staff development."

On the final day before the half term holiday, Charlotte Rhys-Jones announces to her language class that there's a French film showing at a cinema near her on the first Monday back. No-one expresses an interest in tickets except for the teacher.

"There weren't that many seats left when my mum and I booked," she says, "so if you want to go, Al, I suggest you ring up as soon as possible."

Charlotte scribbles down the name of the cinema and a number to call on a scrap of paper, then hands it to me with a typically infectious smile.

Just as I'm about to leave at the end of the day, Yvonne comes bustling out of the tiny language office.

"There's one of your students on the phone," she says. "Apparently, it's quite urgent."

I place my bag on the desk and jog next door to the office. Yvonne tactfully leaves me alone with the caller.

"Hi, it's me – Charlotte," a soft voice says. "Hope I'm not interrupting anything, but my mum says you can have her ticket for the French film."

"Oh, right," I say. "Doesn't she want to see it herself?"

"No, her French is pants. She was only coming along to keep me company."

Having already met Mrs Rhys-Jones, I have little doubt that she'd make such a gesture. They seem a close-knit family.

"Well, er … it's very kind of her. I'll settle up for the ticket after half term, if that's ok."

Just as I'm contemplating life in a monastery, I have a stroke of luck on a trip to *James Dean's* over half term. I get chatting to a lad who turns out to be the older brother of a girl I taught for A level French at *Royal David's*. Together, we manage to initiate conversation with a couple of girls. I hit it off immediately with one of them, Cindy, a pretty, friendly, high-spirited brunette. We end up kissing on one of the sofas and she willingly hands over her number.

"I like you, Al," she says before parting. "I'm more than happy for you to call me, but I think it's only fair to tell you that I met a really nice guy last week and have agreed to go on a date with him next Friday."

"Oh, that's a shame!" I reply. "But thanks for being honest."

"I think it's the best way. But look, please do call me cos it might not work out with this other bloke."

I phone Cindy at the end of half term. She seems pleased to hear from me, but announces that her date was a success and that she's arranged to see the other bloke again. Impeccable timing once more, Al!

On Monday morning back at work, it occurs to me that I should perhaps mention to Yvonne that I'll be going on an educational trip to the cinema with one of my female students. She doesn't express any objections, but suggests I speak to Charlotte's parents first – just to cover my back.

"I hope you haven't forgotten we're going to see a film tonight," Charlotte says at the end of her French lesson.

"No, I haven't," I reply, "but I do need to have a quick word with you about it."

"Really? What's up?"

"Nothing major. It's just that I think I should speak to your mum first – out of courtesy."

"Oh, okay. Here, I'll give you her work number. Save you having to look it up."

Mrs Rhys-Jones confirms that she's more than happy to relinquish her ticket and thanks me for helping her daughter to settle in so well at the College.

"I can drive if you like," Charlotte says once I've hung up. "I'm hopeless at giving directions. Anyway, it seems silly to take two cars. Give me your number and I'll ring later and let you know what time I'll be leaving."

I oblige.

In keeping with tradition, the French film proves to be somewhat off-the-wall, although the extra exposure to the language it provides is of definite benefit to an A level student like Charlotte. It's just a pity that her classmates weren't prepared to sacrifice a few precious hours out of College to join us. Both at the cinema and in her car, Charlotte behaves with great maturity and appears at ease in my company.

"There's another French film showing next month," she says on the way home.

"Maybe we can persuade some of the others to tag along," I reply.

She smiles, but doesn't say anything.

During the first week in March, I return to the cinema with Charlotte and one of her female friends from the French group. Once again, the evening turns out to be as enjoyable as it is educational.

As a result of our evening excursions, Charlotte becomes friendlier than ever towards me at College without for one second allowing this to affect our relationship during lessons. In many ways, she reminds me of Cara Mitchell and Mandy 'Mandarin' Bailey from *Mardall's* in terms of her maturity and thirst for academic success. She even talks openly to me about more personal aspects of her life, including her boyfriend, and I'm willing to offer advice whenever she seeks it.

Rupert joins me at *James Dean's* on Saturday with a couple of his friends, having finally plucked up the courage to finish with his seventeen-year-old girlfriend. It only took him four months. Whilst there, we strike up conversation with a group of girls sitting on a settee located near the toilets. It transpires that they're all students at the City's university. One of them, a pretty blonde called Dawn, really sets my heart racing. She seems genuinely interested in what I have to say to her and, during the course of our discussion, discloses that she prefers older men and serious relationships. This provides my confidence with a much-needed boost.

Later, on the dance floor, Dawn kisses me briefly. Convinced that the brevity of our kiss is not a good sign, I return to Rupert and the other two lads. After all, I wouldn't want to scare her away by being too pushy.

Towards the end of the evening, Dawn tracks me down and insists on putting my number on her mobile.

"I promise I'll call you soon," she says.

"Good," I reply, suddenly uplifted once again. "I look forward to hearing from you."

A week has now passed since my meeting with Dawn at *James Dean's* and, needless to say, she hasn't rung me. If she had been drunk or had taken my number under duress, I could understand her lack of contact, yet none of these was the case. I suppose I should've asked for her number, but then I didn't want to appear too keen. Anyway, we're no longer living in the dark ages. Dawn's silence leads me to acknowledge that whilst my move to the City has considerably increased the amount of starts I've had with the opposite sex, it hasn't so far resulted in anything really long-term. Surely the law of averages must state that cupid will soon fire his bow.

Just before Easter, a further trip to *Deans* leads to an encounter with a twenty-two-year-old lad called Andy Best, one of only a handful of male students at *Mardall's* who ever attended my extra-curricular gym club.

"I only came along to get closer to Rachel Hill," he says. "But then none of us had a chance with the muscleman gym coach around, did we?"

With a smile, I say: "Oh, I don't know about that."

"You lucky bastard! I don't think there was a single male student at the College who didn't want to get into her knickers. What was she like?"

In stark contrast to the behaviour of Scott Dixon a few weeks back, I detect no malice whatsoever in Andy's words of envy.

"You up for chatting up some birds?" he asks, once I've dodged his previous question.

"I would be, but I think I've lost my touch these days."

The reality, of course, is that I've never had much touch, yet Andy seems so much in awe of my pulling power that this is something he really doesn't need to know.

"C'mon, mate. If you can get a bird like Hill, you can have anyone. Hey, what about those two over there? Follow me, my friend."

Andy leads me in the direction of two young women who, at a guess, are in their early twenties. Once we're standing in front of them, however, he loses his bottle and turns to his former teacher for assistance. Eager not to disappoint my protégé, I find myself taking a deep inhalation of polluted nightclub air before moving in on the two ladies. To my relief, they're a friendly pair and more than happy to make polite conversation.

After a while, Andy accompanies one of the girls to a seat further away, leaving me with Rhianne who I find the more attractive of the two.

"I ought to tell you that I've got a boyfriend," she says once we're alone.

"That's okay," I say. "It's just good to have someone intelligent to talk to."

"Oh, that's all right, then. Let me get you another drink."

Before I have chance to protest, my new friend is on her feet and heading for the bar. By the time she's returned, I feel more relaxed than earlier, probably as a result of knowing where I stand. The conversation that ensues is one of surprising frankness, considering we've only just met. Rhianne insists on paying for more drinks and seems quite put out when I object. For a quiet life, I end up bowing down to her generosity.

After roughly an hour, Rhianne suddenly and unexpectedly places one hand firmly around the back of my neck and plants her lips onto mine. What follows is a deep and sensuous kiss that seems to last forever. There is, of course, a break for air eventually, although this is brief and gives way to an intense desire on both sides for more of the same. With no additional mention of her boyfriend, I continue to enjoy Rhianne's therapy right up until the close. Andy, on the other hand, isn't so fortunate with her friend.

Once outside the club, I take a step closer to Rhianne and, with both hands placed gently round her triceps, ask impulsively: "Will you come back with me? I'd love to spend more time with you. I mean, we don't have to do any…"

She cuts me short: "I really need to find my friends. I'm sure they won't have left without me. Back in a sec."

With no obvious signs that she's been drinking, she then skips off down the road.

A couple of minutes later, I spot Rhianne heading back towards me, presumably to say that she's found her friends and decided to leave with them. At this point, an empty cab pulls up outside the club. Rhianne moves towards it and exchanges a word with the driver before opening the rear door and jumping inside.

"Come on, then, Mr Teacher," she calls out. "It's back to your place."

Ecstatic at such a dramatic turn-about in my fortune, I leap into the taxi before she can change her mind.

My night with Rhianne proves to be one of great intimacy and meaningful conversation.

"You don't know how great it is to spend the night with someone I can talk to," she says. "I think you're really lovely."

Her threat that she'll have to leave early in the morning to continue work on her dissertation doesn't materialise. In fact, we stay in bed until 1.00. During our extended time together, I learn that Rhianne has been with her boyfriend, a student at another university about thirty miles away, for three years, but that sex has all but dried up.

"He never seems to be interested any more," she tells me regretfully. "I really do love him, though, and I'm pretty sure he does me."

Unwilling to reassume my role of marriage guidance counsellor, I change the subject. Part of me feels a pang of guilt for the deception despite the fact that I'm not the one doing the cheating and I'm unlikely to ever meet her other half.

By the time I've dropped Rhianne back to her student dwellings – a flat above a bakery on the outskirts of the City – my head is spinning. Whilst I may well have had one of the most pleasurable nocturnal experiences of my life, the fact that it came about as the result of a woman cheating on her long-term boyfriend causes me a degree of consternation. If by some miracle she decided to trade him in for me, then how could I ever be sure she wouldn't go behind *my* back? Given my insecurities and distrust of women, it just wouldn't work. A real pity, though.

SUMMER TERM

It's now the last week in April and I'm travelling on a train out of London with Yvonne, the Senior Curriculum Manager for Modern Languages. Having both attended a course for teachers laid on by one of the Examining Boards, we're on our way back to the College. Sitting in the seat beside me is Moira, a brunette in her mid-twenties with as broad a

Scottish accent as you can imagine. She works in an office. Something to do with computers. I know this because I've already broken the ice and conversation has been flowing. Yvonne has remained a silent observer throughout, although I can tell from the intermittent raising of her eyebrows that she's impressed by my confident approach.

Despite a few weak moments over the Easter holidays when I almost picked up the phone and called Rhianne, I decided in the end to listen to my head rather than to my heart. Surely it wasn't realistic to expect that she'd consider chucking in a three-year relationship with a man she loved for a bloke she'd seduced in a nightclub on a Saturday night whilst under the influence. I'd prefer to avoid almost certain rejection and just preserve the special memory. Whether I'm right or wrong in my negative assessment of the situation doesn't alter the fact that the whole experience has injected a new lease of life into my flagging ego, hence my bravado on the train.

Moira has to alight several stops before Yvonne and me. Not wishing to see this apparently charming young lady walk out of my life forever, I manage to secure her number – all part of a day's work.

At the weekend, I ring Moira. She seems pleased to hear from me and suggests we get together in the City on the first May Bank Holiday. The fact that we met outside a pub or club environment and without the influence of alcohol has left me feeling uncharacteristically positive about this date.

When the Monday arrives, I fetch Moira from the train station. We stop off for a snack lunch at *Yates's*, one of several trendy bars that have sprung up recently just round the corner from the High Street. The conversation at the table is relaxed and good-humoured.

Afterwards, back at the house, I crack open a bottle of wine and the familiarisation process continues. After several glasses, Moira begins to open up.

"My ideal man would be a redhead covered in freckles," she says out of the blue, just as I've convinced myself that she definitely fancies me.

Whether this is a random remark that I should ignore or an attempt on her behalf to inform me that I haven't got a hope is too early to say.

In the evening, we go for a meal at the restaurant that adjoins *James Dean's*. Strangely, the young waitress refuses to look at Moira once and takes all our orders through me. The latter is visibly miffed. After I've settled the bill, she hangs back and hands one of the unused white serviettes to the waitress.

"What was that all about?" I ask when she catches up with me outside the door.

"I've just given that stupid cow your phone number," she replies, almost spitefully. "She obviously fancies you. No' much of a waitress, though."

I laugh off her suggestion, but reason that her apparent jealousy is almost certainly an encouraging sign.

As I'm on half term and Moira isnt working in the morning, we agree to drop into *Dean's*.

"A'll be interested tae see what the clubs are like here," she says, perking up.

Once inside, my date – or is she just a visitor? – sticks with me for twenty minutes or so before announcing that she needs the toilet.

"Here, hud ma drink for me," she says sharply. "And promise me you won't move from this spot."

I obey, yet Moira fails to return. Concerned that she may've lost her bearings, I do a swift circuit of the club. No sign. It's only on my third lap that I catch sight of her on the edge of the dance floor in the middle of a passionate kiss with a tall bloke with – wait for it – red hair and freckles. Infuriated that my guest could treat me so shabbily, I approach her and make it known that I'm fed up and heading home. She doesn't reply or budge an inch.

By the time I've reached the exit, I've calmed down sufficiently to reason that it'd be harsh to leave her alone in a club in an unfamiliar City. Anyway, the night is young and I'm hardly ready to turn in.

During the course of the next hour, I have no joy whatsoever trying to find Moira and come to the regrettable conclusion that she must've left with her 'ideal' man. I set off home shortly after midnight, ruing my misfortune once again.

Back at the house, I drift wearily into the lounge and have to do a double take at the sight of Moira sitting bolt upright on the sofa bed glaring towards me. One of the Spanish girls must've let her in. Before I have chance to open my mouth, she leaps up out of her seat and rushes towards me as if about to unleash an attack of terrifying ferocity. Just short of me, however, she stops in her tracks and launches into, not a physical assault, but the most brutal and vicious verbal one I've ever witnessed in my life, one expletive after another emanating from her tiger-like snarl. With her accent at its broadest, I'm only just able to decipher the motive for her ambush – she's convinced I abandoned her, a vulnerable young woman, in an unfamiliar nightclub in a strange City. Apparently, there's a string of colourful messages on my answer machine. I try to explain that my threat to leave was made at the heat of the moment and that I'd not actually gone through with it, but she's not in the mood to listen. The profanity continues.

"Just get me a fucking cab!" she roars, as if attempting to impersonate a psychopath. "Ah don't want tae have tae look at you for another fucking second, you fucking, fucking wanker. I was fucking shiteing masel walking back here. What sort of a fucking arsehole are you? Ah could've been murdered!"

Aware that my explanation has fallen on deaf ears and irritated by the intensity of her attack, I adopt a different approach: "So you think it's acceptable to go on a first date with a bloke, then drift off and pull someone else?"

Not unexpectedly, she ignores my question and persists with her demands for a cab. I explain that it'll cost her an arm and a leg at this time of night. In a noticeably gentler tone, I suggest she kips on the sofa bed and catches a train first thing in the morning. She shakes her head dramatically, utters further obscenities, then grabs the phone with her right hand. I leave her to it. Calm at long last.

On hearing confirmation that a taxi will cost in excess of fifty pounds, Moira finally slumps down onto the sofa and mutters something about staying. I fetch some bedding and a glass of orange juice as a peace offering. She snatches both from me without a word. I take this as my cue to leave.

When I wake in the morning, I find that my irate visitor has made a stealthy departure. I listen to my answer machine messages from last night – there are three in total – and am bombarded by language even more obscene than I heard in person, the broad Scottish accent enhancing the effect perfectly.

"Why can't I just meet someone normal?" I ask myself before joining mum and dad on a trip to Bristol Zoo to meet up with my sister and her family.

Chloë marvels at the sight of so many large animals and we have a really super time – such a contrast to the rather miserable, unsettling events of yesterday. Sometimes, I wonder where I'd be without the reassuring sanity of my family. With hindsight, I suppose it's quite amusing that my attempt to search for a girlfriend outside a pub or club environment proved so disastrous. Mum, dad, Jayne and Joe certainly think so.

Towards the end of May, Ben Connery, the precocious sound engineer from my old amateur dramatics group, comes out with me in the City. Having heard on the grapevine that the management has changed hands at *The William Pitt*, I return to the pub to speak to the new landlord. He announces rather dismissively that my ban will remain in force for the foreseeable future since his predecessors claimed that I used to encourage under-age drinking by not grassing on my offending ex-students. I wonder why Lynne or Stu or even Heather couldn't have told me this.

Ben and I hit the new bars – *Yates's* and *Bar Med* – instead. We then move on to *Dean's* where for once I'm almost relieved to have an uneventful evening. The last thing I need right now is another hostile encounter with Scott Dixon who, since the last incident, has been conspicuous by his absence. My family wonder why I continue to frequent the club. I suppose it's because the good times considerably outweigh the bad ones. Anyway, I've never been one to run away from a tricky situation.

With the sudden departure of two of my Spanish lodgers, Vicky and Natalia – the latter complete with the mattress from her bed – a replacement moves in on the second May Bank Holiday. She's a black French girl called Sylvie who was introduced to me by Hans, the German assistant at College.

"She's a lovely girl," he assured me. "She won't give any trouble."

Now where have I heard this before? I have to confess, though, that my first impressions concur with his view.

Now that the Upper Sixth have gone on exam leave, life at *Lower Valley* has become appreciably less manic. Unlike at *Mardall's*, the staff aren't expected to take on invigilation duties other than for exams with an extra large sitting. The responsibility for this rests with local people who are in need of some additional cash.

There's no disputing that the second half of the summer term is one of the perks of teaching in a Sixth Form College, a payback for working in such an intense exam-factory environment from September to May. I'm sure this is what prompts some in the secondary sector to claim that they have a harder life. Having had experience of both sectors, I'd say they're right on the discipline front, but wrong when it comes to overall workload. Sixth Form preparation and marking generally need to be more in-depth, and the pressure to achieve good exam results is even greater. After all, university places depend on them.

My twenty-strong Upper Sixth German group seem, on the whole, to be pleased with this year's exam papers, though I've been in this game long enough not to pay too much attention to students' assessment of their own performance. Some are unrealistically optimistic – often the lads – whereas others are ridiculously pessimistic – often the girls. Although I'm anxious to know how my latest charges have fared, I'll just have to be patient and wait until the results come out in August to see if I've made the grade as a Curriculum Manager.

On the middle Saturday in June, Rupert and I take a taxi from his house in the direction of a Rugby Club Hall in a nearby town where Charlotte Rhys-Jones is due to celebrate her eighteenth birthday.

"I'll be really upset if you don't come," she told me whilst handing over two tickets during a recent French lesson.

The taxi driver bores the two of us to death with tales of women undressing for him in his cab late at night. He's so wrapped up in his explicit accounts that he loses his way to the hall, then charges us for the extra mileage. This incenses Rupert who, although on an annual salary approaching eighty-five grand, is without doubt the most tightfisted person I've ever met. It's not uncommon for him to announce jubilantly on a Saturday night that his shares have gone up and that drinks will be on him. He then proceeds to buy the first round with a flourish, only to wait expectantly for me to cough up for the second, which is how we normally operate on a lads' night out. When I remind him of his earlier offer of generosity, his standard reply is that his shares could easily tumble in such a fickle market and that he needs to exercise a degree of caution. Surely he can't have been so stingy with his numerous girlfriends. I seem to recall that he lent one of them money to buy a horse. I know he's also been generous with various other male friends.

Charlotte greets us warmly on the door. Later, when all the guests have arrived, she takes hold of my hand.

"Come and meet my brother," she says and escorts me across to the other side of the hall.

Her parents are also in attendance. Mrs Rhys-Jones makes time for an extended chat with Rupert and me.

"It's so good of you to come," she says gratefully, "although I think you're very brave mixing with all these unruly teenagers."

She thanks me once more for supporting her daughter over the last academic year, then adds: "You've had such a positive influence on her, Al. You can't imagine how reassuring it is for my husband and me to see her blooming again. She was so low last year when struck down by glandular fever."

With the party over at midnight, Rupert and I move on to a club just up the road. The former is itching to tell me something.

"Charlotte had a quiet word in my ear and told me she fancies the pants off you," he says with an air of excitement. "If I were you, I'd get right in there."

Cackle, cackle, cackle.

I try to explain that it's unprofessional for a teacher to have any form of romantic involvement with a present student, but Rupert, who attended a boys' grammar school, isn't listening.

"I think I'm gonna retrain to become a teacher," he says, squeezing a pair of imaginary boobs and uttering something along the lines of "Coorrrr!"

Rupert on twenty-five grand a year? I can't see it, somehow.

Back home, I reflect briefly on Rupert's revelation about Charlotte. Part of me feels certain that he's exaggerated her words since she's only ever given off friendship vibes in my company. My memories of Rachel Hill before we got together convince me that Charlotte's manner is far too upfront and flirty for someone who harbours interest of a romantic nature. I don't think I've got anything to worry about.

Two weeks have passed since Charlotte's eighteenth and I'm back at *James Dean's* with one of Rupert's friends, Leslie. Whilst I'm enjoying a quiet drink on a settee in the far corner of the club, Leslie goes off in search of female talent. During his absence, a gorgeous pony-tailed brunette with a stunning figure plonks herself down next to me, surprisingly close up, in fact.

"I know you," she says with a flourish. "You're a language teacher who does gymnastics. Haven't you also got several Italian cars?"

"Er, y...es," I reply slowly, trying to recall where we could've met. Her face certainly isn't familiar. "How d'you know that?"

"Don't you remember? We had a long chat in here sometime last year, but then you left suddenly without saying goodbye. I was really disappointed, actually."

I take a closer look at the 'hot chick' pressing her thigh tightly up against mine and wonder how in a million years I could've walked away from her on our previous encounter. Was I struck by temporary blindness? What's more, how come I can't remember her? I normally have an excellent long-term memory for faces. Most peculiar.

I apologise for my rudeness on our last meeting. She's so willing to forgive me that within five minutes she's got her tongue down my throat. The look of total astonishment and admiration on Leslie's face when he returns is a real sight to behold.

"I model part-time for Schwarzkopf. You know, the hair products firm," my mystery woman (Kimberley) tells Leslie and me. Neither of us is surprised.

After another bout of sensuous kissing, Kimberley excuses herself and disappears amongst the crowd. Just as I'm beginning to fear that I won't see her again, she reappears with an enormous grin on her face.

"You'll never guess what I've just done," she says.

"No idea," I reply, pressing my lips together tightly and shaking my head.

"I've just shagged the bouncer!"

Before I have a second to absorb her shocking confession, Kimberley kisses me again with great aplomb. She then rises from her seat without a word and heads off to chat to a friend at the bar. Sensing that I'm struggling to hold onto my position on cloud nine, I suggest to Leslie that it may be a good time to leave. He agrees. I pass Kimberley on the way out and make a point of saying goodbye.

"Wait a minute," she says, grabbing me by the wrist. "I want your number before you go. Maybe we can meet up in the week."

Somewhat confused, I oblige. What a bizarre evening!

Just after 7.00 in the morning, the phone rings. Assuming it's for Arancha or Sylvie, I decide not to pick up. After a few seconds, I hear the answer machine click in down below in the lounge. Shortly afterwards, the phone goes again and there's a further message.

I get up at about 8.00 and listen to the messages whilst waiting for my toast to pop up. To my surprise, they're both from Kimberley, claiming that she hasn't made it to bed yet. I have things to do, so decide to call her back later.

By the time I've returned to the house in the afternoon, there's another message.

"Blimey, this girl's keen," I tell myself. "I get it – she was just joking about her antics with the bouncer to make me jealous."

Lying on my bed in a pair of shorts – the temperature is well into the seventies – I return Kimberley's calls. She's delighted to hear from me and eager to know what I'm wearing on such a hot day. I enlighten her.

"The thought of you with not many clothes on really excites me," she whispers down the line. "When am I gonna be able to see you again?"

We discuss our availability. Kimberley then invites me to a barbecue party on Friday.

"I won't be able to make it till about 10.30," I inform her. "It's just that I coach at a gym club for three hours on a Friday evening."

"Don't worry about that," she says. "Just make sure you're there."

Seconds before I'm ready to set off for the gym on Friday, Kimberley rings.

"I'm sorry, I'm gonna have to cancel our date tonight," she says. "My friend's a nurse and she's on a late shift. She doesn't drive and needs me to pick her up."

As I'm running late, I leave it that I'll be in touch soon to arrange an alternative date.

After gym, I call into *Dean's*. Just as I'm emptying my first drink, I spot Kimberley sprawled across the settee with one of the regular doorman called Gary. He's off-duty and all over her. Angered by her deception, I find myself half-filling my pint glass with water from the drinking fountain nearby. Before I have chance to engage my brain, I've stalked the cavorting couple and surreptitiously emptied the contents of my glass all over them. I then make a hasty retreat to the other side of the club. Over the next hour, no-one tracks me down.

On the way out, I pass Kimberley in the lobby. We exchange glances, but no words. The guilt betrayed by her expression leaves me in no doubt that she's aware of the identity of her water attacker.

It's only on the way home that it occurs to me how short my temper has become in recent months when under the influence of alcohol. My reaction tonight was definitely out of character. I think this is simply a sign of monumental frustration on my behalf. Nothing ever seems to go right romantically.

The following Friday, I bump into Dawn, the university student who insisted on taking my number after we'd kissed a few weeks ago. She seems pleased to see me and makes it known that she's started a holiday job with an insurance company that just happens to be located close to *Lower Valley Sixth Form College*.

"I like the job," she says, "but public transport is so bad, I have to leave home at 7.30 in the morning."

Sensing divine intervention, I offer her a lift in with me – at least until the end of term.

"Oh, thanks. That'd be great," she says. "I'll call you tomorrow or Sunday to arrange something."

It's now bedtime on Sunday and there hasn't been a word from Dawn. I wonder why some people waste their breath saying they'll do something when they know they won't. I suppose it's just a cowardly way of saying "no". But then why did she ask for my number originally?

With my first year at *Lower Valley* over in mid-July, Martin Studd joins me for an evening out at *James Dean's*. We're early and the club is relatively empty. I take the opportunity to tell Martin about my adventure with Kimberley and the bouncer.

"Is it that bouncer over there?" Martin asks, pointing across the dance floor.

"Er … yes, it is actually," I reply. "How on earth did you know that?"

"Cos he's got one of those lazer pointer things on you. Oh, look out! I think he's coming over."

Before I have time to work out my story, Gary takes me to one side.

"Did you throw water over me and m' girlfriend a few weeks ago?" he asks perfectly reasonably.

Caught on the hop and fearing for my life, I deny any knowledge of the incident. It's only later that my conscience kicks in and, spurred on by Martin, I decide to come clean.

"I'm really sorry," I say with my head bowed, "but Kimberley and I were supposed to be meeting up that night and she blew me out at the last minute with some feeble excuse." Gary nods, his fists held firmly by his sides. "It was a bit of a pathetic reaction and I'm quite embarrassed about it, actually. I can assure you it's not something I make a habit of doing."

"Okay, mate. No problem," he says, then turns and walks away.

I utter a private "phew" and return to Martin who was looking on anxiously throughout my exchange with Gary.

"There you are," he says. "That proves that honesty's the best policy."

With no work in the morning, I drop into *Dean's* the following Wednesday and am immediately summoned over to the 'quiet' area by Kimberley.

"Sit down and have a chat," she says, patting the seat beside her.

At this point, I spot Gary glaring across at us from the other side of the club.

"I'd better not," I reply. "I don't want to upset your boyfriend any more than I've done already."

"Don't worry about him, he's a pussycat. 'Boyfriend' did you say? I don't think so. He's got a wife and baby."

Kimberley grabs my arm and pulls me down next to her. I attempt to escape, but she's having none of it. In the end, I resign myself to staying put.

"Why should I feel guilty about talking to her when Gary's married with a kid?" I ask myself. "It's not right that blokes like him should have the best of both worlds."

Rather bizarrely, Kimberley decides to remove the laces from my trainers and uses them to tie my hands together.

"You're the one that I want," she says, "but it's a bit awkward finishing with Gary at the moment."

"Why's that?" I ask. "Is he violent?"

"No! I told you, he's a big pussycat. It's just that he's paid for my holiday and I'd be a real bitch if I dumped him now. By the way, I don't spose you've got any spare rooms in your house?"

"Spare rooms? Who for?"

"For me. I can't stay where I am now for much longer."

I tell her that both rooms are currently taken, but promise she'll be the first to hear if the situation changes. The thought of a beauty queen like Kimberley running round my house in skimpy underwear makes me go weak at the knees.

Gary becomes increasingly irritated at the sight of me with my hands tied. Eventually, I manage to persuade Kimberley to release me rather than antagonise him any further.

On my weekend visit to *James Dean's*, Gary accosts me once again.

"Follow me," he says and leads me into a small room to the side of the main bar.

To my horror, he locks the door behind us.

"Oh, my God, I'm going to get a real beating," I tell myself.

I look up at Gary and try as hard as I can to imagine a fluffy, harmless pussycat, yet all I can see is a large, solidly built individual with a number one haircut preparing himself for battle.

"Don't worry, mate," he says suddenly as if detecting my unease. "I'm not gonna hurt ya."

At first, I wonder if he's bluffing, but then I notice a blatant relaxing of his stance.

"I just wanna know what Kimberley's been sayin' to ya. All the details."

Sensing that he could easily turn nasty if he felt I was lying or holding back information, I decide to be straight with him. I relate the whole story from the outset, not forgetting what Kimberley had told me about her holiday.

"That's ridiculous!" he says. "I'm not paying for her to go away."

When I've finished my account, he pats me gently on the back. "Thanks, mate, I appreciate your honesty. At least I now know where I stand."

He unlocks the door and the two of us return into the main arena. I breathe a huge sigh of relief.

"Well, I've almost certainly blown it with Kimberley," I mutter to myself. "But as much as she turns me on, I think I'd rather come out of all this with a full set of teeth."

In the early hours of the morning, the phone rings. Feeling certain that it's an indignant Schwarzkopf model, I roll over and ignore it. By her third attempt, however, I relent and pick up. I barely have chance to say "hello" before Kimberley hurls a barrage of abuse into my right ear.

"I can't believe the rubbish you told Gary tonight," she rages. "As if I'd wanna break up with him to go out with a muppet like you."

I let her finish before closing the one-sided conversation with a polite, non-grudging "Bye, then". As my head returns to the pillow, it occurs to me that I should've listened to the alarm bells that were ringing in my head when Kimberley first announced that she'd "shagged the bouncer". To be honest, I probably would've done had she not been so magnetically beautiful. I think it must be part of human nature to allow external beauty to mask the flaws that lie beneath. In this respect, I suppose good-looking people always have it easier than their less attractive counterparts. And she did flatter me beyond belief at times, which is always a cunning ploy when dealing with someone whose self-esteem is as fragile as mine has become. Oh well, a lucky escape, I guess. What was I saying recently about meeting someone normal?

All in all, it's been an exhausting year and I don't think I've ever felt in more need of a rest. Thank God for the summer holidays!

If I Fell

(Year 8)

*If I fell in love with you, would you promise to be true
And help me understand?
Cos I've been in love before and I found that love is more
Than just holding hands.*

AUTUMN TERM

A couple of days before the start of the new academic year, there's an unexpected phone call for me at home.

"Hi ya," whispers a morose-sounding voice down the other end of the line. Has someone died?

After a moment's hesitation, I recognise it as belonging to Charlotte Rhys-Jones.

"Oh hello," I say. "Is everything okay?"

"Hm, not really. I've been ill again and my mum suggested I rang you. Hope you don't mind."

"No, it's fine. So ... er ... what's the problem, then?"

"Oh, it's my glandular fever. It's come back and I'm freaking out about my French coursework."

"I see. Kissed too many of the local lads out in Spain, did we?"

"No!" she says, sounding more like her old self. "What're you like?"

I chuckle. "Sorry, couldn't resist that. Listen, Charlotte. Try not to worry too much. It's a good five to six weeks until the first essay's due, so there's no cause for alarm."

"Spose not."

"And I'm sure the College will be flexible about deadlines if you can produce a medical certificate. Just get plenty of rest."

"Okay, doctor."

"And not too much going out," I add, aware of her compulsion for socialising.

She laughs and then suddenly changes the subject: "By the way, I've got a really cool tan, so you'd better get your Spider out."

It takes a good few seconds to register. Did I really agree in a light-hearted moment at the end of the summer term to give her a ride in my classic car if she came back in September with a better tan than I did? I guess I hadn't taken her suggestion seriously at the time. Trust Charlotte to remember.

"Ah, but you haven't seen *my* tan yet."

She giggles. "You've got no chance."

As I head down the corridor on the first day back at work, the Principal stops me in my tracks.

"Look, Al, um ... well done!" he says with a congratulatory nod.

I realise at once that he's referring to the A level German results that were published a couple of weeks back. Of the twenty Upper Sixth students I took on single-handed this time last year, eighteen passed – ten with grades A to C. Not that achievement is the only key factor any more. Here at *Lower Valley*, retention – the number of students we hang on to – is also a top priority and I managed one hundred per cent in this area. Considering the lack of optimism for the group's future success voiced by my two predecessors when I took over, I am, to coin a student phrase, 'well happy' with the outcome.

My redundancy two years ago has made me only too aware how easy it is to feel undervalued by senior management, so the Principal's words put an even broader smile on my face. Despite the rumours that were circulating when I first arrived, he obviously knows a thing or two about man-management, which, in my humble opinion, is an often overlooked quality amidst the modern obsession with league tables and balancing the books. Privately, I'm just relieved to have dispelled any lingering doubts I may've had about my ability to combine effective teaching with the successful running of the department. Looks like the world ain't such a bad place, after all.

Following the last-minute departure of Yvonne Lambert to try her hand at professional translation, Margaret Becker, the Curriculum Manager for Spanish, has been asked to take charge of the Language Department, pending a replacement. If she really considered herself to be the most heavily burdened teacher at the College before her appointment, she may well have a shock in store now.

Romantically, the summer holidays have thrown up two possibilities: Lisa, a small, blonde, olive-skinned Canadian who works behind the bar at *Razzmatazz* nightclub and Anika, a taller Swedish *au pair* with closely-cropped brown hair and the largest breasts I've ever seen outside a Pamela

Anderson poster. I know this because she shared my bed a couple of weeks back and I was fortunate enough to view them at close quarters. Not that I'd ever class myself as a 'tit' man as such, but these were a real eye-opener and a definite turn-on.

Actually, it all came as a bit of a surprise as Anika had told me quite firmly during our previous encounters that she wouldn't go any further than kissing because she had a dream boyfriend back home who she was intending to marry. Where have I heard this before? Then, one evening at my place, she proceeded to harp on about wanting more experience before settling down and ... well, one thing just led to another. As for Lisa, I've got a date with her at the weekend.

My date with Lisa is an odd one. We meet for lunch, chat a bit about her life in Canada, then trail around the town aimlessly at her request. In *Disney World*, we bump into Joanna Black and David Marsden, two live wires from my new Lower Sixth German group. To be honest, they seem more interested in talking to me than my date is. I am, therefore, slightly surprised when Lisa takes me up on my offer to come back to the house.

Since the lodgers are entertaining downstairs, we have little option but to head for my bedroom. Just for some peace and quiet, of course. Clueless as to whether she fancies me or not, I throw caution to the wind and kiss her. She responds at once, but then just as I'm starting to feel a bit more relaxed, suddenly withdraws with a sigh and says: "Al, I'm sorry – I can't do this."

"What's the problem?" I ask, wondering whether the chef accidentally slipped an excessive amount of garlic in my lunch.

"It's not you. It's just that I ... I'm still in love with this guy in Canada and it ... it doesn't feel right."

"What d'you mean? Were you ... er ... together?"

"Yeah, two years back." Her large, protruding eyeballs retreat dolefully into their sockets. "I'm still hoping we might get it on again when I return to Canada."

Defeated once more, I slump down onto my bed with a whole array of expletives on my tongue, contemplating whether there are other blokes out there who are also blessed with such amazing good fortune.

"Why the hell did she agree to meet me in the first place?" I ask myself. "She knew I fancied her."

But there seems little sense in creating a scene, so I take a few deep breaths and attempt to carry on some sort of polite conversation. Before long, Lisa looks at her watch and mutters something about her evening shift at the club. I offer to drop her there, but she needs to change first, so we head for the house round the corner where she's lodging.

As she jumps out of the car, I leave the engine running.

"Not coming in, then?" she asks with an air of disappointment.

"Thought you were in a hurry."

"Well, I've got about … um … twenty minutes. Come on up. I'll show you my room."

Upstairs in her box room, I plonk myself onto the single bed in the corner whilst she slowly strips to her knickers, ensuring that I get a bird's eye view of more than just the upper section of the house.

"Is this girl feeling sorry for me or getting off on being a mega tease?" I ask myself despairingly.

Aroused, but determined not to let her walk all over me, I remain seated and settle for lapping up the view.

Later on, I bump into Anika in town. Against all expectations, we end up in bed a second time. What isn't so surprising, however, is the guilt that follows and her promise that it definitely won't happen again. Just in case she means it, I grab one final admiring look at her truly remarkable assets. Page three girls eat your heart out!

It's the following Monday and I'm sitting at *Bar Med*, reflecting on one of the most memorable weekends of my life over a quiet pint. All thoughts of Anika and Lisa were temporarily sidelined by the sight of some of the legends of motor racing history hurtling round the famous Goodwood circuit in examples of the most beautiful automotive machinery ever designed. It was the annual Revival Meeting.

"At least if a car decides to be temperamental, you can usually get out the spanners and fix it," I tell myself with a grin.

The modern era of stars was represented by Brits Damon Hill and Martin Brundle. However, it was the Golden Oldies John Surtees, Jack Brabham and Stirling Moss – the latter two in their seventies – who captivated me with their outstanding displays of undiminished skill.

"There can't be many sports where the advancing years detract so little from performance," I reflect.

For a person who's increasingly concerned about the physical restrictions imposed by old age and, at the same time, more determined than ever to fulfil his childhood dream of racing, it was all a very uplifting experience.

Both mum and dad were keen motor sport fans, and some of my earliest childhood memories are of race meetings at circuits like *Thruxton* and *Brands Hatch*, with that unforgettable smell of Castrol in the air. As I'm sure I've mentioned before, my first ambition in life was to be world motor racing champion – as well as a successful dairy farmer and Olympic gymnast – and here I am now as a mere French and German teacher. Funny how things work out. Still, at least I'd be capable of a good old chinwag with Michael Schumacher in his mother tongue.

I take another sip of my beer and wonder whether Moss and co would substitute their glorious era for the highly commercialised, rather soulless modern world of Formula One. I console myself with the thought that they probably wouldn't. Sarah, the pretty brunette behind the bar, recognises me from my time at the girls' Convent, even though I didn't teach her. She listens attentively as I enthuse over my awe-inspiring weekend and seems to understand.

"Yes, I think you should definitely start racing yourself," she says avidly.

I smile to myself. "I wonder if she'd be quite so supportive if I were her husband and we had a young family."

But since my chances of becoming a family man appear to be growing more remote by the day, I reckon I'll just have to settle for donning a helmet and a set of fireproof overalls.

Still with my head in the clouds and dreaming of a racing debut in a classic car, the Spider gets a handful of rare post-summer outings. After several gentle reminders, I find myself leaving College late on the following Wednesday afternoon with Charlotte Rhys-Jones in the passenger seat. Since the start of term, she's been in high spirits and, thank goodness, there've been no signs whatsoever of a recurrence of glandular fever. I am, however, a tad uneasy about the prospect of being spotted in a convertible with a student alongside me, given the modern predisposition for scandal-mongering and blowing things out of proportion. Moreover, I haven't completely forgotten the comment she reputedly made to Rupert at her eighteenth.

"So you definitely told your parents where you were going?" I ask slightly uncomfortably.

"Yeah, I told my mum," she says with a mock yawn.

"And she was okay about it?"

She flashes me a look, which seems to say: Were you born paranoid or what? "She thought it was a bit unusual. But she's cool."

Once we've left the immediate vicinity of the College, I start to chill out. After all, Charlotte is over eighteen – old enough to vote, drink alcohol and even tie the knot without parental consent. And anyway, worrying constantly is exhausting.

Back at the house, I introduce my guest to Sylvie, then set about preparing something to eat. Sylvie has other plans, so it's just Charlotte and I who sit down at the table to brave my attempt at a homemade pizza. The conversation flows naturally and I realise more than ever what a sweet, fun-loving person she is. As she eagerly tells me more about herself, I can't fail to notice the almost permanent radiance of her stunning brown eyes and the gleaming whiteness of her teeth against the background of a face darkened by two weeks in the Spanish sun. Somehow, it seems impossible to believe that just a few weeks back, the very same person was struck down by glandular fever, so convincing is her impersonation of vibrant health. In spite of myself, I have to acknowledge personally that the young woman in front of me looks particularly alluring on this mild September evening.

Slightly concerned that there may be an ulterior motive for wanting the ride in my car, I ask about the lad Charlotte was dating last term.

"Well, we did split up over the summer," she says, "but have met up a couple of times recently."

There follows a twinkle in her eye, which convinces me that she has aspirations of full reconciliation with her ex. The sensible side of me is reassured, although I can't help wondering why I've had so much difficulty finding an older woman with all Charlotte's qualities in the 'real' world.

To wash down the pizza – particularly the hard bits round the edge – we pay *Bar Med* a brief visit. Afterwards, I drop her home.

On my way back, I can't help conceding how much I enjoyed Charlotte's company tonight.

During the course of the next two weeks, it becomes obvious from their more distant behaviour that Anika has no intention of breaking her promise and Lisa of changing her mind. I've seriously lost count of the number of times another bloke has got in first and left the sort of indelible impression I've been incapable of achieving with anyone. What have they got that I haven't?

Charlotte, however, rings every other evening for a light-hearted, informal chat, which helps counter my mood of despair. At College, she's as friendly as ever but respectful and I begin to wonder why I was dubious of her intentions in the first place.

"Yes, she just sees you as an older brother figure," I tell myself.

But then one morning at the start of break, when I'm cleaning the white board from the previous lesson, a voice from behind makes my hair stand on end.

"So are you going out with Charlotte, then?" it asks.

I turn to catch sight of a fully laden Begonia entering the room to set up for her beginners' Spanish lesson.

As a native speaker, Begonia originally came to the College to help out with conversation classes, but has enjoyed the experience so much that she's in the process of taking a formal teaching qualification. Her slim build and youthful Mediterranean appearance mask the fact that she's a double divorcee and the mother of two grown-up sons.

"Charlotte?" I ask, a picture of innocence. "What d'you mean?"

"I see the way she look at you and I wonder if something is going on."

"Oh, right. Er, no … not at all. We … er … we just talk on the phone every now 'n' again," I decide to confess, trusting her discretion. After all, she recently confided in me about her secret admirer amongst the staff – a long-standing member of the middle management who lost his wife in tragic circumstances – and it'd be harsh not to return the compliment.

"She is a very, very nice girl, you know."

"Yes, she certainly is. So … er … what exactly did you mean about noticing the way she looks at me?"

"She has love in her eyes when she see you. That is obvious."

My eyes almost pop out of their sockets. "Really? I … I don't think so, somehow. Actually, I think she's still in love with her ex-boyfriend. She goes on about him all the time. I'm sure she just sees me as a … a sort of sounding board."

"But I tell you what I see is true."

Not persuaded, I try another angle: "Okay, but it'd be extremely unprofessional for a teacher here to go out with one of the students. Surely it must be the same in Spain."

"Yes, of course. But love is a very special thing."

Still taken aback by Begonia's comments, I'm anxious to continue the conversation. At this point, however, the first arrivals for her lesson begin to drift into the room, forcing us to adjourn.

Later, in the evening, Charlotte calls to find out what I'm up to on Friday night. With Begonia's words still fresh in my head, I'm aware of the need for a more guarded approach, yet at the same time I'm keen to find out the truth.

"Oh, just the usual, I guess," I answer vaguely. "Down the pub, you know."

"Oh, okay."

"Why d'you ask?"

"Just wondered if you fancied meeting up again."

"Right. Well, I'm not so sure that's a good idea."

"Really? Why not?"

"Us teachers, you see, we're not really supposed to arrange to socialise with students outside College."

There's a momentary silence before Charlotte speaks again. "Yes, but don't forget I'm a year older than the others."

"Nevertheless, it's a kind of unwritten law."

"But that's pants! We're just friends, aren't we?"

"That's right, we are."

The problem with Charlotte is that she's a persistent young lady who just won't take no for an answer. What's more, she possesses masterful social skills, which help reinforce her powers of persuasion. If her manner weren't so pleasant and down-to-earth, I'd find it easier to be assertive and put my foot down. On reflection, I suppose she does have a point. She'd be at university now if she hadn't lost a year through glandular fever.

"So how about it, then?" she says.

"What exactly did you have in mind?" I ask, conscious that I'm fighting a losing battle.

"I'm not sure. You choose. I can drive over to your place, if you like."

In the light of Begonia's observation earlier in the day, I change my mind and decide that a further meeting with Charlotte might not be such a bad idea, after all. It'd provide a perfect opportunity to have a proper chat with her about the teacher-student situation. It should be easier to convince her face to face. I suggest we go out for a bite to eat. She accepts and leaves me to decide on the venue.

When Friday evening arrives, Charlotte drives us to a large pub overlooking a lake, located in the vicinity of *Mardall's*. It's renowned for good food and a mellow ambience. I choose a table that's well out of earshot. As I've got a chauffeur, I decide to have a few drinks. After all, it could be tricky trying to establish once and for all whether Charlotte's motives for wanting to see me outside College are purely platonic. If they are, I don't want to overreact.

What follows is a perfect continuation of the pizza evening at my place, the only differences being the public setting and the fact that we're both more formally dressed. Charlotte is immaculately made-up and sports a grey and black skirt with knee-length boots. Along with her curvy proportions, she could easily be mistaken for a woman five years her senior.

As the evening progresses, I realise more than ever what great company she is. I try to read her body language to ascertain whether there's any truth in Begonia's remarks and can't help acknowledging once again what an attractive young woman I've got sitting in front of me. In my head, I'm trying to brace myself for a frank talk about our situation, yet it seems so inappropriate to spoil such a lovely evening. And ... and I just can't take my eyes off her.

"I'll do it later," I tell myself.

After the meal, we stand outside by the lake, admiring the moon's reflection on the water and breathing in the cool, tranquil September air. For some reason, the three pints of lager I consumed with my steak seem to have gone straight to my head. I'm conscious of the proximity of Charlotte's body to mine, the loud thud of our hearts drowning out the animated chatter of the ducks paddling just a few feet away. Then, with my prudence temporarily on vacation, it happens. Entranced by the beauty before me on this sublime autumnal evening and weary from years of dead-ends and forbidden paths, my defences finally crack as I lean forward and kiss Charlotte Rhys-Jones beneath the star-studded sky. Her lips are warm and inviting, and for a full two minutes the real world is forgotten as a sensation of profound happiness pervades every limb in my body.

As our lips part, interrupting the highly emotive moment, there's an awkward silence.

"What d'you ... er ... fancy doing now?" I ask, attempting to break it.

"Get out of the cold," she replies with a nervous giggle.

We climb into her car.

"We could go for a drink somewhere else, if you like. Or d'you need to get back?"

Charlotte's answer is as rapid as it is decisive: "I'd prefer to go back to your place."

The journey home is brief but long enough in the silence for the bane of my life, that wretched conscience, to rear its ugly head.

Lying together on my bed fully clothed – oh, if only she weren't my student and we were naked – I try to recapture my composure and self-control, but it's an agonising battle. The conversation is slightly more stilted than before, but my overcooked brain tells me that words and not actions must dominate the rest of this encounter. So I continue to ramble on – about anything that comes into my head.

Waving goodbye to Charlotte about an hour later, the sense of relief that nothing further happened is as strong as my desire that it had. Scarcely before have my head and heart been in such direct conflict. In reality, though, it wasn't so much the instinctive sexual desire that was so hard to resist, but the recognition that I was so close to being reminded, maybe for just a brief interval, what it was like to be intimate with a woman who really appreciated me.

"Have I been denying my feelings for the last year out of professional obligation?" I ask myself, as I attempt in vain to get some much-needed sleep.

Then, for the first time, a bizarre thought enters my head. What if she's THE ONE? What if after all the trials and tribulations that have accompanied my search for true love, Charlotte Rhys-Jones is THE ONE? After all, the path to true love never runs smooth. Isn't that how the saying goes? My sensible side tries to take over and persuade me that if she really loved me, she'd wait. But isn't that the stuff of black and white films and fairy tales, not the real world on the eve of the millennium? My mind is in turmoil.

I try to divert my thoughts as it's really 'doing my head in', but fail woefully. I know what those close to me would say: "She's just got a crush on you because you're her teacher. Remember what happened with Rachel." If this is a teenage crush, then I'd be putting my heart on the line once again. But even more significantly, I could potentially jeopardise my professional future if we got caught. But then if I tarnish everyone with the same brush, that makes me a cynic, doesn't it? And surely there's nothing more reprehensible than that.

When I wake in the morning, I've sobered up completely. The previous evening's trip to fantasy land is ... well, just that – a fantasy. All weekend, I can't rid myself of an abhorrent feeling of guilt. Okay, I'd be the first to put my hand up and acknowledge that during my eleven-year teaching career, I've been attracted to some of the female students. Rachel and Maria are living proof of this. Are there any straight male Sixth Form teachers who haven't? But never, never in my wildest dreams did I think that I'd ever give in to temptation with a *current* student. My moral values and sense of professional duty are far too strong for that. And yet, I have. Charlotte, the temptress, has worn me down and discovered a chink in my armour after all these years. What scares me is that I really do like her, but somehow I'm going to have to find a way of letting her down gently.

My lesson with Charlotte's group on the following Monday runs smoothly. Thank heavens! I'm desperate to talk to her in private, but the opportunity evades me all day.

Just as I'm on the verge of phoning her in the evening, she calls me. She's as eager as I am to discuss the events of Friday night, implying that she too has had reservations. There seems to be a reluctant mutual understanding that we should forget what happened.

I am, therefore, slightly surprised when Charlotte rings the following evening, expressing concern that I may've misunderstood her.

"Al," she says. "I don't think I really said what I meant last night."

I'm intrigued.

"Oh, in what way?" I ask.

"It's just that I think I gave the impression we shouldn't meet up any more and that's not what I want."

"Okay, but ..."

"I mean, it's all right for us to carry on seeing each other as friends, isn't it?"

"Er, I don't know."

"I really do understand why we can't have a relationship."

"You do?"

"Yeah, 'course. Don't you believe me?"

"Yes, I do, but if we're seen together, other ... other people'll probably get the wrong idea."

"Then we'll just have to be careful."

In the end, I'm impressed by Charlotte's maturity. I decide that if we continue seeing each other as friends until June, I should have a clearer idea of whether Begonia is right and this is more than just a crush on a teacher.

"Well, okay, then," I say, happy with the compromise.

And so we do meet up – several times over the next fortnight, in fact. In early October, we go to see another French film, which involves picking up Charlotte from her house and dropping her back later. Her parents are there and receive me warmly. Her dad even offers me a beer. Am I imagining it or are they genuinely pleased about my friendship with their daughter? They certainly appear to be giving it their blessing, which helps put my mind at rest.

At the end of the evening when we part, Charlotte kisses me again on the lips – no tongues, but not exactly a grandparent's farewell kiss either.

"Thought we're sposed to be just friends," I say in mild protest.

She smiles sweetly and, with a shrug, says: "I like your kisses. They're very warm."

But there's a lot on at work at the moment and I haven't got the time or energy to question the situation once again. Anyway, it's not as if we're going out with each other or even sleeping together. Moreover, I really enjoy Charlotte's company and I'm considerably more contented than I've been for a long time.

Over the next couple of weeks, however, there's one thing that leads me to question for the first time the extent of Charlotte's maturity and that's her irritating habit of continuously discussing her encounters with other men. The Will Smith look-alike who's desperate for her number. The bloke from an internet chat room who she's arranged to meet. And, of course, her ex-boyfriend who wants her back.

"Is her interest in me merely superficial, after all?" I ask myself. "Or is she trying to make me jealous?"

Just before half term and Charlotte's planned trip to the Med with her parents, I decide to test the water – purely for future reference. I suggest that we shouldn't perhaps see so much of each other if what she really wants is more time to play the field like many eighteen-year-olds. She listens carefully to what I'm saying and promises to have a think whilst she's away.

Towards the end of half term, a letter arrives with familiar writing and a foreign postmark. It's from Charlotte. The first page contains a description of the resort and an account of what she's been up to with her parents. What appears on the second fills me with consternation:

*... I know for sure now that I want to
be with you! Just thinking about you makes
me smile, and I love the times that I spend
with you. I know that things are hard because
of the situation, but I want to take the risk
and get to know you better! "J'ai envie de toi!"
and I don't mean that in just a sexual way,
I want to be close to you in every possible way!*

All my love, with big hugs and kisses!

Charlotte

As I lower the letter onto my lap, I can't help feeling flattered. No-one has ever written to me in such a tender, romantic way. Not even Rachel or Sam. But I'm anxious too. This wasn't the reaction I was after before her trip. Her words attempt to revoke the wise decision we both made after our Friday night misadventure and so put our friendship on an entirely different plane, one that would play havoc with my conscience and nervous system.

This is typical of my life. Here is a gorgeous young woman who really wants me and I can't do anything about it without placing my whole teaching career on the line. If only we could jump forward eight months, it would make the situation so much less complicated. I'm ashamed to admit it, but I think I've fallen for Charlotte Rhys-Jones hook, line and sinker. How the hell am I going to respond to her letter?

It's my birthday the following Sunday. Charlotte is keen to see me. I arrange to meet her after lunch with my parents, with every intention of reiterating the 'just good friends' option.

I'm running late, but I find Charlotte still waiting for me in the Leisure Centre car park near where she lives. We go for a walk in the woods, then have a quiet drink in a pub that she assures me is 'safe'. Just as I'm stealing myself to broach the contents of her letter, her phone bleeps. She reads the message with a grin.

"Anyone interesting?" I ask.

She shrugs.

"No, not really," she says. "Just this guy I met down the pub last night who made me give him my number."

Over the next few minutes, there's a frantic texting session between Charlotte and the mysterious man from the pub whilst I sit twiddling my thumbs. Being from the pre-mobile generation and not exactly the greatest fan of the antisocial nature of 'messaging' whilst in someone else's company, I can't help feeling irritated by her behaviour. She appears to sense this, but makes no attempt to stop. In spite of myself, I'm suddenly overcome by a wave of jealousy, yet my hands couldn't be more firmly tied. At this point, I remember Kimberley, the *Schwarzkopf* model, and the evening at *James Dean's* when she bound my wrists with my shoelaces. Seems as symbolic now as it was then, although the circumstances are hardly the same.

Back at the car park, Charlotte produces a birthday card and a large box of chocolates from her bag, which partially help to counter my feelings of rejection. I return to the house with my head in a massive spin and my emotions all over the place. The prospect of another man vying for Charlotte's affections is playing havoc with my increasingly fragile heart.

"Who was I kidding thinking we could just be friends for eight months?" I ask myself. "The feelings on both sides are far too intense for that."

It's no good. I'm going to have to make a decision one way or another. Either I stop seeing Charlotte altogether and accept that someone else will snap her up or I throw caution to the wind and give our romance a real go – now. If it can work for my former colleague, Jerome, surely with the right girl it can work for me too. And with all the bad luck I've endured over the last fifteen years, surely I'm entitled to a break. Only, why does it have to be so dangerous?

Back at work the following week, there's an Open Evening. Margaret informs us that she's invited a number of the more mature language students to assist in the marketing of the department. Charlotte R-J is among them. Before the customary invasion of the College by hoards of fifteen- and sixteen-year-olds with their parents begins, she asks if it's okay for me to drop her home at the end. I accept.

Unfortunately, just as we're winding up after four solid hours of hard grind, Margaret approaches Charlotte and offers her a lift.

"Er ... it's okay, thanks," she says awkwardly. "Al's taking me."

As we're making our way out to the College car park, I turn to Charlotte and say: "I can't believe you told Margaret I was taking you home."

"I know. I'm really sorry," she says. "She caught me by surprise and I couldn't think of what to say. D'you think it'll matter?"

"Don't know. Hope not."

But it does matter. The following morning at College, Margaret accosts me in the corridor.

"I'm sorry to have to ask this, Al," she says, "but is there anything going on between you and Charlotte Rhys-Jones?"

I clear my throat, realising how crucial my answer could be.

"Er ... no, 'course not," I reply. "She's just a ..."

"A very attractive young woman," she says, nodding feverishly.

"Well, yes, she is. But I was going to say that she … she's just a very friendly person."

What happened to the calm delivery I'd rehearsed in my head?

At this point, we arrive at Margaret's Spanish lesson. With her class already waiting, our conversation ends abruptly.

"Oh, bugger!" I mutter to myself, not in the slightest bit convinced that I've managed to waylay suspicion.

It doesn't help when Begonia catches up with me later for a confidential chat.

"What were you two up to last night?" she asks reproachfully. "You have made it so obvious the way you look at each other how you feel. Even Margaret has noticed."

I bite my bottom lip. "Yes, I know. She's already spoken to me."

There's a long silence as I try to figure out my next move, but I'm starved of inspiration and desperate for guidance.

"Help me out, Begonia," I say, almost pleading with her. "Tell me what I have to do now."

"You must be very, very careful," she says, aware of the events of the last ten days.

"It's no good – I'm going to have to stop meeting up with her. At least until next summer. Aren't I?"

"But you will break her heart. And the heart of an eighteen-year-old girl is very fragile."

"And so is the heart of this thirty-four-year-old man," I retort, only partly in jest.

Somewhat overwrought and certainly not thinking straight, I race home and dial Charlotte's number.

"Hi, it's me," I say, catching my breath.

She seems to sense my anxiety.

"Oh, hi ya," she whispers. "What's up?"

"Not good news, I'm afraid. Margaret's onto us."

"What, cos of what I said last night?"

"Yes, but not just that. Begonia reckons we aroused suspicion by being over friendly during the Open Evening itself."

"Oh, pants!"

"Listen, Charlotte. This is the last thing in the world I want to do, but things are getting out of hand and …"

"And *what*?"

"And so I … I think we shouldn't meet up for a while."

There's a pregnant pause before she responds, an unmistakable note of melancholy in her voice. "You mean *completely*?"

"Well, yes. At least until things've quietened down a bit."

"Right."

There's a painful silence. Concerned that my heart will intervene and force me to back down, I try to escape. "Well, I'd better go. We can talk more on Monday, if you like. You know, after the French cinema outing."

"Spose."

"Okay, er … have a good weekend, then."

But it's not a good weekend – at least not for me. Once I've calmed down a bit, I can't help wondering whether I overreacted. I know for sure that, in an attempt to be assertive, I was too callous, too matter-of-fact on the phone. But then expressing my feelings spontaneously when under pressure has never been my forte. I decide to write a letter to Charlotte explaining how I really feel – that I hope we can pick up our friendship again, and maybe more, once she's left College and everything's above board. Still in need of moral support, I call Begonia. She agrees to meet for a drink.

"I think you should definitely give her the letter," she says. "It will help her heart to cope if she knows for sure that you will wait for her."

We then proceed to discuss her own situation with Godfrey and how what started as a sloppy, unwanted kiss has developed into something a bit special. Begonia has fears of her own, on the grounds that some colleagues may disapprove of an inter-faculty romance, particularly given that it's less than a year since the high-profile murder abroad of Godfrey's wife. I do my best to reassure her.

On Monday evening, there's a season of French films showing at the City cinema. Charlotte is the only second-year student among the small party led by Simone and myself.

Afterwards, the two of us sneak off to *Bar Med* for a chat. Any plans I have of relaying the contents of my letter in person are thwarted by Charlotte's manic texting. I don't have to be brain of Britain to realise that her mind is on other things. Or do I mean 'another bloke'? She does, however, look up when I mention the letter and is keen to take it with her. I hesitate, but then she flutters her eyelids, so I yield.

A week later, it's official. Charlotte and the mysterious bloke from the pub are seeing each other and she's already stayed over at his place. And all I can do is stand by and take it on the chin.

"I'll be a bit late for tomorrow's lesson," she says one morning on her way out of the classroom.

"Oh, how come?" I ask.

"I've got a doctor's appointment."

With knitted brows, I take several slow-motion steps towards her. Surely her glandular fever hasn't struck again. "You're not ill again, are you?"

"No, nothing like that."

She grins smugly and marches off.

With this, the humiliation of Al is complete. Although common sense tells me that her new lover has probably saved my skin, I can't help feeling severely wounded. Whether this is because I now realise how stupid I've been believing in Charlotte's maturity or because I really care about her, I'm not sure. Probably a combination of the two.

It's now December and I'm depressed. Not clinically, of course, just severely down in the dumps. Exactly as I'd feared, Charlotte has forgotten me after five minutes and there I was putting my whole teaching career on the line because I thought she was special and worth getting to know better. That I've misread the signs once again doesn't surprise me. After all, I've been doing this consistently since the Wombles made their last appearance on BBC TV. What does puzzle me, though, is how Begonia managed to get it all wrong too. I mean, I thought she was supposed to be the resident expert on affairs of the heart.

But my life is rarely dull for long. On the first Saturday of the month, I arrive home to catch Sylvie, another rejected soul, frantically massacring an official England World Cup tie with the kitchen scissors.

"Bastard, bastard!" she sobs, as the tiny pieces cascade to the floor.

"What's up?" I ask, horrified by such an act of brutality that would've impressed Napoleon himself.

She stamps her foot twice before replying: "'e stand me up again. Why 'e do zhis to me? I 'ate 'im, I 'ate 'im!"

It's on occasions like this that I'm eternally grateful for my knowledge of French, which reassures me that, despite Sylvie's undoubted wrath, an act of cannibalism has in fact not taken place. Apparently, Andy Best, the ex-*Mardall's* student who attended my gym club, gave her his beloved tie as assurance that he wouldn't stand her up twice in succession. Not for the first time in his life, the booze must've stripped him of his memory. What is it they say? *Hell hath no greater fury than a woman scorned.* Poor Sylvie. I take her for lunch at *Wetherspoons*, one of the new bars in the City, in an attempt to cheer her up.

A few days later, Gabrielle, a twenty-nine-year-old Brazilian who moved into the house a couple of weeks back after Arancha returned to Spain and who's engaged to an American pilot, suddenly bursts into the lounge during a gripping episode of *EastEnders*, sinks to her knees in front of me, unzips my trousers and …

"Gabi, what you doing?" I ask, covering my private parts with both hands.

She raises her eyebrows above her glasses and says: "You not like?"

"Well, yes, of course. I mean, no – not with, you know, Sylvie in the ..."

Unable to force the words out, I gesture in the direction of the kitchen. After all, the poor girl was educated in a French convent.

"Where do I get this amazing propensity for attracting attached women and students exclusively?" I ask myself despairingly as *EastEnders* ends with that familiar Grant stare. I zip up my jeans.

Just before Christmas, Sylvie returns to France, her decision prompted not so much by the fear of catching her landlord with his trousers down in front of the TV, but by an accident which involved her Renault 5 ploughing into the side wall of a house on the back road into town. She claimed that her foot had slipped as she was negotiating a u-turn. And guess who had to fetch her from Casualty at 2.00 in the morning and escort her home whilst still in a state of intense shock? Who said a landlord's duties never extend beyond collecting the rent? I'll miss her, though.

Gabrielle heads off to visit her man who flies – as opposed to visiting my flies – and, just as I'm looking forward to a few weeks of peace and quiet, a Spanish friend of Arancha's talks me into temporarily offering Gabrielle's room to a French guy called Thierry. An Italian girl, Katherina, has already agreed to have Sylvie's old room after Christmas. In view of my increasingly dire financial situation – the result of taking on too large a mortgage – I have little option but to continue juggling the rooms in my hostel for foreign workers.

Despite the gloom and doom of recent weeks, I guess I should be grateful for small mercies. If it was inevitable that at some stage I'd risk my career in the pursuit of potential future love, it's fortunate that it was with someone of Charlotte R-J's good nature. Since our 'split', she's been not only the model of discretion but also friendly and cooperative in class. I mention this to Paul Redhead, the CM for RE and Philosophy, who, in addition to Begonia, is the only colleague officially 'in the know'. As a man in his late twenties with a teenage fiancée, he has little difficulty relating to my predicament.

"Yes, she always seemed pretty mature to me," he says. "You never know, things might still work out when she's left. But if it's any consolation, I'm sure you've done the right thing even if it doesn't feel like it."

With the exams fast approaching, my primary concern is for the lack of College work Charlotte has been doing at home. She tells me that her parents share my sentiments, but blames this on the upsurge in her social life. By this, I assume she's referring to her new man. Anyway, with the millennium just round the corner, I'm determined to put her out of my head and find a licit partner I can date before I'm in my dotage. There must be one out there somewhere.

As a regular customer, *Bar Med* sells me tickets for New Year's Eve for twenty pounds instead of forty, breakfast included. The new millennium gets off to a positive start thanks to a highly enjoyable kiss with a young woman with braids and a cowboy hat. Unfortunately, she doesn't stay through till breakfast, but then nor do I after crashing on my own at about 2.30 in the morning, adamant that 2000 will be my year.

SPRING TERM

Two weeks into the New Year, the pantomime season gets underway and I make a comeback appearance on stage with my old amateur dramatics group in their rendition of *Puss in Boots*. As before, I try to flog tickets to the students, but only Dave Marsden and Jo Black from the first year express an interest.

Late on Friday afternoon, just as I'm about to set off for the second performance, there's a call out of the blue from Charlotte Rhys-Jones, requesting tickets for Saturday for her and her boyfriend's eight-year-old brother. I promise to leave some on the door.

When I come off stage on Saturday evening, I'm surprised to find Charlotte alone in the bar. "What happened to the boyfriend's little brother," I wonder, but decide not to ask. She's in an affable mood and sticks around for a chat. Dave and Jo are also keen to talk, taking the mickey out of my rather excessive make-up. Apparently, photos will be e-mailed to every member of the College. I reckon I'll have to watch out for these two.

Since Christmas, I've been covering the topic of Food and Health with my two Lower Sixth German groups. Towards the end of one of the lessons, Jo Black's 'neighbour', Lucy Vaughan, a sweet-natured, conscientious brunette, suddenly throws down the gauntlet after I've revealed that I sometimes bake my own bread.

"I bet you couldn't make a chocolate cake," she says.

"No problem," I reply confidently, although I've got no experience whatsoever of cake making.

"You'll have to bring it in so we can all have a slice," Jo chips in.

I don't know – the things I let myself in for.

Following her appearance at the panto, Charlotte rings for the occasional chat. As a result, I begin to wonder whether she's as happy as she made out before Christmas. I see this as an excellent opportunity to gently coax her into doing some more work. However, she confides in me that she's having serious doubts about going to university, but doesn't want to disappoint her parents. Not exactly an uncommon problem.

Margaret is quick to pick up on the fact that Charlotte is back to spending more time in my room between lessons and decides to confront me again. Since she's met Charlotte's boyfriend and I've nothing to hide, I confess that we talk on the phone every now and again.

"That's not a problem is it?" I ask. "I think she needs some extra support at the moment. You mentioned yourself that her Spanish has deteriorated."

"I don't know," she replies. "I suppose she is a mature girl. But then again, other people may get the wrong idea. I'd keep schtum about it if I were you."

Relieved to have got Margaret off my back, I feel vindicated in my belief that honesty is often the best tack. But I couldn't be more wrong. In the evening, Charlotte rings in a state of fury. She explains that her tutor demanded to see her this afternoon, and then gave her a rocket about harassing a member of staff with unwanted phone calls.

"She spoke to me like I was a little kid!" she fumes.

Under normal circumstances, I'd refuse to discuss a colleague with a student, but on this occasion Margaret's actions have left me with my back against the wall. After brief reflection, I inform Charlotte of our conversation earlier. There's a deadly silence at the other end of the line.

"Come on, Charlotte, you don't think I'd do something like that, do you?" I say. "Surely you know me well enough by now."

"Do I?"

I persist in my effort to convince her of my innocence, but my reassurances fall on deaf ears. I'm put out by Margaret's act of deceit, yet the damage has already been done and there seems little I can do.

The repercussions, however, are drastic as Charlotte is transformed overnight from the polite, happy-go-lucky young woman I've known for sixteen months into an awkward schoolgirl with scant respect for her teacher.

It all begins in a fairly minor fashion – refusal to explain lateness, insistence on eating an iced bun in class and open criticism of the contents of my lessons. But then she steps it up a gear by refusing to do a mock oral exam, on the grounds that I was obstructive over her initial choice of topic and then didn't give her enough time to find an alternative. It's true that I expressed doubts about the suitability of her initial proposal, but that was six weeks ago.

A few days later, Margaret receives a letter from Charlotte's mum, supporting her daughter's claims, and any hopes I harboured of being able to keep her dissent under wraps fade fast.

Surprisingly, Charlotte phones at the weekend to apologise, blaming her odd behaviour on a recurrence of glandular fever.

Back at College the following week, however, Charlotte is up to her old tricks again, leaving me in a state of confusion.

"Why's she doing this to me?" I ask Begonia, throwing both arms up in the air.

"That is quite simple," she replies. "She thinks you don't care for her any more."

"What, a woman scorned and all that?"

"Yes, that is it exactly."

"So d'you think I should tell the Principal about it? He always says ..."

"No!" she says sharply. "That would make things worse for Charlotte."

"What can I do then to pacify her?"

"You have to find a way of showing her that you still care."

On 13th February, I take a massive gamble and send Charlotte a Valentine's card with a typed message that I hope she'll be able to decipher. I'm careful not to leave any obvious signs that would incriminate me should she decide to disclose it. Whilst not totally persuaded of the wisdom of this move, I'm desperate to appease her before the situation gets even further out of hand. Anyway, with her vast experience of life and relationships, I still trust Begonia's judgement.

On the evening of the 14th, Charlotte rings to thank me for the Valentine's card. Apparently, it was one of three that she received.

"I recognised your granny writing straight away," she says good-naturedly.

Considering that my message wasn't hand-written, she's obviously got her wires crossed. Never mind. The main thing, judging from the pleasant, upbeat tone of her voice, is that it looks like Begonia's plan has worked. I breathe a huge sigh of relief.

This year, the students have been provided with the facility to e-mail staff about their work. After releasing pictures of me as a country bumpkin in the panto for general staff and student consumption – not to mention ridicule – Jo Black and Dave Marsden have been downloading jokes from the Internet – some of them bordering on the vulgar – and mailing them to me. Whilst not wishing to be a party pooper, I have little option but to insist they stop in view of the fact that messages are monitored regularly by the IT team to combat abuse of the system.

Eventually, after several reminders, I get round to baking that eagerly awaited chocolate cake for Lucy Vaughan. Even though I say it myself, it turns out to be a highly respectable maiden effort. Full of pride, I take it along to the German lesson and some of the group are even brave enough to sample a piece. Hugh Granger, the visiting student teacher, defies his diet by helping himself to two slices.

The following day outside my classroom, Lucy presents me with the most magnificently decorated cake you'll ever see – far superior to my humble effort.

"This is *my* attempt at a chocolate cake," she says proudly with a grin that stretches the width of the corridor. What's more, she's even iced my name on the top.

By chance, Charlotte R-J is nearby, waiting for the start of her Spanish lesson in the room opposite, and witnesses the entire ceremony. I can't help noticing her reaction out of the corner of my eye and … if looks could kill. I'm flattered by Lucy's gesture and can't thank her enough. If only her timing had been a touch better, though.

"Fucking hell!" I curse aloud on a Friday afternoon in late February as a hazardous guy rope all but sends me sprawling in front of my own back door, complete with three bags of *Tesco* shopping. "When will that flaming Frenchman get his bloody tent off my lawn?"

Away from the wheel of a car, it's almost unheard of for me to use the 'F' word, but I really am at the end of my tether right now. Unable to afford alternative accommodation after his brief spell in Gabrielle's room over Christmas, Thierry persuaded me to allow him to pitch his tent in the garden for a few days on her return. But that was over three weeks ago and he's been showering and using the kitchen during the day for nothing. It's not as if I'm made of money. Actually, I'm so heavily in debt I've had to put the house on the market.

Realistically, though, my problems at home pale into insignificance when compared to the stress I'm under at work at the moment. Hugh, the demon chocolate cake gorger, is not a natural in the classroom and I've had to follow up complaints from colleagues about his train spotter attire, the constant reek of stale cigarette smoke and his tendency to fall asleep in front of students in the Resource Centre with his headphones on. The mock exams need to be marked, as does the written coursework for French and German. And then there's the Exchange, which is hardly renowned for organising itself, not to mention a mere fourteen one-and-a-half hour lessons a week that have to be planned and taught, and the related marking that's mounting by the day. Nothing new for this time of year, I guess, but I was wrong about the Valentine's card keeping Charlotte's wrath at bay. She's been really unpleasant again since the cake incident and it's starting to undermine my ability to cope. In fact, at times I feel I'm about to lose the plot completely. But there doesn't seem to be any way of stopping her and, mentally exhausted, I find myself seeking refuge in alcohol.

By Sunday, I'm hung over. The prospect of having to face it all again on Monday morning places me closer to the edge than ever before. I decide to ring Charlotte in an effort to appeal to her better judgement, but her mobile is switched off. I leave a message for her to call me urgently. A few hours later, I leave another message. And then another. All in vain.

In the end, I pay the pub a further visit and sink a few more pints. On my return, I try Charlotte's mobile one more time. It's 11.00 pm. But again, it's just the voice mail service.

"Charlotte, please call me back. We've really got to sort this out," I say, almost pathetically. "The exams are just round the corner and I want to help you."

But she doesn't return my call, not on this evening or on any other during the following week.

About ten days later, I find myself at a College desk with Charlotte and Mrs Rhys-Jones sitting opposite. It's Parents' Evening.

"It seems obvious to me, Al, that Charlotte's French has deteriorated dramatically this term," Mrs R-J says. "Can you offer an explanation?"

I try my utmost to explain that I've been unable to persuade her daughter to put her College work ahead of her social life. Fortunately for me, it transpires that Charlotte's performance in her other subjects has also declined. Throughout the duration of the conversation with her mother, she just sits and scowls, offering little more than a grunt when I try to involve her in the discussion.

Finally, just after 9.00 pm, my evening of torture comes to an end. Or so I think. As I make my way down the main corridor towards the car park, Kevin Gough, the Vice-Principal, steps out in front of me and beckons me into his office. The Assistant Principal, Diane Brown, joins us. It's the latter who speaks first: "Earlier today, Al, I had a visit from a female student and her boyfriend. I'm afraid to say that she has made a formal accusation of harassment against you and is anxious for us to take action."

With these words, my whole world caves in on top of me.

I leave the College car park at about 10.00 in the knowledge that my predominantly successful eleven-year teaching career could well be on the verge of an abrupt, premature conclusion. My future, it seems, lies not so much in the lap of the Gods, but in the lap of Charlotte Rhys-Jones. How could she do this to someone she's supposed to care about? Boy, do I need a stiff drink!

On my arrival at College the following morning, I'm summoned to the Principal's office. His stern demeanour doesn't exactly inspire me with confidence and I accept his offer of a seat somewhat apprehensively.

"I received this in the post this morning from Mr and Mrs Rhys-Jones," Dr Faulkner says gravely, handing me a typed two-page letter. "I'd like you to read it."

I begin to read, outwardly calm but inwardly 'shitting my pants'. It's individual words and fragmented sentences that jump out at me rather than complete paragraphs. *A formal complaint. Harassment of daughter. Pushing her too hard. Loss of self-esteem and confidence. Glandular fever. Anxiety and panic attacks.*

I pause, unable to comprehend the extent of their accusations. So I start again in the hope that I may've misinterpreted something. But the words convey the same message second time round. I let out a cry of anguish. Surely the Principal, with his years of experience, isn't going to buy this. I glance up at him for reassurance, but realise from his earnest expression that he believes every word. I read on.

> *Charlotte has shown courage, dignity and maturity. The more she's refused Al's advances, the more difficult and manipulative he's become! There've been unwanted phone calls late at night. His intentions have felt sinister and uncomfortable! She doesn't want a formal investigation – it would cause upheaval to other students. A doctor's certificate will be sent to the Examining Board. We'd like the College to enclose a covering note requesting special consideration. We'll be taking her away over Easter to recover from her ordeal and hope she'll be fit to take up her rightful place at university!*

I fold the letter carefully and return it to its envelope, my head shaking almost uncontrollably in disbelief. After all, this is the stuff of *Corrie* and *EastEnders*, not the real world that I live in. I fight to retain my composure, but the pain of seeing myself described in such cruelly harsh terms is starting to kick in and I sense the tears welling up behind my eyes. But I'm a teacher and a man, and in my world, teachers and men don't cry. At least not in public.

"Well?" Dr Faulkner asks, raising his bushy eyebrows and stroking his greying beard.

"It's ... it's outrageous," I reply. "I mean, it's such a distortion of the truth that it ... it just isn't real."

"I can assure you, Al, that this is *very* real."

He gives me an option. Either we deal with the matter straight away informally, or I can request the presence of a Union Representative or friend and a more formal hearing can be arranged. I pause for reflection. Although my head is crammed with a maze of thoughts and emotions, all jostling for position, I still manage to reason that since there appear to be no false sexual allegations – thank God – I ought to be able to handle this on my own. And in any case, there's my letter. What if Charlotte were to produce it during the course of a formal investigation? I agree to an informal hearing.

When the hearing begins, my natural inclination is to throw up my hands and confess everything. After all, I am guilty. Not of the crime suggested by Charlotte and her parents, that's for sure, but of betraying my professional duties as a teacher. I feel a desperate urge to tell Dr Faulkner how I gave in to temptation and kissed Charlotte because my self-esteem was in the gutter and she flattered me beyond belief. Yet if I've learnt one thing in recent weeks, it's that honesty doesn't always pay. If he gets wind of the fact that I kissed her on several occasions, he'll conclude that worse followed and I'll definitely lose my job. And surely, surely I haven't sinned enough to deserve this. Or have I?

In the end, I opt for a compromise and tell Dr Faulkner exactly how our friendship developed. How Charlotte had insisted on being pushed hard and always craved my attention. How we went to see French films together with her parents' and Yvonne's consent. I stress the fact that I felt sorry for her because she'd missed a year through glandular fever and wanted to help as much as I could. He listens attentively, but doesn't take notes. Then comes the question I've been dreading: "Charlotte's parents have indicated that you sent her a Valentine's card. Is this true, Al? Did you send Charlotte Rhys-Jones a Valentine's card?"

I've no choice. I'm going to have to deceive him on this point. There's no way he'll ever believe my explanation. Anyway, how could I attempt to justify my actions without incriminating Begonia? Whilst it might help my cause to reveal her involvement, I've always valued loyalty to friends and I couldn't do this without her permission. I brace myself, take a deep breath, then firmly deny any knowledge of a Valentine's card. Not satisfied with my reply, Faulkner repeats his question, glaring at me through his large, rimless glasses, hoping no doubt to spot the slightest flicker of unease. I retain eye-contact, my chin raised in an exaggeratedly confident pose, and confirm my answer. Throughout the remainder of the hearing,

I sense that he's already made up his mind whose story he believes and it certainly isn't mine.

A little later, Diane, an immaculately turned-out lady in her late fifties, catches up with me to relay the fact that Charlotte and her mum called into College first thing for a chat.

"Charlotte admitted that she had a crush on you," she says congenially. "What's more, her mother confirmed that she and her husband were aware of this, but did nothing about it. It's just like fatal attraction."

I smile and say: "I think she was worried about her exams and saw me as a scapegoat."

"Yes, she was certainly very uptight about something. And it wouldn't be the first time that the imminence of exams has brought a student to breaking point."

Whilst Diane has a reputation for being highly supportive of the staff – unlike the Principal, it seems – I don't think somehow that she'd be talking to me in such an understanding fashion if she thought I was solely to blame for this regrettable situation. She places her head on one side before continuing: "I suggested to Mrs Rhys-Jones that Charlotte might like to renew her acquaintanceship with you after the exams. Unfortunately, she wasn't overly enthusiastic about my proposition."

"I always thought she and her husband approved of our friendship."

"Maybe they saw you as a respectable future partner for their daughter. Or maybe her mother took a shine to you herself. You just don't know. But then when the chips are down, blood always runs thicker than water, I'm afraid."

I leave Diane's office with the impression that she's got a much clearer idea of what's going on than Dr Faulkner. Perhaps it's because she's a woman. Or is it because she spends more time on site and isn't always away attending 'important' external meetings? I just hope they liaise before our leader decides what action to take.

Later in the day, a letter from the Principal appears in my pigeonhole, transcribing almost word for word the content of our discussion and formally warning me for allowing such an inappropriate friendship to develop with a student.

"How," I ask myself, "did he remember everything so accurately? Did he record our conversation?"

The letter goes on to threaten that a recurrence of similar conduct will almost certainly result in my dismissal from the College. The final paragraph particularly catches my eye. It contains an acknowledgement of my exceptional linguistic ability and impressive teaching skills, and goes on to wish that I'll be able to put this unfortunate incident behind me. With these words, it appears that my nightmare is finally over. The sense of relief is immense.

Sadly, my run-in with the management seems to have taken its toll on my close friendship with Begonia. As my constant confidante over the past few months, I'd continued to hope, perhaps rather optimistically, that she'd offer to defend me in front of the Principal once it was clear what Charlotte and her parents were alleging. But of course, she's got her own professional future to think of. Moreover, she wouldn't want to jeopardise her now public romance with Godfrey, our Head of Faculty and a prominent member of the middle management. Having expressed her opinion that Charlotte had behaved very badly, she's barely exchanged a word with me since. Looks like I'll be paying a high price for involving her in my dilemma.

Charlotte returns for one lesson, but can't cope with the strain, so arrangements are made for her to receive one-to-one tuition until the exams – with a new part-timer called Georgia who's been helping out in the French Department since Yvonne's departure. I'm still expected to mark Charlotte's work, though.

On the Tuesday before the start of the Easter holiday, one of the ladies from the Main Office catches me in the corridor and hands over an urgent message from Georgia to Charlotte, requesting that they rearrange their French lesson scheduled for lunchtime. On the way over to the language block, I pass Charlotte. With Margaret off sick, Simone on a course and Begonia nowhere to be found, I decide to give her the message myself. I do so promptly and politely, then move on.

The following day, Margaret informs me that Charlotte came to see her first thing to complain that I'd spoken to her. Heaven forbid!

As if life hasn't been dramatic enough lately, Rupert flies off the handle on the last Friday of the term when I kiss a girl he calls Ruby – she frequently wears a top of this colour – who he once fancied but never made a move on. Earlier on, he was stressing how much he'd started to dislike her and put his thumbs up in approval when he saw her coming on to me. Perhaps unwisely, I give him my front door keys when he informs me he's tired and wants to go back early.

When I return myself about half an hour later, I find him rummaging through my drawers for Charlotte's phone number.

"I was gonna ring her parents and get you sacked!" he rages.

"So you think that's a reasonable response to my actions tonight?" I ask, almost dumbfounded.

"Yes, definitely!"

I knew Rupert had a temper, but I've never seen him like this before. I try my best to appease him. However, he's still furious and tears down one of my curtain rails before kicking my vacuum cleaner out of existence. On reflection, I probably should've ignored Ruby's advances, but since Rupert sees a different girl he likes virtually every week, it's hard to take his interest seriously.

In the morning, Rupert claims that he'd never have actually phoned Charlotte's parents had he found the number, but I'm left once more to question the state of our friendship. He's made me a tempting offer on the house, yet I'm not sure whether, in my present frame of mind, I could cope with him living in the same town. And I certainly wouldn't want to move to another one myself. I'm starting to wonder whether the world around me has gone completely barmy. How I miss Mario Campbell's sanity!

SUMMER TERM

With bankruptcy looming, I finally sell the house to Rupert in early May in view of the fact that it'll save me a considerable sum of money in estate agents' fees. I pay off my debts and move to a lodger-free, one-bedroom flat on the other side of town. With some of the leftover profit, I buy my dream car – a Lancia Delta integrale. Okay, I've gone downmarket in accommodation terms, but with my finances as they were, I had little choice.

When the final phone bill arrives for my old house, I discover to my horror that my last two lodgers, Gabrielle and Katherina, made eighty pounds' worth of calls to Brazil and Italy between the time I informed them of my imminent move and their departure.

One Friday evening, I head along to *Opportunity Knox*, where the two girls work, in search of reimbursement. On my arrival, I'm confronted by a furious Katherina at the entrance.

"There's no way you get the money," she seethes. "We 'ave to pay eighty pounds rent per week now. Thirty pounds more than with you. No way!"

"But I did give you well over a month's notice," I say calmly.

"You not listen to me. Eighty pounds we pay. Eighty pounds!"

"Okay, that's a lot, but …"

"No, you leave now!" she roars from her opera singer frame. "Or I tell the bouncer to throw you out. Go! Go!"

Before I have chance to contemplate my next move, Katherina shoves me out onto the street herself to the amusement of the two doormen who've just arrived on the scene. And to think both girls left my place with hugs and kisses all round, and a firm promise to pay their share of any outstanding bills when they arrived. Given that they always used international phone cards before, it didn't even occur to me to withhold their deposit.

I drift away from the club, wishing that I hadn't bothered to tell them about my move until the last minute. That way, I would've benefited from additional rental income.

"No wonder people become cynical as they get older," I reflect. "Then again, I did make a killing on the house."

Rupert partially redeems himself by giving Katherina a hard time when we next go clubbing.

Relieved to be solvent once again, I pay *James Dean's* a mid-week visit to celebrate in style and pull Carla, a twenty-three-year-old Law student from Guernsey. By all accounts, she's an intelligent, level-headed woman – dare I say it – so I'm delighted when she volunteers her phone number.

I ring Carla a few days later and she suggests meeting up after I've nervously beaten about the bush for a good twenty minutes or so. Stunned by my apparent change in fortune, I accept enthusiastically and we agree to go for dinner.

When I arrive home from work on the afternoon of my date, there's an unwanted but highly predictable message on the answer phone: *Hi Al, it's Carla. Hope this is the right number. Um ... just wanted to let you know that ... er ... I can't make it tonight. I ... I'd forgotten that I'd been invited to a dinner party. Um ...I guess I'll see you around, then. Byeee!*

At first, I consider returning the call in an attempt to persuade her to invite me along to the dinner party, but on listening to the message again, I deduce from her tone of voice that it was nothing more than a feeble excuse.

"How is it," I ask myself, "that a mature adult can be really up for something one minute, then cry off the next?"

An hour or two later, mum rings and provides me with the perfect answer. After uttering her condolences, she informs me that Carla probably just got a better offer. Thanks mum! I know she didn't mean it.

But all is not lost. The following week, *James Dean's* is packed out with paralytic university students, celebrating the completion of their Finals. Among them is Leila Batchelor who decides in her drunken stupor that I'm 'a bit of all right'. At the end of the evening, she wisely agrees that my bed would be the best place to nurse a hangover. After all, a taxi home at 2.00 am would cost an arm and a leg. As for her breasts, Anika has got a serious rival in town.

Determined to give Leila a first date to remember, I invite her to join me at one of my male French student's eighteenth birthday party two days later. The evening is a resounding success and she agrees to be my girlfriend, proving beyond doubt that there's always light at the end of even the darkest tunnel.

It's chucking it down on the way home from the party, so I decide to exploit the extra traction provided by the integrale's rally-derived four-wheel drive system. There's a series of short dual-carriageway stretches followed by roundabouts and, with no-one else on the road, I have the time of my life. That is until I see a blue flashing light in my rear-view mirror as we're heading along the M3.

"We haven't got a problem with your speed here on the motorway," one of the officers informs me, "but you were pushing it somewhat coming out of the town. In fact, we couldn't get anywhere near you until you slowed down."

Thanks to my profuse apologies and Leila cleverly wiggling her double Fs in front of both men in blue, I'm allowed to proceed with nothing more than a caution.

"I love the fact that you're a teacher," Leila discloses back at the flat. "The thought of you putting ticks in exercise books makes me go weak at the knees."

Guess I'll just have to set my classes more homework from now on.

Shortly after the speeding incident, I receive an anonymous typed letter in a small white envelope. The contents give rise to a considerable amount of head scratching on my behalf.

> *Alan,*
>
> *You are probably wondering who this is from and why you have got a letter!!! Well I'm just letting you know now that you will never know who has written this. It isn't a scary stalker or secret admirer. You really won't guess who it is has written this and who ever you suspect that it might be believe me it isn't them. It's not some ex girlfriend or anyone you might wish that it was (like Rachel out of S Club, even though she is perfect for you!). I'm nothing special as a woman and to be honest this type of letter is one that I have never written before.*
>
> *I don't really care if you never find out that it was me who wrote this but I just wanted to let you know how unappreciated you are by everyone. I'm just writing to tell you some things that you may not have been told before by anyone however close you were to them, but you may have been told this by many people. I just had to write and let you know.*
>
> *All of the people that I know realise that I feel this way but you will never know in a million years and they would never tell you, or anyone else. This*

is purely an innocent letter and I mean no harm by it so don't get worried about it.

I just feel that the luck that you have had with love at the moment hasn't really reflected how great you are to people and how you make people laugh. You are a great man and in many ways you have no flaws what so ever. Many people have total respect for you and the way you are in your job really is amazing.

I don't know anyone that has had such a great impact on my life from afar like you have Al and I can't believe that women can be so harsh and mean to you. I can't really say that I know you as a person just like I'm sure that you couldn't say that about me either but I'm not sure why I felt the urge to say all this to you.
There is never anyway that I could say this to you, face to face. May be in a couple of years I might admit to you that it was me, I would be totally embarrassed though mind you! Please don't think that this is me coming on to you not that it would matter as you have no clue who it could be that has written to you, I just felt that with the luck and all the pressure with moving and all you needed someone to tell you how great you are.

So I guess that I have let know now. You can take this in anyway that you want but it is purely meant innocently. If you want just forget about it and pretend it never happened.

Ciao
xxx

When I read it for a second time, it occurs to me that it might be a practical joke – from someone like Rupert, perhaps. Then again, it does seem to be written from the heart. *No flaws whatsoever*, eh? If it is genuine, then the author can't be anyone who knows me that well. I pass the letter over to Leila, on the grounds that a bit of healthy competition never goes amiss, but decide otherwise to keep it under wraps – at least for the time being.

A week later, another anonymous letter arrives in an identical envelope. This time, it's dated.

25th May 2000
Alan,
This is another letter but again its not one to freak you out or for you to think that I'm weird about. Even though it doesn't matter if you think that I am strange coz you have no idea who I am. You haven't said anything to me about the last letter. I thought that you might hint to me that you were

sent a letter from someone who admires you greatly, but then again I guess that you don't rate me highly enough or important enough to tell me that.

This is just another letter I guess to let you know that I still can't believe how much of a great person you are and about how people can like you so much and you can be so naïve to not even notice it. I can't explain how stupid I feel when I see you and my heart skips a beat but I have never really felt like that. It is a totally cliched saying but it is just so true Al.

You put yourself down too much and you just don't realise how good you are at so many things. Some people would give many things to be like you Al and you just don't know it. You are an amazing sports man and can probably do most things if you just set your mind to it but then I guess that you don't think that. You are a great teacher and so many people just love you.

Just a few more things. Please be careful in love. Don't jump in too deep to fast and whatever happens don't let whoever it maybe change you or try to rule what you do. You are a great person Al and you obviously don't realise how I feel though, if you did you would never talk to me again!!!

I feel as if I can talk to you about loads of things and be totally at ease with you but then you always tell me that I don't really know you and that there are many things about you that I don't and shouldn't know. Well this is one thing that you don't know about me which shows you that you can never know everything about a person whatever you may think. There is always something, at least one thing about everybody that no-one knows.

Please don't take all of this the wrong way Al as it is not a joke. I'm totally serious and as I said I may admit, one day that it was me who wrote these pathetic little letters. I'm sorry if you find this all a little weird but I have to let you know how I feel as it frustrates me to not be able to say anything about all of this in person.

Ciao xxx

Now convinced beyond any shadow of doubt that the two letters are authentic, I wrack my brain to figure out who could've composed them. My initial suspicions fall on Charlotte Rhys-Jones, yet it just doesn't add up in the light of her harassment claims. There are other female students at College who chat to me in between lessons, but none that I could imagine opening her heart on paper to such an extent. Surely it can't be one of my colleagues. This really is a mystery.

The exam season gets underway towards the end of May and the Board sends us a German oral examiner who suffered a stroke two years ago.

Anxious to explain why he has to walk with a stick, he tells everyone he meets of his misfortune.

On the second day of the orals, I arrive at 8.30 and unlock the German room for the examiner. Whilst we're sitting chatting, a whole army of ladies from the office suddenly descends upon us.

"Do we need to call an ambulance?" one of them asks with genuine concern.

"Erm, I know the oral exams can be stressful, but isn't having an ambulance on standby a bit excessive?" I reply, wondering if I'm at the centre of a practical joke.

"Well, a few minutes ago a student came to the office claiming the German oral examiner had had a stroke."

It transpires that the examiner had arrived early and, wanting immediate access to the classroom to sit down, had accosted a passing student.

"D'you think you could find Al, the German teacher, to open up the classroom for me?" he'd asked. "You see, I've had a stroke."

Alarmed, the student had rushed to the office to pass on the worrying news.

One Sunday in early June, Leila joins me for lunch at mum and dad's. My sister and her family are there, and I sense a great interest in my new romance. After all, it's not often that Al brings a woman home. My little niece, Chloë, takes an immediate shine to Leila and plies her with questions in the middle of roast chicken.

"Are you and Al going to get married?" she asks excitedly.

Leila chokes on a bone, so I intercept: "I think we'll have to wait just a little bit longer, Chloë, before we decide to get married."

"How long? Seven weeks?"

There's general laughter at the table and Chloë seems puzzled as if to say "what's so unreasonable about that?" It wasn't that long ago that she told Jayne she was going to marry me herself. When Jayne explained that nieces don't normally marry their uncles, she responded as good-naturedly as ever: "Well, in that case, I'm going to *help* him find a wife."

If I ever do get married – perhaps I'll manage it by the age of seventy – I'd love to have a child like Chloë. I know I'm biased as her proud uncle and godfather, but she really is a little angel.

Towards the end of June, the College Leavers' Ball takes place. Leila seizes the opportunity to wear her favourite evening dress, a low-cut one at that. She looks extremely sexy and I feel proud to be seen with her. Dr Faulkner appears with his camera, so I make a point of introducing him to my new woman in the belief that it might offer some reassurance. Judging from the downward focus of his eyes, I think he likes her.

Charlotte R-J fails to show, which I'm sure is for the best. Looking round, I notice that there are quite a few first-year students present and soon discover that this was an attempt by the organisers to boost ticket sales.

Half way through the evening, I nip off to the loo, only to be confronted by one of the Lower Sixth lads when I reappear.

"David Marsden's trying to pull your girlfriend," he says with apparent glee.

Intrigued, I return to the sight of a drunken Dave Marsden with his head practically buried in Leila's cleavage. He stands bolt upright as soon as he sees me, totters, then leans forward and whispers a slurred but perfectly intelligible sentence into my ear: "Your girlfriend. She's got an amazing pair of knockers!"

On Monday morning at College, a sheepish Dave Marsden apologises for his comment at the Ball.

The Exchange trip to Munich couldn't arrive at a more perfect moment for me. However, I suppose it was simply too much to ask to expect everything to run smoothly. At 9.00 on the evening before our departure, I receive a call from Germany, informing me that some of the German partners have been in recent contact with two classmates suspected of having contracted meningitis. I ring the Principal at once.

After liaising with a medical expert on the NHS helpline, Dr Faulkner decides that the trip should go ahead. All the families are given the option to withdraw, an offer that two of the ten-strong group decide to take.

Fortunately, there are no major problems out in Germany and I get the opportunity to unwind properly for what seems like the first time this year. I stay in a spacious two-bedroom flat with Reinhardt Schmutzer, an English teacher responsible for Exchanges.

During the daily excursions, Jo Black follows me round almost constantly. She's turned out to be one of the friendliest students I've ever taught, very much in the mould of Cara, Mandy, Rachel and Amanda at *Mardall's* and, dare I say it, Charlotte Rhys-Jones. As a result of my unpleasant experiences with the latter, I'm careful not to put myself in any potentially compromising situations with Jo. It occurs to me that she might in fact be the author of my mysterious letters.

By the end of the week, the suspense is too much to bear and, perhaps unwisely, I decide to tackle Jo over the letters. However, she just stares back at me as if I'm from outer space. Somewhat embarrassed, I rapidly change the subject. Who the hell could've written them, then? She could be my dream woman, for all I know.

Just as I'm looking forward to a peaceful conclusion to the academic year, I return from Munich to discover that in my absence, Kevin, the Vice-Principal, authorised the search of one of my College bags, which I'd left in the cupboard in the German room. All courtesy of a tip-off from my dear colleague Margaret. As a result, the Principal would like to see me urgently to discuss the contents of their find. Guessing at once what this is likely to be about, I approach his office with trepidation.

Dr Faulkner explains that he'd received a letter from the mother of one of my French students, complaining about the College's choice of syllabus and the fact that she was informed too late in the day that her daughter was struggling. Anxious to disprove the latter, a copy of the girl's statement of progress (report) from the first year was requested from her tutor, but she couldn't locate it in the file. Illustrating once again the importance of allegiance to colleagues in her department, Margaret stepped in at this point and told the management about the existence of my bag. Unable to wait a couple of days for my return from Munich, the search was carried out. Among the various bank statements and other items of a personal nature, the management found what the Principal describes as "a large quantity of unmarked work" – in files I paid for myself.

"This is an insult to your students," he says, "and unacceptable professional conduct."

I challenge his definition of 'large', on the grounds that the bulk of what he found was a couple of past papers, of which the students had done many. I plead mitigating circumstances, but my words fall on deaf ears.

"I shall be writing to warn you formally that if you fail to mark work in future in line with College policy, your contract here will be terminated," Faulkner continues ruthlessly. "It may well be that your excellent results from last year were achieved with a similar lacklustre approach to marking, but that's beside the point."

I feel certain that a teacher with poor results but an immaculately-kept, up-to-date mark book would be unlikely to find themselves the unfortunate recipient of a formal warning. Surely this is bureaucracy gone mad. He goes on to promise that he'll be monitoring my marking during the course of the following year. Then, suddenly and rather unexpectedly, he softens his tone: "I'd like to add that, should you decide to apply for a post at another College, no mention of your two formal warnings will be made in a reference."

My immediate interpretation is that my boss is indirectly urging me to seek alternative employment. It's only later when I've calmed down a bit that I realise that this is just the generous, Christian side of his nature coming out. There is, therefore, no need for me to appeal against his sanctions. In any case, this academic year has sapped every last ounce of strength from my body and I'm desperate to put all the misery behind me. And what better place to do this than a Greek island with the lovely Leila, my page three pin-up.

Girl

Was she told when she was young that pain would lead to pleasure?
Did she understand it when they said
That a man must break his back to earn his day of leisure?
Will she still believe it when he's dead?

AUTUMN TERM

As the world's leading exponent of the consequences of delayed puberty, I have to confess that my two-week holiday in Crete in the summer was my first spent in the company of a proper girlfriend. Following the ordeals of last term, I was more than happy to pass the daylight hours crashed out on the beach soaking up the sun and the evenings savouring the local delicacies over a beer or three. Leila, however, is a woman of action and insisted that we squeezed in our daily dose of exercise. You know, strolls along the coastline, that sort of thing. With her double Fs and sexy persona, she attracted many admiring glances, both from the locals and our fellow tourists, whilst her enormous Karaoke repertoire never failed to impress. As well as belting out popular 'rockers', she touched the romantic in me with her emotive renditions of *How Do I Live?* and *I Will Always Love You.*

Ever since our first date at my student's eighteenth, she's been a model partner and, despite my previous experiences, I've begun to wonder whether our relationship might in fact have a future. Although anxious not to tempt fate, we've been together for almost four months now and there's been no indication whatsoever that she finds me 'too nice' or that I've become the 'big brother' she always dreamt of.

Incidentally, on our return from abroad, we attended the wedding reception of Ali Carlisle, one of my gymnasts and trampolinists from *Mardall's*, who kept the promise she'd made a while back at *James Dean's* to include me in her marriage celebrations. It was a highly entertaining evening, with Leila attempting to teach me the dance moves to some of the Steps' and S-Club 7 hits. Not a pretty sight!

It's now the first day back at College and the Principal is bending over backwards to impress the staff with a Power Point presentation of our students' record-breaking performances in last summer's exams. That is, how the first 87.32 candidates outperformed those of any of the famous public schools blah, blah, blah. Whilst Dr Faulkner's handling of the events of last term may not exactly have accelerated him to the top of my Christmas card list, you have to give credit where it's due. When it comes to manipulating statistics in order to portray the College as the best educational establishment in the entire country, our leader is an unrivalled master. Harrow and St Paul's eat your heart out!

"Maybe he should try his hand at politics," I chuckle to myself cynically.

And there I was naively believing education to be about individual learners across the *whole* ability range developing their skills and preparing for life, not schools and colleges all trying to outdo each other in the league tables by boasting the achievements of their most able students. Hm.

I mustn't, however, be too cynical since my one hundred per cent pass rate has guaranteed German a prime position among the group of best performing curriculum areas that Faulkner has displayed on screen for all the staff to see. In addition, my retention rate for the last two years was significantly high enough to lift the subject into the leading band. It appears that this latest set of results has not only saved my reputation but also my self-esteem, so perhaps I should keep my criticisms under wraps on this particular occasion.

Charlotte Rhys-Jones scraped a C for French, but to Margaret and Begonia's horror could only muster a D for Spanish. According to the former, she managed to convince her parents that it'd be wise to take a gap year before going to university and is working for a local car dealership. Trust Charlotte to get her own way!

This is the first term of Curriculum 2000, which has been introduced by the Government to broaden post-sixteen education. It means effectively that the average A level student will now be selecting up to five one-year AS subjects in the first year as opposed to making a two-year commitment to three or four A levels under the old system. The changes have had a positive effect on the uptake of German, which has increased by a hundred and fifty per cent in comparison to last September. In practical terms, I'll be responsible for three groups of about eighteen students in the Lower Sixth alone – a personal record.

To my irritation, I discover that my two excellent groups from last year have been collapsed into one of twenty-three for the Upper Sixth. Since there are now too many bums to pack into the tiny German room, we've been timetabled to use a rather bland Maths room upstairs, which lacks the necessary resources such as dictionaries. I head off to see Kevin

Gough, the Vice-Principal, to protest that it's educationally unsound and detrimental to the students' best interests to allow such a large, mixed ability A level language group. But in an age where financial considerations take priority, Kevin declares that his hands are firmly tied and that the decision must stand.

Now that I finally have a girlfriend, I've been inundated recently with other women buzzing around me like flies over a corpse. How come they never noticed me when I was single? It's almost as if my unavailable status is stamped across my forehead, offering a challenge to any local woman I meet. One of life's mysteries, I guess. Despite this sudden abundance of interested female 'talent', I think I'll count my blessings and stick with my Karaoke star. After all, the grass is rarely greener on the other side.

My decision continues to appear sound until one morning in early September when Leila and I have a conversation that sets the alarm bells ringing, prompting me to wonder whether she's too good to be true, after all.

"Where's he going to sleep, then?" I ask routinely after she's informed me that her best friend and former lover, Grant, will be staying over in her flat after a night out.

"In my bed, like he always does," she replies as if it's the most natural thing in the world. "You know you can trust me."

I'm aware of Leila's reluctance to wear clothes at the best of times. "Please don't tell me you've been sharing your bed with him naked whilst you've been going out with me." She bows her head. I'm annoyed, but determined not to be the jealous boyfriend, seeing as it's never worked for me in the past. I take a deep breath and endeavour to keep my voice down. "Why can't he sleep on the settee?"

"He's got a bad back and it's not really big enough for a six-footer."

As is often the case when a crack of doubt appears in a relationship, other apparently minor details immediately leap to the fore and take on much greater significance. I suddenly remember Leila's confession that she'd woken up one morning months after splitting up with Grant to discover that they'd made love again, but had no recollection of it happening. It seemed odd at the time, but not worth pursuing. Not any more, though.

"In that case, I guess it's okay if I invite Sam Woodfield over and sleep naked alongside her?"

The look of horror on Leila's face tells me exactly what she thinks of my proposal. Then she says: "Okay, I'll make sure I'm wearing PJ's from now on."

I pause in anticipation of the second half of this sentence: "… and he can lump it and curl up on the sofa", but my wait is in vain.

My reference to Sam stems from the fact that I've bumped into her in town quite a lot recently. On one occasion, I actually introduced her to Leila. The latter took an instant dislike due to the fact that Sam was skinnier. What is it with modern-day women and their obsession with looking like giant stick insects? Some of the blame has to be levelled at the media, I suppose. Considering that Leila has suffered from bulimia for a number of years, my comment about Sam was, on reflection, perhaps rather insensitive. Realising that I've overstepped the mark, I decide to leave the Grant issue.

A few days later, when I'm out at *Bar Med* with Rupert, we stumble across Sam again.

"Al, I need to talk to you about something," she says, biting on her bottom lip. "It's really important."

We move to one side. There's a long silence before Sam opens her mouth again to speak: "Um … you know when we split up, I … I promised that one day I'd explain why?"

"Er … yes, vaguely," I reply.

I'm bluffing, of course. In truth, I've relived this moment a thousand times.

"Well, I … I want to tell you now."

Intrigued, I turn to make sure Rupert isn't eavesdropping, but he's 'miles away' eyeing up another leggy brunette. Anyway, the music is probably too loud. Sam looks visibly uncomfortable and sways nervously. Then she says rather awkwardly: "Oh God, this is difficult. I really don't know how to put it."

"Go on, just spit it out. I'm not going to think badly of you."

My impatience is blatant. Well, let's face it, I have been kept in limbo for some two and a half years.

"Okay. Well … the reason. Um … the reason I couldn't carry on going out with you is … is that …"

"That *what*?" The suspense is almost unbearable. I extend my neck forwards towards her in ostrich fashion, my eyes full moon-like in anticipation.

"That I … I'd started seeing a teacher from my school. A … a female one."

My pint glass oscillates frenetically in my right hand, forcing me to tighten my grip to prevent it dropping over the upstairs banister that I'm leaning on.

"Not Miss Ford?"

Sam screws up her forehead. "How on earth d'you remember that?"

"There's very little about our relationship, Sam, that I don't remember."

Blimey! So I was right, after all. Sam wasn't just fobbing me off when we split up. More than two years down the line, I finally discover that there's a genuine explanation for her disquiet – she was uncertain about her sexuality.

"I'm not a lesbian, though!" she protests as if reading my thoughts. "It was just this one person that I really admired and I'm completely over her now."

"So did it start whilst you were still at school?" I ask, hungry for more detail.

"Yes. Apparently, she's been involved with other girls too."

"Really?" This just gets better. "So … er … who broke it off, then?"

"Well, she did. After about a year. I was really upset at the time, but I'm completely over her now. Honest."

Right. So maybe it was just a phase, a bit like it was for my friend Nicky in her late teens. However, this is not something I find particularly easy to relate to. I just can't imagine a bloke going through a gay period and coming out at the other end – if you can excuse the pun – reassured that it's a vagina and not an anus he prefers, after all. Then again, I suppose she could be bisexual. Somewhat baffled and still reeling from the shock, I get in another pint.

"I bet Miss Ford doesn't have a warning on file for harassment of a student," I tell myself.

Later in bed, I can't help feeling angry and hurt by Sam's revelations. Whether my fury is fuelled by the fact that Miss Ford came between me and the woman I loved or by the simple acknowledgement that she unforgivably abused her position as a teacher and got away with it is hard to say. If it is due to the latter, it just goes to show how easy it is as an outsider to condemn the actions of others without full possession of the facts. Mind you, I'm sure that a homosexual scandal involving a female teacher at a selective girls' private school would cause more of a stir amongst the tabloids than the rather fumbling heterosexual antics of a male teacher at a Sixth Form College. That I can in some way be connected to both scenarios doesn't even bear reflection. With my imagination still working overtime, I envisage the exclusive centre-page feature in *The News of the World*: *Why I ditched schoolmaster lover for games mistress. 18-year-old schoolgirl reveals all.*

Over the next few days, I can't stop thinking about Leila and Sam, wondering whether their confessions actually alter the way I feel. It's certainly true that I've never really stopped caring about Sam and maybe I don't know Leila as well as I'd like to think I do.

Prompted by a firm conviction that it'd be in my best interest to win back the Principal's trust, I decide to come clean about my anonymous letters from last summer. After all, he did make me promise following the Charlotte incident that I wouldn't hesitate to inform him of any other potential difficulties with students. Anyway, it won't do any harm for him to read the paragraph praising my teaching abilities. However, rather than showing appreciation for my willingness to cooperate, Dr Faulkner appears more concerned than ever. As a result, I leave his office about ten minutes later, fearing that my good intentions may've backfired.

Shortly afterwards, my cousin organises a hen night and invites Leila. I head out into town on my own and, perhaps inevitably, end up at *James Dean's*. As if by magic, Sam appears with her younger sister, Claire. For some reason, they're really happy to see me.

We spend about an hour together drinking and generally having a laugh, then Sam suddenly comes out with a question that throws me off-balance: "Al, d'you think you're going to marry Leila?"

Whether she has an ulterior motive in asking or it's just one of those random questions that often accompany a heavy drinking session is unclear. Whatever's the case, I resist the temptation to wind her up.

"Er, well, we haven't exactly known each other for that long," I reply. "So I … I can't possibly say. You know, it's just too soon."

At this point, we take a seat in the quiet corner of the club and Claire does a miraculous disappearing act. I look into Sam's eyes and begin to realise that she's genuinely jealous of my relationship with Leila. Okay, I know I'm a bit slow on the uptake, but with Sam Woodfield, nothing is ever crystal clear. What does become clear, though, in the hazy, drunken moments that follow is that I'm slowly falling under her spell once again.

When our lips are finally reunited, I'm completely overcome by one of the top compliments a man can get – confirmation that the woman who broke his heart has matured and come to realise her mistake. But my paralysis – or do I mean paralyticness? – is short-lived as it suddenly dawns on me that I've got a girlfriend who, apart from a bizarre penchant for sleeping naked alongside her ex, claims that she really loves me. I withdraw in protest: "Sam, what're we doing? I'm sorry, I can't do this to Leila – it … it's just not right."

"But if we both feel the same way?" she says.

"It's not as simple as that. I was crazy about you before and you finished with me three times without even bothering to offer a proper explanation, remember?"

"I know, but I have explained everything now, though."

"You have and I'm pleased you told me, but you can't just waltz back into my life years later because it's now convenient for you and expect me to dump my girlfriend of four months."

And that's how we leave it, with Sam looking miffed and yours truly suffering from a severe attack of remorse. As far as I know, there are two main schools of thought when it comes to honesty in a relationship. Either you hold the view that, if you love someone, secrets and lies should never enter your head or you believe that anything likely to cause a partner pain and destroy trust should be avoided at all costs. It'll come as no great surprise that I've always subscribed to the first theory, yet I'm terrified of Leila's reaction, given her dislike for Sam. But then what if they were to meet by chance and the truth came out? Or what about Claire who must surely have witnessed my act of deceit and her sister's compliance? Hearing it from them would be even worse, wouldn't it?

Unable to decide on the best course of action, I end up sleeping on my guilt with one question in my head: "Why couldn't Sam have sorted out her sexuality issues whilst I was still single?"

At the end of September, my cousin – another Samantha – marries Gordon Chambers. The reception is held at a nearby hotel overlooking a marina and provides a perfect opportunity to catch up with more distant members of the family who I haven't seen for years. Although only one person actually verbalises it, I sense a feeling going round that that 'professional bachelor', Al, might well be the next to get hitched. Whilst this is, of course, the last thing on my mind at the moment, the beauty and romance of the occasion bring Leila and me close together.

At dusk, the celebrations are almost brought to a catastrophic premature conclusion when my sister discovers that her three-year-old autistic son, James, has gone missing. A panic search is carried out and he's spotted almost immediately stranded on a boat moored in the marina. How he managed to step across onto the bows without falling in and drowning convinces me beyond doubt that there are such things as miracles. All we need now is one more to cure dad's returning cancer.

When the two of us attend the Goodwood Revival Meeting the following day, I promise myself that it won't be long now before I make my racing debut. Dad's only serious regret is that he allowed mum to talk him out of accepting a friend's offer to race his car back in the fifties and I'm determined he'll get to share the experience with me whilst still in reasonable health. In spite of my move last spring, I don't really have the finance. But hey, since when has life been a dress rehearsal? And I do have three credit cards.

Still wracked by guilt, I've made up my mind to come clean with Leila about Sam W. Unfortunately, the right moment never seems to present itself.

Then one evening after yet another drinking session together in town – we've become rather too proficient at this lately – Leila says out of the blue: "There's definitely nothing going on between you and Sam, is there?"

The opportunity is too good to miss.

"Er, no," I mumble, nervously concealing my lower lip with the fingertips of my left hand. "There's nothing going on … now."

Leila jumps down my throat. "What d'you mean 'now'? Something's happened between you two, hasn't it?" She looks deeply into my eyes, searching for the truth.

Even though part of me wants to back out cowardly, I grit my teeth and force myself to confront her penetrating glare. "Well, yes, we did have a bit of a drunken kiss a while back, but I realised …"

"No, no, no!" she wails. "Not again! I knew it, I knew it. My problem's ruined everything again. No, no, no!"

At this juncture, she launches herself onto the settee and boxes the back of it with all her might, sobbing pitifully in the process. I try to restrain her, offering words of comfort, but she refuses to stop her relentless demolition attempt on my sofa, let alone take note of my reassurances. And for me, the helpless onlooker, her hysteria is so painful to witness. I knew that she wouldn't take it well, but never in my wildest dreams could I have foreseen the extent of her anguish. All too late, I realise that on this particular occasion my honesty is a crime even greater than my original act of deceit. But the damage is done and, somehow, I'll have to find a rapid way of healing her ravaged heart.

I try to explain: "Leila, please listen to me. It's you I want to be with, not Sam. It was a mistake. Just a drunken, sentimental kiss."

"Just a kiss, just a kiss!" she screams. "That's more intimate than shagging her, you bastard. And no, I'm not going to discuss it with you. There's only one person I want to speak to now – someone who really cares about me."

She grabs her mobile and scampers off into the kitchen to phone – yes, you've guessed it – Grant.

"You can't ring him now, it's 2.30 in the morning," I yell after her, but she ignores me.

Whether her actions are a deliberate attempt to get back at me or confirmation that she's closer to Grant than she's prepared to let on, I've no idea. All I know is that the guilt and pain from watching her 'breakdown' are tempered by a feeling of considerable irritation. Surely she should be having it out with me not sobbing her heart out to her ex.

After talking to Grant for over an hour, Leila returns to the bedroom in a considerably calmer state.

"I'm sorry, Al, it's over," she announces as she slips under the duvet beside me. "It has to be."

"I presume that's the advice of your former lover who wants you back?"

"He's just got my best interests at heart, that's all."

That she can be so naive winds me up further and I can't help trying to explain how I came to make such a blunder in the first place. I suppose I just want her to understand me and appreciate that I'm not a complete arsehole, but really this is the last thing she wants to hear from me right now. Why is it we often feel compelled to explain and justify our inappropriate actions when a simple apology would be so much more effective?

"Sex a more minor offence than kissing, eh?" I reflect impishly as my head finally hits the pillow. "Bugger, if only I'd known this at the time!"

It's official. Leila and I are no longer girlfriend and boyfriend. We're now 'just good friends' who see each other most days and who under no circumstances whatsoever are allowed to have sex. Leila has decided this. I'm hardly in a position to complain, so I'm just going along with it in the hope that I'll be forgiven before I start drawing my pension.

At the end of October, I appear in the Players' autumn production. Leila comes to support me for two of the three performances. On the last night, I encounter her wrath once more when I mistakenly introduce her to Marjory Smith – a long-serving fellow player – as my girlfriend. For years, Marjory has been desperate to see me with 'a nice young lady' – her youngest daughter included – and I was anxious not to disappoint her once again.

Then at the cast party, my careless tongue gets me into trouble a second time. Only, on this occasion, it prompts Leila's disappearance. Gordon, my cousin's new husband who was helping out backstage, joins me in a search of the house and gardens. There's no sign, so we jump into my car and scour the local area. No joy.

Back at the house, I circle the building once more in the rain and there she is, huddled in a tiny ball in a recess, whimpering pitifully. I give her a big hug and tell her what a silly thing she is. Eventually, with gentle persuasion, she agrees to join the rest of us inside. Within twenty minutes, she's back to her old self and nobody would know anything had ever been amiss.

A few days later, I discover rather worryingly that my act of disloyalty has thrown up an additional problem. Prior to the 'Sam' incident, Leila managed to limit her self-induced vomiting to about two or three times a fortnight. Post-Sam, this figure has increased alarmingly to up to four times a day. It seems that my words and actions have a direct hold on the extent of her bulimia. Oh my God, what have I done?

At College, Jo Black asks me in passing how I'm getting on with Leila. Since I introduced the two on our return from Munich in July, Jo has kept her distance outside lesson time.

"Well, okay, I spose," I reply.

But this isn't going to fool a bright spark like Jo.

"Oh no, what've you done?" she asks, forming her shoulder-length blonde hair into a ponytail.

"Why *me*?"

"Cos you're a man. It's bound to be your fault."

"What happened to equal opp...? Yes, you're spot on. It was *my* fault."

"Don't tell me you slept with someone else."

"Joanna, who d'you take me for? Well, no, not exactly."

At this point in the conversation, I accept that I'm not going to be left in peace until she's squeezed the truth out of me, so I tell her briefly about my encounter with Sam.

"Oh, Al, you're so stupid!" she says. "Leila's lovely."

Suddenly recalling her previous confession of infidelity to her boyfriend, I'm tempted to prolong our amusing interchange, but then I remember that it's the year 2000 and that young women are now probably allowed to do that sort of thing. So I change the subject. Apart from being able to outdo even me in the 'how to talk the hind legs off a donkey' stakes, Jo is also remarkably candid and down-to-earth. If it wasn't her that sent me those letters, I wonder who it could've been.

Good news at long last. It looks like I may make my fortune as a classroom teacher, after all. According to the Principal at this morning's weekly staff briefing, the Government has agreed plans to introduce a two-thousand-pound-a-year bonus for teachers at the top of the basic pay scale. It's to be called the Professional Standards Payment or PSP for short. Apparently, its prime objective is to reward quality teaching. Application forms should be available in the spring or summer term of next year. Maybe this is just what I need to get my racing plans afoot. Who said God had been pensioned off?

Seriously, though, let's get one thing straight. Nobody enters the teaching profession for its financial rewards. It is purely and simply a vocation. After five years' post-A level studying and training, and eleven years in the job, I only earn annually two thousand pounds more than the average salary in the entire country. But with the dramatic upsurge in property prices over the last few years – not to mention the high cost of beer – any additional income would be received like a gift from heaven, particularly if it's to reward teaching rather than administrative skills. I've always struggled to grasp why the most able teachers are forced to renounce most of their teaching duties and take up a desk job that any Tom, Dick or Harry could do – well, almost – in order to progress significantly up the pay scale. With the staff shortages that have hit the profession so hard in recent times, it always seems such a criminal waste of talent. I like the sound of the PSP.

In early November, Leila joins me at the auditions for the Players' Christmas panto. With her flair for singing, good looks and … well, you know, she lands the part of the princess. Soon afterwards, she takes me out to dinner to celebrate my thirty-fifth birthday, but reiterates the fact that she's doing so purely on a 'best mates' basis. Still no sex, then. Bugger!

Her present is a CD of her singing one of her most emotive karaoke ballads, *Show me heaven*, which she produced in conjunction with my sound engineer friend, Ben Connery. To do this, she had to make clandestine excursions to his house late at night. Given that Leila claims he tried to pull her in the summer behind my back – Ben denies this – I can only assume that their secret rendezvous were of a strictly business nature.

I'm having a bit of a crisis. Although Leila's present was really touching and I can live without sex for a while – twenty-six years, in fact – I'm not sure now whether it'd be a sensible idea for the two of us to get back together. Being totally honest, I just don't know if I can cope with the consequences of her eating disorder. Okay, everyone's got their faults – just look at me, for example – but this is a heavy load to take on board, no pun intended. It's hardly fair on Leila either. I can't help feeling that what she needs is a man who, in the words of Dylan, will *die for her and more*, and maybe, with my deep-rooted distrust of women, *it ain't me babe*. This is my head talking, of course. As for my heart, well that's a different story altogether.

In theory, I'd probably be of more use to her right now continuing in the role of friend, but I reckon we've been far too close physically over the last six months for this to be a realistic proposition. A lengthy chat on the phone with my sister, whose marriage has lasted almost a decade, convinces me that I really ought to put my concerns to one side and give my romance with Leila another go. Otherwise, I may live to regret it. I decide to give her an ultimatum – either we try again properly or knock it on the head completely. None of this namby-pamby, in-between stuff.

A couple of days later, Leila is up in town visiting a friend and due to meet me at *Bar Med* at 10.00 on her return. With my speech carefully mapped out in my head, I go there at 9.00 to try to muster up some Dutch courage. I hope I'm not developing an addiction to alcohol. I seem to be relying on it quite heavily at the moment.

On the stroke of 10.00, she arrives – rather the worse for wear, but oozing sex appeal as usual. Before I have chance to act out my well-rehearsed part, Leila makes a major announcement.

"Al, I miss you so much," she says emphatically. "I'd like us to try again. If you'll have me, that is."

And so it happens. Leila and I are reconciled. And with my reservations shelved for the time being, I'm happy enough.

Back at work, Jennifer Warwick, Yvonne Lambert's permanent replacement as Senior Curriculum Manager for Modern Languages – Head of Department to you and me – informs us that she's had orders from above to supervise the implementation of course forums with all the language classes. Godfrey has shown her how this trendy test of student satisfaction should be conducted. She volunteers to show me the ropes with the Upper Sixth German group.

The students are asked as a class to draw up positive statements relating to various aspects of the course, and then each one is required to express the extent of his/her agreement. Comments are not supposed to be personal, but in her inexperience Jennifer allows the statement *The authority of the teacher is respected* to stand. Even though it has, as I'd feared, proved rather tricky teaching such a large mixed ability group, I feel confident enough of the outcome not to intervene. But I couldn't be more wrong. To my dismay, all but one student 'disagrees' or 'strongly disagrees' with this statement. Jennifer suggests meeting all the students alone in small groups to find out exactly what's wrong, but I react furiously.

"My results last year were excellent," I rage, "and I'll resign on the spot if you try to interview my students behind my back."

But it's not just her proposal that's at the heart of my wrath. I had a first-class relationship with the two groups last year, and I'm livid with the management for interfering with that arrangement and with the students for having such a short-term memory. After my redundancy and the two formal warnings, I find it the most upsetting experience of my teaching career.

Incidentally, it's funny how there appears to be sufficient money in the College kitty to finance the extensive building work that's been authorised for the relocation of the Staff Room and Staff Canteen – for the second time since my arrival here – yet not enough to assure reasonable class sizes. Priorities, eh!

Jennifer and I eventually agree to question the students together. It transpires that what they were intimating in the forum was that *they* were responsible for not respecting the difficult *teaching situation* that's arisen following the amalgamation of last year's two classes. In other words, they level blame at themselves, not at me. Everyone expresses major disapproval of the large group, so it's decided that after Christmas we'll split the class in two and that I'll teach both halves in different classrooms at the same time. Work that one out!

I don't like course forums. To my mind, they're just another modern gimmick, designed in a vague attempt to establish quality assurance. In reality, however, I feel they're a perfect way of undermining a teacher's authority. After all, aren't we supposed to be specialists in our field and, therefore, know what we're doing? Are students really in a position to tell us where we're going wrong?

Despite my apparent reprieve, I drive home at 5.00, wondering whether the events of last year and the uncertainty with Leila have hit my overall level of self-confidence more than I've realised. I must admit, I do feel rather sensitive and on edge at the moment.

Why is it that reconciliations are so overrated? Leila and I have been back together for several weeks now and it just ain't what it was. After one reluctant attempt at intimacy – reluctant on Leila's part, that is – she's now declared officially that she's "gone off sex". If you knew Leila, this is tantamount to the Pope expressing a lack of interest in saying his prayers. Although she assures me that it's a transitory phase and has nothing whatsoever to do with my act of infidelity, I can't help wondering whether she just doesn't fancy me any more.

My suspicions are reinforced by the increased interest she appears to be taking in Robin Goodfellow, the one current member of the Players with professional acting experience. The only thing is, Robin is married to another Player. He also happens to be the uncle of one of my former secondary school pupils. I just can't understand what Leila is playing at. It was only a couple of weeks ago that she was highly critical of Robin for flirting with one of the other female members of the cast. I don't know, she can be a touch hypocritical at times.

In view of my reservations about the sense of getting back together in the first place and the fact that I'm beginning to feel completely unloved, recriminations start to flow.

"Well, if you hadn't screwed things up by snogging your ex," Leila says one evening after I've complained about her constant criticism of my behaviour. Funny how the phrase "I adore you" seems to have been dropped from her vocabulary just lately.

"What did you expect when you were sleeping naked with *your* ex?"

I retort rather childishly. Then again, is there such a thing as an adult argument?

Shortly afterwards, on a Saturday evening, Leila goes AWOL, only to reappear the following morning, claiming to have spent the night crashed out on the sofa of her former boyfriend from university. In contrast to the situation with Grant, he dumped her. My mind is in turmoil.

Things go from bad to worse over the next couple of weeks. Almost inevitably, I suppose, Leila initiates a split soon after the Players' Christmas dinner. When she arrives at the final panto rehearsal of the year, laden with immaculately wrapped presents for each member of my family, my heart, more fragile than it's been for a long while, all but explodes. This has, after all, been the longest relationship of my life, and probably the only one that's been conducted on vaguely adult terms and, therefore, resembled the 'real thing' – whatever this may be. Somehow, contemplating a split is always so much easier than dealing with it when it actually happens. Break-ups have never been my specialty.

The only consolation for me is that we'll be seeing each other again after Christmas for the duration of the pantomime. Who knows, with tempers less frayed, we may well be able to talk more rationally.

All in all, the events of the last few weeks have taken their toll and left me feeling rather downcast. Therefore, when Sam rings and invites me to join her, Claire and a friend for a Christmas party at the sports club where she temps during the holidays, I jump at the opportunity. Just before hanging up, she tells me to bring my overnight gear so I can have a drink.

The party itself is good fun, although Sam seems to prefer the company of a male work colleague to mine. Whether she's attempting to make me jealous or just confirm beyond any shadow of doubt that her lesbian days are a thing of the past isn't easy to fathom. In order not to feel totally abandoned, I decide to hang out with Claire and her attractive friend, Rosanna. Full of Christmas spirit, poor Claire overindulges slightly and deposits a colourful cocktail of Bicardi Breezer, Smirnoff Ice and Reef all over the carpet, narrowly missing my shoes. Strangely enough, this is not the first time that my presence has prompted such a dramatic reaction from a woman.

During my first year as a Sixth Form College student, a friend, Owen, invited a large crowd of us to a house-warming party at his parents' as yet unfurnished four-storey house in Wimbledon. Two other single lads and I all tried at the same time to chat up a blatantly tipsy Miranda Williams, my first love from secondary school – first love in my head, that is. Within minutes, she managed to cover us with the entire contents of her tea, thrilled as she was by the exciting nature of our conversation. A fourth friend, Henry, a master at comforting women in distress, devoted the rest of the evening to nursing Miranda over the upstairs loo, finally giving her a fireman carry back downstairs when her lift home arrived.

"What a star!" I remember thinking at the time. "Why couldn't I have thought of that myself?"

A couple of days later, I returned from shopping in town to discover that Miranda had dropped by and insisted on singing *my* praises to mum for looking after her at the party. Since Henry and I could hardly be mistaken for twins, I wasn't sure at first what to make of this. Miranda, however, revisited about ten minutes later, apparently unconcerned that she'd got the wrong man. With my sister and dad's business partner, Marcel, visibly taking the mickey inside the house, I was far too embarrassed to invite the poor girl in. It seems that I was destined to be hesitant with the opposite sex and it wasn't until the following year, just a few weeks before setting off for university, that I started dating my first girlfriend. Sadly, I let Miranda slip through the net.

Anyway, Sam shares a flat with her brother in the grounds of their parents' house – not a dissimilar arrangement to the one I had between '91 and '94. Back from the party, she makes up a bed for me on her bedroom floor. However, after a trip to the loo, I lose my bearings in the dark and mistakenly end up in the wrong bed – one that just happens to have Sam in it. Before long, we're both naked and kissing intimately – just like old times. At this stage, it seems a foregone conclusion that we'll go a step further and rekindle our long-lost romance. But, of course, Sam has other ideas. Just as I'm starting to feel incredibly turned on, she drops another bombshell.

"Al, I don't really want to do this," she says.

"Why not?" I ask. "I thought you … Is it the bloke you were with earlier?"

"No, it's not *him*."

"Well, what *is* the problem, then?"

"It's … it's Miss Ford – Olivia. I've been thinking about her again," she replies, this time without the slightest compunction. "In fact, I rang her the other day."

I spend Christmas with mum, dad, Jayne and her family, relieved to be free from any reminder of my disastrous love life. We have a cracking time, although trying to explain to Chloë, now six, why her new-found friend, Leila, won't be making an appearance isn't easy. After all, if she'd had her way, we'd have been married weeks ago.

On New Year's Eve, I make a now customary visit to *Bar Med* with Rupert and a few other friends. We have such a good time that I temporarily forget that I'm supposed to be down in the dumps. My flagging ego and expanding waistline – too much booze lately – are soon forgotten as I pull three times after midnight. Oh well, I'll be an old geezer soon – sooner than most if I have anything more to do with the likes of Sam and Leila – so I might as well jump at the opportunities while they're still there.

The excitement continues with a trip to Oxford a few days later to buy a twenty-five-year-old classic Fiat that's to be converted into my first racing car by Pat Baines, a Design Technology teacher from one of the College's feeder schools. Cost: three hundred and fifty quid. Bargain!

SPRING TERM

Following the pre-Christmas debacle with the wretched course forum, the new term at College begins slightly more nervously for me than usual. Will I really be able to teach the Upper Sixth in two classrooms at the same time?

The mid-January panto turns out to be the worst production I've ever been involved with. This has nothing whatsoever to do with the quality of the show, but with the fact that Leila has returned from spending Christmas with her parents – including a visit from Grant – adamant that she's completely over me. And I think she means it.

Okay, we're not right for each other. That's become clear. However, just because I'm not going to spend the rest of my life with her doesn't automatically mean that I can switch off my emotions overnight. In my stupid, dumb male mind, it feels like her love for me couldn't have been genuine in the first place if it can die so rapidly. I wonder if I'd be feeling this way if things had turned out differently with Sam. Perhaps rather selfishly, I tell Leila that I'm disappointed she's not suffering a bit more like I am.

"Yeah, well people fall out of love with each other all the time," she says, without appearing to give a monkey's. "Just look at the divorce rate."

I hold quite firm views on the subject of divorce, but sense that this is neither the appropriate time nor place to air them. Instead, I think of all the stories of blokes who cheat on their wives and girlfriends frequently, and are forgiven every time. Rupert is a prime example. Despite his acts of infidelity, his Austrian ex still sends him birthday cards and postcards, and looks him up whenever she's in England.

"C'mon, Al, pull yourself together! You can't compare the behaviour of two different people," I hear Jayne berate me and she'd be right, of course.

It's just that it's hard, really hard being constantly in the presence of somebody I still care about who obviously has the ability to move on without grieving for very long. What an enviable quality!

Just to rub salt into the wounds, Grant is in the audience on the last night of the panto and presents Leila with the largest bunch of flowers I've ever seen as she steps off stage. To my great relief, he doesn't show at the cast party, but then who needs Grant when Robin is around?

I decide not to drink, which is no mean feat for me at the moment. Elisabeth, the host, offers Leila a bed for the night, which prompts her to knock back the booze like there's no tomorrow. Unwisely, I try to have a serious chat with her, on the grounds that we might not meet again, but this only results in more recriminations and tears. Leila then runs off into Robin's arms to be comforted. Determined not to spoil the party, I make a hasty exit.

Back home, I can't sleep. I decide to write a letter – like you do when you're high on emotion.

Overtired and still feeling rather deflated, I drive back to Elisabeth's house in the morning to deliver my epic composition. She's up, but eager to point out that Leila has locked herself in the loo, so I don't stop. What is it with me and women over the last ten years? If they're not chucking up all over me, then they're barricading themselves in the toilet. Am I missing something here?

A couple of days later, Ben Connery cheers me up no end by revealing that after I'd left the party, a drunken Leila declared in front of everyone that she fancied Robin.

Towards the end of the month, my roll cage for the car is delivered to the College. Maggie on Reception is fascinated by it and holds an imitation sweepstake on what it might be. Needless to say, none of the staff has the faintest idea. Teachers, what planet are they on?

Shortly afterwards, I'm on my way out of the City in the future race car when it runs out of fuel three hundred yards short of the nearest filling station. Since the petrol gauge doesn't work, I've had to rely on rough calculations for determining refuelling intervals. Far too rough, as it turns out. The gradient of the road is too steep to contemplate pushing the car. Consequently, I switch on the hazard warning lights and leg it to the garage in search of a plastic petrol container. They're out of them, so I decide to sprint back to the flat – about half a mile away – to fetch my own one.

I return breathless about fifteen minutes later just as a police car draws up and parks some fifty yards behind the Fiat – right on the exit of a tight bend. Whilst I'm in the process of explaining my situation to the young officer, there's an almighty collision. We turn round in unison to discover that another vehicle has driven round the blind corner and crashed right into the back of the patrol car. Red in the face, the policeman takes down my contact details in case he should require a witness. I carry on to work, sensing that my racing career may well turn out to be as dramatic as my love life. Oh dear!

Rather tentatively, Leila and I exchange e-mails towards the end of January, and agree to meet at her flat. When I arrive, she appears very much at ease and introduces me to her new flatmate. Her manner couldn't be more amicable, in fact. Given that some of her belongings are still scattered around my flat, I suggest she comes over next Wednesday to sort through them. What's more, the CD I promised her for Christmas should finally be in the shops by then. I offer to cook dinner.

"I'm off to Manchester with work the day before," she says with a friendly smile. "I'll have to ring and let you know."

It's 8.00 pm on Wednesday. I've been food shopping, but there's been no call from Leila. I know I should ring her, but my pride is holding me back. Tired of waiting, I decide to eat alone. I then agree to meet Rupert in town.

A few drinks in *Bar Med* turn into a hell of a lot more at *Opportunity Knox*. When Rupert leaves, I start to lose the plot.

"Falling out of love with me in five minutes is one thing, but not having the respect to … you know … call me is another," I protest to my invisible drinking partner.

Then it occurs to me that Leila might've had an accident on her way to or from Manchester. Although any sober person would conclude that I'm overreacting, I'm too far gone to think straight.

When I finally stumble into my bedroom, I pick up the phone and, even though it's late, can't prevent myself dialling Leila's number.

"Thanks a lot for … for l…letting me know … about d…dinner tonight," I stutter as the answer phone clicks in. "I … I r…really appreciated it."

Woken by my alarm a few hours later, I'm furious with myself a) for clubbing b) for getting drunk midweek and c) for losing a grip and phoning so late. I'm shattered at work, but hopefully too experienced now to let it show in my teaching.

At lunchtime, I nip over to Leila's office and leave her belated

Christmas present on Reception with a College compliment slip as a light-hearted gesture. As I'm pushed for time, I don't ask to see her. Besides, I assume from the lack of communication last night that she wouldn't want to see me, anyway. It's a small firm and if anything had happened to Leila, I'm sure the receptionist would tell me.

Over the next four days, there's still no call from the elusive Leila. This surprises me because I know how much she was looking forward to the CD and she's always been such a 'well-mannered young lady'. It's not that I'm trying to win her back – the same complications would still be there – but I'm wounded by her dismissive behaviour. It hurts my pride that I can be forgotten so easily. Part of me is now convinced that I'm incapable of securing anything other than fickle love. Men and their pride, eh! Then again, aren't we the ones who are supposed to be the lousy communicators?

On Monday morning, I send an e-mail to Leila, but there's no reply.

As I'm leaving College at the end of the day, I decide on the spur of the moment to call in on her and put an end to the mystery once and for all.

As I search for a parking place outside the block of flats, I notice that her bedroom light is on.

"Good, she's back from work already," I tell myself.

I buzz Leila's flat at the main entrance and wait. No reply. I try again, but with the same outcome. Noticing that the window is open, I call up to her. But once more, there's no response. I'm puzzled. Surely she can't be asleep at 6.00 o'clock. Moreover, she's a light sleeper.

"Oh bugger! Why haven't I got a mobile like everyone else?" I curse, uncertain of my next move. "I can't keep living in the dark ages forever."

Looking round, I spot a phone box nearby and make straight for it. To my relief, it's not been vandalised, so I dial Leila's number and wait nervously. It's the answer machine. I'm about to hang up, but figure at the last minute that it won't do any harm to leave a message. "Leila, it's Al. Please pick the phone up. I'm … I've been worried about you. You haven't called or anything. Er, I'll try again at the door." I pause momentarily, but there's still no reaction, so I replace the receiver.

Back at the entrance to Leila's block, one of her neighbours lets me in. I climb the once so familiar stairs to her apartment, my heart pounding with anticipation. As I reach her door, I can hear music from inside, confirming that she must be at home. And then for the first time, it hits me. Maybe she's entertaining another bloke. Maybe it's Grant or Robin … or even Ben. Oh no, please not! It would explain everything, though. High on emotion and determined to get at the truth, I bang feverishly on the door.

"Leila, this is crazy. Please let me in," I cry out. "I won't stay. I just want to know that everything's all right."

Silence. The old lady opposite opens her door on the chain and peers through the gap, then closes rapidly as I turn and our eyes meet.

"Okay, I'm going to stop knocking now, but I'm not leaving until I know what's going on," I whisper through the letterbox in the calmest voice I can muster from my adrenaline-pumped body. "I'm sitting down here on the landing until you open up."

So I sit and wait. Five minutes. Fifteen minutes. Half an hour. Nothing. And yet all this time, I feel as if I'm back on stage with the Players or making my debut on the set of a romantic comedy. It certainly has little to do with the 'ordinary' life of Al Bentley, a mere language teacher – sorry, Curriculum Manager – who's completely lost a grip on his love life and taken to the bottle.

And then suddenly, it happens. There's movement inside. The key turns slowly in the lock. And, finally, the door opens. Almost simultaneously, a large male figure rushes up the stairs behind me in the obscurity and, before I have chance to take a step forward, brushes past me into the flat and into ... Leila's arms. It's Grant.

"What the hell's going on?" I ask.

"I was so scared, I was hiding in the broom cupboard," Leila sobs, her head resting on the broad shoulders of her tall, stocky 'knight in shining armour'. "My neighbour was going to call the police."

"What, so you called Mr Guardian Angel here to come to your rescue instead?" She nods, her flushed face full of tears. "I don't get it. What've I ever done to make you feel so scared?" There's no reply. "Oh, for God's sake, Leila. How long've we known each other? Nine months? And when've I ever done anything to hurt you? This ... this is crazy!"

In spite of myself, I'm furious now. Furious that her bloody ex-boyfriend, part of the reason I never fully trusted her in the first place, has been summoned to protect her ... against me, a man who's never laid a finger on anyone is his life. If this really were a film, I'd be taking a swing at him now out of self-respect. But my teaching career has taught me far too well how to avoid confrontation. My head is confused and overflowing with questions. Somehow, they all spill out at once. "If you didn't want me to come up, why didn't you just shout down to me or tell me on the phone? I'd've listened to you. Why all this drama and why didn't you let me know about dinner?"

"I wrote you a letter," Leila says tearfully, finally breaking her silence.

"What letter? When?"

She sniffs, blows her nose, then shrugs. "I think I sent it on Friday."

"Well, I haven't got it yet. What did it say?"

"Just explains everything. You'll have to read it."

She sobs once again, prompting Grant to tighten his grip and pull her closer to him. I want to know more, but I can't bear the humiliation any longer. She told me that she adored me, that I was her dream come true. Yet all the time, she was carrying on an unusually close relationship with her former boyfriend, the one who she'd ditched because it didn't feel right. And now, here he is again standing in my way. Both angry and bewildered, I turn to go.

"I've had a lucky escape," I say, shaking my head in despair. "I'm out of here."

Back at the car, I sit motionless for a few minutes, a strong sensation of numbness pervading my shell-shocked body.

On my way home, I castigate myself for making such a mess of my part. In my head, I compose all the things I should've said – all the things that would've come naturally to a fictional TV or movie character in my position. As for my parting words, she'll never forgive me for those, will she?

Considering that the post rarely arrives before I leave for work, I'm confident that Leila's letter will be waiting for me when I get back to the flat. But it's not. Was she lying to me on top of everything else?

Late the following afternoon, after another day of faked happiness at work, I arrive home to find the long-awaited letter in the hallway. As I climb the stairs to my front door, I tear open the envelope and scan the main paragraph.

> … *I thought I only needed to ring you if*
> *I could make it to dinner. Why didn't you*
> *call at a reasonable hour when I didn't?*
> *You woke my flatmate up with your message*
> *in the early hours. Yes, I liked the CD, but*
> *what the hell were you playing at delivering*
> *it to my office with a compliment slip? Why*
> *didn't you ask to speak to me? You were*
> *acting as if you're frightened of me.*

Me frightened of her? Is she having a laugh? I look at the stamp. She was right – it was posted on Friday, first class. Well done, Royal Mail! I wonder how many romances or friendships have broken down due to a delayed or lost letter in the history of the postal service. This prompts me to remember my all-time favourite French films *Jean de Florette* and *Manon des Sources*, adopted from the novel by Marcel Pagnol. Highly recommended!

I decide to write back. Although Leila's letter was written before the rather dramatic events of last night, it'd be rude not to answer her questions. As I drop my reply into the letterbox round the corner, I can't help reflecting rather sadly that this is probably the last contact we'll ever have. I've no regrets that we met, even though my lack of experience of longer relationships left me feeling woefully out of my depth at times.

With half term fast approaching and my romance with Leila consigned to history, I'm beginning to appreciate in my present state of mind that the grass really isn't always greener on the other side. I worked out the other day that, since going to university at eighteen, I've been single for at least fifteen of the last seventeen years. On the surface, this is a hugely depressing statistic, yet virtually all the relationships I've been involved in have led me to question whether I was in fact missing out. I mean, preserving one's own sanity has to be a top priority, doesn't it?

Twice now since our rather bizarre pre-Christmas encounter in her bed, Sam Woodfield has pulled other BLOKES right in front of my nose. As if this isn't humiliating enough, an old friend, Roger 'Sailor', tipped me off the other day that Rupert also kissed her recently to avenge the Ruby incident back in the spring. Apparently, he was also keen to sleep with her – in my old house. Talk about adding insult to injury! Fortunately, Sam declined his generous offer. As usual, Rupert, a master of apologies and excuses, worms his way out of the situation and I find myself forgiving him once again.

Right, then, it's official. For the foreseeable future, I'm not going to bother with girlfriends. I'm just going to enjoy female company – hopefully in the plural – without looking for any form of commitment. Well, after a year of high emotion, I've decided that my poor nervous system is entitled to a vacation.

I'm well aware that teaching, with its 9.00 to 4.00 workday and long holidays, is often perceived by the general public as a cushy profession. There are, however, many taxing aspects of the job that tend to pass by unnoticed. Apart from the many additional hours of preparation, marking and general paperwork, putting oneself on public display day-in day-out, year after year is incredibly demanding. I'll never understand what it must've been like for my amateur dramatic friend and fellow teacher, Martin Studd, to be left by his wife who he adored and still have to stand up in front of all his classes, acting as if nothing had happened. A situation requiring an Oscar-winning performance, no doubt. And I think I had it bad after splitting up with Rachel and Sam – not to mention Leila, of course – and yet none of these relationships lasted more than six months. At least in an office job, you can, to a certain extent, hide away behind your desk and grieve in private.

With the recent drama well and truly over, I must confess that I seem to have re-established my grip on the Upper Sixth German group. To

Jennifer Warwick's credit, her suggestion that I divide the class into two manageable units appears to be working a treat. What's more, considering that a staircase separates the two classrooms, my cardiovascular fitness has been given a timely boost.

On the first Saturday of half term, Rupert and Ben join me for a few beers in town. Once the pubs have closed, we follow the predictable path to *James Dean's*. With the weight of recent events off my shoulders, I feel in great form and initiate conversation with two girls who I guess are in their mid-twenties. The taller and darker of the two, Jodi, comes from Zimbabwe.

By the end of the evening, I've pulled Jodi and she's given me her number.

"Did I remember to tell her that I've officially retired from relationships?" I ask myself as I leave the club with the two lads.

The following Tuesday, Jodi and I go out for dinner. I soon discover that she's had a rather traumatic life. Firstly, her dad died from AIDS. Then, more recently, she split up with her boyfriend of four years after it came to light that he was having an affair with her best friend. This is her first date since then and she tells me quite openly that she's not after commitment.

"I'm just going to use you for intellectual stimulation," she adds.

Wow, I can't believe my good fortune. Divine intervention at long last!

On the Sunday before returning to work, I go for a reflective walk across the local stretch of hills. This is a beautifully tranquil spot with a spectacular view of the City and surrounding countryside, and it always inspires deep and meaningful thought. I turn over the events of recent months and start to wonder exactly in what direction my life is heading. We spend so much of our younger years dreaming about and planning for the future, then all of a sudden we're grown up and life starts to pass us by. I'm thirty-five now and seem to have got so little done. Most of my time and energy is spent desperately trying to keep my head above water as I jump from one financial or emotional mini-crisis to the next. But then I guess this is par for the course in the frenzied modern civilised world.

Back down to earth, my cousin, Susannah, calls in the evening. She informs me, amongst other things, that she met up with Leila for a drink a few days ago for the latter to return some books she'd borrowed. Apparently, my name didn't crop up once in their conversation. However, Susi tells me that Leila seemed fine, which puts my mind at rest.

The following Friday, there's a face from the past in *Bar Med* that sets my pulse racing – Maria Grey, the *Mardall's* student I had a huge crush on between '93 and '95. Apart from spotting her once in *WH Smiths* from a distance, this is our first encounter in six years. Even though it feels like a lifetime ago that she rebuked me for sending her roses, it's not difficult to understand what it was that attracted me to her in the first place: her eyes, her hair, her physique, her mannerisms. Everything about her, in fact.

Eventually, I pluck up the courage to go over and talk to her and her friend Natasha who I taught for French. To my irritation, I'm all nervous and awkward in Maria's company. Apart from saying hello, she makes it perfectly obvious that she doesn't want to chat. Natasha, however, is much friendlier and explains what she's been up to since leaving College. That is until Maria gives her a sign of disapproval and she breaks off mid-sentence, leaving me standing on my own in the middle of the bar looking as if I've got a severe personal hygiene problem.

As I turn out the light back at the flat, I can't help feeling miffed that Maria reacted in the way she did. After all, the only crime I ever committed was to send her those flowers. Oh, and the Valentine's tape, I suppose. I couldn't be any worse off if I'd sent her a daisy chain – and thirty odd quid wealthier. I suppose my subsequent relationship with Rachel Hill might've given her the wrong impression of me as it seems to have done with others. Boy, I think I'd still give my right arm for a date with her – even if she refused to communicate with me throughout it.

I'm up early the following morning and drive to Donington racetrack to learn how to be a racing driver. After an hour's on-circuit tuition – the first time I've ever been round a track – I have to undergo an assessment of my driving skill and take a written theory test (ARDS). I manage one hundred per cent for the latter, but only just squeeze through the practical test.

I return home enormously relieved. I can now apply for my National B racing driver's licence and will be able to compete in the first race of the season at the end of March – in just three weeks' time.

I call into *James Dean's* in the evening to celebrate my achievement and am chatted up at the bar by a diminutive student nurse with two names – Lib or Dee – whilst waiting to be served. We dance a bit together and share a brief kiss on the dance floor. Before leaving, she gives me her number. Apparently, she only has one name, but uses the other with blokes she's trying to ward off. Problem is, I can't remember which one is which.

Later in the week, I give Lib/Dee a call. Or should I say Lib/Dem? She seems pleased to hear from me. We arrange to meet on Saturday. In my new role as a male tart, I phone Jodi immediately afterwards to see what she's up to on Friday. Unfortunately, she's already got tickets to see some male strippers with friends from work, so I book her up provisionally for Saturday lunchtime to view this stripper.

As it happens, I manage to shift my date with Lib/Dem forward to Friday, so should be able to extend lunch with Jodi. Mm, this could get complicated. How some people are able to juggle multiple lovers without getting caught, I'll never know.

I meet Lib/Dem in *Bar Med* as planned. Gary, the junior chef, cooks us duck on the house. We get on famously and before I know it, I'm sharing a bed with her at her friend's house round the corner where she's staying for the weekend. As it's our first date, I've come out unequipped – old habits die hard – but Lib/Dem pulls off my boxers and proceeds to tease me to the point of near explosion. Never before have I been required to exercise such a high level of restraint – apart from in Norway back in '93 and with Charlotte Rhys-Jones, perhaps.

In the morning, Lib/Dem repeats her performance and it's with great difficulty that I drag myself away in time to meet Jodi for lunch and … intellectual you know what. We also have a good time together. Although I haven't completely cleared it with my moral conscience, my new carefree approach seems to be a lot less emotionally demanding than my old one.

The following Sunday morning, the phone wakes me with a start. I glance across at the digital clock on my radio alarm and notice that it's only 3.30. With visions of a sudden death in the family, I pick up nervously: "Hello, Al speaking."

"Oh hi, Al, it's Kate here," comes the reply, as fresh as a daisy. "You gave me your number a couple of weeks back. Hope you don't mind me calling."

"Er, did I?" I answer tentatively, still half asleep. Kate? I don't recall meeting anyone of that name.

"You don't remember me, do you?"

"Er, I'm not sure. I … I've only just woken up."

I scratch my head madly in an effort to think back.

The mystery caller becomes impatient and throws a direct question at me: "All right. Where did you meet me, then?"

I stick my neck out. "Was it *Bar Med*?"

"No, it wasn't. You're just guessing, aren't you?"

At this point, I'm sure I can hear another female voice in the background. "Is there someone else there with you?"

"No, it's just my music. I'm tucked up in my lovely warm bed all on my own."

I've now woken up sufficiently to be certain that it's a wind up, but I haven't the foggiest who it can be. Somehow, I don't think Rupert,

Martin, Ben or Roger are capable of performing such miracles with their vocal cords.

The farce continues for a good ten minutes without any flashes of inspiration on my part. In the end, bored no doubt with her game, the voice at the other end confesses. It's Lib/Dem with help from her friend, Kate. Very funny! Just as well I won't have to get up for work in a few hours.

On Sunday evening, I ring Lib/Dem to congratulate her on the previous night's prank.

"I only spoke to you briefly on a couple of occasions," she laughs. "The rest of the time, it was Kate."

"Yes, but it was you at the end, though, wasn't it?" I ask.

"No, that was definitely Kate. She said you spoke to her rather intimately."

Mystified, I suggest meeting up again on Friday, but the joker is still playing the fool and refuses to give me an answer one way or another. In the end, I say goodbye and hang up, uncertain what's behind Lib/Dem's little game. Not that I object to practical jokes, of course. It's just that I've no idea whether she wanted to see me again or not. I suppose if she's keen, she'll ring back. Hopefully, at a more respectable hour and without the assistance of Kate.

The eve of my long-awaited motor racing debut is a rather fraught affair. The car only just reaches a state of legality by early evening, but has yet to be painted and looks like it's been pulled off the scrap heap. Nevertheless, there's no underestimating what Pat Baines and I have achieved in our spare time in less than three months. More Pat than me, to be precise. Mum and dad are on holiday, and Pat is tied up, so I'll have to face the music single-handed tomorrow.

Just before setting off early on Sunday, I remember that I haven't made a will. I hurriedly place a scruffy note on my bed, leaving everything to my immediate family. I haven't managed to sort out a car with a tow hitch or a trailer, so leave for *Donington Park* in the race car itself, with the numbers carefully masked over and boxes of spares in the back.

I arrive in good time – or so I think – and sign on at my leisure. The paddock is full of immaculate machinery prepared by incredibly professional-looking racing outfits with enormous car transporters and awnings.

"Mm, David and Goliath," I decide at once.

It's only a good half an hour later that I discover to my horror that the clocks have gone forward and that qualifying for my championship is due to start in fifteen minutes. Panic, panic, panic! I make myself unpopular by pushing to the front of the scrutineering queue, but to my profound relief the car passes.

Back in the main part of the paddock, I hand William, an old friend and experienced racer, all my belongings from inside the car and make frantically for the main gate onto the track. I can hear from the roar in the background that qualifying has already got underway. When I get there, I discover that the marshals won't let me through without my scrutineering ticket, which I presume I erroneously gave to Will. Shit! With my heart pounding at what feels like double its normal rate, I do a u-turn and scour the paddock in search of Will. Thank God, I find him almost at once and make it out onto the track with ten minutes of the session left to run.

It's 8.30 and I'm back from a cold, damp *Donington*, wondering why for the best part of thirty years I've wanted to be a racing driver. Apart from my blunder with the clocks, my four laps of practice produced a qualifying time that was twenty-six seconds off the pace. In motor racing terms, this is half a lifetime. Things didn't improve much in the race when a carburettor problem prevented me running at more than five thousand revs and prompted my retirement after two laps. Still, I got home in one piece and live to fight another day.

Whilst at the circuit, I came across two former *Mardall's* students competing in the *Mighty Mini Championship* – Merv Fitzgerald and his younger brother, Dennis, otherwise known as my stalker. Merv was as convivial as ever, but advised me to give Dennis a wide berth.

"He's still bitter about your involvement with Rachel Hill," he warned.

"He's not the only one," I replied and explained about my encounter with Scott Dixon.

Despite what they say, it appears that there are some wounds that time simply cannot heal.

Just before Easter, the Principal brings us the latest on the PSP. There's good and bad news. The good news is that application forms will be available from early June and everyone who's successful in passing the threshold will have payment backdated to 1st April. The bad news is that only one of the three box-ticking sections of the form relates directly to performance in the classroom. The other two cover administrative duties. Glancing at the sample application displayed on the OHP, there doesn't appear to be any area that'd cause me undue concern, but it's disappointing once again to see paperwork take precedence. Easier to quantify, I guess.

On Easter Monday at *Castle Combe*, I make history by completing my first motor race. As a reward for my achievement, I get a signature on my licence. Another nine of these and I'll lose my 'rookie' status and be able to remove the black cross from the rear of the car. My best lap was just over fifteen seconds off the pace, so I am making some sort of progress.

During the remainder of the holiday, I make a conscious effort to cut back on my drinking. After all, forty to sixty units per week is far too much. My tactic is to alternate an alcoholic drink with a soft one like lime and soda. At sixty pence a pint, it's a bargain. In a more sober state, it's not hard to appreciate the destructive nature of heavy drinking. Fortunately, I've never been physically violent, but the bouts of paranoia and temporary depression I've suffered on occasions have been quite alarming. Somehow, though, it's so much easier to drink sensibly when one's life is calmer.

Jodi and I meet up a couple of times over Easter, still without any hint of commitment on either side. I may not be a natural when it comes to casual relationships, but I think I'm gradually learning to adjust.

Jo Black makes several appearances in town with her friend, Vicki. It's a half-hour journey for them by car, but it seems there's more happening 'here' than 'there'. Obviously enough for Jo to drive and have to abstain from drinking. Our meetings are in public and, with the official leaving day just around the corner, I'm not too worried any more. Anyway, I don't think Jo is quite from the same mould as Charlotte R-J.

SUMMER TERM

Back at College, Hollie Skinner, one of my Lower Sixth German students, returns from the French Exchange full of beans.

"Did you have a good time?" I ask.

"Yeah, it was well cool, thanks," she replies. "Oh, by the way, Al. Did you know that the French say "Hollie" to their kids when it's bedtime?"

I brace myself for a punch line, but realise almost immediately that Hollie isn't joking.

"Oh, really?" There's a hint of sarcasm in my voice as I try to make sense of her bizarre observation.

"No, honestly, they do. My Exchange partner's mum said it to her little brother every night."

After chewing it over for a few seconds, it finally registers. What she must've heard was "Au lit!" [*Oh lee*], meaning "Off to bed!" Whilst dear Hollie may not be the most able linguist I've ever taught, no-one could ever accuse her of a lack of enthusiasm. I'd much prefer to teach a spirited trier like her than a lazy, arrogant student with a gift for languages, of which I've come across several during my teaching career.

I can hardly believe it, but it's the end of May already and the exam season is with us once again. The new AS exams have prompted a huge demand for external oral examiners for languages and exceeded the Board's expectations. As a large Centre, it can only accommodate us by extending the original examining period. The poor bloke they send has to test over fifty German students in less than two days. This is really too many for any mortal being, so I hope his marks will prove to be consistent.

As regards the new AS writing, reading and listening exams, Curriculum 2000 was rushed through so quickly that our Board apparently didn't have time to put together proper sample papers. All we got was a mishmash of old two-year A level style questions that the students found too difficult.

New exams always make me nervous. You can never fully trust the Boards to keep to the promises they make at the various courses we attend. With this year's Upper Sixth, it's plain sailing in comparison. As the final year group to take the old A level exam, they've had years' worth of past papers to practise on. There's one thing I've noticed during my twelve years in the classroom. Governments, examining boards and senior management groups generally get away with mediocrity when time has been against them. For teachers, however, such allowances are rarely made.

There is one major advantage for us, though, that comes with the new system of exams. Since both year groups are now tested in May and June, we get a complete break from teaching for several weeks. This provides a perfect opportunity to make a start on the University Reference Statements and complete any outstanding paperwork. I'll also have time to fill in and submit my application for the PSP.

It's a Thursday evening in early June. Given that I won't have to teach in the morning, I head for *James Dean's* with Rupert and Martin. On our arrival in the club, we're immediately greeted with a now customary hug and kiss from a girl called Tracy who used to have a crush on my friend Champagne Charlie, the main chef at *Bar Med*. According to Charlie, she stayed over at his place a couple of times and revealed a bizarre fetish for ironing. In fact, on one occasion, he fell asleep in front of her on the sofa and awoke several hours later to discover that she'd ironed every item of clothing she could lay her hands on. I'm not sure whether this included his dirty underwear.

It's a busy night full of university students, reminiscent of a year ago when Leila and I met. It's not a sad memory – just brings a sentimental smile to my lips.

Half way through the evening, I take a seat on one of the tall chairs, located on the periphery of the dance floor, and watch the world go by. Suddenly, an over-exuberant Tracy comes bounding across and accidentally knocks the contents of my pint glass over the girl next to me. I apologise profusely and prepare to take evasive action. To my relief, my neighbour is okay about it.

We get chatting and I realise immediately that she's Australian. She tells me her name is Kelly and that she's over here till September. After a while, she asks if I want to dance. We get quite close on the dance floor and sort of kiss. I say 'sort of' because, whilst not exactly throwing up all over me in disgust, Kelly seems a bit hesitant.

Before making tracks, she does, however, tell me the name of the pub where she works, so all is not lost.

On Saturday, I take a trip cross-country to Kelly's pub. She's in the middle of her shift, but not unhappy to see me. She suggests I call back at 3.00 when she's finished.

I comply with her request and we spend the rest of a very mild, sunny afternoon in the beer garden of a nearby pub that's renowned for attracting local celebrities. Just not today, apparently.

It transpires that Kelly is in fact 'Shellie', short for Michelle. Either I'm experiencing the premature onset of deafness or they must've cranked up the music at *Dean's* on Thursday night. Shellie tells me about her life in Australia, her travels to date and her plans for the future, which include a two-month trip across Asia in September. Whilst she's talking, I can't fail to notice her huge blue eyes that frequently light up with excitement and her blonde hair tied back tightly in a small ponytail, revealing a pale but attractive face. I also notice her 'hiking gear', complete with DM's, that detracts slightly from an otherwise feminine appearance.

I invite Shellie back to my place and she accepts willingly with the proviso that I won't expect her to sleep with me straight away. As if such a thought would enter my head!

When I drop Shellie home the following morning, she jumps out of the car hurriedly, mutters "Thanks" and disappears into the pub without looking back. I know from past experience that I shouldn't be too surprised by this, but I can't help feeling that I've failed to make an impression.

"We got on so well," I announce dejectedly to the Spider dashboard. "I was sure she'd want to see me again."

But hey, what am I talking about? I'm supposed to be Mr No-commitment.

At work the following week, the annual College photo is taken with a warning from the Principal that should breasts and bums appear on the 'fun' shot as they did last year, it won't, under any circumstances, be released for public consumption. The students duly oblige by keeping their private parts under wraps.

Leavers' Day follows soon afterwards. Unlike at *Mardall's*, where flour and eggs littered the campus, it's a surprisingly sober, uneventful affair.

On the Friday immediately after Leavers' Day, Jo Black rings and asks if I'd be up for meeting her in town for a celebratory end-of-year drink. Since I haven't made other plans, I'm happy to accept.

It's a warm evening and Jo comes round to the flat first, dressed in summer gear that shows off her superbly toned body to the full. Even taking into account my years of competing at gym, I don't think I've ever seen a more perfectly tuned figure on a woman and it's hard to take my eyes off this now licit beauty.

She sits down next to me on the settee. As we talk, I can feel her thigh rubbing up against mine. The discussion flows as naturally as it's always done with such an adept conversationalist. Only, this time, Jo reveals intimate secrets that would never have found expression in our previous 'roles'.

"Al, I fancied you from the very first lesson," she says.

"Oh, right. Thanks," I say, as uncomfortable as ever in the face of praise. Inside, however, my inherently wobbly ego swells instantaneously. "Don't tell me that it was you who ...?"

"Sent the anonymous letters? Yes, it was. Sorry! I was just too embarrassed to own up before."

"Don't be. I'm glad you didn't. Actually, it was unfair of me to ask you about them in the first place. You were very convincing, though."

Jo smiles and, at this point, my eyes are drawn almost magnetically towards her visibly dilating pupils. Even though this is a face that's become so familiar over the past two years, at such close proximity and with the ties of professional responsibility no longer hanging over me, it suddenly takes on a completely different guise. This is not Jo, the student, I'm looking at any more, but Jo, a sexy, desirable young woman who, for some inexplicable reason, has singled me out as the object of her affection. She has so many qualities that I admire in the opposite sex and if I felt for one tiny second that she were capable of loving me properly at the exclusion of all others, I'd be easily coaxed out of my safe refuge back into the emotionally dangerous world of commitment. But I'm under no illusions this time. This is the real world and Jo's romantic voyage of self-discovery is as close to the beginning as mine is to the end. All I'd be for her with university beckoning is an overnight stop on the long, winding road of experience.

In the past, I'd never have allowed such pessimism to influence my judgement. If I had, I probably would've walked away from the likes of

Rachel Hill, Sam Woodfield and Charlotte Rhys-Jones, sparing myself considerable heartache in the process. But my outlook is so different now. With my faith in relationships with women in general at an all-time low, the prospect of transient passion without pain makes Jo's advances well-nigh impossible to resist. As our lips meet, I feel sure that on my deathbed this won't prove to be a decision I'll 'live' to regret.

Somewhat delayed, we do eventually make it into town for that drink. Foolishly, I allow Rupert to join us. Having never seen Jo and me so close, he senses that something has happened. I thought he might be pleased for me, but hey – this is Rupert we're talking about. Instead, he devotes the rest of the evening at *Bar Med* to flirting outrageously with Jo in an attempt to divert her attention away from me. He even puts her on his shoulders. Oh what it is to have good mates!

Jo leaves for home soon after closing time. Rupert and I, spring chickens that we are, go off clubbing. Inside *James Dean's*, Rupert does a customary circuit and returns with a large grin on his face.

"Your Australian friend's here," he says.

"Really? Whereabouts?" I ask.

"Over the other side of the dance floor."

It doesn't take long to find Shellie bopping away in front of the spot where we met. As soon as she catches sight of me, her previously contented expression turns decidedly dour.

"Hi," I say buoyantly.

"I don't wanna talk to you!" she snarls, turning her back on me.

I skip round to the front of her. "Michelle, would you mind telling me what the problem is? I really haven't got a clue." Surely she couldn't have bugged the flat. She ignores my question and carries on dancing as if oblivious of my presence. "Look, I think there's been a bit of a misunderstanding."

Shellie is still not a happy bunny. But eventually, my persistence pays off.

"It's well over a week and you haven't called or anything," she says. "I've felt really rejected."

"I didn't think you were interested. Actually, it's only five days."

There's a vague flicker of a smile. "How d'you work out that I wasn't interested?"

"I've never seen anyone get out of my car as quickly as you did on Sunday and I assumed you didn't like me."

She changes her tune. "Yeah, all right, then. Fair enough."

The witch-like demeanour disappears and the more familiar Shellie returns. Isn't it strange how the most attractive female faces are capable of the most evil glares? With our misunderstanding cleared up, we agree to meet up again tomorrow.

When I hit the sack in the early hours, I can't help chuckling over the day's bizarre events.

"All those years of being single and the moment I adopt a more carefree approach, I'm fighting them off," I inform the area of ceiling above my bed. "Al Bentley and three women at one time. Has the world gone completely bonkers?"

As I lie here in the obscurity, I can't help feeling certain that I wouldn't have been sucked in by the attentions of Charlotte Rhys-Jones had I felt this positive eighteen months ago. How things have changed!

The following morning, Rupert rings in a state of fury. Before leaving *Dean's* last night, I told him quite firmly that his conduct with Jo wasn't what I'd expect from a good friend. He's obviously been mulling it over and is up for a fight. He proceeds to rant and rave for a good ten minutes, bringing up the Ruby incident for the umpteenth time, until I lose interest and hang up. Surely he can't be jealous of me. What a role reversal this would be!

I fetch Shellie in the race car and let her behind the wheel for a quick spin. She's chuffed.

Back at the flat, there are three messages waiting for me on the answer machine. Without thinking, I press the play button, only to hear Rupert at his most confrontational. *And another thing. I'm sure Shellie would be more than interested to hear what you were up to yesterday before you went clubbing,* the first instalment concludes – I assume the other messages are from him – just as Shellie wanders into the bedroom. My index finger searches frantically for the stop button, but it's too late.

"What would Shellie be interested in hearing?" she asks.

"Oh, nothing," I reply feebly.

To my relief, she doesn't pursue the matter. Phew!

On Sunday, there's another significant message, not from an irate Rupert this time, but a remorseful Jo.

"I feel really bad about the other night," she says, "seeing as Ric and I are still sort of seeing each other. We mustn't let it happen again."

Hm. So much for insisting she'd knocked it on the head with her boyfriend with university approaching.

Shortly afterwards, Shellie and I have our first proper altercation. It all kicks off when I catch her counting the condoms in the drawer by my bed. When I explain that I can't commit to a full-on relationship with her departure date only a few months away, that evil glare returns and Shellie storms off out of the flat.

"It's a proper, exclusive relationship or nothing!" she roars out of the half-open window of her Mini Metro, then speeds away without glancing back.

I didn't really expect to hear from Shellie again, so I'm pleasantly surprised when I return home from work a couple of days later to find a message from her on the answer machine. *Hello, it's me. I've been thinking about it and I'm not so sure I want a serious relationship either.*

I call her back and we make up. It seems a good time to mention that I still meet up with Jodi every now and again. Given that the condom audit tallied the other day, Shellie doesn't kick up a fuss.

One Wednesday evening in the middle of June, whilst I'm enjoying a quiet night in with Shellie, the phone rings.

"Hello, Al speaking," I say on picking up the receiver.

Shellie sniggers at my telephone manner.

"Would that be the Al Bentley who worked as a language assistant in Austria in '86?" asks a male voice with a Scottish accent.

I'm virtually speechless. It's my old mate Mario Campbell! He tells me that he found my number on the Internet and apologises for leaving it so long. Just a mere seven years, in fact. Mario's explanation is a complicated one, but involves an unsuccessful marriage to Liza who we met in Corfu in '93. The crafty old bugger! Realising that I would've discouraged such a permanent liaison, on the grounds that the pair were blatantly ill-matched, Mario broke off contact initially to concentrate on what he believed was his last chance at married life. After all, he was knocking on a bit at thirty. Apparently, as the years rolled by, it became more and more difficult to get back in touch. And all this time, I thought he'd just moved on with his life.

Whilst Mario's story interests me, the reasons behind his silence are no longer of any great significance. What counts is that my old sparring partner is back and I'm over the moon. Bearing grudges rarely does anyone any favours.

With so much catching up to do, Mario and I decide a few days later to return to Austria together for a week in the summer.

Despite her recent message, Jo continues to ring on a regular basis and makes numerous appearances in town. On one occasion, she joins me, Jodi, Martin and Rupert at *Wetherspoons*. Apart from the fact that the two girls regularly look daggers at each other, the evening is a success.

However, it's more my relationship with Shellie that seems to meet with Jo's disapproval. *I get so jealous when I think of you together with that*

Australian girl! reads one of her frequent e-mails. So it is true, after all. The way to a woman's heart is through jealousy. Although I'm sorely tempted to fall for Jo again, I decide to respect her initial request.

I can hardly believe it, but it's mid-July already and another academic year is over. After the trials and tribulations of '99 to 2000, this year has, course forum apart, been much more like what I'm used to, although I have felt under pressure to prove myself once again in the eyes of the management. I'm proud of the way I've fought back, particularly considering there were moments last summer when I really wondered if changing colleges was my only option. I just hope the A and AS results will confirm my returning optimism.

Since *Castle Combe*, I've finished two further races at *Croft* and *Mallory Park*. At the latter circuit, I was only six seconds a lap slower than the top man. Schumacher beware!

As for my private life, I have to admit that I've proved a dead loss at continuing with the 'playing the field' game. I was so overcome by guilt following a kiss with Jo in my car after the Leavers' Ball and then a more serious offence with Jodi at roughly the same time that I've settled into a more monogamous relationship with Shellie. Not committed, just monogamous. The more risks you take, the more likely you are to get caught, particularly when you're as hopeless at deception as I am. Shellie can also be a seriously scary woman when the situation demands it. Besides, we've become good friends, which doesn't make infidelity particularly easy to live with. Needless to say, my decision hasn't gone down too well with Jo or Jodi. Retaining a conscience and pleasing everyone at the same time is proving an impossible task.

Following England's defeat in the first Test Match against the Aussies and a lost bet, I'm now facing the prospect of being Shellie's slave for twenty-four hours. I told you she was a hard woman. I wonder what'll happen if I refuse to obey her.

In a week's time, Mario and I will be off to Austria to revisit the scene of our sadly not misspent youth. This should prove a perfect start to the summer. Kevin, the Vice-Principal, is allowing me to miss In-Service Training (INSET) on the last day of term to fly off, on the condition that I collect some up-to-date resources for the German Department. Who said teaching was a part-time occupation?

All Things Must Pass

(Year 10)

All things must pass,
None of life's strings can last,
So I must be on my way
And face another day.

AUTUMN TERM

Holidaying in a town where you spent nine months of your life almost fifteen years before is a strange experience. If that town happened to be in the UK, you'd expect to find many new buildings and signs of considerable modernization. To our pleasant surprise, however, good old Klagenfurt in southern Austria was very much as Mario and I remembered it. Even the restaurant where we used to dine out on a regular basis hadn't altered its décor or menu. Once inside, we couldn't wait to turn back the clock by stuffing our now finely lined faces with a delicious *Hausplatte* – a mixed grill for two like you've never tasted – whilst catching up over several litres of wheat beer.

Despite a seven-year gap, Mario hadn't changed a bit and, caught in a time warp, the two of us reminisced like a pair of geriatrics. Every night, we hit the local bars till late and remembered all those Austrian beauties who, thanks to a combination of hesitancy and youthful naivety on our part, ultimately slipped through our clutches.

Overcome by nostalgia, we then found ourselves scanning the local telephone directory in an attempt to track down two of these Carinthian heartthrobs. It proved a more straightforward exercise than we'd anticipated. With a touch of British charm, we even managed to wangle invitations to afternoon tea. We could scarcely have imagined the warmth of the ladies' welcomes and the great pleasure they took in introducing us to their respective husbands. Bianca, my old favourite, looked as striking as ever and had married a doctor almost twenty years her senior. Their two young children, Steffi and Manuel, were very sweet and impeccably mannered. Somehow, I always knew those *Fawlty Towers* videos I showed B's English class all those years ago would make a lasting impression.

Looking back, it was Bianca who first provided me with a clear insight into the inherent dangers of flirting with the young female mind. I suppose I've only myself to blame for ignoring this warning for a further fourteen years in the belief that she was the exception rather than the rule. All I can say in my defence is that the world I grew up in, where those close to me always meant what they said, probably lulled me into a false sense of security.

My lasting memory of the Austrian trip, however, is of Mario sitting in a pedal boat in the middle of a vast lake surrounded by mountains, chatting away on his mobile to his new girlfriend, Lesley, with the reception as clear as the water beneath him. Klagenfurt may not have changed since '87, but the world certainly has.

Back here in England, I'm more determined than ever to bury the ghosts of the past and tackle the future with renewed confidence. The new year at College begins on 29th August. Is it my imagination or is the summer holiday a few days shorter every year? Heartened by my week in Austria with Mario, I feel almost as positive about the term ahead as I did back in '92. To my profound relief, last summer's A level results served as confirmation that I've been successful in putting the events of 2000 behind me. Not quite the hundred per cent pass rate of the previous year – two out of twenty-one failed – but there was a higher proportion of top grades, which I'm sure would've gone down well with Dr Faulkner. The AS results weren't quite as impressive, but then it was the first year of the new exam and most students did achieve their predicted grades. Judging from the feedback, it looks like I've done more than enough to justify my position as Curriculum Manager for German. At last I can shed that unsettling feeling of being under scrutiny, which never left me last year.

As far as I'm concerned, the whole Charlotte Rhys-Jones business is done and dusted, and I've learnt from my mistakes. On reflection, I find it hard to comprehend how I could've been so wayward, but then I suppose I hadn't met the likes of Leila and Shellie, and my experience of relationships was probably on a par with that of someone fifteen years my junior. Oh well, enough said.

To accompany my new-found mood of optimism, the Modern Language Department has been moved to the main building. I now have a large, bright classroom to replace the dark, dingy box that was my base over the last three years. This means that I'm able to accommodate not only all the German resources but also the most sizeable classes the budget-conscious management decides to throw at me. No more sitting on laps, then!

The first day back begins with the customary staff meeting, enabling Dr Faulkner to remind us all how wonderful we are. We then split into our curriculum areas to review the results and discuss the year ahead.

At breaktime, I check my pigeonhole. Aside from the usual bumf, I find a rather formal-looking internal letter with my name hand-written on the envelope. As I flip it open, it registers that it must be confirmation that I've passed the threshold for the Professional Standards Payment. I pull out the contents eagerly. How I could do with some extra cash right now. Backdated too. After a rapid scan of the type-written page, I feel my blood pressure hit the roof.

"The miserable, tight-fisted, vindictive sod!" I curse under my breath.

With enrolment due to kick off this afternoon, there's no time to waste. I shove the bad news into my pocket and sprint along the main corridor to the new Staff Room where I know there's a copy of the PSP manual. It doesn't take me long to sift through the relevant pages. I resurface with renewed confidence. "I knew it, he's got it wrong."

Just over a year after reassuring me that my two formal written warnings weren't severe enough to be included in a reference, the Principal has only decided to use them to bar my access to the PSP. But here in front of me in the 'Bible', there's no mention whatsoever of formal warnings preventing a teacher passing the threshold. In fact, it confirms that the whole emphasis should be placed on accumulating positive evidence alone from the previous three years, not countering it with negative. If there's sufficient evidence to enable the boxes to be ticked, then the standards have been met, simple as that. I resolve to catch up with the boss straight away to point out his error. After all, even a powerful man like Dr Faulkner can't contravene the national regulations, can he? I feel calmer now.

The Principal has a busy schedule today, but agrees to see me for five minutes. Returning to the dreaded armchair brings back unpleasant memories of 2000, although this time I'm considerably more confident of my position. I outline briefly the reason for my visit. Dr Faulkner fondles his jaw with one hand before uttering some assertive, collected words.

"I'm sorry, Al," he says, "but there's not a single Principal or Head Teacher in the country who would've passed your application as it stands."

"Really?" I reply, attempting to match his assertive manner. "Then perhaps you'd be good enough to show me the appropriate paragraph in the manual that explains this. I must've overlooked it."

Faulkner plays with his beard uncomfortably. "Look, you were issued with two formal written warnings resulting from very serious incidents and there's no way that I, as Principal of this highly revered College, could ignore them."

"But the warnings were expunged from my file in July."

"True, but the payment, as you well know, is backdated to 1st April. And at that time, the warnings were still in force."

His tone has become more threatening and I can sense my own anger mounting dramatically.

"So let me get this straight. What you're saying is that the warnings are serious enough to stand in the way of a two-thousand-pound pay rise, but not serious enough to be mentioned in a reference?"

"What are you talking about?"

"You gave verbal assurance back in 2000 that, should I apply for another job, you wouldn't refer to the warnings in a reference, remember?"

"I don't recall mentioning anything of the sort. Look, I've got a busy day ahead of me and I'm not prepared to discuss this any more. As I stated in my letter, I'll be more than happy to consider another application from you for this October."

"But then I'll lose six months' backdated payment."

"Look, if you think you've got a case, then you have the right to appeal, although I can assure you you'll be wasting your time. Your immediate managers support my decision as does the senior verifier."

With these closing words, he ushers me out of his office, my morale at rock bottom. Despite all my efforts over the past year to put my indiscretions behind me – and I'm convinced I've done so successfully – the stubborn so-and-so just won't let them drop. What's more, he seems to be making up the rules as he goes along in an attempt to reprimand me further. Surely, though, I've been punished enough, haven't I? My nervous system certainly thinks so.

Another quick glance at the manual confirms my suspicions that an October application would be illegal. Any applicant who fails to meet the standards is not at liberty to reapply until a year has elapsed. I head off back to our new, spacious language office, along from my classroom and the Language Lab, wondering if Dr Faulkner has even bothered to familiarise himself with the rules and regulations for the PSP.

Eager to share my plight, I inform the diminutive Jennifer of my discussion with the Principal.

"Well, it's not as if you were an innocent recipient of the written warnings," she replies without a hint of diplomacy.

Even though I've become accustomed to her rather straitlaced approach to running the department and obsession with paying lip service to the management, Jennifer's reaction surprises me. Since I only provided her with a brief résumé of the Charlotte incident when she first arrived, I'm left contemplating how she's in a position to pass such a judgement. Looks like the College grapevine has been working overtime.

With the wretched PSP rejection buzzing around my head, I find it harder than usual to enthuse about the enrolment process. Part of me can't wait to return home to notify the Union.

"Don't worry, you've got forty days to lodge a complaint," a calm, sympathetic Union advisor reassures me when I call. "I'll give you the number of Mr Moyer, your regional representative."

I try this number immediately. There's an answer phone message telling me that the local Field Officer is on annual leave until next week and that any urgent matters should be directed to a colleague. The latter is most helpful. He suggests I send an e-mail to Mr Moyer at once so it's waiting for him on his return.

"As you've got forty days," he adds, "a slight delay in appealing shouldn't be a problem."

Poor Shellie has to endure the full story of my fall from grace during 2000. Over the last eighteen months, I've become more dependent on those close to me to air my frustrations, even at the expense of their own nervous systems. The more I review the events of last year, the more incensed I feel about the Principal's decision. I can't help thinking that I'd be in a far better position now had I given up at the first hurdle and turned my back on the College for a fresh start. But then throwing in the towel when the chips are down has never been part of my nature.

Just as I'm becoming more and more absorbed in my own misfortune, something happens which rocks the world and temporarily changes my perspective – September 11th. For the next few days, it's hard to think of anything else as every news broadcast brings further reports and pictures of human suffering. But somehow, knowledge that there are others around the world far, far worse off than ourselves only seems to postpone our own troubles, not dispel them. Is this human nature or has the communication revolution, with its constant exposure of misery, made us largely immune long-term to catastrophes that don't touch us personally? For Shellie, however, the consequences of this dark day in history do influence her plans for the immediate future. The travel company cancels her eagerly awaited trip across Asia, leaving her majorly disgruntled. It will mean we get to spend a few more weeks together before she heads off back to Australia, though.

Mr Moyer, the Union Rep, returns from annual leave and confirms that I should appeal within the forty-day period. I put my decision in writing and, at the start of the third week of term, hand it personally to Cynthia Thomas, the Principal's PA. Just as I'm leaving her office, Dr Faulkner calls after me, requesting a quick word in private.

Back in his office, I'm half expecting to hear that he's decided to backtrack, but then naivety has always been my middle name.

"Al, I'm afraid you only had two weeks to appeal," he says, glancing at his watch. "And you've just missed the deadline."

Did I detect a note of triumph in his voice? I protest, but he explains that the forty-day deadline applies only to the secondary sector. The Union has made a huge blunder. I slump down into his armchair with egg all over my face, his smug, bearded grin only serving to heighten my fury. I know that I should hold my tongue, but I can't resist the temptation to throw my arguments at him one more time. After all, they're valid ones, aren't they? And he's an intelligent man. But I'm wasting my breath. His defence begins with that same old line: "No other Principal in the country blah, blah, blah."

In my frustration, I consider one further line of attack. My better judgement advises me not to proceed, but I … I just can't restrain myself.

"Why did you lie to me by claiming that my immediate managers had endorsed your decision?" I ask. "Both Jennifer and Godfrey are adamant that you didn't ask for their op…"

There's an eruption of volcanic proportions. "How dare you accuse me of lying! In my own office as well!"

For the first time in the three years that I've known the Principal, he's no longer in control, his bear-like frame shaking feverishly. I take this as a cue to leave, my honour partially reinstated.

I return to the language area, reeling at the shock of my audacious comment. I'd never have spoken to any of my previous bosses in such a way. But then would they have allowed such a situation to arise in the first place? I'm beginning to realise that, for all his strengths, Dr Faulkner is unlikely to win the Nobel Prize for Peace. Mind you, on today's showing, nor am I.

With the bit between my teeth, I find myself composing two letters, one to the Principal, formally challenging his decision, and one to the Union, complaining that I was misinformed on a very important issue. To avoid the risk of missing any further deadlines, I immediately submit a second 'illegal' PSP application.

The following day, Dr Faulkner catches up with me in the computer room and, rather patronisingly, places his hand on my shoulder.

"Al, thank you for your letter," he says calmly. "I've filed it away with your records."

Rather than pacify me, his actions only serve to refuel my anger. On this occasion, however, I manage to bite my lip.

For the rest of the week, I struggle to approach work in my usual positive frame of mind. It's as if all that boundless optimism that I rediscovered after the holiday has been sucked out of me overnight. The great thing about education, however, is that it's usually possible to find solace somewhere. In my case, it's with my two new Lower Sixth German groups. They're so enthusiastic and well motivated that I'm reminded of all the reasons why I wanted to be a teacher in the first place, and why I've stuck at it through thick and thin for over twelve years. It's only when their ninety-minute lessons come to an end that the blues make an unwelcome return. Not that there's any problem with the second-year group, but they're so wrapped up in written course work at the moment that it would be unreasonable to expect the same degree of dynamism.

I'm conscious that, with both legs of this year's Munich Exchange just round the corner, I'm going to have to put my current predicament to the back of my mind. Simone offers some kind, sympathetic words, which help to lift my flagging spirits.

"It doesn't surprise me what 'as 'appened," she adds. "You know what reputation the management 'as 'ere."

In many ways, she reminds me of Marilyn Butcher, my former language boss – somewhat brusque and prickly on the surface, but deeply caring below it. Our discussion is halted abruptly by the arrival of Jennifer in the language office.

"Have you completed full schemes of work for the whole year for AS and A2, and put together that oral handbook yet?" she asks over formally.

I'm lost for words. Surely with an OfSTED Inspection due later in the term, a harmonious team has to be one of the top priorities of any Senior Curriculum Manager. Moreover, there's never been any College requirement to submit full schemes of work (SoW) by the beginning of term. And we've always managed without a specific oral handbook before. Of course, the impending Inspection has nothing whatsoever to do with this. During my teaching career, I've experienced several Inspections and I have to say that it irritates me the way the system instils such a high degree of panic amongst managers, which then leads to a massive administrative overkill. Wouldn't it be less artificial if the inspectors turned up unannounced or perhaps with just a couple of days' notice? This way, the chief inspector's report would be a much more accurate reflection of a school or college's day-to-day performance.

Whilst I'm more than willing to meet Jennifer's demands in time for the inspectors' arrival, that won't be until after half term and I just can't see why she's so bent on putting even more pressure on me at such a difficult time.

Instead of waiting an hour or two to calm down, I write her a memo expressing my disappointment that she's unable to offer me more support and understanding at such a make or break point in my teaching career. I stress that the documents aren't exactly urgent, given that the AS SoW is in place from last year and she already has a copy of the A2 version up to Christmas. As for the handbook, exam-related oral work won't begin until January. I promise Jennifer I'll deliver everything after I've resolved my future with Dr Faulkner and the Union, and certainly well before Inspection.

Once again, however, I underestimate the consequences of my actions. A couple of days later, I'm summoned to an emergency meeting with my two immediate managers. The atmosphere in the room is extremely unpleasant from the outset. Sitting side by side, Jennifer and Godfrey fire questions at me across the table as if conducting a disciplinary hearing. If I were a failing, non-committed colleague with an appalling attendance rate and below average results, I'd have some sympathy for the style of their approach. But none of these is the case. In fact, the only feedback I've ever received from Godfrey in the past was a pat on the back for excellent achievement and retention rates. And here he is telling me that my detailed schemes of work from last year resemble those produced in the 1950s. No matter how hard I try, I fail to comprehend why they're incapable of empathizing with my current predicament. The longer the meeting goes on, the more I realise that the management is closing ranks in order to bring me into line. I'm in danger of being trampled on. Finally, Godfrey dreams up post-Exchange deadlines for the submission of full schemes of work and the oral handbook.

Later in the day, he hands me a copy of the minutes of the meeting, which contain over a dozen inaccuracies – all in an attempt to portray me in an unfavourable light. I then have to waste another hour typing up a response to the minutes. One thing I've learnt in recent years about the modern world is that any form of complaint must be submitted in writing, otherwise you haven't got a leg to stand on.

Purely out of curiosity, I question a couple of other Curriculum Managers about schemes of work. Both admit they haven't produced full-year versions and have never been required to do so for September. When I show them my '1950s' version from last year, they're amazed at the amount of detail. One of the Economics teachers even shows me the SoW Godfrey produced for his own subject. Guess what – it contains about half the detail present in my 'outdated' version.

I must admit, Godfrey's attitude this term has taken me by surprise. In the past, he was always such a friendly, supportive colleague. Has Dr Faulkner had words with him? Or has it got something to do with his relationship with Begonia? If she'd told him an abridged version of my dealings with Charlotte, leaving out her involvement, he may well have got a false impression of me. At the end of the day, however, I don't suppose it really matters what's behind his behaviour. The significant factor is that he appears to be searching for reasons to undermine my role as Curriculum Manager for German. Since Dr Faulkner has asked him to report back on my performance prior to assessing my second PSP application, I should be kissing his feet. But then why should I tolerate a situation where the hurdles are greater for me than for my colleagues? After all, surely the integrity of the system relies on consistency across the board, not personal preference. Let's face it, we are talking about a relatively significant sum of money.

For the first time since I came to *Lower Valley*, the Exchange runs back-to-back, with the Germans descending on us first. I have to dig deep to find the inner strength to entertain with enthusiasm and self-confidence. Reinhardt Schmutzer is once again in charge of the German party. Since he's staying with the Principal and we've shared many personal experiences before, I decide to brief him on the PSP dispute.

At about the same time, Martina Heidfeld, the new German assistant, arrives in England. As is the case every year, accommodation proves hard to find in advance as most landlords want to meet their new tenants before signing a contract. With other things on my mind, I agree to give her the run of my flat whilst I'm in Germany. From our first meeting, it's clear that Martina is a strong-minded woman with superb social skills.

"Will make an excellent assistant," I decide immediately, "but would eat me for breakfast as a girlfriend."

The second leg of the Exchange – in Munich – provides a welcome breath of fresh air. Our visit coincides with the October Beer Festival, so there's every opportunity to drink and be merry. One of the joys of accompanying Sixth Formers on trips to Germany is that they can legally drink beer and wine from the age of sixteen, removing the added burden of having to check up on clandestine boozing.

This year's group is the smallest ever – just five of the Upper Sixth. French and Spanish have also experienced a decline in interest in Exchanges recently. It appears that modern-day students are not particularly keen on receiving 'strangers' into their home. Funny how 'not enough trips' is still the number one criticism emerging from course forums.

As in previous years, I get to stay with Reinhardt and his other half who's given birth to a cute baby boy. The former is extremely busy with schoolwork, which leaves me with a perfect opportunity to do some serious soul-searching alone. In a quiet moment in one of the beer tents – if there is such a thing – I find myself wondering whether this will turn out to be my last Exchange trip. In my present frame of mind, I can't imagine that I'll still be in the teaching profession this time next year. Despite all the magical moments of the past, things have just gone from bad to worse since my foolish transgression with Charlotte R-J and I've simply had enough. As I slowly knock back a beer, I reflect on the highlights of my many previous school trips to France and Germany.

The French trip to a south-eastern suburb of Paris during my second year in teaching was a real eye-opener. It was scheduled to be the last of many for the retiring Head of Languages, Sybil Compton, one of the old school. Keen to involve her junior colleague, she left me to look in on the disco that our French hosts had kindly organised for the Friday night.

"You go, dear," she'd said with a dismissive wave of her hand. "Discotheques are not really my cup of tea."

When I arrived at the hall at around 9.30, I was confronted by a paralytic Tara Burton, a bright, usually responsible fourteen-year-old, screaming dementedly at her Exchange partner's bewildered parents.

"Qu'est-ce qu'il y a?" I asked, coming to the rescue.

"Elle est bourrée et refuse de monter dans la voiture," the anxious father said.

"He says you've had too much to drink and won't get in the car," I tried to inform Tara.

She then bellowed hysterically: "I'm not going with him. Never, never, never!"

"Why not? What's the big deal?"

"He won't wear a seatbelt and a friend of the family was killed not wearing one a few months ago." Further shrieking followed. She had a fair pair of lungs, Tara Burton.

Whilst I persisted in my efforts to pacify her, one of the young lads approached me, out of breath.

"Hazel Morley's been taken off in an ambulance to have her stomach pumped, sir," he said.

I glanced up at the French couple still waiting expectantly for Tara to climb into their car and caught the mother nodding in confirmation.

"Oh, and Polly Wiseman is puking her guts up behind the hall," the boy added.

As a junior member of staff, I had little option but to break the news to poor old Sybil. She was distraught at first, having previously survived fifteen trouble-free visits to the same town. It was only after sincere letters of apology from all three girls that, much to my relief, she retracted her threat to abandon our eagerly awaited trip to EuroDisney. Incidentally, stomach pumping abroad is definitely not to be recommended. Hazel Morley's parents had to fork out a hundred and eighty quid on our return to cover the cost, and that was over ten years ago.

"Mm, much less stressful travelling abroad with Sixth Formers," I nod to myself.

I then recall the case of Catherine Bream, the painfully shy daughter of devoutly Christian parents. She'd surprised me by agreeing to take part in the Munich trip here from *Lower Valley* a couple of years ago. I found it well-nigh impossible to match her accurately with one of the German students, given that she claimed to have no hobbies, to dislike parties and to hate going out. To my relief, I eventually stumbled across a common interest. Like one of the German girls on my list, Catherine had a pet guinea pig. In my usual whimsical manner, I mentioned this to reassure her. A year later, after she'd completed the course, Dr Faulkner received a letter from her parents, in which they accused me of displaying a lack of professionalism when matching up their daughter for the Exchange. Apparently, she'd been subjected to frequent late night parties in Germany and, feeling completely out of place at one of them, had slipped away at midnight and walked back to the house on her own. Funny thing was, every morning when I asked Catherine if there were any problems, she just shook her head. With hindsight, maybe I was fortunate not to receive a formal warning from the Principal for making a fickle reference to a family pet during the course of my professional duties. Now, now!

"Mm, Exchanges have certainly been a highly entertaining part of my teaching career," I reflect nostalgically as I empty my glass.

As in previous years, the five students away with me this time get to experience life in a German school. The passionate but slightly eccentric History/English teacher, Friedrich Kotz, then takes us on a highly enjoyable guided tour of the town, recounting the numerous legends associated with the area. Other excursions during the week involve visits to the 1972 Olympic Stadium/ Bayern München Football Ground, the IMAX Cinema and the impressive Science Museum, amongst other things. 'Other things' this year meaning *Oktoberfest*, naturally.

Any fears that terrorists might target the festival are soon put to the back of our minds as the students and I climb onto our table in one of the beer tents and join in with the traditional drinking songs. Throughout our stay, my troubles back at College seem a million miles away. But all good things must come to an end and I have to return to face the music. As the Germans say: "Alles hat ein Ende, nur die Wurst hat zwei." [Everything has an end, only sausages have two].

Back home, I discover that Martina has been successful in finding accommodation off her own back, which is one less worry for me. At College, I submit the oral handbook and schemes of work for the whole year as requested. Unfortunately, although perhaps not surprisingly,

Godfrey complains that the AS SoW from last year doesn't contain any modifications and needs to be rejigged. As an Economics teacher, I'm not so sure he's adequately qualified to pass judgement. Yvonne, our former Head of Department, once told me an amusing story, which underlines Godfrey's lack of empathy for language teaching. In response to a French student's comment in the end of course review that greater emphasis should've been placed on preparing the class for the *Contemporary Society* paper as opposed to its *Work and Leisure* counterpart, Godfrey had suggested that Yvonne organise a French wine tasting evening for students.

Fed up with my Head of Faculty's pettiness, I decide to air my frustrations with Kevin, the Vice-Principal.

"What's the point," I ask him, "of me being Curriculum Manager for German when someone else, a non-linguist, insists on telling me how to organise my teaching?"

As usual, Kevin finds time to listen carefully to my side of the story.

"Godfrey's written down some stuff about you too, but I haven't had chance to look at that yet," he tells me with a sympathetic smile. "Once the Inspection's out of the way, I'll endeavour to get to the bottom of this. If you can just bear with me ..."

Whilst I'm aware that Kevin is powerless to override any Principal-led incentive – in fact, he was once disciplined himself – at least I've voiced my concerns. What's more, he's a good listener and a strong supporter of Al Bentley, the teacher, which counts for a lot at this demoralising stage in my teaching career.

Shortly after my latest altercation with Godfrey, I enter the language office to find Begonia in floods of tears.

"What's up?" I ask.

She sobs several times. "I don't know what is going on between you and Godfrey," she says, "but I can't stand it."

"Well, if you want me to put you in the picture, I ..."

"No, no, please don't! I don't want to take sides."

To be honest, I was bruised by the way Begonia dropped me as a friend the moment Charlotte R-J went public. And in a funny way, it's almost comforting to know that she's not completely blasé about the whole situation. Is that harsh?

Amidst the madness at work, the day of Shellie's return to Australia finally arrives. Having agreed to avoid anything bordering on the over-emotional – we both hate goodbyes – we spend an amusing final few hours in each other's company.

As the car ferrying her to the airport disappears into the distance – I couldn't take her myself because of work – I feel a large lump in my throat.

Although we're essentially quite different people, circumstances and a mutual aversion to dishonesty and game playing have brought us close together. Well, as close as my defences would allow, anyway. And we certainly shared some great moments. I'll miss her, that's for sure. Before her departure, Shellie made me promise that I'll visit Down Under at some point in the near future and this is a promise I have no intention of breaking.

It's half term and I'm just beginning to get used to life as a single man again. Out of the blue, Jo Black rings from university.

"Hi ya, Al," she says, as chirpy as ever. "How's it going?"

"Oh, hi, Jo. I'm fine, thanks. How about you?"

"Yeah, good, thanks. I've made loads of new friends and got a really cool bloke."

"Oh, have you? C'mon, then, let's hear all about him."

"Well, he's black and over six foot."

"Wow!"

I'm tempted to ask whether she's referring to her new boyfriend's height, but then I remember we're living in the modern world and there's such a thing as political correctness.

"I've gone off white men completely now. They just don't turn me on at all."

Political correctness has obviously passed Jo by. I sense that there must be a cryptic message here somewhere, but I've never been good at reading through the lines, so I decide to take it literally. "Just as well I didn't fall in love with you, then."

"Hm. Has Shellie gone home yet?"

"Er … yes, she has."

"So who've you got lined up next?"

"Give me a chance. She's only been gone a couple of weeks."

"Yeah, but that's never stopped you in the past."

I like Jo. She has this unparalleled capacity for convincing me that I'm the greatest stud that ever lived. Ironically, through trying to protect my heart over the last year, I seem to have made myself into more of a catch. Maybe this is where I went wrong in the past – being too keen, too soon. I think there's definitely a lesson to be learnt here.

On the Friday afternoon before the week of the OfSTED Inspection, I find Kevin Gough hovering at my classroom door as I'm about to leave for home.

"Have you got a minute, Al?" he asks.

"Yes, of course," I reply, trying to guess what he's so eager to discuss. After all, he's never come to see me before in over three years. Surely he hasn't managed to have a word with Godfrey already.

"Al, I … I wanted to say something about Inspection," he says, as if treading on thin ice. "I … I know you're very unhappy here at the moment. You've made that perfectly clear. And … and I can understand why. I'm no great fan of the Professional Standards Payment myself." He pauses for breath. "As you already know, I have enormous respect for you as a language teacher. In fact, you're the best German teacher I've come across in twenty years. The very best!"

"Oh, thanks."

"What I'd like you to do next week is forget about your disagreement with the Principal and go out there and prove to the inspectors what a great teacher you are. Show 'em what you're made of!"

With my morale as low as it is, I'm on the verge of falling for his kind, uplifting words. But only on the verge. I don't have to be brain of Britain to deduce that there's a hidden agenda behind his unexpected visit.

"So the management genuinely thought I was going to scupper their precious Inspection," I smile to myself once Kevin is out of the door.

In reality, however, his words were superfluous. Irrespective of my current state of mind, I'm far too proud to seriously consider deliberately underperforming in front of Her Majesty's inspectors. That just wouldn't be my style.

Before we know it, the week-long invasion of the College by the old enemy is underway. I'm observed teaching just one of my classes in the Language Lab and the hour passes without undue trauma.

On the Thursday afternoon, I'm busy teaching another group in the Lab when Dr Faulkner comes dancing through the door as if all his birthdays have come at once. He apologises for the intrusion and asks if he can address the class briefly.

"I have great pleasure in announcing that every department in the College has been awarded a grade two or above by Her Majesty's inspectors," he says. "This is an exceptional achievement and one that no other Sixth Form College in the country has ever matched." The Master pauses for a reaction, which is low-key at best. He then says: "May I take this opportunity to thank all of you for contributing to the success of this outstanding College."

One of the girls raises her hand.

"Does that mean the inspectors will be leaving now?" she asks.

"No, not yet. They've still got to grade my management team before making tracks."

With this, Dr Faulkner turns on his heels and exits the room, as proud as punch.

"So there's still time for a grade three," I find myself muttering, unaware that the door hasn't clicked shut.

Accustomed to my dry humour, the students scarcely bat an eyelid, with only a handful emitting a modest snigger.

My light-hearted prediction proves, however, to be way off the mark. Instead of letting the side down, the management receives a highly coveted grade one. Furthermore, the local press releases the Principal's beaming photo on the front page of the weekly. Champagne flows throughout the College.

Shortly afterwards, back down on planet earth, one of my German students brings sad news early one morning that I've been expecting but dreading – the death of George Harrison, 'the quiet Beatle', from throat cancer. It seems inconceivable that only two members of the Fab Four, the greatest musical and artistic inspiration of my life, are left. Apart from his often-understated role in the Beatles, George's solo compositions, particularly from the triple album *All Things Must Pass*, lit up many a dark hour in my late teens and early twenties. RIP, George!

Just before the end of term, Dr Faulkner presents me with just the Christmas gift I've been longing for – confirmation that he's rejected my second application for the PSP. I say 'confirmation' since his actions in recent weeks, ably assisted by his loyal servant Godfrey, have left me in little doubt that this would be the outcome. For a split second, though, I did wonder whether he'd be carried away by the post-Inspection euphoria. Oh dear – when will I learn?

With my two written warnings no longer on file, Faulkner has decided to use my 'lack of cooperation' since September as a reason for withholding the payment. Apparently, deadlines have also been missed for schemes of work and the oral handbook. This, in his humble opinion, constitutes 'unprofessional conduct'. I challenge him to produce written evidence that deadlines ever existed, but he waves me away impatiently.

"Godfrey has explained in writing that you've been a difficult and non-cooperative colleague this term and, therefore, my decision is final."

If defending myself in the face of injustice can be equated with being difficult, then I suppose I'm guilty as charged.

A few weeks back, one of the top dogs in the Union rang me at home to discuss my situation. He apologised profusely for the fact that I was wrongly advised about the timescale of my appeal, but promised full Union support through Mr Moyer should my second application fail to be endorsed. A rapid call to the latter confirms that I should appeal at once.

Since evidence is supposed to be drawn from a three-year period up to 12th October 2001, Faulkner's argument about lack of cooperation can logically only refer to a six-week period at the very most, given that it wasn't mentioned as a reason for failing my first application. This is getting complicated.

"I hate to have to tell you this," Mr Moyer says gravely, "but it appears that your Principal has manufactured evidence to prevent you getting the money."

It's no good. Sooner or later, I'm going to have to face up to reality and accept what's been blatantly obvious for some time now. Despite all my efforts over the last eighteen months to get back on track following two indiscretions in almost thirteen years of teaching, Dr Faulkner is trying to alienate me, no doubt in the hope I'll pack my bags and leave. Maybe he's concerned that his picture will appear in the paper one day for entirely the wrong reasons. After all, no College's reputation can possibly be safe with a predatory male like me on the loose, can it? What makes the whole situation even more unbearable is that my two immediate managers, Jennifer and Godfrey, seem to have turned against me too. And I thought they liked me, not just as a teaching colleague, but also as a person.

Not even my redundancy in '97 came close to causing such strong feelings of isolation and rejection. Everyone was so kind and supportive then. Just like in the world of celebrities, where you're only as good as your last performance, I'm being judged purely on the grounds that I was the recipient of two formal written warnings in the space of a term. It's as if my past triumphs have been forgotten or simply negated by the fact that for one tiny part of my professional teaching career I showed signs of human fallibility. The modern world is a tough place to live in, particularly when you're in the public eye.

When the Christmas holiday finally arrives, my sense of relief is enormous. The last thing I need is someone else questioning my integrity as a teacher, especially when 'someone else' turns out to be a female former *Mardall's* student. Visibly under the influence, she approaches me at *Yates's Bar* and asks if there was any truth in the rumour that I was dismissed from the College for sexual misconduct.

A couple of days later at *Bar Med*, another tipsy young lady accuses me of sleeping with Rachel Hill whilst she was still the College.

"She was stunning and it was common knowledge she fancied the pants off you," she says. "C'mon, be honest. No bloke in his right mind would've resisted her."

Why now? Talk about adding insult to injury.

With my drinking partners engaged in pre-Christmas celebrations with their other halves or other friends, I decide to spend the first Saturday of the holiday at *Opportunity Knox* on my own. Well, it was either that or a night stuck in front of the telly. The club is as busy as I can remember it.

About half way through the evening, I head towards the nearest bar, tip-toeing my way round the jubilant party-goers strutting their stuff on the dance floor. My progress, however, is suddenly and rather rudely checked by a hefty shove from behind, which sends me almost cartwheeling into an innocent couple in the midst of a passionate embrace. I spin round instinctively in anticipation of an apology, but realise at once that this won't be forthcoming. The face glaring down at me from the broad, six-foot plus frame belongs to Scott Dixon, the former *Mardall's* student who unleashed a ferocious assault on my reputation a few years ago at *James Dean's*.

"Piss off, Bentley!" he says. "We don't want you anywhere near us, you fucking arsehole."

As I'm reeling from the shock, it soon becomes clear that Dixon is accompanied by an unfamiliar group of mates. Judging by the hostile expression on their faces, they're not exactly overjoyed to see me either. The serene 'teacher voice' in my head urges me to summon up that unflappable veneer honed to perfection during twelve years in the classroom, but on this occasion it eludes me. Not surprisingly, I suppose, the pent-up frustrations and feelings of injustice of recent times have taken their toll. After all, I'm only human – not *just* a teacher, an android devoid of all emotion – aren't I?

"I'm not going anywhere, Scott. If you've got a problem with me, then you can piss … you can *get lost* yourself," I say, struggling to contain my fury.

The words have scarcely left my mouth when the most intimidating-looking member of the gang takes a step closer and places his shaven skull about three inches from my uneasy glare.

"Listen, perv," he says. "Just do as ya fucking told or ya gonna get 'urt."

Teacher bullied by ex-students in Opportunity Knox Night Club – I can see the headline in the weekly rag. Great, just what I need right now. I stand my ground, motionless, bracing myself for a seemingly inevitable onslaught of vindictive blows. Surely it'll only be a matter of seconds. At this point, a young woman I don't recognise emerges from the gathering crowd and parks herself between me and the lads, cupping my head in her hands as if I were a disobedient child about to be admonished.

"Don't be stupid. Just walk away!" she says. "I'd hate to see you get hurt."

Her concern is appreciated, of course, but I'm no coward and backtracking now simply doesn't enter into the equation. I dig in my heels. As she removes her clammy palms from my cheeks, I steal an anxious look around me and can't fail to catch the anticipation, almost excitement, on the faces of those nearby who've abandoned the dance floor in search of something potentially more thrilling.

"We could easily be in the school playground now," I reflect, my heart rate rising by the second.

There's a tense, pregnant pause followed by exchanged glances between the lads, shrugged shoulders and, finally, a retreat.

"Phew, that was a close one!" I sigh, the tension ebbing rapidly from every sinew.

Whether they've decided that I'm just not worth the aggravation or the heavy presence of bouncers has forced them to adjourn is hard to say. Whatever the case, it looks like I've got off lightly … on this occasion.

My sense of relief soon gives way to one of sadness and bewilderment as the numerous alcoholic concoctions that follow start to take effect.

It's a long, reflective walk home, interrupted by frequent about-turns to ensure there's no-one in hot pursuit, pearls of rain streaming down my cheeks. Or are they tears? My teaching career has, without doubt, provided me with more magical moments than I could ever have believed possible when I first braved the classroom back in '89. But now, it seems that the respect I've enjoyed for so many years from those who came into contact with me in a professional capacity is gradually being eroded.

Safely back in the sanctuary of my one-bed bachelor pad, yet blatantly the worse for wear, I sit disgruntled on the lounge floor, with over a decade's worth of my diaries spread out in front of me. I flip through page after page – days, weeks, months and then years – trying desperately to figure out whether I have, after all, been solely responsible for my own demise. Has my quest for true love allowed my professional and private lives to become too closely entangled or have I simply been a victim of unfortunate circumstances? I'm beginning to wonder if we're all allotted a quota of good fortune to last a lifetime and I just happen to have exhausted mine. But I can't go on like this, feeling so heavily downtrodden. Some drastic steps have to be taken.

When I finally hit the sack, I lie awake, trying to figure out exactly why the likes of Scott Dixon harbour such strong feelings of hostility towards me. Would they feel the same way if they'd been a fly on the wall during the last ten years of my life? But maybe I'm missing the point. Whilst I may consider myself to be a monumental failure in the game of love because I've been unable to find lasting romance with one person, perhaps my 'enemies' see it differently. Maybe for them in their early twenties, success with the opposite sex is measured by the number of notches on the bed post with the word 'commitment' nowhere to be found.

SPRING TERM

No matter how much satisfaction an individual derives from his/her job, I think it's fair to say that the majority of employees struggle to approach the post-Christmas return to work with anything more than a modicum of zest. A level language teaching may well be my dream profession, but I'm no exception in this respect. On the eve of the 2002 spring term, however, I find myself experiencing not so much mild reluctance as out and out refusal – like a horse that no longer wishes to jump. The prospect of resuming at *Lower Valley* in the knowledge that I'm the only current member of staff at the top of the main pay scale who hasn't received the two-thousand-pound Professional Standards Payment seems to have sapped my final reserves of energy and enthusiasm. It feels as if Dr Faulkner's additional punishment has nullified all the positive contributions I've made over the last three years and, therefore, stripped me of my dignity. I've considered breaking my contract, yet with important exams just round the corner the students would suffer and I won't have that. It appears that my professional conscience is in direct conflict with my quest for personal happiness, leaving me clueless how to reconcile both.

Why is it I have this nagging feeling I'd be in a more favourable position now had I caved in completely to Charlotte Rhys-Jones' attentions two years ago and engaged in a full-blown romance? Is it because I've finally wised up to the fact that, for her, the novelty of dating an older man – a teacher at that – would've almost certainly subsided quickly, and I'd have been dumped without the bat of an eyelid and, possibly, without the management ever knowing. I'm not suggesting for one moment that this is a course of action I should've pursued. However, it does rankle that my attempts to do the right thing after initially stepping out of line have proved so heavily counter-productive. I suppose the same could be said of Margaret Becker's actions. I'm sure her decision to inform Charlotte's tutor about the former's phone calls to me was motivated by a desire to do the right thing. Only, it backfired massively.

After considerable soul-searching, I make up my mind to steal myself for one final fling at *Lower Valley* until the May 31st deadline. Then, regardless of the outcome of my PSP appeal, I'll hand in my notice and move on to pastures new at the end of the academic year. I'm even contemplating selling the flat and relocating to the West Country where, according to the *Rightmove* website, property is significantly more favourably priced. If my calculations prove accurate, I should be able to afford a three-bed semi again and have enough spare cash to take a six-month sabbatical from teaching. Right now, I can't think of anything more appealing.

During the first week back at work, Dr Faulkner passes me in the corridor and announces that the Sixth Form College Forum that deals with PSP appeals has faxed him the date of my hearing – 26th March in Havant. I relay the news at once to Mr Moyer, the Union Rep, who receives it with scepticism.

"The Forum is supposed to be an independent body, there to provide an unbiased hearing," he says. "You should've been sent written confirmation of the date of your hearing, not informed verbally by the Principal, your opponent."

"What are you intimating?" I ask.

"Well, considering that Robert Faulkner served on the Forum himself until relatively recently, it's beginning to resemble a gentlemen's club. I was worried this might happen."

"But surely there's no way the hearing can be anything other than neutral, particularly when there's so much money at stake."

"One would hope not, but I do have my concerns. You're in the unfortunate position of working under a Principal who is well-respected in the sector and has many contacts."

Feeling certain that a lack of professionalism of this order couldn't possibly exist in a national institution like our education system, I take Mr Moyer's comments with a pinch of salt.

On the final Saturday in January, I drive down to Yeovil in Somerset, accompanied by Martina Heidfeld, the German assistant. We book into a double room for the night above a pub. Whilst this may, on the surface, appear to be the perfect dirty weekend away, it is in fact a house-hunting expedition. Rather than tackle it alone, I thought Martina could offer advice from a female perspective. What's more, it'll give her the chance to see another part of the country. The two of us have become good friends recently and although Martina considers me not bad-looking, there is, apparently, 'something' missing. Now where have I heard that before? As for the double room, well, that's all they had available.

The first two three-bed semis that we view are ideal in terms of size, location and affordability. Both are on the market for twenty-five grand less than the valuation given for my one-bed flat in the City. There's the added bonus in both cases of a garage and off-road parking – as much of a priority for me now as before.

The third house is older and in urgent need of modernization. With the owner on holiday, we're given a guided tour by an American tenant in his early twenties. He's not much of a looker, yet there's no mistaking the immediate chemistry between him and Martina. Once it's clear that I'm not interested in the house, a friendly conversation ensues, during which I disclose that we're staying overnight to get a taste of the local nightlife. Aware that my companion and I are just friends, the American, Troy, proposes we meet later in town so he can show us the hot spots. Subtle move, mate!

After dinner, Martina and I catch up with Troy as planned and he takes us on a tour of the busiest pubs. Any fears I may've harboured about the town being too quiet are quickly allayed.

"The chicks here are so easy," our American friend reveals with Martina out of earshot. "I've screwed fifty-seven of them in the past six months."

In the light of his confident, almost arrogant, persona, I've no reason to doubt him. During the course of the evening, he gives me a discreet nod each time we pass one of his conquests. I try to memorise their faces for future reference.

Inevitably, Troy pulls Martina, in a club not dissimilar in layout to *James Dean's*, leaving me to acknowledge once again that men who show little respect for women often only have to snap their fingers to attract them. Much to my relief, however, Troy fails to get his leg over on this occasion and I'm left to share the pub's double bed with whom I'm sure he'd already pencilled in as number fifty-eight.

Martina and I return home on Sunday morning in total agreement about which house was the most desirable. Since it'd fit my needs perfectly, I decide there's no point in looking any further and put in an offer, which is duly accepted. With a buyer for my flat already lined up, the ball is set in motion.

Back at work, there's an extra spring in my step that's been missing for some time.

"Did I ever tell you about my first girlfriend?" I ask one of my two *Lower Sixth* German groups at the end of their Tuesday lesson.

"Yes, several times," two or three of them answer in unison.

"Tell us again, though," one of the girls urges. "I can't remember the punch line."

"Okay. Well, it's a very short one. Basically, the girl dumped me to go out with a baker. Apparently, he *kneaded* her more than I did."

An almighty groan fills the classroom.

"Oh, and he could also offer her more dough."

Further groans follow from all sides, meaning, of course, that they like my joke. As it happens, my first girlfriend really did go out with a baker after me and they ended up tying the knot. There were no flowers or confetti at the wedding, just flour.

Valentine's Day arrives on the Thursday of half term. I agree to spend the evening in the company of Martin Studd down in Chichester, which is where his parents live. To the disappointment of the two lonely-heart teachers, there's a noticeable lack of women in the town's main pubs and bars. All having dinner with their boyfriends, no doubt. Martin entertains me with stories from his relatively short teaching career. By far the best one revolves around a night out with some of his colleagues that resulted in frequent encounters with members of their school's Sixth Form.

"I got so wasted," Martin says, "that two other teachers had to carry me out of the pub to a nearby taxi in full view of our students. I was then whisked back to the flat of one of my house-proud colleagues, only to throw up all over her new carpet."

I cringe and say: "Oh dear!"

"Rather than disapprove, the Sixth Form now think I'm a real star, particularly the girls."

Students, eh – they're so easy to please. Martin, however, has always preferred the attentions of more mature women and it doesn't take him long to pick out two ladies in their mid- to late-thirties sitting alone. Before I have chance to stall him, he rises from his seat and sidles across to their table. After a few moments, he signals for me to join him. I oblige somewhat grudgingly.

My reluctance to play the game is all too blatant, which prompts Kirsty, the more outspoken and intimidating of the two, to bombard me with criticism.

"You really think you're it, don't you," she says rather harshly, "with your leather jacket and boots?"

I protest that I think nothing of the sort, but my words fall on deaf ears. Further attempts at character assassination follow and I breathe a sigh of relief when closing time arrives. But Martin has other ideas and accepts an invitation for the two of us to join both ladies for drinks at Kirsty's house. It appears that he has his sights on her friend, Maureen.

Back at the house, there are pictures of Kirsty's two teenage children on the wall. Both seem angelic in comparison to their rather formidable mother. It transpires that their father moved out a while back. As the evening progresses and more alcohol is consumed, Kirsty gradually changes her tune towards me. She even asks if she can put my number on her mobile. Not thinking anything of it, I comply with her request.

"He's not really that bad, after all," she tells her friend, Maureen, whose affections Martin has already won over.

By about 2.00, we're all done in and ready for bed. Kirsty organises her guests for the night.

"Right, you two can sleep down here on the sofa," she tells the two Ms assertively. "And you, Al, can come upstairs with me. You must be really quiet, though, cos I don't want my kids to know that you're sleeping in my bed."

Dressed in a T-shirt and boxers, I climb under the duvet with Kirsty. We chat freely for a good half an hour and – shock, horror – there's even a small amount of kissing. I think this is what's generally referred to as 'going with the flow'. After all, it was Valentine's Day yesterday.

In the morning, Kirsty sneaks me out of her room back down into the lounge. She introduces Martin and me to her two children, implying that all three visitors slept downstairs. After breakfast, Martin and I thank Kirsty for her hospitality. Maureen then kindly drops us back to Martin's parents' house.

"How did you get on?" I ask Martin as Maureen's car disappears out of sight.

"She gave me a wicked blow job," he says. "But that's all."

"D'you think you'll be seeing her again?"

"I doubt it. She's plagued with psychological disorders and on medication. How 'bout you?"

"She was actually really nice on a one-to-one, but you know me – I still haven't given up hope of meeting someone who hasn't been married and doesn't have kids. Still, it was a new experience – kissing a woman over the age of thirty-five."

"Mm, it was a bit of a bizarre evening all round."

In the early hours of Monday morning, I'm awoken by the phone. I pick up to the noise of excessive giggling down the other end of the line. When it stops, a familiar voice says: "Hello, my little pork sausage. How are you this morning?"

It's Kirsty. She explains that she's doing a night shift with Maureen at the nursing home where they both work and that she fancied a chat. She sounds drunk. I engage in a conversation just to be polite, but soon draw it to a close, given that I'll have to get up for work in less than five hours. Kirsty appears to understand. However, as soon as I've replaced the receiver, she calls again with further talk of little pork sausages. I wonder where she got that from. She certainly didn't get to see my 'little banger' on Saturday night. Just a term of endearment, I guess (hope). After wishing her goodnight for the second time, the phone rings again. On this occasion, I allow the answer machine to cut in. *Hello, my little pork sausage,* the message goes. *Is my little pork sausage not going to talk to me this time, then? So you've got work in the morning, have you, my little pork sausage, blah, blah, blah.*

When she finally shuts up, I curl up again with the duvet wrapped round me, relieved that I can now finally get some more kip. No sooner have I done so, however, than the phone rings once more. With my patience and sense of humour wearing thin, I pull the lead out of the socket.

"What possessed me to let her have my number?" I ask myself. "She's completely nuts. What was it Martin was saying about women of our age being more mature?"

Over the next few days, there are further messages from a drunken Kirsty. In addition to "little pork sausage", she refers to me as "little willy". I decide not to return her calls.

I don't think I've mentioned this before, but one of my current neighbours is a teacher in the Economics and Business Studies Department at work. Her name is Lindsay and she's a couple of years younger than I am. Occasionally, we give each other a lift to and from College and, consequently, have got to know each other quite well.

One afternoon in late February, we're heading back to the City in Lindsay's car when she asks about the origins of my dispute with Godfrey, one of her immediate colleagues. Trusting her discretion, I relate the whole story from my transgression with Charlotte through to the failed PSP application. She empathizes with my position, but then goes on to make a rather depressing observation.

"Your problem," she says, "is that you won't let go of the idea that there's a sweet, lovely young lady out there for you who's honest and genuine, and who'll never let you down. But I'm telling you, she doesn't exist. Sure, most women – me included – are capable of behaving like that if they think it'll get them what they want. But in reality, we're all devious, manipulative cows who'll stop at nothing to get our own way."

Whilst I have to admit that Lindsay is spot on in her assessment of the type of woman I'm looking for, I really hope her rather damning attack on the female of the species is off the mark.

At the beginning of March, I drive to Wimbledon Station in the company of Minty Brooker, my best friend at junior school. Now a carpenter, he recently built some stylish wardrobes for mum and dad. It was while he was in the process of fitting them that I called in on the folks one evening. Minty and I hadn't spoken for years and we really enjoyed catching up on each other's news. He mentioned that he'd made contact with a few other old schoolmates via the *Friends Reunited* website and was planning to arrange a get-together in London. He suggested I joined him.

I park the car round the corner from the station and we catch the tube to *The Strand*. In one of the popular pubs, we meet up with four other lads. Of the six of us, it transpires that four are married with children, one has a girlfriend but no kids, and the other – a certain Alan Bentley – has no wife, no girlfriend and no offspring. It's great to see them all again, although I can't help feeling that I've been left behind in the game of life.

About half way through the evening, a young woman passes us on her way back from the toilet. She stops and asks me if I have a light. She's rather attractive and I curse myself for the umpteenth time for forgetting to carry a lighter in my pocket. Fortunately, one of my old school chums comes to the rescue. With her fag lit, the woman, Sian, sticks around and strikes up conversation with me. Behind her back, I can see raised eyebrows and nods of approval from the other lads.

"I work for a computer company round the corner," she tells me, handing over her card. "I often come here after work with some of my colleagues."

She points in their direction at the far side of the pub by the door.

Over the next hour, Sian and I go through the usual 'getting to know each other' routine. She's remarkably easy to talk to and appears fascinated to hear about my language teaching, gym coaching and motor racing. I apologise to the others when she nips off to the toilet, but they're not particularly bothered, urging me to "keep up the good work".

By closing time, it's come to my attention that Sian is starting to slur her words rather badly. Each time she takes her hand off the bar, she has to replace it rapidly to avoid collapsing in a heap on the floor.

"Al, we're all going to make a move now," Minty whispers into my ear.

"Oh, okay," I reply, turning round to face him. "I'll be right there."

"Don't worry, I've had a word with Anthony and he's going to give me a lift back in his Porsche Boxter."

"You sure?"

"Yeah, 'course. Looks like you're well in there." He gives me a wink. "And she's a bit of all right."

I say goodnight to the five lads and return to Sian, just in time to prop her up as she attempts to move away from the bar.

"Where're all your friends?" I ask.

"They've l...left," she says. "They th...thought you l...looked tru...trust...worthy enough."

With me supporting her right arm, the two of us exit the pub cautiously. Once out in the fresh air, Sian spots a brand new Landrover Discovery parked directly in front of the entrance.

"Oh n...no, no way!" she says, trying to free herself. "There's n...no way I'm ... I'm g...going in that. I c...can't stand that. P...public d...displays of wealth. Get off me!"

I remind her of our earlier conversation about my exclusive interest in sporty Italian cars, but she doesn't take a blind bit of notice and pushes me away. With no-one to hold onto, she then loses her footing and slumps down onto the pavement, her back thudding up against the lower part of the pub's façade. I step forward to help her to her feet.

"N...no, not in th...that," she says. "I kn...now men like y...you. You only w...want one thing."

"Sian, that's not my car," I say firmly. "Mine's parked at Wimbledon Station and I'm taking the tube back there once I've made sure that you've got home safely, okay? There's no way I'm leaving you here in this state."

At last my words seem to have registered and she allows me to haul her back up onto her feet. We then proceed in the direction of the underground station at little more than a snail's pace. Negotiating the long staircase accessing the platforms proves to be a major undertaking. It requires all my strength to prevent Sian pulling both of us head first to the bottom, her limp, dead-weight frame attracting amused glances from passers-by.

Once on the train, I breathe a huge sigh of relief. Sitting opposite me, Sian opens her mouth to speak.

"I w...want you to f...fuck me se...senseless," she says, attempting to keep her voice down.

Unfortunately, the handful of other midnight travellers in our carriage aren't engaged in conversation and hear every word. Out of the corner of my eye, I catch them wriggling uneasily in their seats.

"I think we'll just concentrate on getting you home," I tell her, for want of something better to say.

"H...home? You w...want to take me h...home? I kn...know your s...sort. St...stay away fr...from me."

I smile awkwardly at the onlookers before trying to change the subject: "I wish they had a toilet on board. I'm bursting."

With a surge of energy from nowhere, Sian levers herself to her feet, staggers across towards me and starts pressing vigorously on my bladder. The result only increases my desire to go and, with my legs crossed, I wrestle playfully with her until she's back in her seat. By this time, our fellow travellers have relaxed noticeably and it's even possible to detect a flicker of a smile on the lips of a couple of them.

"How the hell did I manage to end up in this situation?" I ponder as the train rattles on towards its destination.

Before arriving at her stop, Sian contradicts herself several more times by claiming, on the one hand, that she wants me to "fuck her brains out" and, on the other, that she's not going to allow me to take advantage of her. And all I can think of is not wetting myself.

At the sight of me remaining on the platform after helping her to alight safely, Sian expresses further concern that I'm planning to use and abuse her. I reassure her that I just want to empty my bladder and make sure she catches the right bus.

I head off for a pee. On my return a few minutes later, I spot Sian already sitting on her bus, which is slowly moving out of the station. Not knowing whether to laugh or cry at the evening's events, I walk wearily back to the platform to pick up the next train to Wimbledon. Once again, I recall Martin Studd's words about more mature women. Mind you, Sian was only twenty-nine. Hm.

A couple of days before my PSP hearing, Cynthia, the Principal's PA, asks to see me.

"I'm afraid your appeal's been cancelled," she says. "I'm not sure why. They haven't given a reason."

I pass on the news to Mr Moyer who again expresses dissatisfaction with the lack of direct contact from the Forum.

Mr Moyer is even more unhappy a week later when I send him a copy of a fax Dr Faulkner received after the appeal date, confirming its cancellation. It begins: *Dear Robert ...*

"What did I tell you?" he says. "It's a gentlemen's club. I'm going to file an official complaint about the procedures. If you hadn't notified me in person, I'd have had a wasted journey to Havant."

Jo Black rings at the start of the Easter holidays and suggests meeting up for a drink. Sitting in a bar in her home town, I'm pleased to discover that she's really taken to university life. Moreover, she seems to be besotted with her boyfriend.

"What about you?" she asks. "Isn't it about time you found someone special?"

"Well, it's not for the want of trying," I reply and relate the Sian story. I also inform her of my imminent move to Somerset and six-month sabbatical.

"What about Shellie? Are you still in contact with her?"

"We speak on the phone every now and again. In fact, I'm planning to visit her just before Christmas."

Jo turns her nose up, but won't explain her reaction when I question it.

With help from my friend Roger 'Sailor' and my parents, I leave the City for good at the start of April to take up residence in Yeovil. With a further two and a half months of the current academic year at *Lower Valley* still to run, my plan is to live with mum and dad during the week, then return to my new home at weekends. Whilst I'm excited at the prospect of making a clean break, there's no way I'd have considered turning my back on the City had my circumstances been different. During my five years there, so much happened. Whilst it may not all have been good, one thing is certain – there was never a dull moment.

SUMMER TERM

My hopes of a smooth, uneventful conclusion to my four-year stint at *Lower Valley* are dashed by a bilingual student called Andreas who's in my Upper Sixth German group. Although a fluent German speaker and an above average writer of the language, he's by no means perfect grammatically and submits a second piece of written coursework on a complex topic that contains no errors whatsoever. When viewed alongside his first submission, there's simply no comparison. Concerned that the Examining Board may reject the work on the grounds of plagiarism, I ask Martina for her opinion. She knows Andreas well from her conversation classes and agrees wholeheartedly with my assessment.

I keep Andreas back after one of the lessons and express my reservations in as tactful a manner as I can muster. He denies that the essay in question is anything other than his own work, but agrees to produce all his resources for my inspection. Before he does so, however, I find myself on the receiving end of a phone call from his irate mother.

"How dare you accuse my son of cheating!" she rages.

I try my utmost to placate her, explaining that it could prove disastrous for Andreas if the matter isn't cleared up before I send the essay off to the Board for moderation.

"If they harbour the same suspicions that I do," I add, "and I have been marking coursework for almost ten years, then it could be too late to do anything about it."

After fifteen minutes or so, she begins to soften her tone and requests more precise details of the resources I'll need to inspect.

Later in the day, the College's Senior Tutor summons me to her office for clarification of the difficult situation brewing with Andreas and his mother. She backs me one hundred per cent, but stresses that we must continue to tread carefully. Whilst I'm confident that I've proceeded in the most professional manner possible, it's just typical that a further controversial issue should rear its ugly head just a few weeks before my rearranged PSP hearing.

After further discussions with Andreas and close analysis of his resources, I'm unable to find sufficient evidence to support my plagiarist theory. Acting on the instructions of my senior colleagues, I send a cover note to the Board with the suspect essay, stating that the author is bilingual and that he's worked hard to improve on the standard of grammar evident in his first submission. I'm not totally happy with this, but I console myself with the thought that Andreas is a grade A student, anyway.

A few days before my PSP hearing, I have a lengthy phone conversation with Mr Moyer, in which we discuss our final moves. Since my two formal warnings didn't feature in my second failed application, our defence is limited to dismantling Dr Faulkner's claim that I behaved unprofessionally during the first six weeks of the autumn term by missing deadlines and being uncooperative. Even though Godfrey had responded to my request for written confirmation that deadlines had in fact existed for the submission of schemes of work by claiming that the case was *sub judice*, I've managed to gather a significant amount of other evidence in my favour.

"I think we've got a good case," Mr Moyer says confidently. "That is, if they'll allow the illegal second application to stand."

Towards the end of May at a school in Havant, the Chairman of the Sixth Form College Forum informs an expectant Mr Moyer and me that the start of my appeal hearing will be delayed for twenty minutes whilst the panel rereads the Rules and Regulations Manual. Mr Moyer raises his eyes to the heavens, then shakes his head in disbelief.

"You wouldn't credit it, would you?" he says. "So unprofessional!"

Eventually, we're summoned to meet the four-strong panel and Forum secretary. We take a seat opposite them around a large table. To our left is Dr Faulkner, trying his best to display an air of quiet confidence. The Chairman coughs nervously before addressing the Principal.

"I'm sorry, Robert," he says, "but I'm afraid you contravened the PSP regulations by allowing Mr Bentley a second bite of the cherry before a year had elapsed."

Mr Moyer nods his head feverishly in the direction of the Principal, whose stiff upper lip fails to conceal a cocktail of indignation and embarrassment. The Chairman then proposes we hold an alternative appeal based on my original application. This is acceptable to all parties, although Mr Moyer requests an adjournment, which is duly granted. After further discussion amongst the eight of us present, it's agreed that my revised case will be heard at the end of June. Dr Faulkner offers *Lower Valley* as a venue. Everyone accepts.

"I can't believe so many people have had to come all this way for that sham," I say to Mr Moyer once we're out in the car park. "Surely someone could've read the regulations beforehand and prevented so many wasted journeys."

"I couldn't agree with you more," he says. "Still, I think it ruffled your Principal's feathers to be told he was in the wrong."

The day before the resignation deadline, I submit a letter to Dr Faulkner, announcing my decision to leave the College at the end of the academic year. I stress that I've found it increasingly difficult over the past year to summon up my usual level of motivation and enthusiasm in an environment where I no longer feel appreciated. He writes back a few lines, expressing his surprise that I was looking for alternative employment, but wishing me all the best for the future.

After initial deliberation, I decide to come clean with my Lower Sixth groups about my imminent departure. Not wishing to fob them off, I explain that a dispute with the Principal over money has left me feeling so undervalued that I've reached the end of my tether. They appear genuinely disappointed and ply me with questions about the exact nature of the dispute, which I manage to evade.

After my first few weekends in Yeovil, my initial impression of the social scene is that it's fairly promising. Troy, America's answer to Don Juan, has now returned to the States, which, in a way, is a relief since his amazing capacity for pulling the local women was beginning to make me feel deeply inadequate. I haven't made any proper friends as yet, but my face is becoming more familiar in town and there are several people who come over for a chat when they see me out. Despite Rupert's warning that I wouldn't find so many 'fit' women in the West Country, I have to say that there isn't a shortage of stunners in the places I've been frequenting.

Back at College, the day of my rearranged PSP appeal hearing arrives before I know it. In addition to those present at the previous fiasco is a Teachers' Union top dog who's supposed to act as an independent observer. Why he didn't attend last time, I'm not sure. I also don't understand why he comes from the Union I'm affiliated to and not one of the others. Mr Moyer is also none the wiser.

"Still, it should ensure that we have access to some decent feedback at the end," he says buoyantly.

The Chairman kicks off the hearing by announcing that it's not the responsibility of the Forum to determine whether Dr Faulkner was right in issuing me with two formal written warnings in 2000. As far as he's concerned, it was and remains a College matter. He stresses that instead focus will be placed purely on the gathered evidence supporting my application. Aware that we're well equipped with proof that I've met all of the required standards, Mr Moyer purses his lips and nods his head slowly in apparent approval. My faith in a fair trial also receives a timely boost.

Mr Moyer is then called upon to present my case. He proceeds to take the panel through the various bits of supporting evidence, of which they all have a copy. He then goes on to state that whilst he agrees in principle with the Chairman's views on the formal warnings, it isn't possible to leave them entirely out of the equation when attempting to defend my entitlement to receive the PSP. He points out that there's no section in the official PSP Regulations Manual which states that formal written warnings can be used to bar a teacher from making a successful application. He also makes it known that the Principal deviated from the agreed PSP procedures by a) not returning the original application form with comments clearly made on it – I received a letter instead – and b) not supplying me with details of the appeals process.

On the subject of the unmarked work found in my bag, he draws attention to the results of several course forums and post course reviews, in which students confirmed the punctual and thorough nature of my marking. In other words, the formal warning was issued for a one-off incident. He then goes on to demonstrate how paper with print on both sides, like the past exam papers in question, is almost double the thickness of blank paper, giving the impression that the sheets found in my file were more numerous than was actually the case. I like it!

Moving on to the more sensitive issue of my improper conduct with a female student, Mr Moyer mentions that he has no intention of passing judgement on the appropriateness of the punishment metered out at the disciplinary hearing. However, he emphasizes the fact that Charlotte's parents didn't request a formal investigation and asks how, in the light of this and the *informal* disciplinary hearing that ensued, a *formal* warning could've resulted. He describes it as "double Dutch". A brief mention of Charlotte's confession to the Assistant Principal that she'd developed a crush on me is also made. He then questions whether, as a highly responsible Principal, Dr Faulkner would've allowed me to travel to Germany alone with an Exchange party just a couple of months after formally warning me of my conduct if he'd thought I posed a serious threat to the girls in the group.

During the course of his defence, Dr Faulkner tries his utmost to convince the panel that I'd made all the running with Charlotte and that he had to punish me with a formal warning to reduce the risk of further acts of inappropriate conduct with other female students. What, he thinks I'd put myself through all that again? He defends his decision to allow the Exchange to go ahead, on the grounds that he had no desire either to jeopardise the students' progress in German or portray the College in an unfavourable light by having to cancel it. After all, I was the only German teacher. He denounces Mr Moyer's views on the quantity of unmarked work and stresses that the punishment was totally appropriate, even for a first offence.

The Chairman concludes the hearing by asking all parties involved whether there are any further questions. When the panel retires to discuss and weigh up the arguments on both sides, I feel confident that Mr Moyer has presented a strong case technically. However, Dr Faulkner spoke with such vehemence and passion that I can't help wondering if I'd have been better off presenting some, if not all, of my case myself – so the Forum could've seen what sort of person I am.

An hour later, the panel resurfaces. The Chairman announces with a flourish that the Principal's decision not to endorse my application will stand.

"I shall be writing to you shortly," the secretary of the Forum tells me.

Dr Faulkner gives a nod of acknowledgement and rises triumphantly from his seat. Inside, I feel an overwhelming sense of defeat, and an intense desire to shout and scream from the rooftops. I want to ask the panel how they arrived at such a crucial decision after Mr Moyer had presented such convincing evidence in my favour. On top of this, I want to ram home to them how tough it's been for such a proud man to have to continue working in a job where he's felt totally unappreciated and undervalued for the best part of nine months. And more than anything else, I want to tell them that they've just driven a teacher away from the profession after thirteen years of continuous service. After all, surely there's no way I'll ever wish to return after this.

Fortunately, I manage to remain tight-lipped and withdraw from the room without a word or hint of overt emotion. Mr Moyer apologises for the outcome. His senior colleague from the Union takes us to one side and relays the information that the panel had deliberated long and hard before deciding that my failure to appeal against my two formal warnings had implied guilt and, therefore, tipped the balance.

"I was rather confused by their reasoning after what the Chairman had said at the start of the hearing," he adds.

His words only serve to heighten my frustration. Only a few days ago, I reminded Mr Moyer of the importance of stating my reasons for not appealing. However, in view of the Chairman's opening words, he deemed it unnecessary.

"If it was such a critical issue, why didn't they ask me about it at the end?" I enquire.

Neither Mr Moyer nor his senior colleague is able to provide a logical explanation. After further discussion, we finally shake hands. I thank both men for their efforts, before strolling disconsolately off to lunch.

On my way back from the refectory, I pass the Principal, providing the Forum's secretary with a guided tour of the new building. They're laughing and joking like old friends. Talk about adding insult to injury!

In my frustration, I pay Margaret a visit a few days later in her Personal Tutor's office.

"You do realise that your decision to interfere in the Charlotte Rhys-Jones business has had huge repercussions," I tell her collectedly. "Had you left well alone and not ignited her wrath, you would've spared me and the College considerable grief."

Margaret keeps her lips tightly shut and refrains from making eye-contact.

"I know it's no good crying over spilt milk," I continue, "but I just wanted to make my feelings known. After all, it has ended up losing me two thousand pounds."

Sometimes, speaking one's mind, however inappropriate, can be richly therapeutic.

Back in the autumn, I failed to mention that my first season of motor racing actually brought me a trophy – for finishing third in the Rookie Cup. With the new season well underway, I find myself setting out for *Mallory Park* from Rupert's house, where the race car is still kept, at 5.00 am on the Sunday immediately after my PSP hearing. With me is my mum's brother, Paul, a keen motor sport enthusiast.

Over ten hours later, we're back home in a far more sombre mood than we'd have believed possible earlier in the day. Before my race had even been run, a driver in another championship was tragically killed after what can only be described as a 'racing accident'. The meeting was subsequently abandoned out of respect for the poor bloke's family. Rupert is busy packing for his holiday and hardly bats an eyelid when, still visibly shaken, I relate the day's events. Seeing that he's agreed to put me up for the night, I ask if I can make a local call to Pat Baines who prepared my car. He agrees.

Ten minutes into our depressing conversation, Rupert screams at me to stop taking the piss and get off the effing line. Rather embarrassingly, Pat hears every word of his verbal assault. Once I've hung up, Rupert proceeds to give me a lecture on abusing someone else's generosity. Infuriated by his insensitivity and unbelievable tight-fistedness, I head off to the pub.

I return three pints later to face more of my so-called friend's wrath. Steeled by the alcohol in my blood and high on emotion after a difficult week, I decide to fight back.

"Somebody died today!" I yell at him. "It could've been me."

And before I know it, I've clouted him with a flat hand round his right jaw.

In response, Rupert unleashes himself on me like a wounded tiger and the two of us wrestle on the kitchen floor like a pair of angry school kids. There's a large bread knife within reach and, concerned by the state of Rupert's now seemingly uncontrollable fury, I decide to back off.

"That's it, I've had enough of all this," I say, rising to my feet. "I'm off now."

I gather up my belongings and pack the car. Aware that I'm almost certainly over the limit and definitely not in a fit state to drive, I give Roger 'Sailor' a quick call from my mobile. As generous as ever, he offers to fetch me and put me up for the night. Before he arrives, however, Rupert attempts to make up, handing back the ten pence piece I left to cover the phone call to Pat.

"It wasn't about the money," he says.

His words, however, fall on deaf ears. I leave shortly afterwards with Roger, determined to put this part of my life behind me.

After a good night's sleep, I awake feeling somewhat embarrassed about my reaction last night. It seems that a whole string of related events simply took me to breaking point. Rupert's undermining of my self-confidence with the ladies. The fact that I was forced to sell my lovely house to him because teaching didn't pay well enough for me to sustain such a high mortgage. My indiscretion with Charlotte brought about by years of failed romance and insecurities about my ability to attract the opposite sex long-term. The effect this had on my PSP application, a long-awaited opportunity to earn a significant amount of extra money. And ... the list goes on. But in the cold light of day, I can see that these events are mere trifles when compared with the loss of a life. Although I feel certain that in the immediate future my blood pressure will rise markedly every time reference is made to those dreaded letters P...S...P, I have to get things in perspective. I now have the opportunity to leave behind my unpleasant experiences and begin a new life somewhere else, a privilege my fellow driver will sadly never enjoy.

My final day at *Lower Valley Sixth Form College* arrives in early July. Dr Faulkner wishes to speak to me in his office.

"You shot yourself in the foot by challenging my decision on your first PSP application," he tells me. "If you'd done as you were told, I'd have passed your second application without batting an eyelid."

"But ... but it would've been illegal," I say. "The Forum made that perfectly clear at the first hearing."

"Nevertheless, I would've put it through and no-one would've noticed."

And they call it the *Professional* Standards Payment. More like *Principal's* Standards Payment, if you ask me.

Astounded by what I'm hearing, I rise from the armchair, ready to leave. But his Lordship hasn't finished. "As it is, I shall not be writing you a good reference. You have to learn to behave in a more respectful manner towards your employer."

I open my mouth to remind him that I've worked under three Head Teachers and one other Principal without the slightest acrimony, but decide that such a retort would serve no purpose and close it again.

"And you just couldn't resist having a snipe at me when I came into the Language Lab during Inspection, could you?" Faulkner says finally as I'm about to leave his office for the last time. "And Margaret. I hear you couldn't refrain from pestering her with your criticisms either."

Bidding farewell to my Lower Sixth classes is no easy task. One of them, however, has a surprise in store. Tom Banks, a good linguist and highly accomplished musician, takes out his guitar and performs a rejigged version of the Oasis hit *Wonderwall*. Apparently, one of the girls, Kelly, helped him alter the original lyrics. After a stunning solo performance, the whole group joins in with a second take.

> *Today is going to be the day that you're moving to Somerset.*
> *I'm sure, you've heard it all before, but a better teacher we won't get.*
> *I don't believe that anybody can speak German the way ... the way that you do.*
> *We'll spit, we'll throw him in a pit, Dr Robert Faulkner we will hit*
> *He's a goon, looks like a spoon, I bet his wife isn't fit.*
> *I don't believe that anybody can speak German the way ... the way that you do.*
> *And even though German is confusing, you make it easier for using.*
> *There is something that we'd like to say to you, but we don't know how.*
> *We said maybe, you made our lessons crazy, and although you travel far,*
> *You are 'wunderbar!'*

On this note, my thirteen-year teaching career draws to a close, with a touching send-off from those who have always been closest to my heart, perhaps too close at times – my students.

I'll Follow the Sun

(Epilogue)

One day you'll look and see I've gone
For tomorrow may rain, so I'll follow the sun.

The months have rolled on since my 'escape' from *Lower Valley* and here I am on the last Sunday in November, sat in the Departure Lounge of Heathrow Airport with my nose stuck in a book – an entertaining one relating the experiences of a former school inspector. The amusing anecdotes are providing a perfect foil to the apprehension I feel about flying in the light of 9/11.

Although a year has elapsed since she left England and there's a new boyfriend on the scene, Shellie, my ex-girlfriend, was only too happy for me to pay her a visit Down Under during my six months of leisure. So for only the second time since I entered the teaching profession in '89 – I had a week in Crete in September – I've been able to take advantage of more favourably priced, out-of-season travel.

Free from the day-to-day pressures of the classroom, there's been ample opportunity to reflect on my life so far, particularly my action-packed thirteen-year teaching career. I think I can say with a degree of conviction that, regardless of our educational backgrounds, the majority of us approaching the dreaded four-zero can lay claim to an A level in hindsight. What a fantastic place the world would be if, with the wave of a magic wand, we could step back in time and transform all our 'if onlys' into reality.

If I could have my time again, I'd enlist at once the services of a guru like Paul McKenna in an attempt to banish my infuriatingly fluctuant self-esteem. I'd start dating from as young an age as possible and certainly endeavour to gain some sexual experience well before the ripe old age of twenty-six. I'd resist all predilections to naivety and downright stupidity, and, above all, steer clear of girls in their late teens in my quest for serious romance, especially if they happened to be my present or ex-students. Oh yes, there'd be no falling for the flattering but ephemeral attentions of the likes of Rachel Hill, Charlotte Rhys-Jones and co.

Then again, in a perfect world, this story would, of course, never have been told. And anyway, since nothing lasts forever, who's to say that a life bereft of true love yet adorned with richly diverse and fascinating experiences is any less rewarding than a more mundane existence spent in the company of an adoring soul mate? Who knows, maybe one day – and that's a huge MAYBE – cupid will fire his bow and I'll be in a position to confirm or refute this theory.

Whether I'll return to the teaching profession when my money runs out, I haven't a clue. The results published in August did, however, set my pulse racing once again. My two Lower Sixth German AS groups performed well, but it was the Upper Sixth A level group, in particular, which crowned both itself and its teacher with glory. All sixteen members of the class passed, with grades ranging from A to D, and seventy-five per cent managed a C or above. Statistically, this constituted my best ever set of results. Bilingual Andreas' smug confession over the summer on a chance encounter in *Bar Med* that his Austrian mother was indeed the author of his second coursework essay did little to detract from my overall sense of achievement. Dr Faulkner eat your heart out!

My thoughts are interrupted by the arrival of a pretty, olive-skinned woman of slim build with long, straight, charcoal-black hair. Of the many available seats, she selects the one directly opposite mine. I flash her a glance over the top of my book and our eyes meet. She smiles sweetly. I smile back before returning to the humorous words in front of me.

"Definitely not English," I mutter under my breath. "More likely Asian."

A little later, as I pass through the Gate marked *Singapore*, I spot my foreign friend in the process of being chatted up by a lad with a northern accent.

"Ah, so she's catching the same flight," I tell myself.

I listen in discreetly to their conversation and am surprised to discover that my mystery woman is not Asian at all, but a native of Dublin. After a few moments, she catches my gaze and we send a nod of acknowledgement in each other's direction.

Once on board the plane, I find that I've been allocated the middle seat of a row of three. There's no-one to my left, but in the window seat is a distraught-looking oriental girl who's anxious to get something off her chest. Her English is broken, yet with the help of some official papers waved under my nose, I manage to establish that she's an illegal immigrant and about to be deported.

Eventually, a body arrives to fill the vacant third seat. I look up and, to my astonishment, see the face of my Irish friend beaming down at me. Stunned by such an extraordinary coincidence, we're both initially lost for words. However, with the cabin crew busily preparing for take-off, I soon learn that her name is Sinead, that she's twenty-nine, highly intelligent, very friendly and – wait for it – single. What's more, there's no indication whatsoever that she suffers from chronic indecision or harbours lesbian tendencies.

"Is this fate?" I ponder excitedly. "Surely this can't be it after all this time."

With the security video out of the way and a request for the passengers to fasten their seatbelts, Alan Bentley, the one-time successful language teacher and gym coach yet hopeless romantic, sits back in his seat, closes his eyes and prays for a less turbulent journey into middle age.

The End

And in the end, the love you take is equal to the love ... you make

9 781786 238368